TRANSCENDENCE

Also by Brad Mathews

Thousand Branches Series
The Thousand Branches
The Venom Storm
The Satyr of Fulton Manor
Tomb of the Phoenix

Era Sinistra Trilogy
Era Sinistra
Era Sinistra-The Shadow
Era Sinistra-Skyglow

Decay
The Girl from South Track
Revelation Trilogy
Revelation (Book 1)
Reflection (Book 2)
Reincarnation (Book 3)

TRANSCENDENCE

TRANSCENDENCE

REVELATION SERIES
BOOK 4

BRAD MATHEWS

Unity Star Books

To creators and artists at heart: You are the spark that keeps the human spirit alive. When anyone in the public arena criticizes your vision, you know you have arrived. Never stop making beauty.

Whoever fights monsters should see to it that in the process he does not become a monster. And if you gaze long enough into an abyss, the abyss will gaze back into you.

Friedrich Nietzsche

Contents

The Laws of Interdimensional Time Travel

(As described in this series)

1. Memory cannot work in reverse. You cannot remember events from a future dimension and your reality belongs only to you.
2. When you travel to another dimension of time, you disappear from your current dimension and replace your future self in the new dimension.
3. If you die in a different dimension of time, you cannot exist in any of them.

I

Plato's Forms

Another Dead Body.

The new *Philadelphia Daily Phoenix* tries to assess the situation by reporting another tragic death, as if bodies hadn't been turning up daily for the past year. Ho hum. Just another dead person.

But this is no ordinary corpse. When I consume news, I make a habit of scanning the first few paragraphs rather than just the headline, to gauge my interest in the story. One name jumped out at me: Former mayor Archinson, or as I call him, Archimedes. The victim. According to the *Phoenix*, authorities uncovered disturbing evidence of foul play.

True enough, the "authorities" these days are little more than paid bounty hunters hired to take on dirty tasks such as bringing in "criminals" dead or alive. Often, the perpetrator is dead. The bounty hunters operate under the auspices of The Freedom Brothers, a well-funded organization that governs the city through unconventional practices, which often include money-laundering, bribery, slander, and outright murder. They keep the city in check, at least in the eyes of Harrisburg and Washington.

To me, the circumstances call for careful consideration of all the known facts. No one ever elected the Freedom Brothers. They command a city of a hundred thousand people. A prominent band of invested citizens has risen over the last year, calling the Freedom Brothers a vast criminal enterprise. And while the description fits, the new group, which calls itself

United Philadelphians for Progress, isn't much better. In under a year, UPP has taken credit for the murders of at least three FB officials, ostensibly to reestablish democracy in its United States birthplace.

Not surprising—and there's nothing I can do about it. If I run off to Philadelphia without her consent, Becky might kick me out for good.

I love her. She maintains a curious sense of humor and style throughout our travails, often chiding me, using that cute little smirk when she knows something is bothering me. And the current state of Philadelphia keeps me up at night, wondering whether Marissa has kept herself out of the FB's attention. It's only secondary to the tremors that wake me at all hours. Citizens in terror. Gunshots. Monsters. Titans. The chilling cries of mourning mothers, husbands, and children haunt my dreams.

Becky has warned me six times that "doom-scrolling" is detrimental to my mental health, but she's suffering, too. Her memories of Ian remain incomplete, as if lengthy periods of his past have been erased from existence forever. I try filling in the holes where I can, but I face the same problems. A week ago, Ian called for the third time and Becky didn't even recognize his voice. After hanging up the phone, she retreated to the bedroom, buried her face in the pillows and sobbed for ten minutes while the moon-washed waves of the lake lapped upon the pebbly beach.

She reaches over to turn the lamp off without my approval, pecks me on the cheek, and rolls to face the hallway while I scan the article.

It should surprise me what has happened to the city I've always loved. In truth, I find that those post-apocalyptic dystopia thrillers miss an important characteristic of humanity. While the typical movies show totalitarian governments raining terror on the hapless citizens of society, the reality is even more chilling.

Although Philly has begun rebuilding from the destruction, its population remains less than ten percent of what it was before the Titans sacked it. The competing criminal enterprises let chaos run rampant without helping those who suffer. So long as the image of justice and order prevails, Harrisburg doesn't care. Lawmakers often say the city deserved its fate, or that the people should have expected that electing fools could never have achieved their desired changes. The concept has merit, although the not-so-shocking cruelty brings headaches that transform my face into something Becky would rather not see, and that somehow makes me angrier.

And if Harrisburg doesn't act to bring order to the city, why should Washington? The Senate pretends Philadelphia doesn't exist, either out of convenience, disdain, or because it provides no funding to keep the power-hungry parties sated. Six months ago, a member of the House of Representatives referred to Philly as "the former City of Brotherly Love." Ten years earlier, that little wisecrack would have caused nationwide outrage. Now it's not even a blip on the radar. Because what Philadelphia became represents a more-nuanced version of what became of the nation.

Increasingly, politicians serve their own ends, using ever-heated rhetoric to get elected and untold sums of dark money to keep their campaigns going strong, while doing nothing to solve the nation's problems. Bickering and finger-pointing have replaced well-reasoned proposals for popularity.

Some days I imagine that if I were anyone important, I could run for office and change everything from the inside, ignoring the proverb that "absolute power corrupts absolutely." When that thought does creep into my mind, I wave it off because I've convinced myself that I'm better than today's politicians. But if I did get elected, would I be better after a year or two? While I consider myself a good person, I'm not ready to exert so much faith in my own moral values.

When I reach the last few words of the article, a tribute to Mayor Archinson, I toss my phone on the floor, roll over to spoon Becky, and when she shrugs me off, grunt and shift toward the window, gazing into the woods. Cars travel along the windy avenue into the forest, skirting the scenic lake, avoiding a few night-owl tourists returning to their cabins.

I sigh and try to will myself to sleep, but my brain conjures images of Philadelphia from the past and the present, forming them into anger and weariness while the echoes of grieving mothers cry in my ears.

Hours pass. Becky has begun snoring, letting her shoulders rise and fall with each breath and twitching every few minutes, as if a disturbing image floats into her subconscious. Maybe if she wakes up, I can ask what's bothering her, but I know her. When she realizes that I've failed to sleep, she'll elbow me in the ribs and lecture me in the morning.

Lying in bed is useless, so I decide to get up, put on my slippers, and sift through the pile of mail that has accumulated in our roadside mailbox during the week. I don't make a habit of checking often. My excuses don't amuse Becky, but why should I go out there to bring in nothing but glossy ads, questionable credit card offers, and fake get-rich-quick schemes? We pay our bills via new technology, assuming that "big brother" has no use prying into the financial lives of an average couple trying to stay as far away from the big cities as possible.

My slippers shuffle on the soft carpet as I walk, the drawn curtains allowing blue moonlight to filter into the living room. We usually deposit the mail on the bay windowsill. It's next to the plush recliner I rest in while escaping reality by watching kids' shows that depict the world as just. It may be propaganda, but it sets my mind at ease for only a few hours, so it's worth the risk.

Sighing as I sit down, I grasp the letter opener in my left hand while searching in the dark for an envelope. The first I shred, regardless of who it's from. I can feel the fake cardboard credit card inside. "Why do these clowns still send snail mail?" I grunt to myself as I toss the shredded envelope aside. A few ad mailers make me feel better. Two pizzas for the price of one at our favorite Erie pizzeria, Romano's. This one goes in the 'worth saving' pile.

A half dozen ads go into the garbage heap before I find the edges of a thin, hand-addressed envelope from Philadelphia. I recognize the return address as Miriam's shop on the corner of Market Street, but the lettering is cleaner and more elegant than the old seer's should be. I gulp as I cut the letter open to reveal the dogeared corner of a photograph printed on copy paper. A single sheet of paper has the same handwriting as the back of the envelope. Excitement runs through me as I read:

Found this: I could use your help Kerry, Conveyor of Light and Shade. Come quick and I'll buy you dinner.

No other words, not even a signature. I'd consider it rude, but then again, the letter might as well be an InstaText sent through the USPS's ridiculous network. If she had left a connection number, I'd have to send a sarcastic "good one," and then forget it.

But there is a photograph.

Flipping to the front side of the page, I feel remorse before I can fully understand what I'm seeing.

The scene is set against a backdrop of cracked, pitted pavement, stained from oil, tire skids, and chewing gum. Mayor Archinson himself peers back at me through helpless eyes. His weary face shows distress and anger. Blood, dried and clotted, trickles toward a fragment of a white line that doesn't resemble paint. Deciding the white must be a rubberized crosswalk coating, I let my eyes scan the foreground.

A thick, rubber-banded manila envelope stuffed with papers and photographs is clutched in his right hand, and some of the contents have spilled onto the street. What little the photograph shows is hard to distinguish. The scene is dark, but enough residual light glints off the glossy surface to hide what the photo reveals. Minor details stand out: In the corner of the photo may be a pediment from a Greek-styled building. I study it for several moments to determine its origin, then turn my attention to a hand-typed message addressed to the National Archives in Washington, D.C. The font is unreadable, but I can guess the title:

RESEARCH MAY UNCOVER THE LOCATION OF AT-LANTIS

"Atlantis," I grumble. Atlantis never existed in the first place, a fictional island said to have disappeared forever, according to Plato For centuries, researchers and explorers have tried to uncover where the island's ruins lie. Even the most promising mission, an exploration backed by data and an enormous grant has exposed only snippets of information and a hazy Sonar image purporting to show lines and columns. Scientists claim that straight edges don't happen in nature; a myth that has outlasted many conspiracy theories.

When you look at nature with a keen eye, you see straight edges everywhere. Central 'veins' of leaves dart from the tip to the stem, basalt dries in hexagonal columns, minerals form crystals in perfect geometric shapes, and water ripples in streams, crisscrossing straight lines in a lattice of waves.

I toss the photograph aside, wondering what she meant by 'needing my help.' My research skills involve analyzing project specifications and documents, comparing construction materials and equipment to find the best fit for cost savings.

"Right," I whisper. "Another mindless conspiracy."

For years disinformation campaigns have labeled conspiracy theories as "proof". Their proponents cite circumstantial evidence.

The media have been complicit in spreading these stories for a long time. I take a moment to gauge my trust in the *Philadelphia Daily Phoenix*. The outlet claims to be the city's sole remaining source of truth, using the coincidental fall of the *Enquirer* as evidence that only the *Phoenix*'s editors are trustworthy, ignoring the fact the *Enquirer* failed because the city itself failed, the *Enquirer* cited facts based on thorough research., while the *Phoenix* deals in suppositions that strike the believable emotional tone, using manipulative language. I've seen it in a variety of stories, including a feel-good piece about a fresh farm-to-table produce supplier feeding the remaining struggling citizens.

For this propaganda to be successful, people must rely on a single major outlet, and the *Phoenix* has in my opinion suppressed any competing sources. Even the most basic research reveals connections between the editors and FB movers and shakers.

If I can't trust the *Phoenix* to tell the whole truth, why should I trust an unconvincing photograph? I can think of only one reason: That the UPP ordered Archinson's assassination to throw FB off track, and the *Phoenix* reporters whitewashed the evidence left behind. The Freedom Brothers don't want the information Archinson had to go public. They couldn't control it because they didn't arrive on the scene first—whoever took the picture had. And that means she's in trouble and definitely needs my help. If the FB hasn't already dumped her in the Delaware River, I'll consider it a miracle.

I consider who may have sent the letter and mutter under my breath. "What the hell are you doing, Marissa?"

"Ker?"

I look up to see Becky standing in the hall entrance, her dark hair laying limp along her gray robe's fluffy collar. The robe shows a glimpse of her thighs.

"Uh, good morning." I croak.

"Come back to bed ... let's discuss it tomorrow."

I follow her to the bedroom, lie down and we settle into a comfortable snuggle while she dozes off. But my demons return as I close my eyes. Meteors crash to the earth, exploding into mushrooms of orange and yellow flames, emitting clouds of acrid smoke as they destroy the city. Amidst it all, the sneer of Cronus infects the scene with the poison of rage. I question whether the Olympians corralled the other eleven.

I've heard nothing in over a year. I know only one way to find out.

2

The Last Ptolemaic Ruler

As the shade from the deciduous trees across the road obscures the sun's glow, I can feel the weight of tired eyes watching me, a clear signal that something's off. From the hallway window, I catch a glimpse of the sun's reflection on tranquil waters before the boats disrupt the peace. Then again, the flitting sunlight is more than sufficient to disrupt my morning rhythm. How long had I slept after Becky had lured me back to bed? Trying to keep track of time while I'm trying to fall asleep would only keep me awake, but when something worries me, tracking the passage of time is the least of my problems.

"Good morning, honey," I croak without turning my head.

A tiny swish in the silent air suggests she's blinking, and when she does that, she's usually concocting a way to pry me out of a stubborn frame of mind. But this time I'm not being stubborn; my mind is digesting what Marissa's letter *really* meant and how I might go about replying.

The Philadelphia Postal Service no longer operates in the central city, forcing unlucky residents to sneak out to the western suburbs. That's a perilous journey even without the gangsters aiming guns at anyone who wanders too near the city limit fences. And since addresses have become useless locators, mail stays at the suburban station for Philadelphia residents who wish to retrieve it.

I doubt Marissa will be anticipating a snail-mail from me. If she wanted to reach me through InstaText or a good, old-fashioned cell call, finding my number probably wouldn't be difficult. She expects me to come visit because she wants my help to break the gang's stranglehold over city governance.

The newspapers claim the city population has climbed to over a hundred thousand, a far cry from the million-and-a-half who called Philly home before the Titan attack. Partisans and government officials from outside the city dismiss any attempt to estimate the number of casualties, as if those lives had ever mattered to them. The level of scorn directed at those who remain is another matter. In remote job site meetings, I can get away with expressing empathy for the survivors once or twice without attracting unwanted attention.

As technology has advanced, leadership coordination takes place mostly offsite, and I communicate virtually with my teams, conduct meetings, and review construction issues via virtual reality goggles. I don't often travel to the city any longer, but I hear the occasional rumor about Philadelphia projects, including a developer promising to build a thirty-story mixed-use project in the financial district. With no reliable city leadership involved, the proposal raises immediate suspicion, but I can't put a stop to it.

"How did you sleep?" Becky rests her hand on my shoulder as I gaze outside.

She taps her toe on the lamp behind her to turn it on. We invest little in trendy tech products, unless they offer real convenience. The ingenuity of the design eliminates the problems of motion-sensors, which would be a major nuisance should we roll over during the night. Now that we don't have to fumble through the dark for a switch, we can sleep in peace until we need the light.

"Well..." I begin, not planning on offering an answer.

It takes two seconds for her to exhale, perhaps a sign of relief. "Deep subject."

"Yeah. Something like that."

"What were you looking at last night?"

Never one to break the ice with marital small talk, she gets right to the point, which is sometimes unnerving even when I expect it. I'm not great at expressing half-formed thoughts without stumbling over awkward phrases or useless filler words.

"Oh, it's just another Philly thing where the gangs are wrestling for control. You know the shenanigans."

"Indeed."

"Yeah," I mumble.

She gazes at me while I turn away from the window, prop up the pillow behind my head, and look into her eyes, kissing her once on the lips. "What's going on this time?"

"I assume you saw the news."

She closes her eyes in solemn mourning. "The former mayor?"

Becky has never lived in Philadelphia. A longtime resident of Harrisburg, she worked in education when we met and stayed in school leadership roles throughout our long separation. I still don't remember how we ended up owning this lake house, but it's home now. Becky excels at empathizing when someone memorable dies, even when she doesn't have a personal connection to them.

Mayor "Archimedes's" death would have made national news in any other era, but now he's just "*another dead body*." Marissa wants me to help uncover his secrets before the gangs can lay claim to them, destroy them, or worse.

"Did you ever meet him?"

"Not personally," I recall. "He was the one who got Secretary Whitworth into public service, realizing his dreams and all that."

"And you still haven't introduced me to him," she whispers.

"Time and place," I argue. "Not really the point. Arch was considered a visionary, drawing the respect of everyone, regardless of party affiliation. That's good leadership."

"Then what has you so worried?"

"Marissa found him—before the FB or UPP did. And he was carrying a document with purported new information about Atlantis. Which means her life is in jeopardy."

She rolls over and rests her face on my chest. I can feel my chin stubble snagging on her hair as I breathe in and out, watching her head rise and fall with each breath. I glance at the television on top of our dresser, its elongated shadow falling over the inlaid wood. A handcrafted piece like this one could fetch a thousand dollars new, but Becky had paid just three hundred, and restored it herself.

She'd always had a good eye for detail, a trait that had attracted me from the beginning.

"So that means you're planning on going to Philly," she says matter-of-factly.

"I'm thinking about it."

"Acting like I don't understand how you feel again? You know better than that."

I have nothing to offer in self-defense but a sheepish sigh.

"You know how I feel about the city," she warns. "It was dangerous when we met, but now, I don't want you to even consider going."

"I have an adequate system of self-defense," I say. "They'd better bring it if they want to get at me."

"Who's *they*?"

Damnit. She knows my clever retorts regarding what I call the 'nefarious they' by heart. Falling into that trap is humiliating, but instead of reacting out of anger, I grunt in confusion.

"Not like you don't know."

She sighs again. "You've already decided. Tell Marissa to be careful. And would you visit Reading on the way? Your son needs a man-to-man."

"Ian?"

She can't hold back the grin. "No, your *other* son, the illegitimate one you had with…"

"Of course I can. It's on the way. What does he need?"

"He'll tell you," she says, "because he trusts you."

"He trusts you, too."

This time, she fakes a smile and lifts her head so she can gaze into my eyes to prepare for a kiss that I hope will never end. Instead, she whispers. "I know that."

With this busy an itinerary, I'd better get going if I'm to reach Philly by nightfall. If the city is dangerous by day, the peril only rises after sunset when it will be harder to cross the razor wire-topped fences ringing the city undetected. Gang members patrol the perimeter at night, ostensibly as a public safety measure. But the guards serve another purpose. By restricting travel into the city, they can keep tabs on whatever opposition may enter, making it easier to deal with before it gathers steam.

Showering, dressing and brushing my hair takes only thirty minutes this morning. I pass the time on the highway to Reading listening to 'oldies,' the rock music I loved in the mid-2010s. The rhythm never gets old. The journey takes a little over five hours in minimal traffic conditions, where the most efficient route involves tolls. I don't bother speeding.

Reading is closer to Philadelphia than Becky is comfortable with, but Ian is a grown man and doesn't need parental protection. When most of Philly's surviving residents fled, many chose to settle in Reading and Scranton, causing crime in those cities to skyrocket.

I pull up to Ian's townhouse after two in the afternoon. I'm suddenly hungry, but I can suppress the urge to eat for a few more hours. That's if Ian doesn't force-feed me one of Brianne's legendary meals.

"Dad!" he shouts from around the corner, as though he could sense me coming.

"How's life treating you?"

He pulls open the door, kicking something metal out of the way before greeting me with his trademark grin. The kid isn't much younger than me, and he looks just like me. "Mom said you were coming. You eat leftovers?"

I can't refuse.

He leads me into the living room through an entryway, a three-foot square of irregular shale tile hemmed in by strips of silver where the carpet stretches into the living room. Cluttered wire storage shelves flank two walls, carrying boxes of bric-à-brac, important papers, childhood memorabilia, and assorted cookware. The bottom shelf is full of dog food, enough to feed a ravenous beast that might as well rival the legendary Cerberus in weight. I can hear the animal panting as it lumbers down the stairs in response to Brianne's call.

"Bernie! Stay!"

The dog's name is Bernie? That name can't have been Ian's choice.

"Brie made a delicious lasagna," Ian says cheerfully. But trouble must occupy the back of his mind, or Becky wouldn't have sent me.

"That'll work," I say.

Parents often yearn to dig the trauma out of their kids, but that's a parenting technique with drawbacks. Instead, I find that allowing Ian to voice his concerns when he feels the time is right leads to greater trust. And while Becky doesn't always agree with my approach, she's understanding enough to let me try—unless the trauma gets the best of him and she must step in.

"You want to know something?" he asks.

I savor the meaty lasagna and the crumbly cheese before mumbling, "Hit me."

"It's actually two things. I found out something that could be dangerous, and I didn't want to bring it up with Brie before I discussed it with you."

"And what's that?"

"It's a funny thing; I didn't even know I was doing it. But the other day, it started snowing."

I screw up my face in a fake grin, "In August."

He nods. "Next thing I know, the neighbor's falling down the steps, getting out the snowblower. I figured out it was me because of another problem—Brie's pregnant."

"Well, damn," I grin. "Congrats, man."

"See, we're not very well prepared. I'm scared out of my mind. The snowstorm went away when I forced myself to see things clearly. And returned as a cyclone when I let the dread overcome me."

"What?"

"I guess I have powers. But I thought that someone had surely given you yours. And I don't recall anyone giving me anything."

"Makes sense," I say, thinking fast. "I'm a descendant of the Six, which means you are too. The problem is, you must try to control your emotions, because they drive it."

"That's what I thought ... which makes me even more nervous."

"It's manageable," I say. "Experiment in a controlled environment so you don't hurt anyone."

He nods and eyes the growing pile of dishes in the sink. If my intuition is correct, he might be considering using his gift to wash them for Brianne. as I'm guessing she assigned him the chore.

We eat in relative silence and then settle into a chat about the complexities of daily life, the increasing danger that long-time Reading citizens fear every day, the consequences of raising a child in perilous times. I can offer him little reassurance. Ian understands that sugar-coating won't solve problems, but that leaning on me can at least lessen the emotional load.

Three hours later, I'm heading out the door, hugging him and Brianne goodbye, sneaking past Bernie's enormous paws, and heading for my car. Storm clouds gather, growing gloomy as I drive away, while Ian watches from the porch. The rain falls in sheets for twenty minutes until I reach the Philadelphia suburbs.

Nightfall is only a couple of hours away, but I may be able to sneak through one of the less-busy gates without raising suspicion. The chain-link fences have already deteriorated, bearing signs of suburbanites attempting to burrow into the city. Long stretches of fence bisect parking lots, zigzagging between residential buildings and tearing through parks. In the park outside the gate is a gathering of protestors, holding signs condemning the opposing factions in the city. A man in dirty khakis smokes a cigar and flicks it through the fence as he watches its red glow peter out in the weeds on the Philadelphia side.

Nobody shows any interest in stopping me, but they watch me until I can no longer see them. I park my car in an abandoned lot that had been bulldozed, hiding my car between the hulking chunks of rebar and towering piles of concrete. Walking the rest of the journey is not without its risks; the destruction makes the trek dangerous, even without the city's controlling interests inflicting violence on innocent civilians. By sunset, I find my way to the wide section of Market Street approaching the historic district. The ruins of the architectural masterpiece create a tantalizing cover for anyone wishing to avoid eye contact with the gangs. A familiar face peers out at me from a makeshift cave. I stare at her for a few moments before she waves me into her temporary residence, welcoming me with a wobbly handshake.

She whispers in the darkness. "Are you ready for your final healing?"

3

Anti-Nemesis

Miriam welcomes me into her temporary home, where the faint glow of candlelight emanates through the cracks. She takes me by the hand, careful to dodge a sphere of concrete with a half-shattered plank leaning against it. Attached to the plank is a makeshift double-twine braid that stretches into the shadows before rising to the ceiling, supported by concrete anchor bolts embedded in the lean-to walls. As I step inside, a glint of steel catches my eye, reflecting the candlelight. Following Miriam around a corner, I pass a plank door into a small room with a beige tiled floor. A broom leans against the rubble wall, a remnant of the collapsed second floor which now stands upright. The single candle stands on a wood-paneled door with its hinges and knob still attached. The door had survived the assault of the Titans and Miriam has repurposed it as a tabletop. A pair of books gathers dust at each end while a small glass of foggy liquid sits near the pewter door handle. The table's 'legs' appear to be stacked cinderblock, tied together with metal straps and strut cables.

She breathes in deeply, approaches the table, and sits down on a pillow placed on the tile. Motioning for me to join her, she cups her hands around the candle flame as if to warm them, closes her eyes, and lets a full minute's silence pass between us.

The crude architecture lets in drafts of night air, creating dank condensation. The pillow is damp, but I sit down without complaining, while *plips* of water drip onto tiles.

She curls her fingers around mine, holding my palms up, and digging her thumbs into my love line, she exerts a pressure wave that hits the nerves all the way up my spine, rendering me immobile. The throb in my back may come back to haunt me later.

Still with her eyes closed, she whispers an incantation to start the session: "Mother Circe, Sorceress Daughter of Helios, channel your grace through me."

I don't dare speak, because whatever she's doing is gluing my tongue to the roof of my mouth.

"You have encountered much, Kerry, Conveyor of Light and Shade. In you I sense the Algean memory, flooding your senses with the pain of tragedy. And the shadow of Perseus, god of destruction..."

My hearing goes fuzzy as she talks, transforming my brain into mush.

Moments after I black out, I sit upright in a marble-floored mausoleum. Its intricate columns support a gabled façade exterior and the domed room where I'm now standing. Candles flicker and glow from chalices set on intricately carved cornices, which line the circular walls at regular intervals. Somewhere overhead in the dark, wings are beating.

I shrink into the shadows as I hear male voices approaching from the adjoining room. The intruders wear tweed jackets with leather elbow patches. One carries a black canvas briefcase, the other a beige blueprint tube. They don't notice me as they talk, which, in my current state, is as intelligible as dueling grunts.

While the taller stranger uncaps the tube, the other deposits the briefcase on a central stone dais, tapping it and glowering at his companion. Unsurprisingly the case contains cash, what looks like six figures in wads of small bills. After a brief handshake, they review the unrolled plans, glancing up at the ceiling while the scene swirls into a vortex of black mist.

When I open my eyes, choking on the humid air, I already know I've seen these shores before. Salty waves smash against the collapsed basalt shoreline, and a sultry afternoon sun heats my skin. These shores were dark the last time I was here, and this time I can see the destruction Cronus caused. Cracks zig-zag through the bedrock and yellowed grass gilds the sandy ridgeline. Plants have rooted in the eroded river channel. I find myself muttering Sarah's name as I glance skyward, where a pair of wings streaks in front of the sun.

Screeches erupt from my right, tearing apart the scene until all that's left is the pulsating darkness of my thoughts. I squeeze my eyes shut to stifle a wave of tears, but my tear ducts leak greasy splotches of mud that twist around me like a cyclone, carrying the debris of my past like a whirling storm of garbage.

"...where the Algea roam, insipid carrier of doom and rage." Miriam's voice murmurs in the darkness before she reappears, still digging her long thumbnails into my flesh. "Kerry must overcome these daimons and unravel the corruption that runs rampant. For if you fail in your mission, the Gods will unleash the greatest enemy of humankind..."

The room spins as I feel pain drag through my spine.

Overhead, the ceiling shakes, showering dirt across the table. The darkness looms hundreds of feet above us, as though an elevator shaft holds the leaning piles of concrete back from smashing us.

Miriam concludes her speech, but keeps her thumbs pressed into my palms. "You must drink from the glass, Kerry. I have prepared this concoction for just such an occasion. You will feel an immediate burst of energy, followed by residual grogginess. You must not fall asleep if the potion is to take hold. Do you agree?"

I still cannot speak, but I don't need to. As though acting of its own accord, my head bobs forward as she guides my hands across the door panels to the pewter handle, turning my palms together until I squeeze the glass. The liquid looks like acrid tap water from a rusted faucet. Clouds of orange and gray swirl as Miriam guides the glass to my lips. I don't want to drink it, but I cannot resist. My hands vibrate with blasts of ice and heat that rip across my skin as an icy sweat builds on my brow.

"Oh my God," I want to say. My tongue peels itself from the roof of my mouth as the rim of the glass touches my lips. With the first taste, white-hot tremors splash through my veins. Convulsing, I swallow the last of it, and heat scours through me. Rage like I've never felt before roils in my stomach.

Tears fall from my face. Miriam's small hands shake. With the sudden ability to speak, the tonic drives me to scream obscenities the gangs could hear six blocks away. "I DON'T KNOW WHERE YOU ARE, BUT I'LL RIP OFF YOUR TESTICLES AND FEED THEM TO CERBERUS!"

"Kerry," a faint voice echoes in my brain. *"You are stronger than this. You found me and transformed me. My energy still radiates through your body. Use it."*

"NOOOO!" Gripping the glass, I shatter the glass and form it into a marble in my grip.

"You should feel better in a few moments," Miriam says, her voice calm. She weathers the storm far better than Becky would. If this had happened in front of Becky, she'd hide her face and mutter under her breath.

"I…" I can't continue. The rage dissolves like powdered sugar in water, and I struggle to breathe. My eyelids droop even as my pupils dart from side to side in the scant light.

"You are experiencing the aftereffects," Miriam assures me. "Let this moment bring you clarity."

"I … can't believe she can still speak to me."

"Sarah," she says, as if reading my thoughts. "Emotional entanglement transcends death."

"It does?"

"Of course," she says, frowning and straightening her back. "Did you assume that death destroys the bridge?"

"Well…"

"It strengthens it," she says. "Our choices put strain on the structure from afar, yet it retains its shape. As one end settles, the vibrations roll like waves from one end to the other, steadying your feelings while communicating with her."

Viewing Miriam through half-closed eyes, I let the candlelight in, blurring shape and light with the surrounding darkness. "I guess if you put it that way."

"You must be familiar with the law of energy conservation?"

Through my exhausted emotions, I swear she's being facetious, but I don't allow myself to get angry again. Instead, I shrug it off. "Might have heard the term once or twice," I say.

"You seem thoroughly surprised that I'm familiar with the basics of physics, at least on issues relating to my work." She gazes at me with a curious smile, raising her eyebrows. Pushing a knot of curly hair behind her ear, she explains, "Energy can neither be created nor destroyed. Therefore, the energy between you and Sarah still persists through the bridge. Without realizing it's happening, you are drawing from it and transferring back to it as you need it. So tell me again what you feel?"

My hands lighten, and although my legs still feel numb, sensation is creeping back into my body. My eyes finally open, showing me the room in greater detail.

Within the lean-to structure, detached lengths of pipe and sheet metal wrapped around crumbling concrete slabs cast complicated shadows in the cavern. Miriam must have glued broken planks together to create the door, but why didn't she just use the door she'd repurposed into a table? I already know the answer to that; she'd already used the door as a table before she'd realized the need for a door to conceal her candlelight from the gangs. By now, they must be aware of her abilities. Wherever Marissa is, she must have her hands full. I came to the city to help her.

The makeshift door moves when weight on the structure opens it, and through it I can see the entryway to her lair. Concrete dust, bits of rat-gnawed insulation, and twisted scrap metal are interspersed with fist-sized chunks of cement along the slab walls, where rebar cages keep the slabs upright. Above the doorway light gathers like golden oil on a steel blade, maybe not visible to intruders. The double-twine rope affixed to a slide bracket holds a four-foot-long knife edge upright. Since the spherical remnant of concrete is tricky to avoid without disturbing the plank, the movement resulting from contact would release the slide holding the blade in place. And should the intruder continue, the blade would slice him in half. A well-conceived booby trap. I'd give Miriam props for it if the newfound energy hadn't been prodding me into motion.

"You seek Marissa," she says, pressing her palms against the door table and getting herself up from the pillow.

"D'you know where she is?"

"Doing the same thing you'd be doing right now, considering."

I frown, "Considering what?"

She tilts her head sideways and approaches the makeshift doorway, which I now realize is trapezoidal. "The Freedom Brothers search for the assassin. They will not hesitate to engage anyone who stands in their way. Their will to destroy their opposition is piling up the bodies. Avoid them at all costs, because they're well-armed."

"My abilities should protect me."

She grips my arm and glares into my eyes. "Refrain from using them unless absolutely necessary. The last thing you want is another war."

"Because they will think I'm on the UPP side," I finish for her.

"And because you're marked, Kerry. You're famous. Regardless of whether you take sides, they will see you as a threat and try to eliminate you."

"I should be okay," I say, struggling to stand up straight on the messy floor. "They won't catch me."

She inhales and closes her eyes, still gripping my forearm. "If you'll forgive the expression, you've just stepped into a hornet's nest."

4

The Defender Owl

My shoes shuffle through the dirt at the entrance, kicking loose gravel onto the door frame. Before Philadelphia was taken over, this entryway might have been a small apartment lobby, but then again, I don't recall much about this neighborhood. Located ten blocks south of Independence Hall, many of the buildings were aging, mixed-use structures, serving as apartments, and repurposed offices with ground-floor shops. From here, I should be able to discern the remains of the financial district's glassy towers. However, the lack of light and the thick smog have shrunk the visible horizon to a half-mile or even less.

"I'm not sure where to look," I say, meeting Miriam's eyes. "Would she be near her old store or on Market Street?"

Miriam frowns, "Market Street is ground zero. You won't make it a block before the Freedom Brothers behead you."

Shaking my head, I press on. "Why don't you use your foresight to predict where I might find her?"

"I cannot," she admits. "And even if I could, the code of Hecate prohibits it."

"I know Zeus. I'll put in a good word for you."

She sighs. "Then perhaps I should relay a rumor that the gods aren't pleased with you. Since you meddled in their affairs, they distrust you, thinking you may one day start another war over something they view as trivial."

I cough out a swear word, "Feeling's mutual. And if they think my family is trivial—"

"You don't grasp the logic," she interrupts. "Your family is everything to you, and it should be. You should assume they feel the same way about theirs."

"It's all hubris," I bite back. "Why are you so quick to believe them?"

"Who said I am? You equate reporting the news to agreeing with it, a tendency that has caused much turmoil in this world."

I shake my head and scowl. "I didn't come here to be lectured."

"Correct. You came here to lecture Marissa."

A simple growl is all I'm willing to go with to communicate my disgust.

She responds by lengthening the syllables of her speech. "I can read your thoughts. She's more than capable of taking care of herself."

"Then why did she ask me for help?"

With a curt smile, she nods toward the doorway. "You'll have to ask her yourself. Reports say the ex-Mayor's body was found eight blocks away in an alley. Marissa may still be in the vicinity, trying to piece it together."

"Right."

"And Kerry, dear? Do exercise caution when you leave. I hate resetting the trap."

I nod and place my feet where they will not disturb the stone.

My heart sinks as I consider the trip I'm about to make. If the Freedom Brothers have chosen Independence Hall as their operating headquarters, then the United Philadelphians for Progress have probably set up shop closer to midtown, an expanse of mid-rise brick and stucco edifices between the financial and industrial districts. And since the UPP is surely behind Arch's assassination, the crime scene must be in their backyard.

The stench of blood and sweat, along with human waste, reaches my nose. Most residential buildings now lie in ruins, their plumbing systems destroyed. Since gravity is no longer balancing pressures, the sewage gases escape into the streets.

A block away, the skeleton of an office high-rise marks the center of midtown. The sloped parking decks remain, having crumbled from the inside as the superstructure now lists from its center of gravity. The interior walls exist only as twisted mounds of steel and mica dust. The glass exterior, which once reflected the azure sky, is now shards of scattered glass on the sidewalk.

Steering clear of the building for safety lengthens my route; eight blocks south and two west. I walk the westerly leg first, getting an altered view. Two blocks over, the two- and three-story buildings that once housed grocery stores, restaurants, dry cleaners, and mom-and-pop clothing stores are now mostly rubble. Where one edifice stays standing, the next has caved in, its metal trusses bent and covered in roof debris. A face pokes out, eyeing me dismally; her clothing torn and filthy.

I only offer her a nod, keeping focused on my journey. Downed power lines and traffic lights look like black scissors, across an intersection where a gargantuan crack cuts through the road. Asphalt droops into the twenty-foot-wide chasm filled with acrid water, rusting cars, and a dozen dead bodies. The opposite bank rises at least ten feet higher. I can't cross it, even if I were able to use the deadened power lines to tightrope across. I turn back and trudge toward the next block, a better-preserved throughway, although the rubble of toppled building makes it difficult.

Confusion makes the journey treacherous. It takes me over an hour to walk less than a half mile. I hear the distant sounds of murmuring voices, and then desperate shouts, increasing my pace so my heart beats a rhythm with the quarrel.

Twenty feet away, I see it—a duel. Two burly men are duking it out with makeshift swords made of struts and insulation shields. "Get up, you loathsome—"

"I'll kill you now!" a man screams. As I get nearer to them, I suppose them to be rival gang members. When his opponent doesn't surrender, he attacks, swiping his blade at the other man's abdomen.

A single parry deflects his blade, allowing the victim to regain control and kick at his attacker's feet, slamming a fist into his abdomen. He produces a bloodstained knife with a four-inch blade, but the attacker twists his arm, doubling him over, and kicking him in the crotch.

But rage mixes with surprise as the victim buries the knife in his assailant's gut, howling ferociously.

I avert my eyes as he turns his attention to me. "Get a good show, barfbag? Come at me! I fight as dirty as you look!"

"I'm not looking for a confrontation," I say, shrinking back.

"Everyone's looking for one. That's all there is anymore. 'Less you want the UPP thugs to eat your liver, I'd say fighting me is a better bet."

"Sorry to disappoint you," I mumble, glancing at the aggressor's writhing body as he groans in pain.

Without wasting another moment, I push through the next few blocks, keeping my eyes forward, where lines of burned-out cars sag under the weight of structural beams. It looks like there's another duel ahead, and fear takes me by surprise.

"That'll do it, bitch!" the man shrieks. His opponent eggs him on with a flick of her wrist, baiting him into charging her. She easily sidesteps his assault, slaps him on the back with a brick as he passes, and turns to face him as he gets up from the street.

He reveals his weapon just before she attacks. A sawed-off shotgun, modified for assault. He aims it at the woman, pulls the trigger, but misses the mark. Without a weapon to match his, she'll have to outwit him to survive.

A strange sensation creeps over me, raising the hairs on the back of my neck. I watch the woman closing her eyes, waiting for the man to reload his gun. He fumbles with it while grunting obscenities. It's like ice water suddenly runs through my veins as I recognize Marissa. She's using the spirits to convince the man to drop the shotgun.

He tosses it aside and charges her with his fists up while cursing at her. As he hesitates to right himself after another wild miss, she pelts him in the face again with the brick, knocking him on his backside. Rather than press her advantage, she waits for him to struggle to his feet. The dead are working on her behalf. He growls and limps away, considering himself out-manned as I run up to them.

"At least tell me that happened for a reason," I call out to her.

She doesn't need to look my way as she nods. "He was trying to kill me. UPP scum."

"I didn't come here to defend you in a fight," I say, cautiously navigating the ridged street, allowing her time to meet me halfway. She places her hands in mine and welcomes me to hell.

"I suspect you weren't ready for this," she says, watching a solitary homeless woman creep along the shadows across the street. "You might think the gangs wage most warfare here, and you'd be wrong. The rest of us know we are competing for whatever scraps the gangs leave behind. Necessities like food, toilet paper, and shelter. These people are desperate; they'll resort to any means to get what you have. It's not that they're evil; they're only pawns. UPP has this entire district locked down. They control the real estate, the power, the water, and the food. They'll take bribes for extra, but they don't give discounts, and no one here has money anyway, so they must steal from each other to survive."

"It looks worse than when I left it," I say, shaking my head.

"Right," she agrees. "But let's cut the small talk—we've gotta get off the streets until morning. I'll take you to my place."

"You have a ... forget I said that."

A grin covers her face. "Just shut up and follow me."

Taking the lead, she sidesteps a pair of dislodged service hole covers. In one of them the concrete utility pit's rebar ladder rungs hang loose, and an explosion has collapsed half its shape. Marissa crouches under a twisted overhang, shrinking into the dark while she waits for me to join her. She quickly scans our surroundings, and deciding that the coast is clear, she crawls through an opening only big enough for a dog to shimmy into. The entryway appears to be a dead end, but she produces a key, holds it up in the scant light before inserting it into a lock on the floor, and pulls on the metal handle in a diamond-shaped plate. A simple padlock wouldn't keep anyone out while she's inside, but she's installed a locking slide latch on the underside of the plate. She pulls a small flashlight from her pocket, peers into the depths, and waits for me to say something.

"You live down there?"

"The rats live down there. I use it as a home base. You first."

There are rebar steps descending into a square shaft. Realizing I'm dropping into an elevator pit, I quicken my pace, as though expecting an elevator to land on top of me. The shaft drops at least forty feet. While the gangs and desperate citizens have likely taken up shelter in the subway tunnels, Marissa has chosen this sanctuary, and it takes me until I reach the floor to understand why.

Above me, she descends the ladder, slides the latch, locks it, and warns me to get out of the way. I shuffle to my right, meeting something iron against the wall. The metal pulses under my palm while the light above me grows brighter.

"There's a power switch above the pipe bend." she says.

"You have electricity?" I feel along the concrete wall for the switch.

When the light flicks on she explains, "Battery, actually. I stole it from someone who attacked me, and I found he left cash, so I used it to pay UPP for the charge, under disguise. We've got about 48 hours of power left, so it's best to keep the lights off when we don't need them. Besides, light attracts attention. Looters are always looking for somewhere to hide from the criminal enterprises."

"Uh-huh."

"And the gangs have got the state and federal governments convinced they're creating law and order. I call it 'scofflaw and disorder.' If you thought Congress was corrupt, you've got another think coming."

"I get why they're doing it," I say, letting my eyes settle on a column of red piping, enormous valves with wheel handles, and a fire alarm system. I assume the fire system no longer works, since the city water distribution network has fallen into disrepair.

There is fire riser, a wall painted with red and blue painted stripes behind it, a concrete masonry partition shielding the vault, and a service door, long since welded and bolted shut, that may lead to a subway platform outside. Had they seen the door, the gangs and desperate citizens would have taken refuge in this room before Marissa set up camp.

She has designed a complex series of measures to keep herself safe. Under a stainless-steel table with plastic caster wheels, a giant pentagram stretches from wall to wall. And bolted under the table is another surprise; an explosive device. Her scheme dawns on me the moment I lay eyes on it. She's wired the room to blow if an intruder trips the system. And she's hidden the wiring in metal tubing fastened to the walls.

I wonder if Miriam helped her rig it, but remember that I've underestimated Marissa before, and to my detriment. At last, I realize that Marissa and Miriam have prepared for the same eventuality: That they would one day need to find different hideouts. Now, Miriam's complaint over an hour ago rings in my mind. She doesn't want to set her booby trap *again.* Because the blade must have already dismembered someone. I suddenly realize how dangerous Philadelphia has become.

"Yeah," Marissa agrees. "They're doing it because they want to control everything. Greed, lust for power, human indulgence, you name it. They're the power brokers. The UPP exists because the FB didn't plan for contingencies well enough, and now they're wrestling for power. And whoever comes out undamaged gets the ultimate prize—unlimited money, unlimited power. They've bent the laws to their will, and because laws no longer exist here, they've taken control of every resource. And once a despot has power, he'll stop at nothing to preserve it. Lucky for us, no other city wants anything to do with us. Because if they did, it would mean war, and even bigger heaps of bodies. I'm weary of hearing their voices crying out for justice all the time, but I'm doing what I can."

"Which leads us to why you asked me to come," I say.

"I need your help to find out the real reason UPP murdered Mayor Archinson. The photo I sent you is a starting point, but I've just stumbled on a bigger piece of the puzzle. And it's a doozy."

"I'm ready for anything."

Raising her eyebrows, she unfurls a roll of paper on the plan table and peers at the markings along the right side of the page. I know a conceptual plan when I see one. And this one ignites white-hot rage in my heart.

5

Temple of Aphaia

The plan shows 'Independence Tower', comprising condos, apartments, and retail. It looks high enough to claw at the sky. On the ground floor a pair of restaurants have thirty-foot-high marble columns, capped by a decorative cornice with curly edges, tucked under the overhanging residential tier. The storefronts are set far enough back to dull the sun's glare during the morning and afternoon. Behind the glass is an expansive seating area with dining options that surrounds a glass-walled escalator up to the retail stores above. Towering above the columns, a gold-flecked glass curtain wall wraps the structural steel. Fluted mullions break up the panes spaced at thirty-foot intervals above the columns. These stretch right up to the middle section, ending at a vaulted faux-brick center. Viewing holes allow people sight of the iron bell suspended from a thick, wooden support in the middle.

Gagging at the opulence, I flatten out the curled corner, slam my left fist on the stainless-steel table and growl.

"And I was afraid you would overreact," Marissa laughs.

"How can they do this? This is federal property. The National Park Service—"

"Sold it six months ago," she says, frowning. "I'm guessing you don't read the *Post*? Despite the biased reporting, it still conveyed that although the government had explored the possibility of revitalizing the entire district, costs got out of hand, and they directed Harrisburg to redevelop it using private-sector contracts. And that's where I lost the trail."

I shake my head. I can hear muted whimpers somewhere behind the steel-plated wall separating Marissa's hideout from the Subway tunnels.

"Stunning, isn't it?"

"Stunning depravity. Architectural masterpiece. Temple students would study this garish nightmare if the school still existed."

"Actually, I heard the university still exists, but underground. When the deans and faculty cleared out, the Freedom Brothers took control, or so the rumors say."

"Doesn't surprise me."

"But look at this."

She runs her fingers up and down the title block on the right-hand edge of the twenty-four by thirty-six sheet. Above the scribbled signature of the chief architect, the recognizable logo of Hart and Harris Architects fills the stamp box. I've worked with that company before and, underhanded tactics aside, even they wouldn't be so brazen. Unless they operated on tax-exempt "donations" worth millions.

These *donations* are sanctioned money-laundering schemes. If the Pennsylvania House of Representatives and the Governor's office has approved the design, it might be that corruption overrules the Pennsylvania constitution.

"And notice this logo," she points to a stylized pictogram of the American flag showing five stars in the blue field shaped like an italic letter F, and blank white spaces backing a red-striped letter B.

"Freedom Brothers. So you're saying UPP murdered Archimedes to make a statement about the Freedom Brothers?"

"A *public* statement," she agrees. "They want the remaining citizens to mistrust the FB, and pardon the expression, but this building might be a giant middle finger to authority."

"But there's gotta to be more to it than that."

She nods and rests her palms on the plan table. During the moment of silence, I peer at the pentagram tattoo on her left hand. "Isn't there always?" she says.

"And this is where the alleged information about Atlantis comes in," I surmise.

A shrug indicates she isn't yet ready to admit this wild tangent, but that she's happy for me to connect them. "I haven't worked out the details. Getting close enough to the right players might get me murdered. And that's where you come in."

I shake my head and look away. "Miriam just got through warning me not to use my abilities, because these gangs know who I am."

"Right," she agrees. "But haven't you considered *how* they know that?"

"I assume the people who formed the gangs were on Ground Zero that day."

"They were," she says. "But you were just *some guy* to them."

I jump in without taking a breath. "You said I was famous."

"As in an urban legend. What makes urban legends so salacious is that not everyone knows them. In fact, it's so rare the masses consider such stories mindless conspiracy theories."

"And now we have a *real* conspiracy," I choke. "I hate it when they're right."

"Because only *you're* allowed a stroke of luck now and then? I mean, you have impossible abilities and all that, but don't give yourself that much credit." She continues, "The point is, an urban legend must be rooted in some hidden truth, which happens to be that you're the luckiest man on earth."

I once believed in luck. Working on job sites, traveling back and forth from home, dreaming about someday having a girlfriend with wavy amber hair. And after I first settled down with Becky, I really did consider myself lucky. It wasn't until decades later—at least in the time travel realm—that I realized 'luck' was better known as putting myself in a position to succeed and working hard at it. "No such thing," I mutter.

"Because you just happened to meet a princess in your adventures. You must admit, impossible odds make for a great story."

Maybe they do. Maybe periodicals and newspapers will one day make me a real legend, a hero to all Philadelphians, instead of the freak who endangered them. I'm unwilling to waste time considering this further, so I let it slide. "I mean, it's ugly."

"It all is," she agrees.

"What if I don't want to unravel it?"

Her chin drops as she hears those words. She drags her left hand across the table, rests it on my shoulder, and gazes into my eyes. "Are you saying you don't love this city anymore?"

"Because I know what happens when I get involved. Again and again, I screw up. You can chalk it up to *bad* luck if you want, but I'm no better than the Freedom Brothers' leader."

"Which brings me to this…" She tilts her head sideways, and suddenly grasps my elbows to pull my arms down to my sides as if to kiss me. "No one really knows who the head is. Not the citizens, not the UPP, not even the rank-and-file FB members themselves. True shadow government. Hell of a superhero movie plot."

"I'm no superhero."

"You're the closest thing we have."

"Everything I've done," I begin, gritting my teeth and scowling at the rendering, "I've done for my family."

"Maybe that's what sets you apart," she says, pausing and considering her next words before continuing. "The gangs let fear and anger drive them, not love."

"Love of power."

She snaps at me, "That's not love, and you know it."

"Like you're an expert."

She hesitates. "Remember what I told you after than run-in with Scylla? About Beau? It took me forever to process it. And maybe you don't expect occult dealers to experience much love, because everything is mysterious and black instead of sunshine and rainbows."

"You don't need to go over it," I mumble. Still, her tone suggests she's ready to do more because I'm here—Kerry, Conveyor of Light and Shade. In my entire lifetime, I haven't spent a moment considering the effect I have on the emotions of other people. It must be an unfortunate side-effect of my abilities that I haven't yet considered, but it makes sense. If light and dark boil down to emotions, and emotions power my abilities, then that energy can transfer into others. It's either delightful or terrible news. Marissa paints it in streaks of gray. While I can detect an air of hope in her voice, her sadness, and even despair, are obvious.

"It had to be love," she whispers, her voice wavering. "Things like that don't affect you so much without love."

"What is it you're *really* saying?" I'm suddenly aware of my sarcastic tone and that Marissa could infer distrust from it.

"You know what I'm saying."

She's not saying much. But sometimes, fewer words speak more important truths. Is she revealing feelings for me?

"Independence Tower," she says, changing the topic, "might be the sign of things to come. If you like corruption with your morning coffee fix, you imbibe it for the rest of the day, if you catch my drift. United Philadelphians for Progress is the one thing standing in the FB's way of changing this city for their own gain. If they're willing to defile important public sites, they won't let an occult dealer with spiritual powers stop them."

"You said it yourself," I interrupt her. "UPP are scum."

"They all are," she says, backing away from the plan table. "You're the only one who can topple the power structure. And I think that it starts with finding Atlantis."

"The gods will do anything for that info," I admit.

"Maybe it's time to call on your Neato friends for a favor."

Marissa's joke refers to the New Titan Order, or NTO. Maybe it's the darkness of the hideout soaking my spirit, but I let it pass without laughing. Suddenly the lights flicker off.

"Power-save mode," she mutters. "I programmed the battery supply that way for two reasons. First, it saves energy for when I'll need it. And second, motion sensors would let me sleep too long, so I make a habit of getting up every two hours to turn the lights back on. When I flip the switch, it resets the timer."

"You want me to get the lights?"

I can sense her yawning in the dark, after which she whispers: "I think we can rest a while. Send your wife an InstaText. Let her know you're safe."

"Won't that cause problems?" I assume she knows what I'm alluding to, but in the darkness I can read her body language or expression.

"Maybe," she says, amending to, "Probably. The power comes from the battery, but you know how InstaTexts transmit. They used to use cell-towers, but that's the old-fashioned way. When the recorder finishes compressing your message, it blasts it out through the earth's energy where only your wife can decode it. But the FB might have techies that can decode any messages sent from within the city."

"How could they?"

She sighs. "Geofencing. The technology goes back decades, but criminals are getting better and better at using it for their own nefarious purposes. Didn't you wonder why they don't have guards at every city entrance? Because they don't need them. When your car comes through the gate, they know."

"Don't tell me that," I grumble. "I haven't renewed my insurance yet."

"Yeah," she says, "They don't care about your car. They care about you."

"But I assume they have cameras," I stammer. "They see my face, they connect my registration, find my car, use the SmartLink system to track my earlier movements, and boom! They've got my wife and son as hostages."

"You've seen too many sci-fi movies."

"This *is* a sci-fi movie."

"Fine then," she says, "Don't send the InstaText. If she rips your head off when you get back home, don't blame me."

Becky would never rip my head off. Over the years, she's proven capable of hurting me in more nuanced ways, not through the power of words, but by the silence between the words. The tactic is really effective; only a woman with superior intellect could do it. And while she only uses it when she's *really* upset, I've known her to do this over dinner when recounting the latest meeting. It sets me off for the rest of the evening, and she never apologizes. Apology is unnecessary because she fully understands my flawed explanations.

The conversation winds down as I stare into the darkness. Usually, talking through dire circumstances until Becky falls asleep helps me, but I don't want to disturb Marissa.

I hear her retreat to a corner next to the fire riser, vinyl and poly fabric scraping across the tile floor as she covers herself. She hasn't planned for a visitor, so I'm on my own.

As time ticks by I parse the events of the day, trying to break them into manageable chunks in order to understand them better. I'm aware of the hardness of the floor, and even the awkwardness of the dark itself. I'm not used to sleeping on my own in pitch black.

More than an hour must have passed by the time my eyes droop, and I enter a harrowing dreamworld.

The frothy seas roar as the black hurricane swirls overhead, the spray from breaking waves indistinguishable from the wind-whipped downpour. Lightning forks across the sky as the watercraft lists hard to port, sending me spiraling into the storm. As the icy water hits my skin, it feels like a million needles peppering my skull with the words:

Now you shall suffer.

"I'm going to die," I croak.

There are things worse than death.

In the maelstrom, Ian calls out to me—"Dad! It's out of control! Get yourself to dry land, fast. I can outlast it, but you can't."

The storm brews a sinister black face that boils with rage as the lightning blinks through the clouds like flashes of fiery blood seen through veins. When its mouth opens, a hundred yellow fangs appear, tipped with blood. Ian yells at me to flee as the boat cracks under the pounding waves.

"I won't make it!" I shriek. "Tell the gods I said…"

I never finish my sentence, cut off by gurgling saltwater entering my lungs and sorrow filling my heart. Somewhere between existence and chaos, I languish, my muscles and skin losing sensation as my soul flits away like a spark in the ether. I cannot reenter my body, but I know the journey is not over yet.

From somewhere, I can still sense the vibrations of Sarah's energy, blinding me with life even in the nothingness. *"Follow me,"* The Phoenix says, dipping its fiery wings in the brackish water surrounding me.

Falling into the unconscious abyss, I allow my heart to answer through a simple rhythmic beat, saying I won't give up, even in death.

The saltwater in my lungs burns, sending my brain a single, blackened word: *Suffer.*

6

Colossus

*S*uffer.

It's amazing how a single-word sentence can evoke such feelings of bitter anguish. I blink awake in the dark, trying to listen for Marissa stirring behind the partition.

I can't tell how long I've been asleep, but if I have battery power in my phone, I should be able to see the time. I'd left home in the morning with a full battery and was using it to navigate to Philadelphia and to enjoy music during the drive—enough usage to drain it—and had neglected to bring my charger. I could ask Marissa to power it from her storage battery, but she probably has better uses for that.

"Kerry?"

Her gentle voice from behind the partition causes me to sit upright and chills to race across my flesh.

"Is that you?"

"Don't mind me," I mumble, uncertain whether she heard me. "Just a dream."

I've suffered before—during my entire adult life, tragedies and crises have come and gone, and ever since the time-travel started, I've endured even more heartache and distress. Because of my history, a command like "Don't mind me" should not drive me to the brink, yet it still punishes me, no matter how I try to distract my mind from going there.

"Eh, time to get up anyway. You want to get out of here?"

This tunnel may be the safest place in the city, but staying also has challenges, chief amongst them the inability to make headway with our investigation. Throughout my career, investigating always meant finding more economical solutions to common construction problems, researching products, and devising new methods of using labor. Auditing a former mayor's assassination had never crossed my mind. And because Philadelphia may be the most dangerous city on earth, I don't really want to venture out. Because Becky has warned me, and because I don't want to *suffer*. Watching this once-great city tear itself apart is more than enough tribulation.

"What do you have in mind?"

She hesitates, perhaps tactfully. "I know a place. Quiet, off-the grid. Perfect sewer for us to pay homage to the past. Last time I went there, I found a sealed-off passage leading somewhere important, with FB's ugly logo stamped on it."

"Great place to get our heads bashed in," I agree.

"We can fight them off."

I remind her, "Miriam warned me not to—"

"Funny thing about oracles: Sometimes their warnings must become prophecies. Even funnier thing about prophecies: They tend to fulfill themselves, especially when you least expect it."

Pushing myself up from the floor makes my muscles hurt and my bones creak. In normal human years, unblemished by time travel, I shouldn't be a grandfather, and I still endure aches and pains from my encounters with Titans and monsters. Entering a fight on so little sleep is a recipe for disaster.

"That's not something she ever described herself as being."

"I would have thought it obvious," she chides. "She frames her sessions as 'healings' because that has a positive connotation."

"And for a sorceress-slash-seer-slash-healer, she seems well-versed in physics. Alarmingly so."

Marissa hesitates, and I can hear the blankets swish as she pushes them into the corner, "Why's it alarming?"

"See, I used to depend on Secretary Harley for that kind of wisdom. In fact, I could use a refresher if we can make it to Washington. Because Harley knew Mayor Archimedes—he's how he got involved in politics."

"No one in their right mind would want to get involved in politics these days," she says. "They make their living by saying outrageous things. Even if none of the innuendo is true, it would drive a normal person crazy. Another self-fulfilling prophecy."

"That's not the point," I interrupt her. "Harley might know something we don't."

"And we're supposed to find him in Washington? He's been out of public office for six years. Or did you not realize that?"

"I guess I got too busy enjoying my family," I snap. "You should try it sometime."

"Running from zealous cults drains your time even when you're in a cult yourself."

Cult accusations have tarnished politics since I can remember, but no one ever admits being in a cult. To politicians, it's nothing more than a special organization supporting a person or cause, and following it comes with the promise of reward, of either money or prestige. "What?"

"Long story," she says, tapping on the light switch next to the fire riser and squinting.

"Do you ever do guerilla warfare? Steal your opponent's weapons after defeating them?"

"You'd have to be insane to try it," she remarks, tilting her head for emphasis. "Not enough people to mask it. Once someone gets word you're armed, they'll hunt you down, shoot you with your own gun, and defend themselves against UPP."

"Okay."

"Good thing I've got my own stash. Never been used." Grunting as she reaches behind the fire riser, she pulls on a shiny steel latch screwed into a plywood box. I watch her open the door, listen to clinks of metal against metal, and see her pull out two guns.

"Police grade," she says, aiming one and checking its 'magazine', which is only a cartridge attached to an electrical pulse. A police-issued stun gun can immobilize enemies, even if it doesn't knock them out or kill them like in the movies.

She passes one to me, while resting her elbow on the red-painted wheel of the manual shut-off valve. I study the weapon's heft in my hand, mentally comparing it to the weight of a nine-millimeter handgun. It feels lighter, yet not as light as I would have thought it should be. Checking whether the safety is engaged, I point it around the room, squinting as I find a target—a narrow stainless-steel cylinder attached to the instrument panel mounted on the partition.

"You'll have to be conservative with it," she warns. "No backups. So don't miss."

"Easier said than done."

"They're more effective at close range."

"Do I even want to know how you got these?" I squint at the sighting mechanism, rest my finger on the trigger guard, and release my pent-up breath. "Stealing from the police department is a felony."

"No such thing as a felony in a lawless city devoid of police." She slips her weapon under her belt and watches me familiarize myself with mine.

"I got there to find it had already been ransacked. Everyone always goes right for the armory, but you can find good stuff in the evidence lockers. They'd pried the lockers open, but I found an unmarked box under a huge pile of debris. Four taser guns, seven knives, and a blowgun. I used the one and only dart on someone chasing me home one night—probably wanted to rape me or something. And that put him in a real bad mood."

I frown. "God, this city is a hellhole."

"You ready to clean it up?"

Either her confidence is a ruse to mask her worries, or she's made bravado part of her overall strategy. I can't decide which is true, or which is worse. But then I remember that she's found a way to survive, and maybe I should give her more credit. That kind of bluster is tough for me to master, even when I try. Becky *hates* ego, so I've had plenty of practice with patience and humility, those oft-discussed, yet seldom-used supports of Biblical faith.

Without speaking, she clicks on her flashlight, clenches it between her teeth and begins to climb. I hadn't noticed how bone-chilling the air forty feet underground was until now. To my bare hands, the rebar ladder rungs feel as if they're coated with frost. I'm shivering before we reach the top. Shining the light on the latch, she slides it open, pushes up the lid, and lets a few rays of pale blue light filter into the pit. Then she waits on her knees for me to pull myself out of the hole. My eyes fall on a painted pictogram behind the top few ladder rungs. In the scant light I swear I can make out *wings.*

And flames. I see them just before she shutters the hatch, examines the lock, and clicks it closed. Cautiously, she lowers the lid into place, stands up, and offers me a hand. Before we make our way to the crawl-through entryway, she pats me down, rests her palms on my shoulders, and says something in a foreign language.

Careful not to offend her, I raise my eyebrows and wait for her to explain.

"Reference from your Book of *Revelation.* I'm surprised you don't know it."

Shrugging, I decide on humor. "Guess I'm not used to hearing it outside the original Hebrew."

"It's an exhortation to wisdom," she explains. "Contrary to what you might expect, it can get you far in this city."

"Make new friends and influence people," I say, squinting. Following her out the door, I gag at the smell of fresh human waste, while she crawls out pretending not to notice. Sunrise should be under an hour away, judging by the emerging orange and yellow light invading the blue sky behind the defaced skyline. A storefront shattered across the street lies twisted beneath foam-insulation wallboards and crumbling siding. On an unbroken segment lying sideways over a rusted sewer grate, among layers of graffiti, I spy the anarchist symbol.

Marissa leads the way along the sidewalks, keeping a low profile should stalkers seek to engage us. Before we make it a block, I notice that she's hidden her weapon while I'm still carrying mine in my hands. Inserting it into my jeans pocket feels awkward, but I'll just have to endure it. Marissa sniffs the air, gauging our direction. She looks at the pre-sunrise glow over New Jersey, and tiptoes into what remains of an alleyway.

"Not a step farther," warns someone in the darkness.

Panicking, I fumble for the weapon as he speaks again, "I'll shoot you right now for trespassing."

"Christ, Dawson, you know who I am," says Marissa, waving at me to settle down.

"You got him to come?" Dawson looks at me and frowns. "Always knew you were persuasive, but damn."

"I'm sorry," I say. "You have *friends?*"

"Allies," she corrects me, squinting into the shadows. "Another thing that pays off. You don't trust anyone unless you have mutual needs. Dawson supplies me with information, I give him protection from the gangs. Favors for favors."

Dawson steps out from under an eave into a brighter patch. His buzz cut might give him away as ex-military, but he also sports a face tattoo depicting a muscular human with a bare, outstretched arm. The subject's torso disappears under his collar, and when Dawson flexes his muscles, the figure opens his eyes and scowls.

"Good night?" Marissa asks, and he nods.

"Managed to stay out of harm's way this time," he agrees. "But those thugs didn't know where to look this time."

If anything is true about Philadelphia the way it is now, it's that it harbors many hiding places, and the less accessible and more dangerous, the better. He's chosen a rotted-out wooden residential building as his fortress for the night. I might consider it a strange choice, but I assume he has his own reasons for staying here.

"Got anything for me? We could use a good lead."

"Not much in the way of leads," Dawson admits, shaking his head. "But good news. You know that sewer you found the other day? I saw people in there last night. Judging by the smell, they hadn't bathed in a month."

"Which means they're not part of the gangs." Marissa explains, glancing at me.

"FB probably still has eyes on it. You going in this morning?"

"We have to find out if there's anything else they're hiding. The UPP didn't kill Arch for nothing."

"That's still an assumption," I interject, earning a dark look from Dawson.

He gathers a fist, and turns back to Marissa with a subtle whisper, which I can't make out. Of course, he didn't intend for me to hear it, but that doesn't inspire trust. I frown as she whispers back, pats him on the forearm, and exchanges a glance with me. They were whispering about me. I can take a hint.

"It's the only thing we've got," she says, raising her voice. "Who cares if it's circumstantial? The real quest is restoring glory to our city. And this is the key."

"Fine…" I say, showing my palms and backing away a step or two, as though they're about to fight me.

As quick as it began, the conversation closes. Dawson retreats into his lair as Marissa stalks on down the alleyway, avoiding piles of debris and human waste. After ten minutes we reach an intersection, which the gangs have cleared to allow unimpeded traffic into the heart of Philadelphia's historic district. Taking this avenue during the day might be dangerous, but Marissa has a different plan.

Abutting the sidewalk near the corner, an open grate allows a trickle of water from the street to drip into a cavernous chamber below. Although it's reinforced steel, citizens have been pulling it out of its concrete anchor bolts, leaving gouged-out holes. Checking both directions for oncoming cars, Marissa pulls the grate off the opening, peers into the darkness, and nods at me.

"Go on," she says. "I've got your six."

"Who's got my midnight?" I ask.

"Be ready for anything," she whispers, "but trust our intelligence. If there are citizens down there, they won't engage with intruders, because any intruders will be FB and *they're* armed to the teeth."

"So are we."

"At least ours aren't lethal."

Crouching and then sitting back on my buttocks, I place my feet on a concrete ledge, peer into the murk, and try to adjust to the darkness. The bent-rebar steps disappear into the black after only a few feet. I'm glad Marissa's backing me up. Ten steps down, I splash into a two-inch deep puddle as my eyes adjust to the dim light.

"Get back," I can hear a woman whisper twenty feet ahead. She shrinks into a narrow side-channel, careful not to disturb the water.

I offer her a sympathetic glance as I pass by, Marissa following behind me. The main channel, I decide, must run the length of the thoroughfare, taking in more and more storm drainage from hundreds of entry points along the way. The utility vault covers, spaced about a hundred feet apart, allow spots of hallucinogenic light to reflect off the puddles that soak the concrete pipes on which we tread.

Marissa takes the lead as a man ducks into a dark side channel. When she reaches a slight dogleg, the pipe splits into parallel runs. The main branch must continue straight into the historic district, while the smaller branch might lead us under the park. She takes that route, her hair skimming the top of the pipe. The smaller size means I need to bow my head as I walk. A single strand of spider silk sticks to my forehead as the humidity increases.

With an abrupt halt, Marissa puts an index finger to her lips, points into the darkness fifty feet ahead, and we prepare our guns. As a shadow shifts, we know we've garnered unwanted attention. Our enemies close on us faster than I'd thought possible. The nearest one swings a punch at me, and I react by pulling the trigger, sending a coiled wire of energy straight at his heart. His fist slams into my head as he collapses into a puddle, slamming his face onto the concrete.

The second man strikes at Marissa. She points the taser at his groin, unleashes her shot, and listens to him howl as he falls to the floor. Now out of ammo, we're down to two-against-one.

The third wastes no time, hitting Marissa in the gut and slamming a fist into my face. Marissa slaps him and kicks at his shin while I shove him away, terrified as I hear muted voices ahead. We're outnumbered, but I can only concentrate my energy on my immediate attacker.

Marissa picks up a broken-off chunk of cement to defend herself with while I punch the attacker's jaw. He retaliates by shoving me sideways so that I trip on my own leg. To catch myself from falling, I twist my ankle out of position, tripping him as he advances. His first swing misses, but he catches his balance by wrapping his arm around my neck and squeezing.

The darkness in my heart plunges deeper as he beats me bloody. I manage a kick to his stomach, but he doesn't seem to notice. And when he zeroes in on me for the kill strike, something strange happens.

Ten more enemies appear, whooping and cheering as my assailant prepares to snap my neck. Instead, he is crying and whimpering in the darkness.

"I was only trying to do what you said," he pleads to no one. "Be brave. But I can't anymore. I'm sorry."

"Marissa, what are you doing?"

"Convincing him to go easy on you," she mumbles.

When he hears her, he regains focus, squares his jaw, and squeezes my neck until I'm ready to pass out. I feel the blackness encroach, and when I hear the crack of a breaking bone, I open my eyes. The attacker is screaming, and our audience has ceased to cheer. My dark energy erases my assailant's arm. Marissa readies herself to fight once again, while the ten foes size us up.

One of them growls at me, "Well, if it isn't *The* Kerry Gearhardt."

My veins turn to ice as I ready for another battle. In the darkness, he watches me shuffling my feet on the cement floor of the pipe. My heart hammers inside my chest as he takes three giant steps toward me, stops, and stares right into my eyes. A spot of light from the utility cover dances on his scalp, ringing his eye with a halo of white encircling a fireball pupil as angry as the sun. With a sudden pang, I know who he is, and it's bad news.

7

The Omphalos Stone

I should have heard his hooves clicking on the cement pipe wall as he approached. Now that he stands before me, my nerves jangle. The great centaur Chiron stands a full six inches taller than I do. His bare, muscular arms sprout from broad shoulders, between which a golden mane grows. His nostrils flare as he stares at us, stamping his hind legs.

Marissa holds a defensive position should any of the group attack, but so far, they hold their ground.

"How—how do you know about me?" I stutter.

Chiron lowers his voice, and says in an enquiring, yet kind tone, "You are legend. I heard you convened with my brother and defeated the Titans. So many heroic accomplishments, yet such a tragic history. I don't suppose you came to help us."

I growl at him. "The Freedom Brothers can burn in hell."

He shakes his head and Marissa steps back toward the tunnel wall, closing her eyes as if to ask the dead to speak. Her posture, while defensive, looks ready to fight should the need arise. But so far, neither Chiron nor his posse have moved to attack us.

"I assumed that you knew I'm not beholden to them. I represent a different group, which seeks to restore this city to its former glory. We've held our own thus far but could use your help."

Glancing at his friends tells me all I need to know. The three women are toned and slender, with sleek sheaths of hair falling down their backs.

The bulky tattooed men wield short swords. Their trimmed beards highlight clenched jaws. They stand still and easy, like a bowling pin arrangement, in three rows.

"United Philadelphians for Progress," I bite. "You murdered Mayor Archinson. Scum."

"The mayor's death was a tragic accident," Chiron murmurs, "but quite necessary."

"Didn't look accidental to me. You pumped him full of bullets."

"The former mayor wasn't fond of being followed," he continues, "much less pursued. The FB leader wanted him on charges ranging from espionage to sedition. While investigating those accusations, we learned he held crucial information and sought to have him meet with us before the FB kidnapped him, or whatever else they do with their victims. But the mayor didn't trust us, tried negotiating his way out, and when the FB arrived, he ran. We aimed for the FB foot soldiers and two errant shots hit him in the back. Had he escaped, we'd have had bigger problems."

"You talk smooth," I say, attempting to swallow my sarcasm. The circle of light from the utility cover reappears above his right eye, shrouding his face in shadow and making him appear mechanical. A horse-cyborg hybrid is more than unnerving, and I lost focus momentarily. "But I know a forked tongue when I hear one."

He flexes his shoulders, tilting his head so that the circle of light disappears into his thick hair. "You don't know what I seek, yet you're here. Which means you were following Archinson before we'd ever heard of him. If either of us has a forked tongue, Kerry, Conveyor of Light and Shade, it must be you."

"You've done your research," I say. His rear hooves kick at scattered concrete gravel, which splashes into a nearby puddle. Over the years, rain has eroded older segments of cement pipes, leaving an uneven surface, and near Marissa's knees the wall disappears into the shadows where I sense faces watching

"As I said,"—he shrugs—"my brother told me stories about you, about your selfish actions, your ulterior motives. And that you freed the Titans, including his despicable father. That you helped where it counted, and he rewarded you. But he underestimated your cunning."

"Because I was a servant of The One," I mumble. "I did it out of necessity, to save my family, something neither you nor Zeus would understand."

"We seek the stone," he says, ignoring this, "Get out of our way, or we will slay you."

"The legends claimed you were kind," I call out to him as he clicks his hind hooves on the pipe and turns his back. "I guess that means the stories never capture the true essence of anyone."

"We all have families," he says, leveling his voice and striking an authoritative pose. "Don't pretend I know nothing about you. We all have different needs, but our methods are the same. That makes us comrades; brothers in arms. You and I have a common enemy. We must unite to defeat them."

Suppressing the urge to spit out a retort, I turn to face Marissa, seeing her open her eyes a sliver. The ten UPP fighters begin hacking at a five-foot-diameter circle of cement and mortar patching a broken pipe wall. Because the access hatch is above this spot, I assume that if there's a room behind the wall this may be a flow-measuring station.

The cement patchwork crumbles as they work at it. Marissa's demeanor has gone cold, a bad sign. A tangle of deep roots hangs through a hole in the pipe above her. The light shifts overhead, and when she emerges from her trance, a familiar emotion spreads across her face, as though the spirits of the dead are manifesting their sentiment through her. Is this a new power? I'll ask her about it later, but now, we must escape.

"Let's get out of here," I mumble, grasping her hand.

She resists without speaking, clenching her knuckles, pulling her fingers from my grip and standing firm, her expression growing frostier. The dead have spoken, warning her that Chiron and his gang may not be trustworthy. Still, she seems intent on lingering here. It may be that her wish to save the city depends on what lies beyond the concrete patch in the pipe wall. We're unlikely to know while we're outnumbered five to one. She looks at me, seeming to ask what my plan is, but no ideas spring to mind.

Thirty feet upstream, a pair of eyes emerge from the mist, growing larger as they move toward us. Someone has heard everything and seeks to join us. But then something changes in Marissa's expression: A mysterious blue glow that vanishes as the citizens arrive. At once, the eyes multiply.

Not one pair, but a hundred yellow eyeballs hover toward us like fireflies, gathering into a battle formation behind the ten UPP fighters.

My heart sinks. "What are you doing?" I whisper to Marissa.

"We needed a distraction, and Miriam never warned *me* to not use my power."

I don't believe it. The eyes float silently behind the ten warriors chipping at the wall, waiting for them to break through—or take notice.

"Getting close, sir," a woman shouts as she slashes her blade at crumbling cement.

"They will help us only a moment," Marissa warns, "but it might be enough."

The chatter intensifies when they gouge an expanding hole in the pipe wall, crowding around it while working to enlarge it. Now there's a hole large enough to step through. They part, allowing Chiron to hurdle the knee-high entrance. As he disappears through it into darkness, the nine soldiers turn, like sentries guarding an entrance to a sacred tomb. In a flash of panic the hundred yellow eyes flicker out, their gathered mist seeping through the soldiers' clothes and entering their bodies like wisps of vapor through open pores.

"Boss," one woman murmurs, "something strange is happening."

I straighten up. As I move to meet them, reaching for the darkness in my soul, the Phoenix's energy fills my spirit and I attack them. But instead of fighting back, they scatter through the tunnels and disappear. Chiron continues to inspect the hidden treasures, and when he sighs, I know the battle is on. The hundreds of eyes blink back into being, glowering as Chiron turns his back on his bounty.

They stand watch, and before I realize what's happening, he steps aside, allowing us to enter the tight chamber while the hovering eyes wait outside.

The small chamber affords us little room to maneuver as we stand around a stone table in the center. Above it, artificial light shines down from a circular fixture in the solid rock. The dust inside refuses to settle. Cobwebs cling to the altar surface, stringing a silky gauze between the stone dais and the room's crown jewel, a boulder carved into the image of a pineapple.

"I never expected to see it again," Chiron gasps reverently. "Behold the navel stone. Taken from its original home at Delphi and brought here for reasons untold. The ultimate symbol of protection, once thought to be an ancient relic that had disappeared into time."

"The ... what?"

"The Titan Cronus had a habit of swallowing his own children," he explains, "deeming them threats to his power. But my mother wanted to protect my brother from him, so she fashioned a stone and wrapped it in swaddling clothes, swapping it with Zeus long before the Titan war. I thought it was a myth."

"You came here to get a rock?" I ask, unable to mask the exasperation in my voice.

"This room holds many secrets," Chiron explains, examining the stone and running his fingertips along its textured sides.

Around the platform, hugging each of the walls, are stone benches with carved backrests. Hundreds of tiny black spiders scurry through the etched cracks, spinning cobwebs in the dust. As I take it all in I suddenly realize what this room is, and dread creeps into my gut.

We have entered the Cella of an ancient temple, hidden in Philadelphia's bedrock for thousands of years. Decorative patterns etched on the walls rise toward carved wooden cornices at each corner of the chamber, with decayed crown mouldings in between. In each corner of the room slender fluted columns taper toward a cracking ceiling, which scatters sand over the treasures within.

Scrolls of ancient papyrus sit on one bench, and as Chiron pays respect to the statue, Marissa sits and unfurls one. As she does so a hairy spider scurries across her lap, pauses on her knee, and gazes up at me. I'm terrified.

"The curse shall be revealed," she reads, translating Ancient Greek. "The powers within shall not be disturbed. Great destruction will rain upon you for defiling this temple."

She sighs, adding, "And I thought the city was already cursed."

"Marissa." My throat goes dry as the spiders multiply, crawling over my feet and running up my pants leg. "The last time they unsealed this room, they unearthed the curse. It's happening again. We need to get out."

"You're still terrified of our tiny eight-legged friends?" she asks, mockingly.

Before I can utter a swear word, the spiders multiply again, covering the walls like churning oil stains. They climb over each other, filling the room as they form an inch-thick carpet. They swarm over my hands as I bolt toward the exit. Impatient, Chiron stamps his hooves on the floor, smashing thousands of them.

I screech as a spider drops onto Marissa's scalp. She takes it gently between her fingers and says to it, "Tell your little friends to give my friend a little space."

"Marissa!"

The ceiling bubbles with spider babies, filling the chamber with a nest of silk. Agony courses through my veins as I leap out of the chamber ahead of Marissa and Chiron. The tunnel rumbles as though an earthquake is in progress, and the spiders chase us through the storm drains. My blood feels like ice as I sprint away from them, even faster than Chiron can gallop.

When we reach the junction, I swipe dozens of arachnids off my pants, arms, and face, howling with terror. Marissa trails behind me at least fifty paces as I make my way back to the grate we entered through. Chiron turns away toward the other end of the channel. As I reach the rebar ladder we'd descended, spiders spread out through the storm drains.

Dozens of civilians watching from the branch tunnels mutter disapproval as we flee the ancient curse. The city trembles as the curse gathers momentum. At street level, echoing screams shrill across the city.

The cloudless sky above me pulses with a flickering sun, as though it's about to explode. Spiders crawl out of the utility lids, covering the towers in strands of silk.

I feel utterly helpless as we flee. The sun looks like a white-hot fireball. A dozen blocks away, a building topples as the earthquake rips a gash through the city's streets, swallowing burned-out cars, dueling citizens, and the detritus from the Titanic destruction unleashed a year ago. I only know one way out of this, but it will destroy Cronus' mending of spacetime that freed Ian from the bonds of death. If we do not escape, the city will cease to exist.

Marissa seems to know this; she tries to keep up with me as I tear through the streets in search of a shadow or an intact elevator shaft. But the destruction has demolished every portal in the city. We're trapped. The city goes dark, as though a monstrous asteroid has eclipsed it. When I gaze up, I can see tentacles wrapping like a dome over Philadelphia. The monster will swallow the city whole.

But terror and rage have carved out a blackened pit in my stomach, rendering my body invisible. I black out as the beast crosses over us and departs. The black clouds of my limbs spread out over the cracked streets. Screams echo as ruins tumble into more ruins. In a flash of blinding light, it all disappears and an eerie silence resumes.

The blank white room I've landed in stretches to infinity, bathing everything in purest white. The light in the room dims for a split second as I hear wings beating in the distance. Closing my eyes does little to shield my senses from the blinding light, but when the colors emerge, they form into a red bird. The Phoenix lands beside me, its heart murmuring strange sentences directly into my soul, as though it no longer needs to speak to fill me with wisdom.

Be the light, Kerry. You must convey it to save Philadelphia. And you will.

My heart races as I open my eyes. The blinding light filters away, leaving Marissa and me alone in a broken city. The fleeing citizens have stopped running, and a temporary peace reigns. Careful to check myself for lingering spiders, I wrap my arms around Marissa, sensing hundreds of eyes looking at us. Marissa glances around, uncertain whether they are the spirits of the dead she'd summoned. But they're the eyes of citizens; citizens dressed in filthy clothes, their hair matted to their faces, whimpering children clinging to their legs.

Then a child steps into the shattered street, gazes into my eyes, grins, and turns to her mother, a tall black woman wearing a puzzled expression. I know what she's about to say before says it: "It's him."

8

Pheme's Trumpet

The child's unwashed face still carries traces of what she last ate, interspersed with many weeks' worth of grime and sweat. Her red stretch jeans had turned maroon after over a month of wandering the city. Matted hair, a few tufts in loosening pigtails, sprouts over her ears like a giraffe's ossicones. She pouts at me before glancing up at her mother's ashen face.

Wordless, the mother stares at me as though trying to scrape a few thoughts together. Before she speaks, Marissa gives a sideways nod, nudging me to glance toward New Jersey.

"You want to explain that?" I ask.

"I assumed you already knew," Marissa says, shaking her head.

Of course I know, but that doesn't help to lighten the tension. Instead, everything about it seems forced, as though the child and her mother shared a common secret without the need to communicate verbally.

"Tell them," Marissa whispers as several sets of eyes appear out of the debris, each regarding me contemptuously.

"Tell them what?"

"Anything."

I clear my throat, look away in order to assemble a sentence, and then look directly at them.

The watching citizens have tripled over the last few minutes. The more I hesitate, the more time the Freedom Brothers have to notice. I can only be brief, and I don't have any reassuring words. Every thought bouncing around inside my cranium is a confused mishmash of conflicting ideas.

"This is your city," I say. "Fight for it before they take that ability away. I can do little—"

"You fought the Titans," a man accuses. "Show a little guts for Christ's sake. 'Less their cowardice rubbed off on you?"

"They know you're here, anyway," the child's mother agrees. "The gangs deprive us of food, shelter, protection. And they hoard all the weapons. We won't get far without a leader."

"There's another possibility," I argue. "If the Governor decides to listen to the corrupt FB about an uprising problem, he'll send in the National Guard to quell it, and your problems multiply. We're working something out, so give us a couple of days to—"

"Good job," Marissa interrupts, mocking my fumbled sentences. "Could you at least try to act human?"

The crowd turns their attention to her instead, realizing that she's mastered the English language better than I have. No argument from me.

"See that?" the child's mother says, eyeing the horizon where a darkening blur wafts in the sky. I don't have the nerve to look up, because every time I do, I overload my senses with the destruction and chaos coursing through this city. Dilapidated piles of ruins on top of smashed cars huddle against the dangerous streets. Hundreds of bodies rot under building carcasses; they're never going to be identifiable. The morning rays of the sun shoot through the maze of rubble, glinting off shards of glass and the foil of a fragment of insulation fluttering on the humid breeze. A broken segment of black iron piping rests on a crushed concrete slab, under twisted ceiling grids and shattered wooden trusses. The ashes of a once-great metropolis, now reduced to embers. I can't cope with this much destruction, and every emaciated face spreads despair through my soul.

"That's what you referred to as a Shade, isn't it?"

I don't bother looking, just give a disinterested nod, as though to cure her doubts.

"Which means the FB has allies."

"Stay away from it," I warn them. "And whatever you do, don't give in to fear."

"Easier said than done," says a man with graying stubble, grimacing. He shuffles his feet in a mound of dirt and shattered gravel without looking up, a signal that he's struggling to find the will for positive emotions. The city in this condition will suck you dry.

"Anything else?"

"You fought them!"

"How can you stand here looking this weak? The rumors called you a hero."

"Guess they were wrong."

Unknown faces, unknown names. And they have all built their opinions around nothing but hearsay. I feel helplessness like a poison eating away at my spirit. I can do nothing for them.

"I still think he's brave," the little girl says, tugging at her mother's top.

Her garment's single button is covered in mud. Her tangled hair hangs over her ear, and her mascara has run into jagged canyons across her face. She frowns, restless. "Don't talk to him, Vanessa," she whispers.

Vanessa? My heart misses a beat. I try to reply, but nothing I say will ease the tension. In fact, trying to guess her identity might detonate the entire conversation.

Too late. The mother scowls at me as I catch myself staring at Vanessa.

"Get the hell out of here, you coward! If I see you again, I'll kill you myself. To think my husband died for you!"

When they say every story has two sides, they never clarify which side is which. In a bleak situation like this one, differentiating allies from foes is hard. Generating a greater understanding of your own position only admits a failure to grasp the intentions of others, leading to a harsher outlook and further division.

"Kerry," Marissa says, "we should get moving. I calculate the FB will arrive in…"

"One damn second," growls a muscular man. He shoves the stubble-faced man aside, clutches Vanessa's forearm, and raises his fist. "Disband, or this one dies!"

Anger sinks into my heart. "The hell she does."

Muscles tosses Vanessa aside like a rag doll and her mother shrieks. If I can't fight for Vanessa, I can't fight for anyone, which would mean that her mother is right. I stagger toward him.

He laughs as a meaty hand grabs the mother by her hair. He swings her back and forth, dragging her feet across the blacktop as he roars with derisive laughter. "You and whose army?" He shows his teeth, and spits. "So you're the one they're talking about. Here to save the day again, just like last time? Maybe you should tell them how much blood is on your hands."

In a single motion, I charge him, channeling power into my fist. Muscles anticipates my first punch, blocking it with his wrist, but the power surging through me snaps his bones and sends his own backhand smashing into his nose. He doubles over, wiping blood from his face, his expression filled with hatred. His bulk slows him down. I can see what his intentions are before he moves a muscle.

His first punch swipes past my ear, and on the rebound, I grab his forearm and twist. Anger pulses through the veins in his neck. He resets his stance, then slams his heel into my knee. A sharp pain spreads through my leg as he makes contact, but not before the energy spinning through my veins recoils. The kickback sends him staggering backward at least ten feet while I lunge at him.

"You can't win, Gearhardt," he snarls, shoving aside Vanessa's mother and squaring his shoulders. Clasping his fists together and making a right angle with his elbow, he plows into me, spitting obscenities and hammering blows on my head.

"I already have," I bark.

Marissa works in the background, summoning the dead to my defense. When I sense them, the hairs on the back of my neck stand up. Muscles hesitates at the wrong moment, indecision slowing his reactions. I know what to do, but it won't be pretty.

Without even moving, I watch the confusion cross his face. Loyalty and devotion clash with shame. Before I know it, he's pulling a knife from his sock, turning it over in his hands.

"I coulda been someone," he growls, curling his fingers around the black plastic handle. "Chose to be nothing. Goodbye, Kerry Gearhardt."

"No, wait!" I cry as he shoves the blade into his own abdomen, drawing a mass of crimson blood. As he twists the blade in its incision, he glances toward the heavens, where the Elder Shade awaits.

Another dead body.

A Freedom Brothers gangster. The spirits of the dead can wield untold trauma. His eyes look up to the sky as he bleeds out. Vanessa's mother tries to shield her little girl from seeing the carnage, but Vanessa can't help but see, shock coursing through her. I fold my hands, glance at Marissa, and say nothing to the dispersing crowd.

As they leave, Vanessa's mother nods at me. "I hope I didn't judge you wrong. Make believers out of us and we can defeat them."

She turns her back to walk away, pausing when she reaches the corner of the buckling sidewalk. A destroyed and decaying sign advertising a popular soft drink sinks into splintered wood framing, crumbling asphalt shingles, and dead wires.

"By the way," she says, "You can call me Mazama."

I watch her walk away before Marissa whisks me back toward her hideout. We share little conversation as faces watch us from the gutters, draped in shadow.

Wings beat in the darkness high above the forested island as the creature of death homes in on us. My heart races as Becky and Ian disappear through the cabin's closet portal. A single scream pierces the night as I hoist a glowing rock, power it up, and hurl it at the beast's serpentine head. It explodes into a fireball as it smashes through the monster's brain, sending fiery embers into the lake's crystal surface.

Blood. Vanessa pleads with me—I must let her go.

"Mazama," Marissa mutters, committing the woman's name to memory as we climb down the ladder into the darkness. She flicks on the light, tiptoes into the protection circle painted on the floor, and moves toward the stainless-steel table.

She unfurls the scroll, plants her fist on the upper edge, and scans the English script scrawled above a faded Greek phrase at the top of the parchment.

"The piece we were looking for, it seems," she says, trying to make better use of the light.

Realizing that I'm leaning close enough to cast a shadow, I back away so she can read it. Before saying anything out loud, she purses her lips while she reads it to herself.

"What is it?"

One confused glance tells me everything I need to know. Taking this as an invitation to read it myself, I step to her shoulder and narrow my eyes to read the words. A map is hand-drawn on the parchment in modern indelible ink. It has seeped into the scroll, spreading blackened spines like a dragon's spikes. In the center of the sketch, an "X" marks an intersection between two unlabeled streets. The handwritten English notation beside it offers only one clue:

"Hear Lies the Second Bank of the United States."

Whether spelled incorrectly on purpose, the map's central message suggests we investigate on the site of the Second Bank of the US. Solving the riddle is outside my skill set. When I glance at Marissa, she unfurls her fist and pushes down on the parchment's top edge.

"You don't know the Second Bank?"

"What's the significance?"

"The design of it," she guesses. "One of the oldest examples of classical Greek architecture in the United States. The Titans destroyed buildings indiscriminately, but old buildings often have robust founda-tions that can withstand even the most violent earthquakes. It's telling us we should go there. I'm betting the FB hid this in that sewer temple to suppress evidence of something big, probably bigger than the mayor himself. This one will take careful planning, because that's ground zero of the FB's Philly operations."

"Now that everyone knows me," I ponder aloud, "I can let my powers take control again."

She nods when I speak, unwrapping more of the scroll as she says, "And that leads us to a bigger problem. Because we're aware of the SBUS, so are the United Philadelphians for Progress. And they'll have a better plan than we do."

Gloom floods my soul as Marissa reads the words written in the background. Centered lines form stanzas like a poem, and when she reaches the end, she holds her fingers over her lips and gasps, then staggers toward the light switch and flicks it off, bathing us in blackness. I want her to explain, but my nerves are vibrating. If she explains what she saw now, I might destroy her lair and consume her in my Shade body. She knows what lurks in the future. Trying to think up a plan to deal with the aftermath, she paces in the dark, bumping into her waferboard partition, rapping her fingers on the red-painted valve wheels, detaching herself. Before long, I realize what she's doing. I don't want to witness the outcome.

9
Wings and Serpents

The darkness doesn't bring sleep. Too many thoughts rampage through my brain, churning into a chaotic nightmare. And while the day's events should have just brought weariness, my muscles twitch, itches needle at my skin, and knots tighten in my back, as though my brain is making excuses to motor on. Judging by my internal clock, it might be near noon, but it's hard to really know in the impenetrable darkness.

Somehow, I can tell that Marissa remains awake. Her faint breathing suggests calm, but the way she skulks through the room without even clicking her heels on the tile floor shows a palpable air of desperation. In case she's making plans, I dare not interrupt her.

Then again, I can't assume she believes I'm asleep either. How could she? I've just faced my most mortal fear, and again I've lived to tell the tale, only to get in a brawl with a Freedom Brothers thug who let his conscience attack him. The realization rings alarm bells. Now, *both* gangs know I'm in Philadelphia. Armed with that understanding, they could either take advantage of my powers, or set out to eliminate me. But which side will do which? Making predictions is futile. Sometimes, one must forge ahead without a plan—a foreign strategy to someone like me, but not to Marissa.

I've made plans my entire life. Failing to abide by my own rules transforms me into a shell of myself. Sacrificing concrete rules for adaptability has never been my way of doing things, no matter how much Becky has chided me for it. But Marissa excels at operating on the fly. And it has led her to more success than I ever could have imagined.

Another drawback of being confused in the darkness is that it makes the perception of time unreliable. When you want time to accelerate, it slows down, stretching your nerves with the hours. When you want it to slow down, it passes away in a flash, leaving you ill-prepared for the consequences.

The FB thug used sheer strength, willpower, and even emotion, yet I emerged from the duel unscathed. Not a scratch on my body. I consider that I should have gone back and pulled the bloody knife out of his abdomen, keeping it for later use. Opportunities are lost on me more often than they should be. By now, the knife will have fallen into either the FB or UPP's hands. Then again, maybe it's better I didn't take it. Because someone could have followed us here, and if that had happened, we'd have the gangs prying open the doors by now.

After an hour or so, Marissa's breathing becomes erratic, her footsteps more pronounced. I can now hear her pacing. Before long, she settles next to me, whispers my name, and touches my forearm as though she can both sense my presence and see my exact position.

"Nice day up there," she says.

A poor icebreaker, even for me, the king of bad icebreakers. Remembering when I'd first met Sarah, my version of breaking the ice would have entailed slipping on it and breaking my arm.

"I thought only the Ancient Egyptians cursed their sacred sites. If I ever see a spider again, I'll hunt Zeus down and smite him with his own lightning rod."

Silence. Either I've offended her or she's taking it as a joke. I can't decide which is worse.

"Which gets me thinking," she says. "We should get to the Second Bank sooner rather than later. The longer we wait, the better organized the FB will be. They know you're here, and they know you're with me. And we have more chance of disrupting their empire if they don't have a strategy in place."

"Then again, rushing in unprepared is a fantastic way of finding trouble. Failure to account for both gangs will be our undoing."

"We have aces up our sleeves," she counters. "If the United Philadelphians for Progress have already learned about Suicide Guy, they'll be enjoying a round of drinks right now. Everyone knows they hoard almost the entire city's wine and spirits in their secret lairs. That might mean the FB is preparing for the worst, because they know what we're capable of."

I shake my head. Marissa's fingers slither across the floor, tangling with mine for a few seconds, giving me conflicting sensations of comfort and dread. Is it an innocent hand-touch in the dark, or does Marissa harbor desires?

"What we're capable of is no longer a surprise to them," I grumble. "They'll see it coming."

"But even in the war, when the Titans knew your abilities better than you did, we still emerged victorious."

This one induces a brief grin. "I guess Cronus misjudged me. Never expected me to junk-punch him, especially with the energy from his own hands. You can call it poetic justice or whatever, but when the chips are down, I don't care about a fair fight."

"What if we strategize around that?"

"They'll expect it." I say, turning my head to where her voice is coming from. "Don't assume they know nothing about me, because that almost lost us the war."

"The funny thing about patterns," she says, trailing away before reasserting her tone. "They don't always lead to predictability. You flip a coin ten times, getting four heads, a tail, two more heads, another tail and two more heads. It's still fifty-fifty whether you get heads again. I used to know a guy in Vegas. He told me the casino moguls program slot machines to anticipate your bets, knowing that an early payout will make the average person spend more time pulling the lever. Even the best gamblers can't beat the odds, because it's not easy to break habits you don't know you have. The computer has memorized them, but a single lapse in concentration might cause an unexpected move, and when that happens luck gives you a big win."

"Uh-huh," I say. "Just like gambling. Only the stakes are higher."

She hesitates. I imagine her hands are clasped behind her head and she's arching her back and relaxing her shoulders. "You know what I'm saying."

"I should change up my habits," I say. "But I can't do that if I'm unaware I have them."

"I have an idea about that," she says with a quick sigh.

"What's that?"

"Not telling you is part of the plan. If I told you, you'd probably overreact."

"Sure. I've had monsters come out of nowhere, goddesses and princesses giving me unexpected gifts, the Titans sending my own son after me, but this is what I'll overreact to?"

"You'll need to stay alert, because things can happen fast. If we don't move today, the Freedom Brothers will have assembled an army and UPP won't be drunk anymore."

"Well, when you say it like that..." I curl my knees up to my chest, lacing my fingers together to support the weight of my legs. Marissa's heels tap as she walks away. She flips on the light, causing me to wince as my pupils adjust.

"We should find weapons," she says, surveying the empty box where she'd stored the taser guns. "And I'm thinking the more lethal the better."

"The gangs have an embargo on weapons," I mutter.

"Not if you know where to look. It's easier to enter the city during the day, am I right? Less surveillance on the fences because their patrols have *real* criminals to track down, people who oppose their power and seek to eradicate their injustice. The point is, suburbanites can get in. Do you think they'd come unarmed?"

"They won't share."

"If we pretend to be enforcers, they might."

"Enforcers don't wear clothing they haven't washed in a year," I say, glancing at the mud stains on her black tee, and the dirt on her knees.

"People wash their clothes in the river," she argues. "Maybe not a hundred percent sanitary, but it beats being a walking incubator for who-knows-what. I have spare jeans and tees. You should get some."

"Should we just run to the clothes store?"

She nods and rests her elbow on the valve wheel, causing it to squeak as it turns under her weight. "The UPP has a store. If you don't have money with any actual value, they're willing to take bribes. Weapons or secret information. The more scandalous the better. And it just so happens that everything these cretins do is scandalous."

"This is gonna get us killed," I say, rubbing my eyelids and straightening my back. I glance at the red pentagram stenciled on the floor. Its ten-foot diameter features a sketch-shaded star like so many advertisements and company logos from the 2010s. Before I move, I glance over at the ring of paint binding the star, noticing voided letters in the two-inch-wide arc. I don't need to stare for long to understand it's Greek. I haven't learned the language. Am I supposed to believe that Marissa has just recently mastered it?

"You're a survivor," she says. "You saw the way the citizens reacted to your victory today. Even the Titans couldn't beat you."

They defeated me ten times over, if not more. I won't argue with her, but I will never forget the scars the Titans inflicted, and not all of them are physical. You would think the continual routs would strengthen me. Instead, I keep finding new ways to lose.

She's come up with a complicated plan. If she expects it to work, every variable must work out. One wrong step, and the UPP will hang us from the El track's iron supports in Kensington. But just maybe ... her plan will thrive on unpredictability. A lesson in High School about Chaos Theory and the Butterfly Effect comes to mind.

Without further explanation, she climbs the rebar ladder steps without shutting off the light. Taking the initiative, I wait for her to make it halfway before beginning to climb in the darkness. With the inconsistent rod spacing, I must feel my way upward before each step, waiting to lurch higher until I feel the cold, ribbed steel in my palms.

When Marissa pops open the hatch and peers through the cracks to survey for intruders, I glance at the moody refracted sunlight falling on the pictogram of the Phoenix. Her wings are spread as she soars through an imaginary sky as limitless as the shaft it's painted in.

Marissa crawls out of the hatch, waits for me to join her on my hands and knees, and then secures the lock. After checking to make sure the entry is secure, she crawls toward the streaking sunlight outside. I sense something is about to happen a split second before it does.

Something big and hairy scurries across my hand, sending a surge of adrenaline pouring through my veins. The shock makes me stretch up, and within a second, I'm back on the floor, groaning from the painful impact of my skull on a dangling strip of angle iron.

The sunlight parches the city from above. Standing in the shadows should help me adjust to the glare, but the shadows hold a darker secret. Not six feet away, I see someone lurking, watching us. The scent of alcohol wafts into my nostrils. Marissa just finished telling me the UPP scum had every drop of alcohol in their personal stores. The man doesn't dress like UPP, but he drinks like them.

"Good afternoon, Sam," he croons, swallowing a mouthful of vodka.

Marissa sidles along the edges of the rubble before wending her way into the open street. Abandoned, burned-out cars and rubble clog the avenue. Closer to the financial district, the heaps grow higher and more chaotic. Many unwashed civilians are probably hiding out in the hollows three stories above street-level, away from the FB's worst extremists. Understanding how they'd purged the city of all they deemed criminal fills me with misery. Neither the state nor the federal government will intervene if the gangs project an image of safety. They've made it safe for themselves by absorbing the violence and the fraud while the scattered citizens duel for necessities. Seeing it myself in such harrowing detail makes me want to retch. The stench of human waste, death, and decay makes that even easier.

"Sam?" I gasp after gazing at a church's detached steeple tilting east where it collects the sun's rays. "Who's that?"

"You are," she says. "When someone addresses you, it's polite to answer if they're not trying to kill you."

I frown as we march to a street corner, where the traffic lights lay smashed and twisted in the middle of the intersection as if bowled over by a wave of seawater and debris. "What am I supposed to call him?"

"Whatever you want. The name isn't as important as the greeting."

"I don't suppose you see Chuck very often," I say, gazing at the cracked asphalt beneath my feet.

"You're calling him Chuck?" She smiles, "Okay."

"Reminds me of a certain celebrity," I say, conjuring the image of a manicured salt-and-pepper beard and a cowboy hat.

"Not that I know of," she says, answering my earlier question. "But I saw him watching a brawl a few weeks ago, seeming to enjoy it."

"Philly has become the Wild Wild West?"

She hesitates, stopping before she trips over the traffic signal en route to the UPP's clothing store. "You know that's a myth, don't you? Two gunslingers duking it out in the dusty streets might make good movies. It never happened like it does here in Wild Wild Philly."

I breathe a curse word and pick up my pace to match hers as she skirts along the rim of a ten-foot diameter crater filled with festering water and scraps of plastic and paper trash.

"You learn to live with it," she says, quickening her pace.

I follow in silence for ten or eleven blocks, glancing back and forth from the crystal azure sky, crisscrossed with contrail streaks, and the mountains of trash and debris piled up against the facades of fallen buildings as far as I can see. My heart leaps in my chest as I see dozens of citizens lined up at a wood-sided shack constructed of recycled studs and siding. The building's plexiglass windows dull the driving sun, casting a blurred circle of reflection back at me.

Men, women, and children in rags linger, dejected. Their shoulders slump when an argument breaks out in front of them. A woman shields her child from the fray as the first combatant throws a bloody fist. The other man fights back by slapping his foe in the chest with a meaty hand.

The violence lasts less than a minute before shouting at the front of the line quells the emotion. "Shut it down, or we beat the living pulp out of you scum!"

"That would be the UPP," Marissa whispers.

"*That's* their store?" I eye the sagging wood frame supporting the wall where holes in the exterior reveal a network of red and white wires that the rats have gnawed. From inside, dull incandescent lights illuminate darkened aisles of first-rate clothing and apparel.

The windows vibrate when the UPP shouts.

"You there!" the guard shouts, glaring at me. "We're closed. Come back tomorrow, bright and early."

"He doesn't know who you are," Marissa comments. "That's good."

"Everyone needs something," the woman in front of me retorts. "Just let him stay."

"I'll make it worth your while," I answer. "Information you won't want to pass up. I need a fresh set of clothes, no designer labels or anything."

"I'm supposed to believe you? Come to the front of the line, you filthy son of a..."

"Blink," Marissa warns, an instant before she closes her eyes. The voices in the line hush as an inexplicable darkness of spirit hangs over them. As if shrouded under thick gray clouds, their skin absorbs all light and emotion, making them pale and forlorn. The dark creeps into my flesh as I seal my eyes shut.

"We'll let you in this once," the guard relents. "Welcome to Progress Goods. Watch your step."

With the color in their faces restored, the citizens grumble as they let us slink to the front of the line. The UPP guard's nametag says HAZEN. It reflects the sunlight with glittering gold as I peer into the dark interior. The store occupies a half-basement six feet deep, accessible via rickety wooden stairs.

A cracked concrete floor spans the length between shattered stem walls coated in dirt and grime a few millimeters thick. A rodent scurries through painted steel racks of plastic and metal hangers. The shelves form unkempt rows illuminated by dangling chain-pull LED bulbs, where a handful of shoppers peruse the overpriced goods. I nearly gag at a sign advertising stone-washed jeans straight out of the 1990s for the bargain price of $189.79. A matching T-shirt on a white plastic hanger displays the faded logo of a once-popular band. The United Philadelphians for Progress wants only forty-seven bucks for it. I grab at it to check the size, holding it up to my chest as Marissa smiles.

"God!" someone shrieks. "It's alive!"

"Okay," Marissa relents. "Maybe they're not completely clean. But they'll do."

"You go to the boss for that," Hazen snarls, eyeing Marissa's body.

I'd love bloody his face up for leering at her, but the gang holds all the power and would kill me for it, even if they didn't identify me as *The* Kerry Gearhardt first.

Hazen points at a tall, bulky man wearing sunglasses and a tweed hat, sizing up a pair of female shoppers. When Hazen catches the stranger's eye, he nods at me, motioning me to join him in a tiny back room with dim light.

"You should screw up your face," Marissa whispers, "so they don't recognize you."

My eyelids droop as I make my way towards Tweed, wondering how I look to an outsider. The stranger glares at me as I approach while the women pause their perusing to glance at my sinister look. I no longer feel like myself. Dark emotion has gutted my expression, leaving only traces of my soul.

The back room has a shag rug, a standing lamp, and a pair of veneered end tables. Tweed studies my complexion as I wander into his lair. Plywood shelves screwed into the wooden studs display an assortment of socks, hats, jewelry, and sunglasses. I look them over, spying a pair of rainbow-tinted glasses that might make me look like a 1990s action star.

Tweed's gruff voice takes me by surprise. He has an even self-assurance and regards me, too calm.

I adjust my voice to crack. "I want to get this shirt, but I don't have forty-seven."

"Then you can get the hell out of our shop," he drones.

"I have information about the Freedom Brothers and the murder of Former Mayor Archinson."

"We know everything we need to," he says dismissively, waving his palm.

"Yeah," I say, glancing at Marissa. "But there's more to it. They know you guys did it. Not that I'm accusing you or anything."

"We didn't do it," he argues. "They did. There's nothing you can offer that's worth that shirt, son. I've been here a long time, and the FB will stop at nothing to defeat their enemies, and they'll sacrifice the citizens of this once-great city to achieve it."

"Then you must know that they had a scroll from an ancient temple beneath the city, a scroll that is evidence for Atlantis."

"Atlantis is a myth. Plato had a slick sense of humor. Good enough to throw off the Romans, even as they plundered Greek artifacts for Nero."

"There's treasure there," I say, strengthening my voice. "Billions' worth, enough to overthrow those assholes and restore our city. If you want them to find it first, be my guest."

"Where's the scroll?" He eyes me with disdain, flexing his pectorals and folding his arms across his midsection. "How am I supposed to know you're not pulling a fast one on me?"

"Atlantis is real," I can feel the trembling in my skull.

Tweed twists his nose and curls his lip. "You're telling the truth. That will earn you twenty-five. Now keep talking and you can have the shirt."

Aware that I'm concocting a wild story without basis, I reach for the thing that will tickle him. "The scroll shows that the city sank to the bottom of the Mediterranean because the people defied the gods, their lavish architecture a tribute to their own wealth. Wild parties, optional clothing, lots of booze, mind-altering narcotics, you name it. Anything went. That is until Zeus cursed them, killing every citizen—men, women, children."

"I don't give a damn what they did to deserve their fate," Tweed answers, frowning and flexing his biceps again. "What does it mean to the FB?"

"They're on the hunt. And I hear they're training divers to go after the treasure as we speak. If they get it first, they'll wipe you out, rebuild the city in the image of their own corruption, the people be damned. I know because I saw the scroll."

"Where is it?" He unfolds his arms, steps closer to me and squeezing my forearms, sends jabbing pain through my body. Then he releases me, looking pensive.

"They took it, of course," I lie, "to the headquarters of the old Philadelphia Enquirer, which they plan to start printing again. Pretty soon, the entire world will know that you guys blew your one shot at redemption. You want that on your conscience?"

He scans me up and down, raises his eyebrows, and relents. "Take the shirt. This better be true, or we'll find you. And we'll kill you. Now get out of here before I change my mind."

Without hesitation, I follow Marissa back to the wooden stairs, past shoppers searching for good deals. Before we make it to the top of the steps, alarm creeps its way up my spine. Realizing that no one recognized me because Marissa was using new tricks to disguise me, I swallow down the darkness within me, forcing it to the bottom of my stomach. I wish I could chide her for it, but I don't have the will.

Before we turn away, I glance back into the store. Something I didn't see before catches my eye, but I dare not stare. A glint of polished steel flickers in the shadows of a sagging wall with loose wires poking through the sheathing. I've seen it depicted a million times. Every time I open my wallet. Emblazoned in blue and green in the top right corner of my plastic insurance card: The caduceus.

10

Alchemy of Mercury

I can't count how many times I've seen the symbol, but seeing the rod in the real world takes me by surprise. It can't be the real thing, can it? And if it is, how did it end up for sale in a UPP-owned store? As corrupt as the gang is, they couldn't have found it by accident. Which means someone in the gang either understands Greek lore or is a descendent of a god. I worry slightly as I remember meeting Chiron.

Marissa gives me a sideways glance as we climb the rotting plank steps, passing the judgmental guard, and up into the sun baking the pavement under our feet. The temperature feels like it might surpass 90 today, and I can feel the humidity against my skin. She mentions nothing about the staff, but I know she saw it too. We need to discuss this where the UPP can't hear us.

A fallen skyscraper's metal innards prod at the sky above a six-story high mound of debris, a lone beam mitered into the shape of an arrow pointing northeast toward the Delaware River. Nestled within the ruins, twisted pipes jut between collapsed concrete decks, crumpled ceiling tiles, and fragments of glass. As we pass by, I glance at it as though it's just another building, but I can smell something burning.

Haze from the citizens' fires hang over the city. Without heating systems, many would freeze to death. Luckily there's no shortage of wood to burn. The smell of meat pings my stomach with a message of hunger. I decide to take the chance before Marissa beats me to it.

"I know what you were looking at. And you probably have a lot of questions."

"Just one," I mumble. "How did they get it?"

She screws up her face and eyes me with a sophisticated air of confidence and disbelief. "Should I tell you who it belonged to and what purpose it served?"

I should know more about Greek legends than she does, even about stories that parallel pagan tales of witchcraft. But then again, I don't know much about the caduceus, only seeing the symbol on my insurance cards, believing it must have something to do with healthcare. It resembles the rod of Asclepius, but how does it differ?

"I'd say the answer to your primary question might come from investigating what it really means," she says offhandedly, as if expecting me to ignore this advice.

After all, we've got bigger plans, such as finding weapons to combat the Freedom Brothers thugs. That thought brings to mind another riddle, which I might discuss with Marissa later.

"I'm going to steal it."

She gives a half-giggle. "You can't be serious."

"Do I look serious?"

A subtle shake of her head tells me she opposes the plan, for now. I don't know why, but I have a vague notion deep in my gut that she's acting on ulterior motives. That breaks down trust, regardless of what we've been through together. Which leads me to another thought.

How close is she to the carnage, the death, the assassination? She's not telling me everything, and until now, I've given her the benefit of the doubt.

"They have around-the-clock surveillance by human eyes. We'll never get in without starting an all-out war between the FB and UPP. Which would mean more innocent lives lost. I'm afraid we'll have to do it the hard way for now."

"How many people are watching? Two? Three?"

"Enough to render my abilities null and void, if that's what you're thinking." She pushes a strand of hair behind her left ear and gazes toward the west.

A few miles away in the suburbs, free people look through fences at the remains of the city. If Marissa wanted to save the city, why didn't she ally with key people from outside the city, feeding them information and relying on them for monetary aid and sustenance? Only one explanation makes sense: She doesn't trust them, excepting Miriam and me.

We pass the building in silence, letting the smell of cooking meat trail away into the confused stench of rotting flesh, putrid water, and human waste. Plodding through the wreckage toward the outskirts of downtown takes far longer than it would have before the city met its doom. Then, I would have been able to log a mile in twenty minutes or less, but the destruction has doubled the time it takes.

The crumbling front of the movie theatre grabs my attention. The white of an old marquee sign hangs down, grimy and stained yellow by the sun. I wonder if we would still find the portal in the janitor's closet.

I stumble over a stone about three inches in diameter, kick it with my toe, wincing as it rolls away. I'm thinking the crumbled and weathered concrete must have been a poured in place above-ground structural member for a parking garage, and I'm just tiptoeing until I see a yellowed scrap of paper attached to the stone.

Marissa looks back at me as I reach down to pick it up, judging its weight in my hand. A rounded stone like this could have been a decoration. I realize its use as I glance to the end of the block. Many years ago, as I fled monsters in the streets, I sped past an ornate iron fence surrounding a nondescript chapel. Its perimeter had four layers of red brick spanning ten feet between columns. And the columns looked like tall tombstones, each inscribed with the symbol for a cardinal direction. Atop each of them, a rough concrete sphere drew the ensemble together.

Squinting at the writing on the paper, I glance over at Marissa, who feigns interest.

"Are you kidding me?" I growl.

"What?"

"Coordinates." I read the ink-scrawled writing twice to myself, attempting to remember basic spatial reasoning.

39°57'08"N, -75°09'50"W

"What does it mean?"

"Degrees, minutes, seconds. I believe these are the coordinates of downtown Philadelphia."

Tilting her head sideways, she says, "Right. Of course you know that."

Her acerbity doesn't bite like it once did. Without knowing why the coordinates to Philadelphia are fixed to a round pillar capstone with a dried-out rubber band, I let my mind wander.

"What if the chapel holds significance? Or maybe someone knowledgeable in science and architecture left it here as a clue, expecting us to stumble on it."

"You know what the odds of that are?"

"Maybe better than you might think." I scan the tiny sheet of paper until I find the initials A.A. printed in tiny ink strokes near the bottom right corner. "How far did you follow the mayor? Did he come to this section of town?"

She shrugs. "Maybe. But maybe not realistic, given the circumstances."

I grip the stone as if I'm about to throw it but then relax my hand. Removing the note and trying to memorize it, I watch as a black bird flutters overhead, darts behind a half-collapsed billboard, and lands on a length of structural steel that has half of its fasteners broken.

"Why's that?"

"Because I found evidence that our UPP pals had been keeping tabs on Archinson for over a week, spying on him because they knew what he was doing. As long as he didn't interfere in their affairs and he stayed affiliated to the Freedom Brothers, they let him do what he wanted. But something changed. He went to them for information, and when it started to look like collaboration, the UPP took him out."

"But Tweed back there in the store claimed they didn't do it. The FB did."

"And you believe him?"

"Well—"

"Listen," she retorts, waving her hands around, "the United Philadelphians for Progress chose their name to give the remaining people hope of a peaceful reconstruction. They curate this image better than any politician ever did, because without the citizens' trust, they won't get far in enacting their fascist agenda. UPP and FB make a big show of being on opposite sides, but they serve the same ends. The sooner you realize it—"

"Did I sign up for a political rant?" I ask.

"Tweed said they didn't do it because he wants you to believe they're on your side, at least until you decide where your allegiance lies. And if you don't make the right decision, and soon, they'll execute you, too."

"We already know the where the Second Bank is. A location within seconds of a degree is—"

"Pretty accurate," she says.

"One degree is very precise from a global standpoint," I explain. "We're talking within a few dozen feet. Only the mayor could have known the exact location. Do you know why? Because along with the city council, a mayor reviews site plans for every construction project with the civil engineers—who must rely on decimals of seconds, using devices that can shoot a distance within a millimeter over three hundred feet—"

"Mumbo jumbo."

"He knows because there was a recent project at these exact coordinates. And I'm guessing it's at the Second Bank."

"Right, and he assumed we'd find his clever little clue rather than the FB already being aware of his plans."

"It makes sense if you really think about it."

"Kerry, this may seem like a fun little mystery, but we're talking about life and death. A hundred thousand lives depend on us beating the gangs to the real prize. Let's not lose sight of that."

She sounds just like Becky when she scolds me. The more I replay the memory in my head, the more I hear Becky's voice. Assuming that Becky is still safe and sound at the lake house, I don't want to betray her trust; I never intended this trip to turn into a long expedition leading to Atlantis, if it even exists. And now I can hear her voice urging me to drop it and head home. *Marissa's smart enough to figure it out on her own. Is it really worth risking your life over ... again?*

Before I can reflect on this, I sense a plan coming together. We'll get firearms from a suburban ideologue, use them to steal the caduceus, find the Second Bank's ruins, and plan to meet former Secretary of Defense Harley K.

Whitworth, Jr., not only because I consider him wise, but because he knew mayor Archinson better than anyone else did.

We walk in silence toward the outskirts until we reach a dried patch of dirt with tuffets of yellowed grass and thistles sprouting up where there was once a neighborhood park. With its trees chopped down and burned, and the pavement broken and scattered, it no longer represents serenity, but decay. The city has forgotten it. The park is nothing more than a footnote on a derelict map, and now that human needs such as shelter, food, and water dominate all life, parks are worth nothing. But being here gives us a chance to discuss the caduceus and what it means. Marissa's knowledge might be relevant.

It is more than an hour since we've left the UPP store, and I can feel the afternoon heat sinking with that oppressive humidity. A splintered park bench with few planks still sitting on concrete footings remains.

But we sit cross-legged on the ground, eyeing each other as we battle over who starts first.

"That symbol is on my insurance cards," I say. "I always knew it came from Greek legend, but never cared much to investigate its significance."

Letting out a slow exhale, she wipes a bead of sweat from her brow with her forearm and straightens up. "It goes back even further than that, to three or four thousand years BCE."

"Before Christ to us Christians," I interrupt.

Do I even qualify as Christian anymore? Even with a trinity, I'd always considered Christianity a monotheistic religion, and now that I've discovered that the immortal Greek gods and goddesses are real, I haven't reevaluated my beliefs. And then there's the fact that theism itself comes from a Greek Titaness. I'd be the most confused person alive if it weren't for the true pillars of my faith—Becky and Ian.

"Whatever," she snaps. "The ancient Mesopotamians used to ascribe actual powers to it, and that carried over into Greek legend, where Hermes used to carry it as a symbol of craftsmanship and invention. Sometimes it's even depicted in the hands of Isis. The stories said it could induce sleep or awaken people, depending on their state. And that if used on someone who was dying, it would bring a gentle death—and reanimate the dead as well. Long ago there was a pagan spiritualist cult that believed in its powers, made wooden replicas, and even searched for the real thing. They thought it could unite the mortal with the immortal, the living with the dead. The sect fizzled millennia ago, and when Greece fell, Rome used it to symbolize the planet Mercury and metallic alchemy."

I almost choke. "Did you say it's sometimes depicted with Isis?"

"Sure ... but no one really knows—"

"Now we do," I assert. "Because we met Isis. And that might explain how the UPP thugs got it."

She shrugs, "Maybe you're onto something. But don't let your curiosity blind you to our intentions. Going on a side quest will only result in deeper trouble."

"We steal it," I argue. "We use it on the Freedom Brothers, make them spill why they killed the mayor, and what Arch knew. Either the United Philadelphians for Progress know exactly what it does, or they think it's a throwaway symbol. Then they have to divulge everything they know, which gives us the power. It's a solid plan, and you know it."

"Not without a mountain of risks," she says.

"Which brings us to my last question," I say, flexing my forearms and stretching my neck. "You're in trouble, and maybe I don't want to know why. But you invited me here for a reason, so if we're to rely on each other, we must be honest."

She nods and pushes her feet together in the dirt, drawing her knees toward her chest as if deep in thought. I notice her eyes twitching before she refocuses on something distant behind me, just above the horizon.

"You know," she says, "The war affected me in more ways than one. It made me realize that maybe life is more than the pursuit of knowledge, or even wisdom. That something in common binds humanity together. You can call it a deity, faith, love, or many other things. But maybe it's only the fact we share this rock in the universe, thinking it belongs to us instead of *them*. When you see the world the way we have, we gain a greater respect for its power and resilience, wouldn't you say?"

I close my eyes and consider what she's saying. True enough, the war made me understand things differently. But it also destroyed more than just the city I've called home; it also devastated my soul, crushing everything I thought I knew about myself and about life. Marissa's message of resilience seems misplaced, because I saw what it did to her. Living out the worst memories and nightmares took its toll. By telling me this, she's admitting something else: That she's in bigger trouble than I first thought.

To gain her trust, I'll have to tell her what transpired the other day when I talked with Ian.

"Kerry, Conveyor of Light and Shade," I start, lowering my voice and cracking my knuckles, "An ancestor of the ancient Six Cretan Titans has a son. Princess Ariadne gave me my powers, and since Ian is a descendant of The Six, he now has powers too. And they may be more exceptional than mine. He can control the weather, bring storms, depending on his mood. And right now, he's afraid. Because his wife is pregnant. I don't know what it means, but it spells worldwide trouble."

"Logical," she says. "But you were right—I am also in trouble."

"Tell me everything."

She hesitates.

"I did something stupid, in retrospect. Sold something I found to a bartender or someone. Just a scrap of metal with some writing etched into it. Like it was supposed to be an item of importance, and if he could investigate its hidden qualities, he could help the city recover and be hailed as a hero. It was bullshit, but I was desperate. When the Freedom Brothers found out, they pursued me. Sent goons to take me down. Every day I live to see the next, I consider a success. But I've survived. And that's a big problem for them. That's why I needed your help; I'm just a common swindler, but you're something else entirely."

"Are you saying all your pagan artifacts are hogwash?" I ask.

"Just that one," she says with a smirk. "I've always been a good salesperson. I guess I exaggerated one too many times."

She lets her eyes express the emotion within, and I sense the sadness and urgency in her voice. Suddenly a gunshot rings out, and a lone silhouette skulks along the fence line, looping in and out of sight. When I see that he's running straight for us, I conclude that he's not the one shooting. He sees us as the saviors, endangering us all.

Hand in hand, Marissa and I sprint away from the man as repeated blasts puncture the silence, filling me with dread. Nothing can prepare me for what comes next. Within seconds, I'm lying flat on my back, surrounded by fire.

II

Pyrophoric Salvation

Marissa dives before I see it coming, skidding at least three feet in the dirt and slamming the top of her head into a rock. To avoid turning crispy, I dig into my bag of emotional tricks, funneling dark energy into my chest. The deflection douses the flames in contact with my skin and absorbs the heat. Thermal shock can cause anything from seizures to total blackout. Instead, my body transforms the fire into pure light, reflecting from the source. My only chance is to use it as a shield.

Another gunshot rings out a split second later. It's followed by confused and agitated voices cursing. Even as the stranger attacks, he holds back as though the flames keep him at bay. The explosive expansion of air sends a shockwave of roaring thunder across the park, rebounding off the derelict residential buildings a quarter mile away.

Rolling onto her back and groaning, Marissa closes her eyes to contact her deceased allies, but they refrain from aiding us this time. The air continues to heat as the fires scorch a tuffet of dried grass, shooting flames higher than our attacker's head.

"GOD!!" The enemy combusts before he can utter another word. Turning tail and sprinting toward the gunshots, he screams as the flames devour his clothing and sear his flesh.

Excited whoops and cheers erupt from beyond the fence line to celebrate the short-lived victory. Before I can figure out what's going on, I roll over to shield Marissa from the heat. She responds by shoving her elbow into my sternum, making me double over. The fire dances at arms' length yet even with little fuel to consume, it expands, encroaching on us. Heat rips at my skin, drawing tears of pain. Marissa uses my body as a shield, but as the towering fire scorches my back, she grasps my free hand and flings me into the dirt behind her head. Landing gut-first on a stone elicits a winded grunt. When I keel over to vomit, the flames collect into a human figure.

Knowing what it means, Marissa transforms her fear into a scowl. The shouts and cheers die away as the shooters flee into the neighborhood. The Fire Guy undulates before us, solid as a normal human, yet embodying every characteristic of fire. He gathers a fireball and bowls it toward the residences, watching it bounce onto our attacker's flaming backside. Within seconds, it renders him motionless, rolling to a stop where it scorches the dilapidated wooden fencing.

When we sit up, Fire Guy sneers. "Keeping a low profile, I see."

Heat of a different kind flares in my brain. "You didn't have to come. Now you've killed someone, and the gangs will blame me for it. Thanks, you bastard."

"He was running from the FB," Marissa agrees. "How does murder fit into your code of ethics?"

Prometheus shrugs. "On second thought, maybe I shouldn't have saved your lives, since you're so grateful. Should I pass your disdain on to Zeus?"

I roll my eyes, patting my shirt as though to extinguish imaginary flames. Since his boss and I share a less-than-cordial relationship, I couldn't care less if he informs him. Recalling how I accused Zeus of subterfuge and how I hadn't thanked him for helping bring Ian back, perhaps I do owe him a reprise. For the life of me, I don't understand why I agreed to join Fire Guy's misfit Titans. He hasn't changed; change is for mortals. Prometheus has existed for millennia, and the only change he's ever shown was his defection from the Titans and swearing loyalty to Zeus. Zeus's zealotry knows no bounds, so I'd rather navigate the perilous streets without his employee's intervention.

"Still a patsy," I growl.

Another shrug. He watches the remains of his fireball consume the fence's splintered planks before igniting the ruins of a nearby dwelling.

"Humanity hasn't changed since the dawn of time. Still regarding loyalty as weakness. Sometimes doing the right thing means standing behind moral values."

Laughing feels unnatural now, but I can't help it. It should feel soothing, yet it doesn't. "Do you really expect me to take moral advice from a Greek Titan-God? You're a bunch of amoral pricks. The Titans, the Olympians. Next-level debauchery."

"But even you have your limits," he reasons. "After all, you helped us save the world."

His comment sparks rage, running the humor right out of my brain. I rise to my knees, clutching the rock like a baseball and squeezing it until it glows. "I did it for my family."

While I size him up, he nods, relaxing his shoulders. "Alliances aren't always borne of shared values. Sometimes they arise out of congruent needs."

"Why did you come?" Marissa shouts. "We don't need you."

"You may not feel that way now," he says, "but you'll come around. It turns out we could use your help, if you're interested, Kerry, Conveyor of Light and Shade."

Raising the glowing stone and holding it ready to throw, I snarl, "I'm a tad busy right now."

Prometheus wears an amused grin. "Are you going to launch that through my feeble body? It won't meet much resistance."

I let my arm down. What an asshole—it wouldn't work on him anyway. I sling the stone to my left. It streaks across the park like a comet, leaving a glittering trail as it arches into the maze of destruction a quarter mile away before its energy expires.

He tilts his head and lets his gaze meet Marissa's. "Perhaps a compromise is in order. You deal with those people shooting at that poor young man, and join us on Crete on your terms so I can get out of your hair."

His phrasing causes me to shake my head and smile. His being in my hair could cause baldness, third-degree burns, and blindness. In only a year, he's picked up American idioms, yet hasn't mastered the arts of subtlety or irony.

"Should I book a plane ticket out of Philadelphia International Airport?"

"You know the way."

The hell I do. I raise my eyebrows as he turns to walk away. If I ever find him again, I'll evaporate his limbs one by one and let him beg for mercy. Because Cronus merged the dimensions and the airport had collapsed into rubble, it might take me years to get to Crete, even if I could afford a flight.

"By the way," he warns, "The person charging you was a Freedom Brother. He was trying to escape individuals—citizens. I saw the whole thing."

Like a flame, his light flickers out and his body vanishes into a puff of black smoke.

Marissa doesn't wait. Sitting up and pulling her tangled hair behind her ear, she glances at the flaming detritus from Prometheus's fireball and says, "Suppose he's right, that the shooters were aiming for the FB thug. What do we do?"

"Track them down, ask them how they got the guns, or if they're UPP," I say. "But we can't assume they have noble purposes. Everyone in this city fends for themselves."

She nods. "You've got the hang of it. We might have to duel them for the guns."

I can't believe I'm about to propose this, but for as long as I can remember, Becky has preached the benefits of non-violence and compromise. In our first argument, I explained the folly of trying to reason with ill-intentioned people who would use their power to hurt others—that the only effective tool was to "fight fire with fire." I'd been on the receiving end of too many conflicts with Prometheus to doubt that belief. Becky claimed that proper negotiation doesn't come from fists or threats, but from love and humility. A week later, she demonstrated this by starting an argument and baiting me into the trap. I realized she was right, and I do hate it when anyone else is right.

"No, there's a mutually beneficial solution. I have an idea, but you won't like it."

She lets a smile crease her cracked, bloody lips. "Anything short of sailing into Scylla's maw, I'm there."

Kicking a pile of dirt at my feet, I mumble, "Don't say *that* again."

"Tell me your plan."

My brow furrow. "I'll need a source of negative energy for this one. The same trick I used to save you from being immolated by the Titan army. Hit me where it hurts and don't relent. Be as cruel as you can. When it hits me, I dissolve into Shade and we sneak into their hideout, materialize, and pose as allies so they don't shoot us."

"You *are* crazy," she scoffs. "But if you're expecting it, does it hurt you?"

I try to relax. "If anyone can do it, you can."

"Nice."

Ten seconds pass before I can exert the strength to skew my expression. My comment, although not intended as an insult, hit her with the force of a cargo ship. Still, I don't care to offer an excuse, so I stutter with filler words. "I mean ... uh..."

"Your wife has taught you all the tact of a nuclear warhead." She forces another smile. "Tell her I mean that as a compliment."

"She'll love it," I say, watching the fire spread to the neighboring houses. A city without municipal services is one where chaos reigns. The water mains that escaped unscathed from the demolition of Philadelphia have a chronic lack of pressure after the criminal gangs subverted the entire system to serve their empire. Every design has its drawbacks, and a lack of water pressure could very well threaten the gangs' assets. It's true that their mismanagement serves them right, and a clever citizen could learn to exploit the flaws to inflict more damage on them.

"Then what?"

"We let them keep the guns if they help us to steal the caduceus. Offer them as backup should the FB be better organized that we expect."

"Right." She looks left and right and then directly into my eyes. She's skeptical and her concerns are legitimate, because I haven't considered every aspect of my plan. But, as I've learned over the years, doing everything the democratic way wastes time and resources, even when concerned about safety.

"Then finding Atlantis and saving Philadelphia will be child's play. I'll let Miriam know before we head off to join your Neato group in another battle to save humanity. What could go wrong?"

Marissa might be clever, but she still sometimes gets things wrong. She masks her weaknesses better than I do, and her willingness to follow an ethical code in the face of impossible odds is admirable. She's always on the right track, and my proverbial train derailed long ago. If my plan doesn't work, I need to depend on her. When things start in accordance with what's planned, unforeseen snags can really cause chaos and one needs luck to snap them back into place. I don't always see the consequences of my actions until it's too late, but luck sometimes has a way of finding me anyway.

Something else Becky taught me rings true; dumb luck is real, but the best players put the correct pieces in motion ahead of time, and that's what guarantees success.

Marissa looks surprised at my lack of a retort. She refuses my help in pulling herself to her feet and stretches. A familiar scent wafts into my nostrils as the smoke curls into the blue sky: Mercaptan. Before we can react, one house explodes into a mushroom of fire as the pressure regulator cuts service for safety. Flaming splinters shoot in every direction and howls erupt from the neighborhood.

"What the hell?"

"Freedom Brothers forgot to end natural gas service to that house," I say, gazing at the fireball and the plumes of roiling black smoke.

"They don't forget," she gasps. "It means we've found another FB hideout. Let's go pillage it before they come back to inspect the damage."

"Another—"

"They have them all over the city," she interrupts me. "They don't make mistakes. Every move they make gives them the best chance of exerting full control over the city and its people. Fire Guy got lucky."

I roll my eyes. "Oh, he knew. I'm going to punch him in the face if I ever see him again, and I don't even care if my fist burns!"

The fireball disperses as we walk toward it. Flaming pieces of debris are scattered across a full block. When we reach the fence, we see glowing coals emitting wispy trails of white smoke. We aren't the first to arrive on scene.

Marissa holds me back by the forearm before I can climb over the collapsed fence. Three individuals are working together, inspecting ground zero, communicating via hand signals like a S.W.A.T. team.

"You!" someone nearby says.

I see a young woman, around sixteen years of age, dressed in a blue skirt over black denim crusted with mud and smoke stains. Her hair is a dull blond mop clinging to a loosened rubber band that once held it in a ponytail. She's peering straight into my eyes. Before I can reply, I find two citizens aiming black-barreled guns at my heart. My blood turns to ice.

"You're the one everyone's been talking about," the teenage girl says. She motions to her gun-toting friends and nods toward me.

Reacting on pure instinct, I raise my palms and wait for Marissa to mirror me. "Listen...we—"

The girl scowls at me, curls her lips into a sneer, and raises one hand like an axe waiting to strike. "Kill him."

12

Victim of the Phonoi

Gunfire erupts from every angle. I have no time to react. I feel the lead bullets plunge through what should be my abdomen, but which comprises only a black, greasy blob of mud. I cannot describe the pain in this moment using words, or even mortal emotions. The black sucks the life from my internal organs, squeezing them into a sticky paste. A dull ache rises through my chest, crushing my larynx. Marissa watches in horror.

Careful not to get shot, she closes her eyes and reaches out through the darkness within me. For the first time, I can hear her emotions playing on my nerves.

You don't die this way.

I mumble something in response that makes no sense, although my heart translates it into the proper urgency.

Always follow the light.

But I see no light. I can only hear my own confused words ringing through my brain as though my head is an empty shell.

I try to speak, but nothing comes out. The words only make sense in my brain. *"Shadows...light...everything dies. All that dies in me."*

Ker—

Becky's voice transforms into the Phoenix, a red and yellow explosion spreading life through what remains of me. When my eyes gloss over, I can see my abdomen boiling like liquid glass.

You know how to find me.

But this time, Sarah's voice has transformed into luscious prose, the pleas of a goddess—or a princess.

"Kerry, Conveyor of Light and Shade, I bestow this gift. Let it..."

Her words filter through my brain, making the rest of her words nothing more than vibrations through my flesh.

"Kerry—"

Marissa speaks to me with her eyes squeezed closed, a painful expression of sorrow on her face, her lips quivering. The gunshots cease. I lie on my side. Opening my eyes, I expect to see my blood spilling into the charred splinters of wood and brick. When the glow subsides, I detect bits of sticky tar oozing into the soil as though it had left my veins.

"Again!" the girl shouts. "Spray him with every bullet you've got! I want pieces of him all over the city!"

Coughing and reaching my hand toward her in a plea for mercy, I rasp my reply. "Please don't—we're on the same side."

The shooters don't listen to me. I squeeze my eyes shut as the gunfire erupts again, yet this time, I only hear metal clacking against metal. *Click, click, click!*

"DO IT!"

"Ash," one shooter warns. "Out of ammo."

She scowls and rips the handgun away from her closest compatriot, and aims the gun straight at Marissa's head.

CLICK!

"Burn him!" Ash screams, her face turning crimson with fury. She throws the gun into the fire and scowls at us.

"I don't—Ash...we're here to defeat the Freedom Brothers. We can't do it without your help."

She holds up a palm and growls, "You're a murderer. Now face justice Philadelphia style."

She doesn't need to explain what that means. I sense she's about to level accusations that I can't hope to defend myself from.

One inhale later, she bites her lip, pushes her grimy hand through her dirty hair, and stares at Marissa, afraid to address me directly.

"I remember where you were that day," she says. "We might have been outnumbered—while they slaughtered us. But then you came in, destroyed six city blocks yourself. There were tourists in those buildings. Family. And you murdered them in cold blood."

I gasp. "They would have—"

"The fate we all must face. If it was necessary, only pure evil should have spilled their blood. Not some ill-intentioned guy masquerading as good. Men, women, children. You owe them your life, you scum."

Marissa swallows and opens her eyes, she gazes into the flames and watches the smoke spiral into a black cloud that dissipates as it drifts toward downtown.

The sun has been diving toward the horizon, burnishing the skylike with orange. My heart sinks, even as agony pounds my abdomen.

"The Titans—" I cut myself off before I can finish the thought. I *hate* it when people are right, especially when they're accusing me of misdeeds I'd never stopped to consider. Then again, it wasn't like I'd had any control over it. When the dark energy reaches depths that low, it replaces all thought.

"You were a coward," she bites. "You think you did it all for someone else. But did you weigh that against the innocent who died? A mother raced home that night to find her two sons had been killed as the building fell. That mother never got to see her babies again. *You* did that. Not the Titans. That family might have escaped, but for you."

The pain rolls through me. "I don't know what to say."

"Every superhero story tells about how the hero saves humanity by destroying the very people they promised to protect. The hero wins, the villain loses. But the innocent lose more. And does the hero ever express regret? You're no different, *The* Kerry Gearhardt. And you know it."

"What were their names?" I almost bite my tongue as I speak, but an idea sparks in the back of my brain.

If Marissa can connect with those children, perhaps she can bring Ash a sense of closure.

But Ash's face drops when she glances around at the other shooters, who still have their barrels trained on my torso. "Doesn't really matter now, does it? You going to erect a shrine for them because you're so benevolent? You don't know how it feels!"

Anger flashes through me. "We've all lost people that matter. I lost my son. My family. The closest friend I ever had. I know why I did it, and I might do it differently if the situation repeated itself. Don't make accusations when you can't see past the end of your own hatred."

A tear drips from her eye, and she dabs at it with her dirty wrist. "I'll never forgive you."

I feel the sadness deep inside me, like a heavy weight in my stomach. I can't ignore the feelings she's sharing. For the first time, I can't make excuses. I never wanted to hurt anyone, but when I see things from Ash's point of view, I realize she's right. Listening to her helps me heal the old wounds I've carried for years. This healing doesn't come from anger or guilt. It comes from the simple need for kindness and understanding. I know I can't change how she feels.

"You don't have to. But we can work together to defeat the gangs. I know a good place to start."

"The gangs mean nothing to me," she seethes. "I'm from the suburbs. We all are. Walked in under the cover of daylight, hoping to solve problems for a local group. They knew about the natural gas service here and decided it would be enough to survive for a while. They wanted us to reconnect it to the suburban grid, bypassing the traps the gangs devised to control the resource. And we were getting close until you showed up."

"You shot at the FB interloper," Marissa surmises, trying to force her voice into something resembling cordiality.

The flames still lick at thin planks, flickering blue above the white coals and undulating like clean wisps of gas vapor jutting into the trails of smoke. A few blocks away, the remains of a four-story upscale apartment building abut new construction. The bundled trusses, interconnected through galvanized stiffener plates, poke at the blue and orange skyline like a symbol of hope. From within the destruction, it rises like a single dandelion in a pitch of dirt.

"Didn't have a choice," Ash admits, shrugging. "He would have returned with enough men to erase the very memory of us. Call it self-preservation."

"He had a family of his own, didn't he?" I say, not meaning to accuse her of anything.

Again, she shrugs. "One of the great contradictions of life. Sometimes you gotta take from others, as much as you hate people taking things from you."

That sentence pops an idea in my mind. I blurt out my plan without so much as considering how Ash might take it. "Speaking of which…United Philadelphians for Progress has the caduceus, and we're gonna take it."

She frowns and glances at Marissa. "Have at it. We have nothing to do with them, either, even if their motives are pure."

"That's where you come in. You have guns…you have a way to get more ammunition, I take it. They'll keep guards on the store, but their patrols will leave a weak spot at night when they're watching the city limits. And there won't be many citizens lined up for semi-clean clothes at a premium willing to put their lives on the line for supplies. We cause a distraction, march in for the caduceus, burn the building down. We attack for something we believe the FB is guarding."

She considers it but shakes her head. "They'll know you did it. Our cover will be blown, and we'll all be dead anyway."

"But that's the beauty of it," I argue. "The FB killed Mayor Archinson because they were worried he had information that would have benefitted the UPP. So they will naturally blame the Freedom Brothers because you guys have guns, which only the gangs should have. If it all lines up, they go for payback, striking somewhere else, spreading the FB's resources thin. Then we uncover the big clue we're looking for and topple the entire structure. Everyone wins."

"They've consolidated power," Ash says, earning a nod of approval from Marissa. "Enough to snuff out any hint of resistance before it even gets rolling. And I'm betting they already know you're around, so they'll be prepared for it."

"Exactly," Marissa agrees. "We've got them right where we want them. Their preparedness will cause them to make other mistakes as it always does. That's how we exploit them."

Ash rests her chin in her greasy palm and stares at our feet. "What clue are you looking for?"

"Can't say for sure," I admit, straightening my spine to compensate for lack of confidence, "but we know the mayor was trying to solve a puzzle and that he had found an important piece. He also assumed they'd kill him for it, which means it's big enough for the gangs to cover up."

"It's a risky plan," one of Ash's gunmen says. His ragged hair covers a bony scalp, and the stubble on his chin is coated in layers of filth and sweat. He glares at me for ten seconds, breaks eye contact, and watches a woman lower her firearm as she gives in. "We'll need careful planning."

"We don't have time for careful planning," I say. "In my experience, too much planning decreases the odds of success."

Ash looks confused. She combs a hand through her hair and raises her eyebrows. "Why do you want this caduceus thing? Is it a weapon?"

I bite my tongue. If I tell her the whole story, she'll laugh it off, refuse to help us, and slink back into the suburbs with her posse in tow. Selling my idea will require old-fashioned luck, which, according to Becky, I have a knack for.

"According to lore, it can reanimate the dead and awaken the weary. And yes, I believe it."

She snarls, "Why's that?"

Shaking my head and breathing in, I say, "Because everything I've experienced has confirmed the old Greek legends. The gods, the Titans, all of it."

"Religion might have had grand intentions," Ash says, lowering her voice, "but they always fall to the same human defects. You're no better than the Taliban. But we aim to get our brothers in the city a slice of freedom, so we have mutual goals. You scratch our back, we scratch yours. When do we start?"

I glance at the darkening horizon where the orange has become deeper and the blue has darkened. "When do the patrols return to the fences?"

"About ten to eleven," Stubble says with a grunt. "They've had their eyes on Millbourne at Cobbs Creek Park, where a camp of opinionated suburbanites hold nightly protests by a campfire. Spirited enough to keep tabs on, not a big enough threat to attack."

"And if they did," Ash adds, "the governor would send in the National Guard, which neither side wants."

"Eleven o'clock," I confirm. "We make way for the UPP trade hub, cause a disturbance, steal the caduceus, and make our way downtown. To the Second Bank of the United States."

Ash frowns. "But there's nothing left of it. The Titans turned it into rubble. Why do you think the Freedom Brothers want it?"

"That's what we don't know," Marissa says, frowning. "We know they're planning a disgusting high rise on the site of Independence Hall with the Centennial Bell at the top. Maybe another corrupt development opportunity, and maybe they know something we don't."

Ash glances at Stubble and raises her voice. "Gus. Head back to the stockroom, bring back six mags apiece." She then turns to the tall, thin girl on Gus's left. "Liana, help Sparta map our route, taking known gang landmarks into account for the safest, quickest way to the trade hub."

After directing her team, she focuses on me, seeming to assess the pain at my midsection as she inches closer. "This had better work. If any of my company dies, I'm gonna hold you accountable. And I'll have enough ammo to turn you into Swiss cheese."

Marissa nods, grabbing Ash's attention.

"And if *you* get in my way, I'll shoot you."

Too much of this plan depends on luck, which makes my palms sweat. I can only hope for the best possible outcome, even if it doesn't meet our goals. Too much rides on this mission. The thought of my life ending in Philadelphia while Ian prepares for the birth of my grandson, and while he grapples with his newfound power, makes the stakes higher. Failure is an option if it saves my life. Still, I exert no power to make the pieces of my plan fall into place. Things will go wrong as they always do. I only hope my luck holds out long enough to survive, because Ash isn't kidding around. She'd kill me, and I'd deserve it.

13

The Delphic Oracle

It had been over an hour since Gus departed for the suburbs. Waiting for him to show up with the extra magazines is stressful. Ash has spent most of this time coordinating plans in secret with her second lieutenant, Liana, a slender teenage girl with bony shoulders and long spindly legs. Her cropped hair bobs at her shoulders and her blonde-tipped bangs highlight green eyes. Liana glances at me only once or twice, each time adding another layer of contempt to her expression. In the meantime, Marissa and I refine our tactics.

"Gonna be a miracle if we can get in without being spotted," she says. "They'll shoot first, ask questions later, even if they don't recognize you."

"That's why we're going at dark," I argue.

"They'll probably have floodlights."

That wouldn't be a surprise, since any group wanting to protect itself and its workers would provide adequate lighting. But then again, they're sometimes placed without much thought. I've spent long enough in the construction industry to witness both.

"That might work to our advantage," I say.

"Maybe. If not, I have a trick. Same one I used last time, which may or may not work."

I swallow. "Wait—"

"You didn't notice? I guess that means I used it right."

Raising my eyebrows and scooting my feet together, I try to ignore Liana's glare. Marissa glances back, and I say, "Maybe we should discuss all your abilities."

"I think," she says, exhaling, "that would destroy their reliability. I've spent the better part of the year perfecting them in the dark. When it's light outside, or if people can understand what I'm doing, they're affected. You're better off just observing."

"Right," I say. "Watch and learn. Good teaching method, but it doesn't always work."

As the hour passes, Ash grows more and more agitated. She glances around at the dying flames. Since the explosion has consumed the gas, the fire is eating away at rubble and paper. I notice a red flame reflecting in her eyes and blink just as it burns into the shape of the Phoenix and extinguishes itself.

"I've been meaning to ask you something," I say to Marissa, "about the Phoenix. You painted it in the shaft by the hatch. And lately, every time I see flames, I can see her looking at me."

She whispers, "There are various properties according to legend, or so Miriam tells me. According to her, she can return in one form or another if you need her. Miriam knows more than you think. You should talk to her about it."

"In various forms, as in supplying an emotionally entangled friend with the energy to feed his abilities?"

A shrug indicates she doesn't assume anything, but something about her suggests she's hiding something. I haven't had a real chance to speak to Miriam since my final healing session. I realize I'll also need to converse with Former Secretary Harley K. Whitworth Junior. He may still live in his rural Maryland manor with his various assistants. Last time I saw him, age had altered his appearance so much that it had surprised me, and I've lost track of how much time has passed since that meeting.

"The biggest thing is, you'll need to stay alert at all times," Marissa says, changing the subject.

"So will you."

"You'll need to warn me of any threats, as I could be ... you might say ... in a trance."

Her powers—if I can call them that—necessitate intense concentration, while mine rely on instinct and emotional energy. I should have asked Ian what supplied his outburst. I should have warned him that using his powers included many perils, but like I always do, I skipped most of that, opting for fatherly love, even if it hasn't always helped him.

Ash interrupts us as Gus arrives at the front side of the building, where decorative craftsman columns support a stone and wood lintel that somehow hasn't yet succumbed to the repeated trauma. The columns' lower thirds form a network of squared stonework under a two-inch wide sloped reveal. Smashed bits of stucco over shredded mesh screens scale the upper two-thirds, lending the residence a quaint suburban quality.

"Hey," Ash says, greeting him and glancing at me.

"Raided the stock." Gus says. "Plenty of mags and an extra Glock, just in case."

"Great plan," Liana says, flexing her neck. Her scapula juts out into a pair of tiny knobs above her sternum. Though her torn shirt conceals her abdomen, she's probably so malnourished that her ribs show through her skin.

"Ash," I say, pressing my palms against the half-burned plank I'm resting on, "let me have the gun. Marissa needs extra defense."

Ash glowers at me. "You shouldn't need a gun. After all, we pumped you with enough lead to kill you twice and yet there you sit, alive. Remarkable."

Her blank expression tells me she doesn't mean it as a compliment. She's testing the limits of my anger, hoping to force me into a mistake on which she can capitalize later. Though she looks nothing like Becky, her tactics resemble Becky's, even if Ash's are honed to inflict lasting damage, while Becky's are employed to teach gentle lessons.

"Besides, I need something."

Remembering Ash had thrown the last gun she'd wielded into the fire in a fit of frustration, I concede the point as she readies the troops.

"Liana and Sparta," Ash calls, "Lead the way."

I've always known Philadelphia for its varied architecture, owed in part to its establishment long before the signing of the Declaration of Independence in 1776. Ornate colonial influences and European religious flourishes complemented sleek glass towers and minimalist design. Now, everything looks the same: Destruction everywhere you look, as though time and decay have ripped open every building to spill its innards into the streets.

The girls, wearing thick, steel-toed combat boots, kick through piles of debris clumped together like sand ridges on a beach. When Ash steps on a one-inch length of plastic tubing, I hear a crunch as it breaks under her foot.

My eyes play tricks on me as the darkness seems to expand. Somewhere ahead, I can hear shouting, perhaps from a block away.

"You'll have to kill me for it!"

"I'd rather not," a woman replies, scorn dripping from her voice. "But if that's what it takes to feed my girls—"

"Bring it, bitch," he snaps, "come on!"

I hear it before I see it. A metallic slap on the pavement tells me the woman is armed. She wields what looks like a PVC advertising flag like a samurai. Waving it around takes skill and balance, but her enemy sees a weakness before she can get at him.

THWACK!

The piping inside the canvas slaps against his skull as he dives at her knees. Too late to react with her heavy weapon, she buckles, drops it, and screams. The man brandishes a brick and hurls it at her head, but not before she retaliates with a fist to his groin. This blindsides him just long enough to give her an opening, which she doesn't waste.

She kicks him in the gut while he's doubled over, reaches for something shiny and metal. With his defenses down, he's vulnerable to a hellish slash across his midsection. The woman slings the two-foot-long aluminum blade with enough precision to knock him over. Blood pours from a fresh wound as his attacker pounces on him, grabs the object she wants, and crushes his ribs with her heel. A crunch rings out and he growls in agony, succumbing to defeat.

Avoiding the melee, Liana and Sparta alter our trajectory around a crumpled hotel sign, its steel girders rusting in the cool night breeze. If the remainder of the structure collapses, it will crush anyone who might call the rubble beneath it home.

Ten minutes pass, then twenty. Crossing under a freeway, we enter the neighborhood with the UPP trade hub, advancing over the bricks, shattered wood, and bits of glass. A line of burned-out, smashed cars rests in the ruins. By the time I wonder if any of the cars contain bodies, I can see the trade hub ahead.

A shanty built in the foundation of a preexisting residential project, the edifice tilts under unbalanced loads. Where crumbling bricks and concrete frame the front entrances, spindly two-by-fours make up the sidewalls, covered with plexiglass siding whose sun-stained valleys show cracks and divots, as though someone has attacked the stronghold before.

Ten feet from the entry door, a broad-shouldered man paces. Ash directs us into the shadows as we skulk toward him. His companion wears a tweed-shouldered jacket and puffs on a pipe while he leans against a sturdy frame, watching, ignoring Shoulder's pacing.

Without warning, bright light illuminates the street. The smoker drops his pipe, launches himself off the siding, and attacks us. Acting in surprise, Marissa is already into her bag of tricks. Something silvery flutters out of the building across the street, distracting Shoulders. Spinning to attack the oncoming spirit, he lets his gaze slip from Ash and Gus, who begin blasting him with bullets.

Shoulders doesn't stand a chance. My ears ring as the repeated blasts knock out my hearing. To disguise me, Marissa directs her energy in my direction, reaching her tattooed fingers through the dank air. My muscles twist and contort as pressure knots in my skin. The resulting pain blinds me as Gus opens fire on the smoker.

After neutralizing our first targets, we advance, stepping over bodies and kicking down the door. A pair of strangers appear just as the light floods in through the entry. They attack, brandishing knives at my midsection. Seeing this, Ash trains her weapon on one of their heads, unleashing a blast that knocks him backward when the bullet plunges into his shoulder. She fires two more shots, missing the mark as the other stranger dodges. He readies a retaliatory blast from a shotgun, shattering a wood joist holding up a teetering awning across the street.

Gus sees it coming and nails him with two shots. He falls backward into the darkness as four more enemies surround us, opening fire one by one. Somehow, every bullet misses as Ash, Gus, and Liana pulverize them. Two attackers fall before I can get my bearings.

With her eyes closed, Marissa lunges toward me, summoning a line of sprits to surround the gunmen. Two assailants sprint away from the spirits, but the other hammers us with a cocaine-fueled barrage of fists and slashes. Gus is on his back as Ash unloads her clip, missing every shot. The man growls and grabs her by the throat with his meaty hand, ignoring the pleas of the ghosts that Marissa brought.

Darkness swamps Ash's eyes as he squeezes her neck. She folds in his hands even as Gus and Liana spray bullets, both missing him. Ash flings out her arm in a desperate move to disarm him, but he overpowers her as a dozen more assailants rush out of the shadows, surrounding us. Marissa overwhelms one of them, a young man with piercings and a mohawk. When he drops his weapon, another loud BOOM shatters the neighborhood. Onlookers arrive to watch the mêlée unfold.

Behind me, a flash of flame bursts through the dark, disorienting our attackers as more gunfire erupts. Energy pierces me as my body glows. My muscles tighten and my face goes rigid as I let it consume me. The darkness within me collapses a split second later. Marissa and the girls hit the floor before lighting zaps through the air in a maelstrom of blinding electricity.

Caught by surprise, Gus unleashes a shot just as a lightning bolt shoots out of my chest and slams into his shoulder, propelling him backward twenty feet, where he collapses. Ash screams as the lightning cuts through every assailant, leaving them paralyzed.

Before I know what's happening, I see Ash sprinting toward me with a contorted expression of pure rage on her face. She screams as she punches me with one hand, curls her fingers around the barrel of her gun and slams its butt into my scalp. With anger flushing through me, I react by shoving her. Enough power still courses through my fingers to send her tumbling ten feet away.

She vaults back to her feet, aims the gun at my head, and shoots. The bullet splinters a stud behind my shoulder. When she aims again, she stops.

Marissa holds her at bay from six feet away with a pulse of spiritual energy. As the rage in Ash's eyes fades, I slink into the basement alone. Knowing Marissa can take care of the rest of them, I scan the darkness until I find the silvery glow of a steel staff.

It rises from the floor, illuminating a pair of wrinkled legs, a tattered skirt, and a tattooed forearm. When the glow dances on her face, fear races through me.

"Do not take this lightly," she says. "It only answers to the power of a god."

My fingers tremble as I stare at her, readying myself for her attack. "Who are you?"

She hesitates, running her knobby fingers along the rims of the wings, feeling the steel feathers, before pointing at me. The coiling snakes glare at me as she hypnotizes me with the staff. "I have gone by many names, Kerry, Conveyor of Light and Shade. I have served Apollo for millennia. If you seek the power of this staff, you must earn it."

"Tell me your name," I croak, my vision going blurry and my eyelids beginning to droop.

"My master calls me Pythia," she says, forcing the power of the staff through me. "You shall answer the call of the bell on the third night when moonlight strikes iron. Fear not. The attack shall happen at midnight two days later. Enemies amass at Gibraltar, eleven strong, ready for war. If you succumb, The One will return."

"The...the..." I try to curse at her, but my lips feel heavy and my voice catches in my throat.

"If this you wish to take," she warns, "you must snatch it from me."

My legs numb as I stand before her. Static snow washes over my eyes as I fall through ages of black and curtains of smoke. The world spins as shooting stars rip through an endless galaxy, surrounding me with brilliant flakes of light.

It feels like hours have passed. Sensation creeps back through my limbs, pulsing with a painful ache. When my eyes wedge open, the glow returns. The woman gazes into my eyes as I blink in awe. My fingers curl around the cold steel as I rise to my feet, trembling as I go.

"Success cannot undo gravity," she warns. "If you do not use it with dignity, it shall resist you. If you use it with malice, it shall destroy you. Hold this knowledge in your heart. I am Pythia, the oracle of Delphi, and I leave you now, Kerry. Conveyor of *Light* and Shade."

She vanishes into a cloud of mist as the darkness coils around me. Chattering arises from behind me as I turn my back on the darkness in the shop. Ash's rage melts into me as I ascend the rickety wooden steps to the concrete precipice and gaze out into the chaotic streets. Hundreds have gathered to witness the mayhem. Marissa grins at me, slings her arms around me, and squeezes. But the fight hasn't ended yet.

14

Achaean Invasion

Steel presses against my scalp, sending a jabbing fear into my spine as I blink in terror. Ash's eyes are fiery orbs of rage. The barrel trembles as her shaking hand pushes it against my head, her finger flirting with the trigger.

"I—"

"PIECE OF SHIT!" she roars.

My heart aches. Marissa rests her palm on my shoulder and exerts spiritual pressure on Ash, but instead of easing the tension, Ash's rage only expands.

"You murdered him! DIE!"

CLICK!

Out of ammunition again. Lucky me. I don't dare smile at her, because before she can say another word, she fumbles through her pocket, finds another magazine, and drops the empty cartridge on the ground while the onlookers gaze at us in shock.

"Ash," Marissa whispers, "do the right thing."

Clicking the fresh magazine into place, Ash seethes. "Don't think you've earned a reprieve. The right thing is your death."

"Uh..." Shuffling sounds come from behind her as a dark silhouette rises in the motion-activated floodlights. "I think I'm ... alive?"

In relief, my nerves sparkle with newfound energy. Marissa's palm grows warm against my shoulder, and Ash lets the barrel's pressure against my scalp abate.

"You…" her speech wavers and a chilly note creeps into her voice. "You electrocuted him."

"Didn't mean to hurt him," I defend myself uselessly.

Ash turns to glare to me and pushes the barrel so hard against my skull that a donut-shaped divot might adorn my forehead now. With the gun's black barrel, she pushes me away as Marissa catches me. Ash lowers the gun, letting her enraged expression fade. "Next time you hurt one of my crew," she breathes, "you get two bullets in your face, and I hope you feel them tear your ugly skin off your skull."

Gus steps closer to his companion, wraps his arms around her, and plants an electrifying kiss on her cheek. In protest, she shoves at his chest with both hands before wiping the grime from her brow.

Many relieved people watch us, sharing comforting remarks between them as our argument cools down. Choosing to ignore me for once, Ash tends to Gus and turns to Liana for help.

"You got it," Marissa mutters. "I thought you'd meet more resistance in there."

I stammer. "Uh … maybe I did. I mean, I passed out, but somehow it ended up in my hands, anyway. Unless I overpowered her while unconscious, I can't explain why."

She raises her eyebrows and glances at Gus, who swats away Liana's hand and bathes Ash in an affectionate gaze.

"Who's 'her?'"

I'm trying to tell a story, but my words feel clumsy. I gloss over how it felt to learn of the ancient city of Delphi and its twisted origins. Why would she appear to me? Does her prophecy matter when it comes to handing the Caduceus to a new owner? I don't want to answer these questions because Marissa might have answers I'm not ready to hear.

Instead of arguing, she just nods when I pause or stop talking. "Goes without saying," she says when I finish, trying not to look surprised.

"What does?"

After thumbing her nose, she flits her eyelids and waits for me to expound on my question. When she decides I don't have a witty reply, she opts for a more concise approach. "That the war may not have ended."

The lack of emotion in her speech surprises me. How can she act so cavalier about something that almost destroyed her, in more ways than one?

"You don't seem upset by that."

"That may be what Fire Guy alluded to," she surmises, hands on hips. "I'd be alarmed, but life in this hellhole, sleeping in that stinky dungeon, makes it hard to feel scared."

There's the in-your-face spirit she used to have. I hadn't realized how much her outlook had changed, until now. And now that she's said it, I can ignore it. "Riddles. But what about her warning not to use it the way she used it on me?"

"Gray area," she replies, rolling her eyes. "Funny thing about serious advice. It is open to interpretation for a reason."

I shake my head. "You don't have that dark a view of humanity."

"Don't I? Every Christian tries to heed the counsel of the Bible, to varying degrees of success, but it's always vague and open to interpretation."

"Another anti-Christian diatribe," I say dismissively.

"Logic," she corrects me. "It's vague because God is supposed to trust your judgement on what you consider right and wrong. So maybe you don't use that thing just because you're pissed, but because you want to protect your friends, your family, and the citizens of Philly."

Now I'm rolling my eyes and shaking my head. "Surely you're not—"

"Stop calling me Shirley."

That joke may have made me laugh a year ago, but today I don't have the sense of humor.

"But what do you think she meant by 'success cannot undo gravity?'"

She glances away. Liana again attempts to dab at Gus's brow, an injury I surely didn't inflict, unless it resulted from him falling down. The high contrast of light and shadows made it hard to see everything.

And that reminds me of the contrast between light and dark within me. Between the polar opposites, could there be a gray area? What if those differences in my abilities weaken how I understand the world? Following that thought to its logical end, I question my commitment to a greater good. Because if light and dark are the only choices, both have fatal flaws. That thought had never occurred to me. The Oracle's warning is making better sense now that I'm exploring it from that point of view. Still, if the vagueness is a feature instead of a bug, I must exert greater caution. With stakes this high, one wrong move can prove the difference between victory and disaster.

"Catching on already," Marissa says, eyeing me with amusement.

"Whatever."

"Sounds like something your wife might say after an argument," she snipes at me.

That was unfair. Becky always makes her point with subtlety, a quality she's perfected after years as an education administrator—or so she says. Working with disgruntled, overworked, and underpaid teachers had taught her tact. Using it on me turned out to be successful, not because it taught me how to use it, but because it taught me what I should expect from others.

"What do you think?" I hear Liana asking Ash.

"Kerry!" Ash shouts. "Ready to move out."

I tighten my expression and turn my attention to her. Matching her intensity might be my best option, even after all these years of Becky trying to calm me down. I nod over my shoulder at the shanty and grit my teeth.

"Burn it down," I say.

She quickly moves with Gus and Liana to follow my command. I raise my voice, knowing dozens of people are watching. "Freedom beats Unity every time! Let the corrupt UPP burn. This is what happens when they mess with our movement."

The words feel heavy in my stomach. Usually, I joke or make my point with sarcasm, but this time I try to sound angry—not just joking around. It's easier to say it that way, but I know it comes with a cost.

Maybe Ash will understand how serious I am. She steps off the plank, disappearing into the dark, walking over bodies while Liana and Gus follow behind. The spectators slink away into the shadows one by one, until only one woman remains. She sneers at me. "You're not FB."

I glare at her.

"You're worse. You all are—insane. Get the hell out of my city."

Marissa waits for the woman to turn her back before letting her attention slide back to me. The smell of smoke wafts into my nostrils as I try making sense of what the stranger has just claimed. What if she's right? I can't stand the idea of being another loose screw in a world of faulty attachments.

"She doesn't know what she's saying," Marissa says, trying to smooth it over. "Trust me."

I nod sadly. "Uh-huh. When people have to follow up their words with 'trust me,' that's when you know it's a lie."

"Kerry."

Bowing my head and letting the dark feelings wind their way through my brain, I turn my back to her. The entrance of the UPP store is dark, and I'm waiting for any sign of fire there. "You don't have to say it."

"Fine," she says. "Maybe when rationality returns to this messed up reality, we'll be able to have an actual conversation that doesn't descend into personal attacks and crude jokes."

"Yeah," I mutter. "That will be the day."

Ash appears at the top of the steps with an enchanting smile. Behind her, the interior light turns gold and orange before thick smoke pours out the door and through the cracks. Time to get out of here.

Ash sprints away in the middle of the street toward the historic district, Liana and Gus at her heels. Marissa and I break into a run as flames consume the UPP trade hub. Watching it go up in smoke might offer catharsis, but we have little time. Soon, the gang leaders will arrive to investigate what happened. They might torture the citizens for clues. The stranger's statement that I'm worse than a Freedom Brother haunts me at every step. She knows that soon the UPP will arrive, and our foes will double.

We streak by wreckage, sprinting twelve blocks into the center of downtown. Marissa leads while I try to keep up. Breathing heavily, Gus growls into the night: "Fight the stars!"

Ash repeats it louder and waits for Liana and her other companion to join the chant. "Fight the stars, fight the stars!"

"Kerry!"

"Fight the stars," I shout, without knowing what it means, until the demolished historic district comes into view. The Freedom Brothers' logo is a stylized star between the F and the B that make up the red and white stripes.

"We're going to lose," Marissa says, panting when she sees the new tower crane on the site of Independence Hall. Shining under a steel-framed shelter is the Centennial Bell, surrounded by firefighters. To conceal our arrival, we slow down and disappear into the shadows.

"There are too many," Ash agrees. "Strategy, or we walk."

My heart hammers in my chest as I gaze at the construction project that will rise as a symbol of pride—and a giant middle finger to everyone in Harrisburg and Washington who ever implied that the city is doomed. The Freedom Brothers and the United Philadelphians for Progress have hammered home the idea that Philadelphia can thrive under their control, but their lies are merely propaganda tools. Whether it works or not, they've consolidated power in under a year and have the citizens under their thumbs. Now, with a chance to shred their empire, I recoil.

"Marissa," I say, "ready to cause a distraction?"

"What do you have in mind?"

"Summon the spirits; make them feel it. When they're confused, Ash and I flank them from the sides. Gus, Liana, and Sparta get ready to shoot—at me."

"I'm good with that," Ash says.

"Make it convincing. Maybe they'll think you're UPP."

"The hell they will!" Liana barks. "They'll know who we are. They'll have connected us to you blowing up their hideout."

"I didn't do that," I remind her. "A guy I know—"

"What's your point?" Ash snaps. She taps her toe and crosses her arms, waiting for me to explain.

"I can't make it clear, for obvious reasons. They can't see me do it or it won't work. They'll kill me first, then hunt you down for sport. I'm going incognito."

"That's code for 'Shade,'" says Marissa. "But it only works when something feeds him with energy. Don't hold back."

"Easy," Ash snarls.

"Let's do it," I say.

No further instruction is necessary. Marissa hides in the shadows as Ash and her crew disappear behind a pile of rubble several blocks away from Market Street. When they are out of earshot, I try explaining how I'm feeling to Marissa, but she blocks me. We tread lightly around the back side of a once-opulent tower that used to scrape the sky along the river. The tower has been stripped of its most valuable components to be repurposed for various projects and now stands as mere scrap. Dirt and grime have rendered the stone's etching unreadable, but there's no mistaking this as one of Philadelphia's finest towers. A hotel and residences once occupied the upper floors, while offices and retail gave it street appeal.

The longer we wait, the darker the night feels, creeping into my bones. Ash and her crew should be ready by now, waiting for Marissa to do her part. I nudge her with my elbow, signaling that it's go time.

She shuts her eyes, taking a deep breath through her nose, her face twitching as she focuses. As the seconds tick by, the Caduceus begins to glow. I grip its chilled staff with both hands as the air temperature drops far enough to produce snow.

Her focus starts to drift with the cold, but she concentrates, pushing herself harder as the air drops even colder.

Instead of producing illuminated spirits or tiny glowing eyeballs, she makes the air sour with a thousand wretched voices pleading, chanting a sorrowful song.

"Caressing the darkness, erasing the blindness."

"...blindness!"

"Avenging the ones that we love..."

"...the ones we love!"

HUSH

The Freedom Brothers fighters flinch as it reaches their ears, yet keep their attention fixed on the Centennial Bell. When the second round of voices comes, an icy breeze blows bits of torn insulation like flakes of yellow and gray snow through the streets. The confetti grows into a gale, twisting into a five-story cyclone of trash and refuse. The voices chill me to the bone, piercing my soul with sadness.

Fighters scurry through the streets, disappearing into their headquarters building, a modern take on Greek architecture. A wood lintel rests atop cracked and fluted pillars standing twenty feet high. Carved from limestone, the members support a rudimentary parapet along the sides while a wood-framed pediment shades the stone entry. I realize furiously that they have robbed the Second Bank of its prominent features to bastardize the design.

When the storm subsides and Marissa opens her eyes, I hear them muttering. Now that we have their attention, I must give into the dark energy once again. Preparing for the ordeal, I step into the center of the street like an old Wild West outlaw standing with my legs apart.

Bright flashes precede concussive blasts as a dozen bullets shred the air, ripping past my ears, close enough for me to feel their heat. I step forward as Ash, Gus, Liana, and Sparta scream into the night.

"Kill him a thousand times!" shouts Ash.

"His wife and son are live-streaming it!" screams Liana.

"They die next," bellows Gus.

The Freedom Brothers react, bouncing out of their lit doorways, and blasting at Ash and her crew with shotguns and pistols. The darkness inside me vibrates as my bones feel like they're turning to dust. As a cloud of soot, I settle through a storm drain grate, eroding a gaping hole into the sewers as I descend. Two blocks away, an hallucinatory light leads us to the exact coordinates Mayor Archinson had left behind. We're about to find his greatest discovery, but the chaos only darkens.

15

Peacock Feather

M y body flows like smoke through an exhaust fan in the storm drain. Somewhere behind me, a muffled voice warns me to slow down. Areas of warmth and cool in an enclosed space should stratify, yet I detect warm and cool breezes rising and falling as I flow through the pipe.

"Kerry!"

It's Marissa. The coal dust making up my body shifts and condenses into a thicker cloud as she runs behind me, skidding to a stop in the inch-deep water. She waits for me to solidify before touching me.

Blood-curdling screams filter through the holes in the utility lid. "…The Hell! … get out … die!" Although I cannot make it out, I hope that's Ash speaking to Freedom Brothers leader.

"I don't think it's that way," Marissa says, running her fingers over the algae coating the flow level near her waist.

I've already lost count of how many turns I've made. The glowing light from several blocks away still attracts me. In the dreadful quiet that descends, I hear a distant trickle of flowing water. Since it hasn't rained in days, I assume irrigation or a leaky hydrant upstream. To supply only their strongholds, the Freedom Brothers must have installed control and balancing valves that might have caused excessive pressure on a hydrant seal.

"We're close," I say. "Why did they deface the Second Bank of the US?"

Marissa shrugs. "Supply routes are a bit tricky right now. But there's plenty of material they can reuse if they have skilled labor."

"Labor skills are marketable, which means they're paying former citizens to work for them. With no regulations governing pay and treatment, they're probably no more than slaves."

"Desperate people will accept any form of work," Marissa agrees, "but that's not the point."

I glare at her. "What is?"

"That way," she says, pointing down a narrower, dark tunnel. "I think you should glow or something."

"Well damn," I say, deadpan. "Guess I forgot how."

Raising her eyebrows and keeping her shoulders hunched to avoid hitting her head on the pipe wall, she says, "I know how it works. You need energy."

"On second thought, maybe I shouldn't have told you everything about my abilities. You never fully explained yours."

She squeezes her eyes closed. "*Learned* abilities. Yours are natural—or should I say, supernatural."

"What's your point?"

Rolling her eyes, she says, "Unless you got a flashlight stuffed up your—"

"We're better off in the dark for now," I interrupt, tightening my lips. Since transforming into a shade requires more dark energy than light, I have little left, and my mood is still sour from Ash's rage, her threats to kill me and my family, and the stench of death everywhere. While it's true I never had many friends in Philadelphia, the friends I had were *close* friends. People like Quin, whom I last saw over a year ago battling against the Titan army the night our city fell.

Marissa protests, "But if we hope to make it there, we'll have to crawl. And slowly, because we don't want them hearing us splashing in this filth through the storm grates."

Hearing her describing the storm drainpipes as 'filth' describes Philly to a tee. Still, I find her use of the word alarming.

The connecting pipe adjoins this tunnel at a wye junction. At three and a half feet in diameter, the route she's suggesting has deeper water, and more trash and disease-carrying bacteria. I'd rather eat raw insects than crawl through the sludge, but there's no other way.

"The sooner we get moving, the better," she says. "They'll find us before long."

I'd never considered the downstream effects of this operation. After we uncover the last clue, what then? How do we escape the sewer without the FB spotting us? I have an idea that it will require spending even more time in this stink-hole.

"When we're done, we must find our way upstream to a territory they don't control."

"Or maybe downstream into the river," she says.

I shake my head. "The bigger the pipe, the more people it attracts."

She kicks at a soggy newspaper floating downstream. It sticks to her shoe, and she makes a retching sound. "I don't envy the person having to clean up the rivers here. If you haven't seen the river yet, I suggest you have a look. It's like they suddenly decided to trash the environment *more.* You don't appreciate clean water until it's gone. And the feds don't want to touch Philly with a hundred-mile pole."

"There's a weir gate at the outlet," I say, "but I see what you're saying."

Getting down on our hands and knees, we crawl into the elliptical hole in the bigger pipe's sidewall. It's impossible to see each other in the dark. Thick swaths of debris coat the utility covers, preventing light from entering from above ground. It would be easy to get lost here.

We slosh upstream, single-file, with me in front. Debris and stealth slow our pace. At every step or two, I sense something sticky brushing against my forearms and my stomach heaves. One would expect sewage gases to make sanitary drains hell on the senses, but whatever this is might be worse. Something oily and solid gets stuck in the hair on my arms.

After perhaps an hour of crawling, we reach a bored-out section of pipe wall secured with concrete.

"This must be it," Marissa says, pausing and running her hands along the wall. "Got a light?"

The distance between my loved ones and myself has lowered my energy. Thinking about Becky and Ian just makes my heart feel tight. Even detecting Sarah's distant flame is more difficult. Concentrating on everything will only make the pain deeper, fueling the wrong kind of energy.

"I might need a boost," I say, grabbing Marisssa's hand and squeezing.

Her warmth thaws my skin, but the physical contact only makes me feel confused. Closing my eyes, I try to detect an energy in her, anything that might spark my abilities.

Searching for it feels like wandering in a cave, seeking a mote of warmth or a futile flame. The spreading darkness invades my soul but I find little sparkles of yellow and purple light, glowing around a series of bends. Honing in on it, I let hope fill my senses. A giant pentagram dances above a stone floor, enclosed in the flickering light as two lovers wrap their arms around it from opposite sides. Her heart seems to beat his name. Turning my head in dismay, I feel a different warmth and as a hushed, sad voice says, "The *Kerry Gearhardt,*" I sense a familiar smile. And then, memory—undying love and loyalty—the reason I spoke to her.

With a sudden lurch, Becky is standing right next to me, clutching my hand and planting a warm kiss on my cheek.

Conveyor of Light *and Shade.*

"Good job," Marissa whispers, as my eyes reopen. A blue glow permeates my skin as I release her hand and press my palm on the block wall separating us from the room beyond. There's no handle or doorway, yet somehow, it doesn't matter.

The caduceus is covered in gunk and soggy paper when I press it to the wall. I'm expecting something to happen, but nothing does. I push with my heart until something calls out to me. It is less a voice than a steady vibration reverberating through my skin, leading me to the source. Before I know what is happening, I find a stone latch buried in a chipped-out section of wall, grip it with my fingers, and pull. It doesn't budge until I put all my weight into it. I sense something moving, inching along like a brass wheel in a muddy track.

Seeing me struggling with the weight, Marissa joins in, pushing with enough leverage to shift the block wall a foot or so. From behind the door, the room belches darkness into the storm pipe. Sidling through, we run our hands along the stone wall inside in search of a light switch. My fingers touch icy steel, and when I grasp a metal protrusion, the vibration intensifies. Energy flashes through my fingers, bathing the room in yellow light.

"How did you do that?" Marissa asks, taking in the scene in surprise. My hand is holding a sconce once used to mount a torch by the door. Its presence suggests the room was constructed before the invention of electricity, long before they built the Second Bank of the United States.

Remembering what happened the last time we entered an ancient temple, I let go of the mounting bracket, my guts peeling away from the inside of my body.

The room is oblong, stretching back to an unmarked steel door in a stone archway. Dust coats everything, making it easy to see foot and handprints. The original inhabitants hadn't treated it like a museum; the prints scatter over every surface from a line of idle pumps, rusted black iron piping, dead electrical panels with gnawed fragments of wire, a cardboard box of spare tools and construction parts, and a wheeled tool cart with a stainless-steel table standing in the center of the room.

Marissa eyes everything in awe, including the high ceiling where a chain-hung light fixture festooned with cobwebs hangs high above us.

And yes, spiders are crawling over everything. My gut lurches. They have built nests in the pumps' finned impeller housing, and around the bolts mounting the equipment to a concrete isolating skid. Every corner has cracks, circling a floor drain with a missing grate.

Centuries later than its construction, this has been turned into a mechanical room. The large diameter piping connects to valves and flow devices through inch-thick flanges. I trace the pipes to where they disappear through a steel plate attached high overhead to the wall. The caulked cracks between the pipe and the hole prevent fire, and also condensation from seeping through the wall.

"This is it?" asks Marissa, sounding disappointed.

Taking in everything I see, I still cringe at a filthy cobweb curling around a bulbous strainer on the pump suction flange. A hairy spider waits there for an unsuspecting insect to wander into its trap. A foot or so above the table wheels, a metal-slide drawer sits ajar. The two-foot by four-foot cart features three drawers on each side to hold screws, fasteners, and tools. Fearing more spider nests, I point at the table, coaxing Marissa into exploring it.

She pulls out a drawer and sifts through cobwebs and fittings, and rummages through the next until she reaches the top drawer. She gasps as she pulls something out. It's a steel orb that might be a giant ball bearing for an enormous wheel. She clutches it in her fingers, staring at it, turning it in her hand, then tosses it to me.

I fumble the catch and hear it clang on the concrete floor. Stopping it with my foot before it rolls between the pumps and into the cobwebs, I bend to pick it up, missing a spider by only a few inches. It's nothing more than a corroded cannonball, maybe from the Civil War. But just as I'm about to toss it into the corner, something catches my eye. Chipped metal and corrosion makes it hard to detect what the etching is.

I hold it up to the light, squinting like an archaeology professor to examine the marking. I get the sense that it resembles a Greek character, *theta*. Next to that one, another—*upsilon*.

Finding Greek writing confirms we've found the basement of the Second Bank. Gangs and construction crews have long since raided and re-distributed the treasure trove, but what we've found is something historical. Yet where is the rest of it?

Marissa thumbs through a stack of dirty papers, scanning hand-writ-ten and typed notes, holding them like a notebook. When a page flutters to the ground, I stop it from skittering into the cobwebs with the caduceus staff. I'm holding it above my head so that I can make out the writing, when something else detaches from the page, swaying toward the floor. It flutters enough for me to pluck it out of the air.

It's a long, slender feather, caked in years' worth of dust. I wipe it on my jeans, and try to let my imagination fill the gaps.

As colorful as it is, I can't look past the spot at the tipped end. I'm holding a peacock's tailfeather. I stare at it until ready to give up trying to figure out its significance in this room. I glance up at Marissa, and I could swear that the spot on the feather winks at me.

What the...

Excited, I read the handwritten note it had fluttered from. The writing resembles the lettering found in the original copy of the Declaration of Independence.

Found this odd feather encased in sand at the foundation cornerstone of SBUS. Committed for archeological study, waiting for age results. What makes it perplexing is the eye. Never seen a peacock's feather with an eye. After studying and consulting history professors, I decided to call it an eye of Argus. Will update more when information becomes available.

Argus? My mind boggles. I know nothing about him, but I will research when I can. Marissa reads a page in her hand in silence as I scan to the bottom of my page, where another scrawled paragraph says,

As he watched over the heifer Io, Argus observed the heavens and Hera tended to her duties. He became known for his alertness and wisdom, and his hundred eyes could foretell events yet to pass. He sees all and knows all. After he died, Hera saved a single feather as a tribute.

Marissa grips the papers she's found while I watch the eye of Argus gaze back at me, its pupil darting back and forth. If the feather could speak, what would it say?

"I don't believe this," Marissa says, gasping. "Delphi, off the Gulf of Corinth, holds the secret. The only true source of knowledge on the resting place of the great city of Atlantis. The Pythia holds the key."

Suddenly my stomach clenches as I hear sloshing behind us. Intruders. Clutching the feather and the note, I dart to the door. We have only seconds to escape. Relying on a miracle, I pull on the handle. It is locked from the outside, trapping us in.

16

The Ten Labors

"**S**tay behind me," Marissa whispers.

I press myself against the door, crouching down, and try to force energy through my veins. My fingers spark but fail, and when the cement block door slides open, some force pushes me back, slamming my head against the metal door.

Stars spin through my peripheral vision as the pain reverberates through my skull.

Marissa conjures a cloud of ash to protect us; it advances toward the Freedom Brothers and collects itself into human form. Naked and gray, the woman entices them to stop, whispering. Moments pass as she blinks at the group's leader, a husky man with a black goatee and cornrows. *I know what you desire.* Her voice cuts through the air and melts into my skull as I gape at her past Marissa.

"You're gonna die," Cornrows spits. The venom in his voice is palpable and he'll take pleasure in inflicting as much pain as he can. One drawback of top henchmen in pretty much every movie ever made is that they talk too much, delaying the punishment they promise to their victims.

The ashen woman spreads her arms as the man advances on her, wrapping them around him, and he disappears.

"Shouldn't have done that," I cough as Marissa again presses me against the door.

As soon as Cornrows disappears, another man takes his place. Bigger and stronger, he has a face tattoo and piercings. He flexes his bare biceps and brandishes a six-inch serrated blade. The ashen woman pounces as he lunges. She yelps as the blade punctures her ribcage. He sneers at her, watching a river of ashen blood trickle between her breasts. Then without warning she explodes, taking Tattoo with her into nowhere.

"Damn," I gasp, incredulous.

"An ash nymph," Marissa whispers. She narrows her eyes at the four remaining invaders. They pull pistols from their pockets and point them at her. Still pressing against me with her back, she shouts at them, "Come no further, or I'll make another one to take you to the underworld."

They're trees, *aren't they?* I dare not ask the question. Marissa's secrets run deeper than I'd thought. If we ever get out of this mess, I'll make her tell me everything—if she wants to keep my trust.

"How'd you like a bullet through your skull?" the new leader asks. She's leaner and meaner, standing a few inches taller than Marissa. Her shaved head leaves a fuzzy stripe of short hair off-center from her cranium ridge, a short bleached-blonde mohawk with a rat's tail at the back of her neck.

"I can do it," says Marissa.

The woman's calm seems to sparkle. "You and your dog will both be dead by the time your defender comes." She snaps her fingers at a stocky man with a shaved head and a salt-and-pepper beard.

Pushing at Marissa's waist, I try to free myself from behind her.

"I wouldn't do that if I were you," Mohawk says, aiming her weapon at my face. "Your powers can't save you now, Kerry."

"Conveyor of Light and Shade," I finish for her sarcastically.

She recognizes it and rests her finger on the trigger. "I've killed seven men with my bare hands, including an ex-mayor who called himself Archimedes."

"Then why do you need a gun, Freedom Sister?"

She nods at the stocky man. "Take them, Django."

"Aye, Misti," he growls, waddling towards us without lowering his weapon. If we're to escape this, we'll need a miracle.

Thinking fast, I brandish the caduceus at him, curling my fingers around the metal staff. It does nothing—at first. Django grabs it by one snake, rips it out of my hands, and curls it under his armpit to admire later. My mood instantly goes sour and the room smolders. Smoke pours from every corner.

Before I can blink, the two men standing at Misti's side collapse. She keeps the gun aimed at my head as Django punches me in the face. My vision blurs as I see what the caduceus caused. One of the downed men got the brunt of it, a red welt appearing on his forehead above his dead, shocked eyes. Next to him, his gangster pal lies prone, leaving only Misti and Django left to take us.

"I'll enjoy this one," Misti says without glancing at her fallen comrades. "Tie them up nice and tight. Don't let them think about trying to escape without feeling any pain first."

I've experienced pain before, possibly more than anyone I know, except Ian. When the memory claws at my consciousness, a remnant of its misery pushes through my bones just to remind me how frail I am. I may be a Titan, but I'm still mortal. My body reminds me of this truth more often than I'd like.

Django clenches his gun between his teeth as the Freedom Sister tilts her head and peers at me through the pistol's sighting groove. He pulls plastic zip ties out of his pocket, yanks one around my wrists, and pulls it tight. Glancing at me to make sure the binding is tight enough, he secures Marissa's wrists and glares at her as she whimpers in pain.

I can see blood at the end of my nose. If I ever get out of this, I'll erode him atom by atom.

"That belongs to me," I cough, eyeing the caduceus.

"Not anymore, it doesn't," he says. "You'll have to pry it from my cold, dead hands."

"Fine," I snarl, "have it your way."

"Don't pretend I don't know about your abilities," Misti says to me. "I don't have a clue how you managed to defeat the Titans with that outlook, so you're not as strong as I thought. Mayor Carlos will be pleased I've caught you, since I'm now his second in command."

Mayor? I could split her skull with rage for that—if only I could channel the energy to make it work.

"I heard UPP had their own mayor," I scoff. "They have more territory than you do. And they know what we just found."

"What you just found?" Misti looks amused. She smiles as she aims at us, reaches down, and crumples the brittle papers in her palms. "It's nothing; a wild goose chase. Yes, we've already sent someone to check it out. You'd be wasting your time."

"You don't have all of it," I sneer, eyeing the blood on my nose. I can feel it thickening at the tip, dribbling toward my upper lip.

She points the gun at my face. "Don't I? Then you'd be wise to share it with the mayor and me."

"Should I do that before or after I disintegrate you?"

"Kerry," Marissa whispers.

I don't care what she says. The back-and-forth feels cathartic and letting my anger speak for me does wonders for my psyche. I sneer at Misti and she glares back. She approaches me, bares her inch-long fingernails, and drags them through the stubble on my cheek. Then, grabbing my hair and pulling tight, she straightens my neck and presses the gun's barrel against my Adam's apple. When she yanks on my hair, pain scrapes across my scalp. "Keep it sealed, Titan. Your friend knows best."

With little effort, she slams the back of my skull into the metal door while letting go of my hair. Turning to face Marissa, she curls her fingers and punctures Marissa's stomach. Retraining my eyes, I see the blood oozing from the wounds. "And you," she says, keeping her voice steady. "I think you'll enjoy your first task, Soothsayer."

"Soothsayer?"

Marissa had never described herself that way, leading me to believe the label was a negative one. Now that Misti's using it as an insult, I decide I'll have to ask Marissa about it later if we survive.

"You'll both have tasks to undertake," Misti says, raising her pitch. "I shall consult with the mayor. From now on, you serve the Freedom Brothers."

And Sister, I think, without daring to speak. The way she reacted to that joke, I might consider it a tiny victory, but then again, I have no clue as to why she lashed out. I can't decide whether it was assuming a masculine job in an organization that hadn't hidden the misogyny in its group name, or something far deeper. I'll reconsider that later.

For now, pain renders rational thought impossible. Although Misti and Django's clothes are soaked, I doubt they'd wasted time and effort crawling through the storm drainpipes with four other men. Their means of travel was clearly more efficient.

Positioning herself behind us, Misti shoves us toward the rolling masonry door. My feet crunch over a pair of spiders as I walk, and out the corner of my eye, I see Marissa cringe. Eight more steps away, I see another spider scurrying toward its home. Stomping on it feels good, regardless of whether it offends Marissa. Seeing an emotional reaction brings an odd satisfaction, not because I offended her, but because it proves she's feeling something. Any emotion could give the spark I need to escape. But smashing her eight-legged friends still doesn't produce the darkness I need. I'll need to think harder about how to hurt her so I can sap the dark energy out of her, but I'm coming up empty.

Django takes the lead, crouching into the drainage pipe. Above him, the masonry door rolls in a stone track only an ich or two wide. Grooves in the top and bottom blocks swallow a metal track where a sturdy steel castor wheel guides the door into a notch in the wall. In a building this old, the foundation walls must be made of thick stone slabs. The ancient slabs must be very thick to allow an eight-inch-thick pocket door to retract into them. The exterior handle must connect through a steel cable where the load transfers into the door frame to keep the heavy door from binding in the tracks. I try to work out why nineteenth century architects would design the SBUS so that they could access the storm drains from the basement.

The idea makes no sense. Crews had retrofitted the building to better serve the public throughout its years of service. City officials had turned the bank into a museum decades ago. Would they have created the passage to move exhibits through the drainpipes? No, perhaps the Freedom Brothers had taken the building's foundation when they came to power and had fitted the door into the basement walls to stash precious artifacts and treasure, a treasure I saw no traces of.

Marissa whimpers as we crouch through a foot of flowing water with a pistol pointed at our backs. I slow down as something slimy sticks to my forearm, gulping in disgust. To prod me along, Misti hammers me in the back with the butt of her weapon, sending a jabbing pain along my spine. We turn right after crawling through the door, and ten minutes later, Django takes us left into a pipe that's only two feet in diameter. It carries less water, but crawling through it without smacking my head on the concrete surface presents another challenge. I can feel the mossy concrete scraping against my back when Django stops at a steel ladder. As if they have memorized this route, Django grips a rung and hoists himself into a two-and-a-half-foot diameter service hole.

"Climb!" Misti commands.

My hands and back ache as I follow Django and Marissa up the ladder. With my head hammering inside my skull, I stop to wait for Django to pry open a hatch. Climbing to the top of the fifteen-foot-deep hole, Marissa lets out a shriek when she pops her head out of the opening.

As I roll onto the stone floor, I have a gruesome view of what made her react that way. A woman's body lies in a pool of blood, flayed open like a fish. Her innards roll out of the deep incision like blobs of congealed jelly. Blood mats her gray hair to her face and her pale white skin reflects the menacing white light in the room. Five people await us.

Next to the woman's chest I see a gold locket in the shape of a seed, and covered with bloody fingerprints. I know I've seen this woman before, but I can't remember where or when.

"Welcome to your new home, Kerry, Conveyor of Light and Shade," says a man in a black robe. He wears a woolen crown on his head that covers his ears with gray fringes. A cool smile on his lips, he reaches out with one hand to four prisoners. I gasp when Ash stares back at me. Blood is smeared across her lips and her cheek, and she's barely conscious. Next to her, Gus hangs limp in iron shackles while Liana's eyes dart back and forth between them.

The man in the robe wears golden rings encrusted with gemstones on each of his fingers. His clean-shaved face has leather-like creases that cut through his stern expression.

"Where are the others?" he asks Misti.

She bows at him. The mayor. "Sir," she starts, "they murdered them in cold blood."

Mayor Carlos nods. "Acceptable, as useless as they've proven. I would like to examine their bodies."

"Sir?"

"Send a crew to bring them up." He glances at Django, who is gaping at a plate of meat simmering on a countertop ten feet away. "And Django, please don't look at our friends' food like that."

"Must be poisoned," I say.

"It's healthy, I assure you," the mayor says, with a chivalrous smile. His wool-covered slippers are quiet on the warped and rotting hardwood floor. The cracks between the nailed-down boards are wide enough to allow spiders and insects to enter, but instead of being dirty, the floor shines as though polished only an hour ago. If you ignore the bloody corpse lying in the center of the room.

I retch when I look at her. Her expression is agonized. They flayed her alive. Horror-struck, I realize she reminds me of someone I know. It couldn't be her, though, because her hair was shorter and curlier, her body more shapely and refined.

"Not a good look," the mayor says, smacking his pouty lips, "wouldn't you say? She worked for us and spectacularly failed in her assignment to catch a witch. The same will happen to you if you fail to carry out the goals I set out for you."

He points his chin toward Marissa. She glowers at him, trying not to look at the gore.

"Let's start with you. A soothsayer, are you not?"

"Spiritualist," Marissa breathes.

Carlos nods and rests his ringed fingers on his chin. "Yes ... we can't have bodies rotting in our streets. That wouldn't be a good look. You will be the collector. You bring them back to headquarters, you get to eat. Your first specimens will be those four men you mauled in the Second Bank's basement."

"Two of them disappeared," Misti warns.

"Taken to the underworld," I growl.

"They told me you were spirited," the mayor says, glaring at me. "Tenacity befitting a Titan. Such tenacity commands titanic conquests. Your first task, Kerry, will be to bring me the Ouroboros ring of our fearless Secretary of Defense. He has failed the city he once called home. Dispose of him how you wish."

I swallow, getting a whiff of the coppery-smelling blood surrounding the dead woman.

"And after that mission," he says, "I would like a word with the goddess Hera. Bring her before me and I shall reward you with the finest meat in Philadelphia."

I glare at the plate, squinting to make it less appetizing. Without a proper meal in a while, my body is not producing the energy to keep me going. My current state of weakness will make it harder to do what Mayor Carlos has laid out for me. Hunger drives deeper into my stomach the longer I wait. But it dissipates when I look at the bloody floorboards, the guts, and the dead woman's eyes. Rage sparks in my fingers.

"I'll come back," I say, "and when I do, you'll answer for murder."

My fingers vibrate as the hunger in my stomach wilts. Then, I point at his four prisoners, letting my expression darken when I see the frustration in Ash's eyes. "You will let them go."

"You're in no position to make demands," Misti growls.

Ignoring her, I glare at the mayor. "Do it, or I won't do anything. And neither will Marissa."

Marissa has a tear running down her cheek, and she's still avoiding looking at the corpse. Her lip trembles, but I won't let us go down this way. Carlos and Misti can skin me alive if they want, but my promise will hold.

17

Maiden Flight of Icarus

Mayor Carlos stares at me until it becomes uncomfortable. To avoid his eye, I glance back and forth between Marissa and the dead woman, trying to unravel the mystery of where I've seen her. Still coming up empty, I focus on Ash, who opens her eyes and lets her rigid gaze fall on me before tilting her head sideways. Her eyeballs dart back and forth as though confusion is shredding her perception of the world, caught in a slow-motion limbo between dreams and conscience.

"You haven't said anything more," Misti says. I can't be sure if she's speaking to me or Carlos, since I refuse to look at her. The half-shaved mohawk with a rat tail looks ridiculous on her, and she's earned my ire.

"Indeed," the mayor says, raising his eyebrows at me. "Don't make it more complicated than necessary. Carry out my commands or I will kill you."

Thinking faster than usual, I bite my lip and steal a quick glance at him before focusing my gaze on Gus. A gash has split his forehead, allowing a line of blood to trickle toward his brow. He has stopped struggling in the shackles and his head has sunk toward his chest.

"I need Marissa's help to kill the ex-secretary. He's more powerful than you realize. And Hera—I can figure out how to reach her, but she's even more powerful than Whitworth."

As if expecting my reply, he licks his lips and considers. "I would expect the descendant of a Titan to overpower him with ease. You must go alone. Your soothsayer friend has important business."

"Why should I believe you're so worried about how things look now? Stop killing innocent people if you want their trust. Just a thought. When I bring Hera back, she'll kill you."

Carlos smacks his lips as if preparing to bite into a marinated chicken leg. "She certainly has a history, but she may be one of the most ambivalent goddesses. You see, I've read everything about her. She will help prevent the senseless slaughter of our citizens. The dead ones are not innocent. They sought to sow chaos, and our laws are strong. Everyone in Harrisburg knows it. And it's not like *you're* innocent."

Frowning, I glare at him. "Stop killing."

"You make me out to be some deranged lunatic," the mayor says icily, "but look at my face and listen to me. Am I a lunatic? Or a leader who will restore order to our city?"

"I see carnage and corruption everywhere I look. You and your gang have hi-jacked every resource, locked down the borders to the city, and made hungry citizens duel for food. And you soil the very landmarks that forged this country. Your death will go a long way towards restoring order."

A flick of his eyebrows signals he's about to change the subject. "Vengeance is a tool of the devil, is it not? I believe you have read the Bible."

"That's not gonna work."

"Then perhaps you can tell your wife how you really feel when you bring Hera back. When she finds out the saint she married is just another cog in the machine of evil."

I point at him with my elbow folded in a right angle, my finger twitching. "Leave my family out of it."

He nods, but under the surface his intentions are sinister. Something unspoken lurks like a pool of acid between us, boiling and ready to corrode me. I can't drag it out of him with banter; he buries it deep within as though harboring an ancient yearning. His lust for power is only the beginning, and understanding him will take a lot more than I've yet discovered.

A library or bookstore might have helped me, but the gangs have confiscated all books to solidify their power. Reading would mean needing to escape into the suburbs or another major city on the Eastern Seaboard.

"Do as I command, Kerry. It may be the only way you'll see your wife and son again."

That sentence tears my heart, filling me with a vengeful agony so deep that I can sense the air beginning to rotate. Suppressing the urge to swallow dark energy requires me to offset it with happier memories. Two things keep it at bay: The day I married Becky, and the moment I reunited with her a year ago. The conflicting emotions engage in battle within my subconscious mind, stopping me from lashing out.

"Fine," I growl, "at least let me discuss the logistics with Marissa."

"And leave the room while you hatch a plan to escape with my prisoners? Don't take me for a fool."

"Then kill me. You'll never get what you want. Is that better?"

"You may have the closet," he says, nodding at a dark rectangle twenty-five feet away, in the wall next to Ash and the other hostages. "Fifteen minutes. My lead enforcer and I have a few matters to discuss as well. If you try anything, we'll kill the prisoners and hunt down your family."

His threat robs me of my best memories, shoving them so far into the back of my mind that accessing them will take a fourth 'healing' with Miriam.

The mayor waits for me to collect Marissa's hand, stepping between the opening to the drainpipe and the woman's entrails toward the closet. Making out shapes and color in low lighting allows distortion to change the room into a doorless dungeon. No windows or other openings are visible, leaving the only point of egress the storm drain service pit. Its hardwood-covered iron disk hatch blocks part of the hole like an annular eclipse, producing a crescent moon of black within the hardwood. The closet cuts a three-foot square divot out of the corner, making a nook for a long table, dining chairs, and a locking cabinet. Without a door, it may not serve a purpose as a closet, but with the Freedom Brothers, architectural choice is deception.

As we step inside, the hardwood shifts. Our uneven weight allows the floor to tilt toward the side wall before the planks' free ends butt against a lip, preventing them from flipping. In that split second, I realize the room's intended purpose: We're standing on the lid of another hatch. What lies below is anyone's guess, but when I glance at Marissa's expression, I can sense the foreboding building within her. Dead bodies lurk beneath our feet, rotting corpses locked away in a subterranean room.

Marissa's lips tremble as I lean against the wall with my face less than two feet away from hers. The room is dim enough to prevent nonverbal communication, but I can see enough of her face to help me understand her thoughts.

"We have a real problem," I whisper, glancing out the opening to make sure that Misti and Carlos have begun consulting.

She breathes her reply. "No shit."

"We need to free Ash, Gus, Liana, and...what's her name again? And we need to do it fast. The mayor will take every precaution to make sure we don't get away together. It might be in our best interest to go along with his demands for now."

"Kerry," she mumbles, her shoulders slumping as though she's about to burst into tears, "I can't do it."

"You're stronger than anyone I've ever met," I say.

Brushing a strand of hair behind her ear with her tattooed hand, she whispers, lowering her voice yet another octave. "I can't be a collector. It doesn't work that way. I must honor the dead's quest for freedom if I wish to communicate, or I will lose the ability and be cut off forever. I don't need to remind you what that entails."

"You should have said something."

"They would have killed me, just like..." Her eyes gloss over and I can see her turning her gaze toward the dead woman before she snaps back to my face.

"I have an idea," I explain, "but I need to understand everything we've found so far. The stone in the spider temple had to mean something. And so do the feather, and the oracle, and the caduceus. It must all be linked somehow. I know Secretary Harley—he has an extensive collection of books, and I think he's hiding something important. He wears the Ouroboros symbol on his left hand, on a ring."

"And?"

"And it's also linked, because the mayor wants it."

"Kerry," she whispers, "the Ouroboros is a symbol of renewal, the cycle between life and death. I've seen it before. And well..."

I wait for her to continue.

"I probably sold it to him."

"What?"

"You didn't see them in my shop, did you? In a bowl on a shelf near the front door. Ten bucks, marked down from fifteen, but they used to make a killing when I did trade shows. They're made of pewter, intricately forged, and a memorable keepsake."

"Harley's too old for you to have sold it to him," I say, trying to estimate his age.

She focuses on a spot beyond my shoulder. *Oh God, please don't let it be a spider.*

"I'm older than you are, Kerry."

I almost choke. In real years, unvarnished by time travel, I should be in my fifties, although I've never taken the time to calculate. Time travel has warped everything about me, including my appearance. How can Marissa claim to be older than me when she doesn't know that?

"You're—"

"Long story, but continue with your plan."

I haven't yet molded my thoughts into a plan. Instead, I'm free-wheeling, letting a wild stream-of-consciousness channel itself into something that may allow a plan to form. "I do what I promised the mayor: Find Secretary Harley, and maybe he lets me study his books. Because I'm betting that stone and the oracle have something to do with Hera. I don't know what Carlos is planning, but it can't be good."

"None of this is good," she says. "The Ouroboros ring is said to have mystical properties if a wearer can use them. The ability to prolong life or cause a premature death—"

"Like the caduceus," I gasp.

She nods, again letting her gaze fall on something in the blackness behind me. Her lip quivers again as the sense of death creeps up through the floorboards. When she shifts her weight, I can feel it. Without knowing what may trigger the hatch to open, I decide to move more cautiously. But if she's looking at a spider above my shoulder, all bets are off. My stomach tightens the longer she gazes at it.

"They're both snakes," she agrees.

"What if the answers to everything are at Delphi?"

She shrugs and looks directly into my eyes. Her pupils dilate as though a sudden realization has struck her, and when she moves, she leans closer to me, causing the floorboards to thump against the lip holding them in place. "I think we're preoccupied."

"We must go to Greece after I talk to Harley. Even though I don't think Becky will like it."

"I thought all the portals were sealed when that dirtbag Titan merged the dimensions. Unless you're thinking we talk Fire Guy into flying us there."

"I don't want to see him," I say. "We get out of town, drive up to New York, and fly American to Athens."

"Kerry."

"I know it makes no sense," I say, "and it's probably dangerous. But I want to see these people burn. Because I'm guessing they think Atlantis has enough treasure to rebuild an empire in the name of the Gods, and they want it."

"Well," she says, her eyes flipping between whatever lurks in the darkness behind me, and the dead woman, "they have the upper hand right now. It won't be easy to get out of this place while freeing them." She nods backward to indicate Ash and her gang. "And staying alive will be a challenge."

"Either the mayor is trying to goad me into unleashing my powers," I say, "or he doesn't understand how dark energy works. Even if I can't control it, choosing the right moment is critical. That's how we escape."

"That doesn't end with their freedom," Marissa protests.

"Maybe not, but we can still save them. Because the mayor let it slip that he intends to keep them alive as a bargaining chip. We'll use it against him."

"And we have another problem," she says, glancing behind me for a fourth time. "The Freedom Brothers and the United Philadelphians for Progress have been fighting for a year, but they seek the same thing—unlimited power. We thought we could use that against them, but now they both see us as a common enemy. If they unite to bring us down, they won't spare Ash and her crew, because they won't have to. Philadelphia will secede from the United States, Congress and Harrisburg will agree, and the American continent will have its first true dictatorship."

"I think they already have it."

"They need to keep the appearance of law and order," she says, "or they wouldn't be trying to make me collect the bodies of their victims."

She relaxes her shoulders, and her lips quiver. "I know what I must do. But you won't like it."

"Tell me."

She refocuses her attention on the wall behind me and lowers her voice to a tiny whisper. "I can't. I don't know how it will play out, but you have to trust me."

"Why wouldn't I—"

"Because you know I've been keeping a secret for a long time. You'll figure it out soon enough. If I don't survive, I want you to tell Miriam something for me."

"You will."

"Tell her thanks. And that I understand how it works now."

A tear wells at the corner of my eye. "How—how what works?"

She grabs me by the hand as though to press me against the wall and kiss me, but as she twists, my body twirls toward the wall. I now see what the object of her attention was, as the floorboards rock and settle again. "She'll know what it means."

A brass knob about a foot above my shoulder is hidden in the shadows. I squint my eyes to adjust for the scant light and see a pair of miniature brass wings with intricate feathers. Just the wings, no staff, no snakes.

Marissa's hand reaches up in the darkness, and I grab her wrist to stop her from touching it. Doing so will cause the floorboards to collapse beneath us, sending us tumbling into the dungeon littered with the bones and decaying flesh of a dozen FB enemies.

I gasp as I remember a warning that seeps into my mind one syllable at a time. *Don't fly too close to the sun.*

Marissa protests, presses her hand against my chest, and looks me in the eye. She's not strong enough to push me out of the closet, but when the energy in her fingers materializes, I feel a pressure wave launch me straight into the room, where I trip and tumble toward the pooling blood. Misti and Carlos glare at me as I glance back into the closet, where Marissa's silhouette reaches for the wings, waves goodbye, and disappears.

18

Astraeus Dominion

I stare at the empty closet for several seconds, waiting for Marissa to call out for help, but when no sound echoes from below, my heart flipflops. Pain stabs at my midsection as I flail near the dead woman's feet. Misti and the mayor break off their conversation, wielding blurry weapons. They're about to slice me from my navel to my neck, but before they pounce on me, Carlos shouts in dismay as he glances at the empty closet.

When Misti squeezes my hand with her sharp fingernails, adrenaline shoots through my veins. Taking advantage of the surge, I clasp my hand around her fingers to use her leverage and stand up. The fresh jolt of energy sends her flipping over me. Inches away from me, her head slams onto the hard floorboards, and the momentum topples her backwards like a domino. When she lands butt-first, I hear something crunch, and I hope she's broken her spine. I scramble to my feet, only to meet the mayor's three-inch blade. It pokes into my skin as I lunge at him, but not with enough force to puncture my gut. It draws a line of stinging blood.

"Your family's gonna die!" he growls, slashing at me again.

He lunges, too late and too weak to inflict any damage. From the corner of my eye, I can see Ash stirring, bobbing her head up and down and blinking.

Carlos lashes out at me, missing again. My body twirls to the right, and my hip collides with his. He spins and grabs my arm to prevent himself from tumbling toward the closet. Desperate to regain my balance, I let the energy course through me, sparking my veins with enough energy to fight back. Just before his blade skims me again, I wedge my shoulder under his armpit, straighten my back, and send him flipping toward the low ceiling. Despite the confusion, he lands on his feet, doing a careful dance with me around the woman's feet. When he lunges with another thrust, I dodge his blade.

A split second later, my fingers graze the hair on his forearm. Instinct guides my fingers to squeeze, yanking out a tuft of arm hair as he screams. The pain somehow tangles his feet with mine, and to stop himself from falling face-first, he locks arms with me. I fight back by clutching his elbow, slinging him around so that I can punch him in the face and end the fight.

Crack!

Carlos bellows with rage and agony as he slashes at my stomach with the knife. For a third time, he misses, but when I feel the blunt edge of icy steel press against my waist, I realize his grip is wrong and the blade is sideways. If I can swing his elbow with enough force, he could stab himself in the face.

Acting fast, I pull at his arm again, lock my knee between his legs, and twist my torso. With another painful grunt, he retaliates by shoving me. The blade's broad side presses against my shirt when he puts his entire weight behind me, pushing me backwards over the floorboards.

I let out a shriek as I see fingernails digging into my ankles. Misti curls her knuckles around my calf, her nails in my skin deep enough to draw blood. I kick her but cannot connect; the miss causes my knee to buckle and my teeth to grit. Without Marissa to help me and with Ash's crew in shackles, I'm on my own.

A face pops up out of the access hole, his eyes wide. I catch him pulling himself out of the hole at the wrong moment. Rather than forcing him back through the hole, the swing of my leg hits him square in the face. He howls as he grabs my foot, twisting me with enough power to send me spinning in midair, and my skull hits something hard. Misti's kneecap collides with my head, and I lose focus. My energy wanes as all three of them land well-placed punches to my gut.

Carlos's rage batters me as his fist smashes my ribcage, knocking me to the floor. *I'll kill your family.* His voice echoes in my brain.

Not if I kill him first. The resultant surge of energy fills the room with smoke. Within me, the vacuum draws it in, twirling it into a violent cyclone. The pressure launches Misti off her feet while I zero in on the mayor. He sizes me up as he tumbles backward. Moments later, a fourth face appears out of the hole, rising and climbing to his feet. I can't react fast enough to push him away, but I don't need to. Dark energy coils through my bones, and as I watch my arm give way to soot, the pressure explodes. The fourth attacker's spine shatters as the pressure squeezes him. I hear him groaning in torturous agony as the dark energy eviscerates him. A second later, he is silent and limp. With another surge, I home in on Carlos, but he has backed away. Desperate for the upper hand, he grabs a fistful of Ash's hair, presses his knife against her neck, and dares me to rush toward him.

Confusion disarms me; I can no longer engage him effectively. Dragging my feet and standing still, I let my body materialize out of the ash cloud while I reach toward him, enraged.

A metallic *click* echoes behind me, and a split second later, I can feel the pistol's polished barrel pressing against my scalp.

"Don't worry," Misti says calmly. Even so, I can feel her muscles twitch through the barrel. She doesn't know how I'll react, but I know I can't survive a gunshot to the head. I must hold back the negative energy coiling within my heart, or Carlos will kill Ash. "Your friend will mop up after you."

"Where is she?" the mayor asks, his pout curling into a sneer.

"Dungeon," I croak. "You may want to pull her out of there before she allies with the spirits."

"You have fifteen seconds to get out," he warns, gripping Ash's hair and slamming her head against the wall. She lets out a weak yelp and falls still.

With his free hand, Carlos pulls something from his pocket, clicks it, and produces a dancing flame near his thumb.

"Let's see how she looks without eyebrows," he says, daring me to reengage. I can't move a muscle. But when I glance to the floor, I see steel shimmering next to the dead woman's legs. The caduceus. My heart pulses in my chest as Misti clicks the pistol, ready to fire.

A split-second later, I'm holding the caduceus in my right hand like a shield.

"Drop it," the mayor warns. But as though it has fastened itself to my hand, I cannot. I clutch it tighter, seeing a flickering glow in the snake's eyes. Tiny yellow flames burst from their eyes, activating the caduceus.

One burst of power later, Misti has collapsed, dropping the gun. It goes off when it crashes into the floorboards, just as I fall into the pit. A twenty-foot fall into concrete should shatter any bone unlucky enough to endure the full force of my momentum, yet I feel nothing when my knees plunge into the soupy water below.

"I'll kill her!" Carlos screams from above, but I already know he won't kill Ash. He needs information from her. And if I know Ash, she'll tell him everything, hoping to cause my death. My body is hemorrhaging as I crawl away. Taking a sharp turn into a larger pipe, I confront my worst nightmare. A hundred spiders scurry toward me on the pipe walls, spinning delicate strands of silk behind them.

Something massive lurks before me, sloshing through the water and dragging its scaly tail through the pipe. Agony skewers me when it strikes, but I still hold the caduceus. The monster ceases to advance as soon as it sets eyes on it. Under the light of the caduceus' soft blue glow, I watch as the monster succumbs, closing its eyes and falling dead before me.

Climbing over its belly, I slither through the pipe the same way we came, seemingly hours ago. Somewhere beyond the walls, a dozen voices murmur and a familiar scream pierces my ears.

"No, don't do it! I won't."

My mind fills in what Carlos says in blistering detail. *Give me everything.*

She screams again. I latch onto the monster's serpentine body and slither hundreds of feet into a larger pipe that has more light. No one is there to meet me; the silence drives a knot into the pit of my stomach with the sudden realization—Pythia, the oracle, is a snake. The caduceus. Snakes. The Ouroboros. A snake. They're linked in more ways than one. I can only hope Secretary Harley holds the answers.

Carlos and Misti, if she survives the caduceus's onslaught, will torture Ash and her entire crew until they give up everything they know about Marissa and myself. We didn't tell them much. If the mayor really wants the goods, he may kill them trying to obtain information they simply don't have.

But they also might confuse him in the hope of staying alive, supplying faulty information to disorient him. The Freedom Brothers will not stop until they own the entire city and its citizens. And when the federal government sees the FB reinvent the city, money will flow once again, and FB power will be concentrated. If Marissa survives, we cannot fail.

Above ground, old sodium bulbs illuminate the Freedom Brothers district, spreading glowing orange circles across the desolate streets. Each time I hear someone speaking, a tremor dies away. With their leaders under assault, the FB should be scurrying through the streets trying to rebuild their strategy. The mayor can't have sealed himself in his throne room with only one exit, at least not without maintaining contact with his hundreds of enforcers. They should be out looking for me, but if they are, their silence is telling.

I think I know why: The mayor will have told them about my abilities and how I'd almost overpowered him. Because of that, two of his minions in the throne room lie dead, hopefully a third. The caduceus may have killed her or merely induced sleep, but for now, her fate doesn't concern me. I press onward, trying to concoct a plan as I set off away from the historic district the FB calls home. A few blocks away, a fallen building with layers of collapsed concrete houses a triangular opening large enough for an average man to walk through. A round stone and a plank guard the entrance, surrounded by splintered wood, piles of shattered glass, broken pipes, twisted metal, and the pieces of a marquee sign with its black letters missing.

Inside the shelter, I hear nothing, see no glowing light, and smell no smoke. Deciding Miriam is either asleep or away from home, I decide to make my way back to my car. Without landmarks to guide me, I don't remember where I parked. I need to contact Becky and tell her I'm all right, knowing I'll have to warn her that the FB may know where she lives. In my mind I can see the crystalline lake water sparkling in the moonlight, and I imagine myself gazing out the living room's bay window at the island.

Memory soaks through me as I tread the ruins in silence, not wanting to see or hear anyone until I can escape. The Freedom Brothers (and Sisters) won't want me to escape. If they're smart, they will have every road in and out of the city guarded. Even if my car is still there, I won't make it out by driving, because I'd be too easy to spot. I know only one way out.

To get there, I must either sneak through the heart of UPP territory or go the long way around it. My chances of doing that unseen are slim, but walking is producing enough adrenaline to keep me going, and the promise of hearing Becky's voice again fills my soul with hope. I'm miserable that I can't contact her without escaping the city, and that will be hard.

Relying on luck, I head toward a collapsed residential building near a deserted freeway underpass. With traffic into and out of Philadelphia restricted, I hear no cars streaking across it, and the highway may be the safest route to the suburbs if I can find the on-ramp.

The caduceus has stopped glowing, its eyes nothing more than pinprick slits in the steel. Holding it close, I creep past the residential building, pushing splintered and rotting joists aside with my feet. The structure's intact face leans against a broken concrete shaft, its upper sections crumbled and falling on exposed lengths of rebar. There is a smell of human waste. I inch closer.

A fallen street sign lies twisted in the debris, its slotted channel mast covered in dirt. A hundred feet away, an enormous crater blocks the intersection. The sign's mounting bracket is missing. Rust coats the bolts connecting the green street sign to the channel member. Bending down, I poke my fingers through the slots in the channel, feeling its heft as I pull it away from the ground. Too heavy to use as a weapon, it strains my arm, causing me to drop it. Still, I may be able to use the sign itself as a shield.

The green metal blank extends eighteen inches from the sheared and rusted bolt holes to bent metal lips protecting its edges from damage. Dents and chips mare the surface of the sign, while a single bullet hole, pierces the 'A' in Washington Avenue. Since Washington is a thoroughfare, it must connect with a freeway onramp. I'm scanning the destruction, looking for it, when I see a pair of green eyes studying me across the twenty-foot-deep crater filled with smashed cars.

Deciding I cannot trust this person, I duck behind the building, tucking myself into a wooden archway supporting a collapsed roof. The floor above reaches down with splintery wooden fingers, while a section of broken plastic piping juts out from between joists. Staying there and waiting for the stranger to pass, I let intuition in.

When I lived in Philadelphia, this building rose five stories. A wooden frame above a concrete parking podium, the sloped roof once sported wrought-iron railings surrounding a rooftop garden. The concrete roofing tiles channeled storm water into a gutter spout that emptied into a concrete channel with a flared end, which then poured into the storm grate.

Now the railings are gone, the tiles crushed, and the basin is smashed. All five floors are now a heap of rotting timbers behind the tilting walls. I realize who lived in this building.

Sarah.

Closing my eyes, I allow specks of red and green to flash through my inner vision. The red sparks turn into flames, the green into a pair of lustrous eyes. Fire forms wings, and when I open my eyes, a bird flutters over the rubble, casting its green gaze over me. Its heart murmurs something, pushing vibrations into my chest.

You know where I am now, Kerry. Above it all, watching you reassemble the world we shared. I know you will succeed, because you always have. You found me. And now you must rely on me.

I shudder as the words pass through me. The remains of her home curl into flames, pushing sparks into the sky. She's home now, patrolling the skies on my behalf.

When I open my eyes again, I balance on a bare section of foundation stem wall, and gaze toward the crater in Washington Avenue, and my heart leaps out of my chest. A freckled little girl with green eyes and fiery red hair gazes back at me. But she vanishes when I reach out to her.

Yet still I'm not alone. Behind her, a man points a gun at me and grins. His voice is deep and gravelly, with a hint of phlegm. "You saw it, didn't you?"

I gulp, holding the sign to my chest and gripping the caduceus in my right hand. "W—what?"

19

The Ouroboros Seal

"The Phoenix."

His face stiffens as he knits his eyebrows together. Maintaining five feet of space between him and me, he emits a hollow-sounding grunt and waits for my reply.

Beyond him, the darkness stretches, rendering the freeway overpass invisible. Measuring at least fifty feet in diameter, the crater spreads outward from the center of the intersection in rays like a wagon wheel. The collapsing asphalt sags over the hole's rim, a foot-deep layer of gravel and compacted sand weathers and erodes. Over the past year, rainfall has carved slots and canyons into the hole's rim, where weeds and grasses grow. The stranger peers into the crater and then rests his eyes on my face.

"Don't know what you're talking about," I say.

"They say the mythical bird has magical properties," he explains. "Exceptional gliding abilities for silence, dimension-bending speed, the ability to heal, and rebirth through fire."

I nod and look away. "Yeah, I know."

"But its most underrated quality, I'd argue—"

"Listen," I interrupt, "I need to get out of here. You're UPP?"

"—it can overcome the boundaries between the physical and the spiritual, the immortal and the living. Something even the gods can't do."

"Interesting," I say, fidgeting and stepping toward him.

He lowers his gun and matches my pace toward the pit. Three or four more steps could send him tumbling into the burned-out cars and the putrid water, where a skeletal hand sprouts from the mud like a beet.

"What's your destination, sir?"

"I gotta get out of the city tonight." I rush my speech. "If the Freedom Brothers...don't wanna see them again."

"You're not UPP," he says, looking me over twice. "Too sloppy, too dirty. And that injury—"

"I'm in a hurry."

"—and you're all wet."

I threaten to take another step, but he stands his ground, his grip on the gun still slack.

"Getting out tonight will be a tall order, since word has it, some troublemaker attacked the mayor. Brave sonofabitch, but foolish as hell. The good news is that smugglers have spent months constructing a tunnel to aid citizens with contraband. I shouldn't tell you about it..."

My fingers are twitching. "Bring me there."

"Gotta make sure you are who you say you are," he says, as if meditating, "else the UPP sends agents to board it up, deploy hounds who can sniff out illegal aid from a half mile away."

"Get. Me. There." I say through my teeth, and realizing I might be deterring his help, add "please" on the end. I don't care if he suspects I'm a gang enforcer or just another down-on-his-luck citizen fancying a way to visit friends in the suburbs. Realizing I haven't even asked his name, I glance at his face, taking in his hardened expression where empathy lurks beneath the surface. His patience may be an asset in normal conversation, but it's wearing my senses thin.

Wearing a blue overcoat with a stiff collar and a lapel, he relaxes the gun and glances into the cavity. Four rusting cars lay at the bottom, half-submerged in murky gray water with a mysterious white foam drifting like soap scum across the calm surface.

"What's your name?" he asks.

"Gus," I blurt out. Gus as in *Ar*gus?

"Well ... *Gus,*" he says, "I haven't seen your friends in over twenty-four hours. What did you do with them?"

Me? "N-nothing," I stutter, hoping I don't sound like an idiot. "I think—heard they got kidnapped. FB."

"Already dead, I presume," he says, shaking his head and frowning. "Sad what this city has come to. I'll lead you to the tunnel entrance. You can make your way after that. But you gotta promise me you won't say a word about our meeting."

"How am I supposed to do that? You haven't told me your name."

"That's the idea," he says, grinning, "but for nostalgia's sake, you can call me Curly. Like the Stooge, only smarter."

"Uh..."

Nodding at me, he turns and sidles around the rim of the crater. Focusing on the path through the debris to keep my balance, I follow. When we tread away from the hole, we turn into a dense alley covered with layers upon layers of wood rubble and dust at least ten feet deep. Stepping away from Washington Avenue and avoiding the freeway seems a roundabout way to reach the suburbs, and I have no idea where the tunnel ends. A clever designer would have hidden the station under mounds of rubble, included three or four changes of direction, and given at least a half mile of distance from the fenced-off city limit, where armed guards patrol.

Climbing onto a steep concrete ramp with rusted steel cabling poking out both ends, he trudges around a broken yellow bucket, pushes up a pair of splintering studs, and stops on a dirty platform six feet above street level. A makeshift set of two-by-four stairs curves around a small square pier, tilting as it rises to a shattered concrete deck that rests on smashed cars. The stairs disappear when we reach street level, and I sense we've left the alley.

We are now climbing through the wreckage of homes and strips of grass. A small side street lies ahead, obscured by fallen trees and piles of wood, rotting sofas, and human bones. Ten feet before we exit onto the street, Curly leads me through a gap in a leaning prefab wall. The roof has caved in, covering a steel-grated floor with the twisted remains of rooftop units and the ripped sheets of tar-based sheathing over the grates. Three pairs of colored cylindrical brushes with long, spongy fibers are attached to frayed wiring harnesses. A car wash in this section of the city should not surprise me, especially buried in a residential neighborhood, although the city council might have started making nonsensical zoning decisions decades ago.

Curly peels back the tar sheath covering the grate and nods at me to help him. With our combined strength, we lift the grate two feet away. Rolling a broken section of concrete slab from a wheel track into place under the lip, we let the iron rest, revealing a pitch-black cavity at least six feet deep.

"Pretty straightforward from here," he grunts, waiting for me to sit down. "After the third bend, there's a light switch on your right. Before you reach the exit, there will be a pair of turns. Turn off the lights before you go up the stairs. Trisha and Barry will be upstairs watching TV. Get their attention and tell them I sent you—fast—before they shoot you. Good luck."

I crouch first, letting my feet dangle into the filthy concrete hole. Halfway down, a groove in the foundation wall carries a strut. When I climb into the hole, Curly rolls the boulder away and lets the grate fall into place. A moment later, he's rolled back the roof covering, and he's gone, leaving me in utter darkness. I swear I can hear scales slipping across moist rocks far in the distance, but I take a breath and press on. I find the light switch after three bends, its galvanized steel box embedded in compacted earth two feet away from the inside corner. I flick the lights on and peer into a long tunnel illuminated by single-bulb pendant fixtures at ten-foot intervals far into the distance. The well-worn floor of compact mud and stone is smooth.

Twenty minutes later, I reach the corridor's end, turn off the lights, and climb the steps. The wooden stairs creak as I ascend. When I reach a door, which stands ajar, I rap at it, and wait. Five seconds later, a man with a gruff voice points a shotgun at my face.

"Just talked to Curly," I explain.

Barry lowers the shotgun and helps me into his twenty-foot-long hardwood hallway. He rasps as he lumbers through the living room, where Trisha munches on popcorn, to the front door. The stoop rests in the shade of a metal awning in front of a modest one-story home. The tiny front yard grows thistle weeds and giant dandelions amidst browning grass.

"Don't come back till morning," Barry barks. "And stay away from the fence. Those Freedom sons of bitches don't like people snooping, and they've been known to shoot at our houses just for fun. And whatever you do, don't tell anyone where you came from. You got that?"

I nod and jog to the end of his street, nearly tripping on uplifted sections of concrete beneath giant old-growth trees. People look out of their houses as I run. I stop at a crosswalk along a busy thoroughfare, standing next to a woman puffing on a vape pen, and wait for the cars to pass. When the light turns red, cars roll to a stop. I point my thumb, hoping someone will offer me a ride. A few seconds later, a driver rolls down his window and pokes his head out. "Where you heading?"

"M-Maryland, I think," I say, trying to hide the parched gruffness in my voice.

"Your lucky day," he says. "Get in. Make any sudden moves and I shoot you."

I wait for him to explain how he happens to be heading to Maryland at the exact moment I need a ride there, but he turns the wheel hard right and drives through less-crowded streets, then turns south toward the state line. Relying on memory, I try explaining where Secretary Harley's lavish colonial home rests in the rural hills northwest of Washington, DC.

He keeps driving without talking, and before long, I drift off to sleep.

Hours later, I wake up when the man turns along a gravel road, glancing over his shoulder. He has sweat on a stubbled cheek. His greasy hair mats to his forehead and he peers at me through wire-rimmed glasses. "This it?"

I look at the two-story colonial home behind a curved gravel driveway. Brick-sided concrete steps ascend to a double front door with pie-shaped glass panels at eye level.

Within a few seconds of ringing the doorbell, the foyer light flips on and a petite middle-aged woman with blond hair lets me in. She glances at my filthy clothes and the scar on my cheek before taking in the caduceus. "Suppose you're looking for Mr. Whitworth," she says.

I notice the five-foot tall urns with red Greek pictograms along the rims as she leads me through an archway into a spacious living room. It has soft leather chairs and a pair of long, button-upholstered sofas.

I sit on the nearest sofa, thank her, and cannot stifle a yawn.

An old man with a cane and a hunched back totters into the room, his black socks scuffing against a threadbare rug spanning from a hutch to the sofa. He peers at me, raises his eyebrows, and sits next to me on the couch. I spy the Ouroboros ring on his finger before I look into his face. Heavy creases fold his sagging skin like creases through old leather. He has a long, white beard. He pushes his square glasses up his nose, puts a bony arm around my shoulders, and greets me.

"Mr. Titan. Good to see you again. I'm entering my final days, I'm afraid. What brings you?"

My lips quiver as a warm sensation spreads through my torso. I still haven't introduced him to Becky, which I'd promised her I would do eventually. Although uncomfortable with only being here to seek advice, I rush into my explanation without slowing to linger on any details. The longer I speak, the more concerned he looks. As I finish, he has a simple smile on his lips; he raises his eyebrows, and pushes himself up from the sofa with his cane.

"Come to my den," he says. "I have important items to show you."

The den is big. A polished desk with carved legs sits in front of a mullioned window, which would flood the room with light in the daytime. An empty mug makes a ring on the desk next to a keyboard projector and a two-button scroll pad. At the end of a sleek monitor, an LED desk lamp shines a square of yellow light onto the center of the desk.

Harley ambles to a bookshelf and takes a leather-bound tome from the third shelf against the left wall. He flips through it and then plops it on the desk before he rolls a pair of chairs to the desk and sits down, groaning as he bends.

Waiting for me to flip through the book, he nods and chatters, wondering about the weather in upstate Pennsylvania and how treacherous the drive was. Answering only in half-sentences, I stumble onto a page depicting a thin woman with a wreath crowning her wavy blonde hair. Her sleek dress bares her shoulders and plunges into a deep vee on her chest, clasped with a brass ring at her waist. I read Hera's introduction paragraph and then glance at Harley, who is wearing a quizzical expression.

"Hera had many servants during her reign," he explains, "including a man with a hundred eyes called Argus, just like you mentioned. Working to protect a princess-turned-heifer called Io, Argus was betrayed and murdered, apparently in an act of revenge. To memorialize her servant, she placed his eyes on a peacock's tailfeathers. Touching tribute. After that, rumor has it she communed with Apollo in his temple, where he was busy writing songs and prophecies. And, just like you suspected, the temple of Apollo is at Delphi.

I nod at the caduceus in my lap and glance down at his ring while he clasps his hands under the keyboard projector. "What do the snakes mean?"

"The caduceus," he says. "How'd you get it?"

I give him the brief explanation without mentioning the shootout with the United Philadelphians for Progress or Ash's group from the suburbs.

He expression is now worried, and he details the caduceus's larger meanings before diving into more obscure facts. "Hermes found two snakes entwined in mortal combat and separated them with his wand to create peace, thus the symbology."

"Too many snakes, too many coincidences," I blurt out. "Your ring, for instance, which a friend of mine thinks she might have sold to you. And an oracle I met who called herself Pythia."

"Snakes represent a wide range of topics in Greek legend," he says, furrowing his brows, his voice straining to stay audible. He clears his throat and continues, "Anything from the cyclical nature of the earth, to wisdom, transformation, renewal, and even fertility."

"But the caduceus isn't just for peace," I argue. "It can kill, put people to sleep, and I heard, reanimate the dead."

He shrugs. "A bit too in the weeds for me to theorize about, I'm afraid. But take the Ouroboros: The snake eats its own tail to symbolize the cycles of life and death. An endless loop of creating and destroying. I can't speak to the oracle, but Pythia's name derives from the ancient serpent *Python*, which Apollo killed at Delphi. That I do know."

The more he speaks, the more excited I get. I can't believe how groggy I was only thirty minutes ago, but sleeping in the car had provided a much-needed rest. "Then why does the symbolism point to Delphi of all places? We even found an intricate oval stone in an underground chamber, guarded by millions of spiders, containing a scroll that pointed us to the Second Bank of the US, known for its Greek-styled architecture."

"An interesting trail," he says, waving his bony hand. "And you believe this stone also pointed to Delphi?"

"I sense it."

"Let's see what we can find," he says, waving at the bookshelf, but struggling to get up.

I nod at him to stay seated and run my fingers along the shelf until I find a volume related to Greek temples, their architecture, and the mythology behind them. Flipping to a section about the temple of Apollo, I bring it over to the table, rest the caduceus on my lap, and flip pages until I find a section on the ancient city of Delphi. I inhale deeply when I notice the heading at the top of the page depicting a stylized Ouroboros ... with a Roman numeral in the center?

No, not a Roman numeral III. A tiny illustration of Greek columns.

I read through the section until I see a sketch of an enormous stone shaped like an egg. "This was it! The omphalos stone, or the navel stone. Zeus, trying to figure the location of the center of the earth, launched two eagles flying at equal speeds who met above Delphi, which was chosen as the location of the center of the earth."

My throat tightens as I continue reading aloud. I can't believe the words on the page, as though they're lifting themselves above the white paper and are wrapping themselves around my throat. "The Titaness Rhea gave the Omphalos to Cronus, pretending it was their son Zeus, so that when he swallowed it..."

"I see."

"Oh my God! He ate his children? I'm glad he's back in Tartarus, where he belongs."

"Delphi is the center of the earth," Harley says, his voice having gone from warm to gravelly. "I assume that means you wish to travel there."

"I don't wish to," I say. "Becky will flip out, but I think Marissa and I have to go ... because the scummy Freedom Brothers mayor wants to make Hera help him with something important ... I don't know what. He also instructed me to—"

"I have read about the Freedom Brothers," he says, and now his voice is frosty. "They're not to be trifled with. Please tell me you haven't crossed them."

I launch into a tirade about how they'd captured Ash and her crew, assigned tasks to Marissa and me, and how Carlos had ordered me to kill him. He doesn't look surprised. Instead, he clasps his hands again and leans backward in the chair.

"It makes sense now," I say. "Everything, including Atlantis. I think the mayor wants the treasure there to buy resources, and favor with Congress, so as to establish his own mini empire."

"Atlantis…" he says, contemplatively. "There are conflicting accounts on whether it's even real. I lean more to the myth side."

We are discussing the logistics of traveling to Greece when he begins musing about the portals still being open.

"I don't see how," I say. "Cronus merged the dimensions to save my son at the behest of Zeus."

"Have you tried?"

"Well … no, but it might be safer to fly to Athens from JFK, rent a car, and drive to Delphi."

"I don't recommend it," he says, his face growing dim. "Travel back home to your wife, see your son."

"He has powers, because he's a descendant of the Cretan Titans, too. He just doesn't recall how he got them. But he's worried, because they can cause far more destruction than mine."

"You should teach him how to control them."

I frown. "I don't even know how to control mine. All I know is that they feed on energy. Cronus is in Tartarus because I punched him in the nuts at full power, while the rest of the Titans ran. And The One … Erebus, is locked up in Tartarus and stripped of his power. Just the way it should be."

"This is too dangerous to do alone," Harley warns, "even if you bring a friend. I understand your sense of urgency, but you should let things play out."

"You were the Secretary of Defense!" I shout. "The point-man to analyze threats to the United States of America. And now you're talking about restraint?"

"That is how I excelled under two administrations," he says, stumbling over his words, but sure of where he wants to go, if I'm reading his expression right. "National security often depends on a cool hand. Archimedes wanted me to serve under him because of my ability to listen and understand without overreacting."

"He's dead," I say flatly.

Again, this information doesn't surprise him. "I understand that, Kerry. But listen, I'm advising you as a friend, because I believe you should enjoy life as much as you can before it's too late. I learned that the hard way, and I don't want you to make the same mistake."

"I'm going to Delphi." I scowl, standing up and clutching the caduceus staff. Leaving the book open at the section on Delphi, I wait for Harley to show me toward the door.

"I understand," he says. "I won't stop you. But do exercise extreme caution, and reach out to your New Titan Order friends to help protect you."

"I don't trust them," I say, almost choking. Weariness brings a tear welling to the corner of my eye as I tell him everything that happened with Sarah, and how I'd spoken to Curly about the Phoenix. Before I speak again, a familiar word sparks in my brain, igniting a warm sensation of energy in my bones.

"Transformation. Renewal. The Phoenix and the Ouroboros."

"You have your answer," he says, reading my eyes. "The Phoenix can protect you, but you must obey the warnings of the oracle. If you misuse the caduceus, the Phoenix may cease protecting you. And you could throw the entire world into another senseless war."

"I don't know how yet," I say, letting my chin droop and shuffling my foot on the den rug. "But we're going to find Atlantis, one way or another. I'm just hoping someone can point the way, how to sail to that location."

He nods. "I know another rumor. It hasn't been confirmed, but I think it's plausible. Decades ago, archaeologists found a mysterious device in the Mediterranean near the island of Antikythera. About the size of a shoe box with intricate gears and carvings on the front, interconnected. It predicts the movements of the sun, the moon, and the planets, and it's accurate, too. They say the *real* Archimedes invented it. If the rumor about a working replica is true, you should be able to measure the positions of the constellations and planets using the Antikythera mechanism to stay on course. But getting your hands on it may be difficult, even if you were to find out where to search for the lost city."

"Antikythera ..." I repeat. "I'll ask around."

I thank him for his time, and we spend a few moments in friendly chatter before I wish him goodbye. I give him a warm hug and a handshake. I want to memorize his advice as I make for the door.

When I exit onto the curving driveway, I try to think of a way back to Philadelphia, indulging in the hope that Marissa is still alive. I can't do this without her. And I must rescue Ash, Gus, Liana, and Sparta from the Freedom Brothers' torture.

20

Theseus and the Bull

Gravel crunches under my feet as I make my way to the end of the driveway, flanked by a pair of white vinyl fences. A four-foot-tall brick sign with bronze lettering marks the entrance to Calvert Manor. Perpendicular to the two-lane road, a rose and tulip garden encircles the sign, with well-placed rosebushes hiding bright LED bulbs. Metal shields illuminate the letters of the house name.

Two hundred feet up and down the road, double yellow lines follow the contour. To my left, a quarter mile away, the lane twists into a series of bends as it curves through a forest. Without knowing which way to travel, I turn to the right, where equestrian fields and small farms create a patchwork grid across the rolling hills, and a grove of gnarled oak trees hangs over a wide gully thick with grasses and shrubs. I walk until the manor disappears into the darkness. A single car tears along the drive in the opposite direction, the unknown driver waving at me out of his open window.

The oaks' shade prevents thick grass from growing, yet provides ample shelter for tiny carpeting plants such as clovers and ivy. Beyond the grove, a wooden fence line stretches from post to post, its runners sagging in the center. An ache gnaws at my stomach; I haven't eaten in days. If I don't stop for a snack soon, I feel like I could starve to death. How far can shops be? I stop at the trees to wipe a bead of sweat from my forehead and look into the shade.

My jaw drops. I adjust my eyes, blinking twice. A woman wearing a long white dress is materializing out of the darkness, her sandals surrounded by clovers and tuffets of grass. She reaches a low branch as if to perch something on it before facing me and straightening her back. Before I can even nod, she addresses me by name.

"It has been a long time, Kerry."

For at least thirty seconds, I don't recognize her, but to avoid offending her, I try to pretend that her appearance isn't a surprise. "Hey. Do you know how I can get to Philly?"

"Tread carefully through the ditch," she says, waving me over.

I hesitate and shrug, trying and failing to think up something witty to say. Perhaps the less I say, the better, because I assume she has an important message for me. As she has advised, I bolt to the road's shoulder, feeling my soles slip in mud under the grass before regaining my balance, before ascending to face her in the oaks' shadows.

"You seek not Philadelphia," she says, as though informing me, "but Greece. Be wary, for the journey is fraught with challenges."

How could she know that? I try to guess her identity as she speaks again. For a few seconds, she waits for me to respond with her hands at her waist.

"Millenia ago," she continues, "I helped another hero to find Athens, traveling from Crete after solving the Labyrinth."

Understanding snaps into place. Princess Ariadne continues, "The creature Theseus defeated now serves my father in Hades. Theseus battled many creatures of the deep along the way."

"Not a problem if you can fly," I say.

"Riding a winged horse is not an easy task."

I've never mounted a horse in my life on the ground, much less a winged one like Pegasus. Ariadne must understand modern modes of transportation, so why is she talking about winged horses?

"I was thinking of flying American Airlines, unless the portals still work. A free in-flight meal might do me good."

She smiles and nods. "With the dimensions altered, an airliner might be your best choice. Why must you return to Philadelphia?"

"A few loose ends to tie up," I say. "Friends to see."

"Including the Spiritualist Marissa?"

I nod. At least she's not calling Marissa a soothsayer. I might consider asking her why she deems that an insult, but that's less of a problem than finding her.

"And I think the Phoenix will help guide me."

The princess nods again. "A wise choice. Now a word of advice about the device you hold. It has great powers, but it will tempt you beyond anything you've ever faced. Do not misuse it."

"Yeah," I say, shrugging. "I remember what the oracle told me. I just have one question: What did she mean when she said 'success cannot undo gravity?'"

"The Delphic Oracle sees all," she says, "including the intentions of your heart. Seek not a literal answer but consider all possibilities."

"Thanks ... I guess," I say, biting my tongue to avoid sounding sarcastic. If she can sense the irony, she might find it tasteless and refuse to help me. Realizing I never asked for this meeting, I figure she has something deeper to discuss rather than rehashing what I already know.

"Why have you come?" I ask her.

After a few seconds' hesitation, she frowns, and flickers with energy. "I wish to impart wisdom regarding your son. He may not fully understand what he possesses or why. It is a potentially terrible force. Containing emotion will be the key to contending with it, as with your gift."

"Who gave it to him?"

Ariadne looks at her sandaled feet. "I know not. But you may soon find out, for he, too, descends from the Six."

"Right," I say, drawing in a tight breath. "You never bothered telling me about that part. I mean, even a word or two of advice such as, 'you know what, you're a bona fide Titan' might have helped."

"A hero must find his own journey," she says, parting her lips and clasping her hands in front of her. "I must now return to my father. Farewell, Kerry."

"Wait," I say, hurrying before she vanishes, "how will I get to Philly?"

"I believe there is a carriage for hire that you can commandeer. In a town one mile away."

I cough. "You mean a taxi?"

"Perhaps," she says, dissolving into thin air. I reach out into the darkness as though to touch her dress, but she's already gone. Inhaling the humid air, I retrace my steps to the roadside after trying to hop over a narrow part of the ditch with minimal success. I feel my shoes sliding backward when I land, but using my arms for balance, I keep myself upright.

Little traffic passes as I speedwalk into the town, a one-stoplight village with a single convenience store, two rows of power lines, and a few dozen one- and two-story houses surrounded by picket fences. Gigantic trees tower over the homes, swaying in the darkness. Across the street, a woman jogs with her German Shepherds, pauses at a chain-link gate, and lets the dogs lead her to a concrete stoop. Finding a taxi here should be easy, but now it's dark, and in the sparse streetlights every car looks the same.

In a stall fifteen feet away from the store's double-glass doors sits a newer Batterycar with a polished chrome grill. The newest models direct their intake through an efficient electrical fan to create power-generating torque. This version has a simple rear deck spoiler and flush door handles to prevent tampering. Peering through the tinted windows, I see a Walle Tap terminal, where users without the Batterycar phone application can rent the vehicle for a one-way trip. From what I understand, the application tracks GPS on every nearby car, allowing drivers to see where one is available.

Seeing that the previous driver has left the doors unlocked, I decide that this is my best option. First, I enter the store and peruse the narrow aisles for something to eat. After grabbing two bags of chips and a bottle of soda, I tap on the reader and wait for my payment to process before hurrying back to the car.

Accessing the driver assistance features without a charged phone presents a challenge, but after I bypass it and use the tap terminal, the motor stars when I press the brake pedal. The touch screen shows fifty percent battery, allowing 297 miles before recharging. Deciding that should be enough to get me to Philadelphia, I enter downtown into the Nav app and ignore the closed roads warnings. The routes into the city won't be accessible at night, but I consider finding the right highways a priority.

Coming up with a scheme to enter the city takes half the trip, before I settle in and navigate into the suburbs. Since Barry warned me not to come back to his home until morning, I won't be able to use the tunnel, and armed

FB guards wait at every road entrance, creating checkpoints. Using another means is more promising, but with no guarantees, I find worry slowing me down.

After spending twenty minutes navigating through the suburbs, an idea sparks in my mind. In its heyday, Philadelphia offered commuter trains using light rail embedded in select routes, as well as proper trains using the old El tracks. The Els lead into a subway downtown, where heavy barricades and fences prevent citizens from exiting the subway tunnels to walk on the rail. The gangs will have barricaded all city-limits stations and erected a fence to stop suburbanites from entering.

Using the navigator to direct me to an El terminal, I find a destination and drive to an empty parking lot. Finding the suburbs have installed minimal chain-link fencing systems for citizen safety, I climb the fence and blend into the dark.

After climbing the fence, I run up the concrete stairway, dart toward the railway, and drop onto the tracks. Traditional railroad ties and runners make up the system, and a series of overhead wires on angle-steel towers keep the trains inline. The train itself must be at another station, probably picked over for parts.

The route offers unobstructed views for almost a mile, which should give me enough warning if danger lurks. At intervals, I peer at colorful graffiti until I make out what looks like a pair of wings. An illustrated eagle sinks its talons into the red-and-white stripe Freedom Brothers logo with the background star shape. No words are necessary. I follow the tracks until I reach a high fence topped with razor wire. A sign warns prospective pedestrians of an electrical current in the wires.

I close my eyes, letting happy memories wash through me. Hands first, I step into the fence as I start to glow. The energy in my body sends sparks of lightning through the fence when I curl my fingers around the metal and climb. But ripping my shirt on the razor wire, I misjudge my fall and twist my ankle.

This rail leads straight to Market Street in the heart of FB territory. I follow it until it dives underground. Deciding to climb over rubble to bypass the fencing, I hurry past weary people, all leering at me like I'm a trespasser. The station may be next to Marissa's hideout, so I knock on the walls where the citizens allow me to approach them. Graffiti covers the treads and walls of the stairwell as it ascends to street level. I spot a sign for Market Street and pass a man heading for shelter. He nods at me as he passes, brushing my elbow.

Then suddenly he shouts at me, "God, that hurt, you bastard!"

In an instant, I understand: A residual energy still glows in my fingers. I have no idea how to access the FB throne room, but when I reach the Second Bank's ruins where they've built their headquarters, I have a sudden intuition. Concrete stairs with metal pipe railing ascend to a false gable that shades a pair of molding-clad double doors, where two men await me with machine guns. I slink into the shadow before they can see me, paying attention to the windows. None are open, but my trek through the shade takes me into the alley between the headquarters building and a demolished skyscraper. A new concrete wall over twenty feet high keeps the shifting rubble from overrunning the narrow walkway. Batches of graffiti accumulate around expansion joints in the wall, and a ground-level door pokes into the FB headquarters building. A single guard stationed at the entrance hears me coming, points his machine gun at me, and pulls the trigger. Signaling that he's didn't unlock the safety, he switches it into place while I raise the caduceus in front of me.

For a moment, the guard stumbles, yanks the trigger, and unloads at least ten rounds into the wall, raining concrete dust and gravel onto the walkway. When he realizes he's missed, he retrains the gun on me an instant after the serpents' eyes in the caduceus begin to glow orange. He falls silent and collapses. I push on the door and find myself in a wood-paneled hallway with several unmarked doors on both sides. Wall-mounted sconce lighting at fifteen-foot intervals span from end to end. I open one door to find a bathroom, and then open more doors until I at last reach the last door on the left. Careful to stay quiet, I press the sole of my shoe against the door and kick. It swings open the instant I hear footsteps behind me. Panic rips through me before I meet her.

She slings her arms around me and squeezes as the tremors of fear roll away. Leading Marissa back the way I came, I pause before we exit into the street. The gunfire will have attracted more guards, blocking the exit. Instead, we turn right into a narrower, darkened hallway, slowing when we reach a door. I turn the handle and push it open, leading us into a stairwell. Trying to piece together a floor plan of the headquarters in my mind, I let Marissa take the lead until we reach the bottom. A series of doors and corridors take us what might be several blocks. The tunnel must lead somewhere, and when I realize where, I halt, pull Marissa back, and retrace our steps.

"The Omphalos stone temple," I whisper, "with the spiders."

She rolls her eyes at me. "Oh, God, you're so cute."

"There's another exit into the drainage," I say, remembering our route through the pipes. I resolve to follow the increasing drainpipe sizes to find an exit.

"Chiron, the UPP thug we met that night, came from somewhere."

She nods at me as we splash through inch-deep water in the pipes' inverts, bypassing the now-sealed temple, and finding another unmarked door a hundred feet away on the same side. Pulling open the doorway, we ascend concrete steps in silence until we hit our heads on a makeshift cellar lid.

Pushing at the lid confirms the FB thugs have left it unlocked. Readying the caduceus, I help Marissa push open the doors and step out into the night. The cellar doors open onto a pathway through mounds of rubble. We press on in the dark until we reach a T-junction leading into a nearby street. It's devoid of foot traffic.

Lingering under a collapsing overhang, Marissa breathes in and sighs, clutching the crook of my elbow with her palms. "You were gone forever. I think it's almost morning."

Bypassing the details, I explain how I'd hitched a ride to see Harley, what we talked about, and how I'd found the Batterycar for the drive home. She watches my eyes as I tell it, glancing back and forth from my face to the caduceus.

"When I fell into the dungeon," she explains, "the spirits caught me, I think, setting me down on my feet. We communicated in silence as I asked for their help, promising their freedom. I could hear you fighting with the FB upstairs through the floorboards. Screaming, Ash, Gus, and Liana a few times. Misti and Carlos got into a heated argument that almost came to blows, when the spirits lifted me from the hole and invaded the throne room. Things flew through the room as they approached, until Misti took the knife and pressed it against the mayor's throat. He had grabbed her wrist when the table cracked into his head, dropping them both. I wanted to untie Ash and her crew, but I couldn't do it and escape at the same time. The room has a trapdoor into a hidden corridor, where I found another doorway and met you."

"Wow," I say. "We need to break in and free Ash. But the mayor will keep them alive just to torture them until I return with Hera and the ring."

Oh, God! I realize I didn't bring the Ouroboros ring. Carlos might kill me for forgetting. I make note of it in my mind while trying to devise a plan for when we return. *If* we return.

"You're really thinking about going to Greece?"

I nod, resting my back against a crumbling wall. "Delphi. The original Omphalos is there, at the center of the world. I believe we will find our next clue at Apollo's temple. I need to call Becky, tell her I'm alive first. Then we hitch a ride to JFK and fly to Athens."

"Good plan," she says. "I've always wanted to visit Greece, just not under these circumstances."

"It will be dangerous," I say, turning the caduceus in my hands. "I need your help. A certain princess who shall remain nameless warned me I'd be tempted to misuse it. I want you to stop me. No matter what, tell me you won't let me use it for evil. Only self-defense."

"Got it," she says.

"I must convince the Phoenix to guide us. Are you up for that?"

She smiles. "You know how I feel about her, Kerry."

She wraps her arm around my waist to draw warmth and energy from me, combs her hand through her dirty hair, and we step into the night. The shadows engulf us as we make our way, uncertain where the road will lead. If we fail, the world may face another war, and that is something I cannot allow. Because not only will it inflame tensions everywhere, but it will destroy me again and shatter my family. And I know Marissa, too, won't be immune.

21
Mustering the New Titan Order

As though its pilings are weakening, the El tracks shift as we hurry back to the station where I'd left the Batterycar a few hours ago. Behind us, the eastern horizon glows with the first signs of dawn. I clench my teeth when my left foot misses a railroad tie and shoves my toes into an awkward position. Stumbling and then regaining balance, I let Marissa stabilize me. The faster we can get away from downtown and the FB territory, the safer we will be.

After less than ten minutes, I hear voices below us. A solitary man needing food for his family threatens to duel a younger man, but when they sense our shadows moving above them, their argument crumbles. Although we're safer up here, the prospect of getting interrupted worries me.

Marissa doesn't speak until five minutes after we've passed the duelists. She pauses to look at the coming sunrise, rests a foot on the rail, and inhales. "It'll take a long time to get to New York—traffic. And I think we should stay in Pennsylvania, avoiding the coast for as long as possible."

"We need to board a flight by this evening," I say, stepping forward a few ties and gazing out over the rubble below us.

Elevated thirty feet, the tracks offer a different perspective on the ransacked city. Homes lie scattered in fragments below us. Buried under shattered roof joists, concrete, sheet metal, and various broken household items, I see a human leg clad in tight denim jeans. A broken lintel has crushed her upper body, and flies swirl around her. A pang of guilt punches my stomach, reminding me that Ash had accused me of murder. Without the Titans attacking Philadelphia, hundreds of thousands of citizens would still be alive. But if I hadn't interfered with time to save Becky, the Titans wouldn't have escaped Tartarus. The fallout from my decisions wracks me with guilt, even though Becky and Ian mean more to me than anything.

"We could try taking a portal," she says, "if you know the way."

Rolling my eyes, I limp along with her until the pain leaves my toes. I've never set foot in New York, via portal or car. I've heard the horror stories about New York my entire life. Muggings, murders, assaults in the park, and a million other perils associated with living in America's biggest city. And though statistics tell of a falling crime rate throughout the twenty-first century, firsthand accounts trigger a more emotional response, and a greater fear. Crime has worsened across much of the northeast since Philadelphia bit the dust. Even in the suburbs, you can never be sure a desperate ex-Philadelphian won't point a gun in your face and demand your purse or wallet. The West Coast and the Great Plains don't have to understand what we go through daily, because their cities are safer, supply chains are intact, and crime hasn't spread that far. News outlets estimate that about half of Philadelphians survived; most fled to various other Atlantic seaboard cities, while others assimilated into another state or country. Canada has grumbled about American expats remaking Toronto.

"Never been," I admit, biting my lip. "You?"

She nods and frowns, stepping over a colony of ants breaking down the body of a dead rat. She exudes a ghostly calm. "Beau took me once. Enjoyed a play, stood in line at an iconic diner featured in one of those 1990s sitcoms, Radio City Music Hall, the Statue of Liberty. A lot to see, but Philly was still home."

"How long ago?"

She changes the subject, wrinkling her nose and trying to speed us up. "Hopefully, the car you rented is still there."

I still carry the etched cannonball in my pocket. It weighs down my jeans with every step, and carrying the caduceus in my right hand also makes the journey harder. To avoid tripping on the leg of my sagging jeans, I must constantly tug at the waist. It's slowing me down. I've lost my phone somewhere, and I haven't seen Marissa using one since I arrived in the city.

If she had energy, why wouldn't she use it to power up her phone as a lifeline to the outside world? The solution might be simpler than I can comprehend now, but to avoid bringing down the mood, I let it pass.

"Don't know," I admit, "but Batterycar has a vast fleet, with some of them marked. We'll find a ride."

"You rented it in the suburbs, drove to Maryland to see your friend, and came back?"

"Rented it in the town the ex-Secretary lives near."

Marissa passes the time by making various assumptions about the progression of technology. "You know, since the ride-sharing apps went out of style, automated cars started to dominate, regardless of safety concerns. You've probably seen dozens of them without even realizing it. Some apps still depend on human operators, thank the gods."

"Artificial intelligence still can't replace actual intelligence."

She gives a cool nod as the Electrofence appears in the distance. "You know why they invented AI in the first place, don't you?"

"To ruin art?"

There's a five second pause while I gauge her possible responses, but what she says surprises me. "To compensate for the dearth of real intelligence. Instead of getting better, it's still getting worse, because it trained using actual humans before it learned to train itself. And now we got a whole military branch dedicated to AI malpractice, proving that smarter isn't always better."

"Oh," I say, not wanting to start an argument. Topics like this might fascinate Marissa, but I think we have bigger problems.

Within a few minutes, we reach the fence, staring at it for several minutes while considering different ways to get her past the barrier without her being electrocuted. My abilities give me the power to climb over, but if she so much as touches metal, she'll receive a shock.

Since the rails rise several inches above the ties and the gravel bed that holds them, the fence's bottom links allow small rodents to pass through. If I can lift the fence, she could shimmy under it. Marissa gazes along the fence gate in both directions. A galvanized metal-framed platform cantilevers above the street level debris ten feet in either direction, so any human would need to hang onto the fence to slink around it. Taut wires span from the fence to the overhead cable supports in four different directions, creating an electrified web truss to keep the fence upright. Foolproof.

But Marissa's no fool. Steadying herself, she taps her toes on the tie behind my right foot, presses her hands against my chest, and shoves me. To avoid falling to my death, I grab onto the fence and feel a surge of energy shoot through my fingers, a bolt of white-hot fury that sparks lightning in every direction.

I could rage at her, but her idea manifests itself the moment I part my lips to shout. The power surge causes the supporting wires to burst into flames as the electricity arcs. Before it subsides, I regain my footing and test the fence for latent energy.

"Oops," she says with a coy grin. "Little short circuit there. The FB will have to fix that."

"Uh…"

She starts climbing before I can wipe the stupor off my face. Backup transformers might restore electricity at any moment, but I doubt the FB engineers will have planned that far ahead. After all, they designed their systems for humans, not for the living descendant of the Six Cretan Titans. After she scales the fence without even tearing her clothes on the wires, I climb over and land next to her.

On the suburban side of city limits, better safety maintenance has kept the El line in good condition. The supports don't sway as much, allowing us to speed up. Street traffic keeps me alert as we advance toward the station. The Batterycar still sits alone in the parking lot, but we're too late. A couple chatters in the distance, fumbling with their apps to rent the car.

Marissa sees it unfold and closes her eyes. When the man swings open the driver's door, the woman shakes her head, crosses her arms, and hesitates.

"What's wrong?" her partner asks before he sits down.

"We need to go see your sister first," the woman says. "She forgot to give us the keys."

Keys? Batterycars don't rely on keys.

The man makes a fist and bats it against the steering wheel. "Fine. Cancel for now. But you're paying the late fee."

"Get your sister to pay!" she snipes back.

They dart away from the car on foot, across the busy road, and disappear into a four-story apartment building. Hurrying down the stairs, we climb the fence and get into the car. It starts without issue. Before we drive out of the parking lot, the couple reemerges from the apartment having an argument.

"How did you do that?" I say, looking over my shoulder to make sure they haven't started chasing us.

Marissa shrugs and smiles.

"Ah, forget it. New York City, here we come."

The voice activation system starts up at the wrong moment. I grip the steering wheel and grimace when it chimes at me. The car's on-board virtual assistant assumes a sunny persona. "You have one new message. Would you like to play it now?"

Marissa raises her eyebrows at me as I glance between the touchscreen and her, trying to understand what's happening. "Uh, sure?"

"Okay!" the cheery, artificial female voice says. "Playing message."

Marissa smiles, but she drops it when a face appears on the touch screen, backing into the frame and glowing with red and orange embers. "Modern magic. You humans *are* good at some things."

I curl my lips, wanting to smash my fist into the touch screen display. Prometheus continues to grin. "Route 432 to Phoenixville. Mount Olympus Games. Don't be late."

"I'm gonna kill you," I growl.

Fire Guy makes no sign he's heard me. Still speaking into the camera, he adds, "I will enjoy seeing you again, too, Marissa."

Before either of us can reply, his face disappears, and the voice assistant chimes again. "Thank you. Would you like to listen to music?"

"Route us to Mount Olympus Games in Phoenixville," I bark. "Then turn yourself off."

"I'm sorry. I may not turn myself off—"

Argh. "Shut up!"

It obeys, and a map to our destination shows on screen. My fingers vibrate with anger and the electric motor whines when I accelerate. Getting onto the freeway, I glance at Marissa, who keeps her eyes on the road.

"Well, that's one way to handle technological intrusion."

"I'm going off grid when we get home," I groan, but I'm following the navigation system's directions.

"What do you think he wants? Neato meeting?"

Avoiding giving her an answer, I listen to the sounds of traffic and road noise as we drive through the suburbs toward Phoenixville. She adds little more to the conversation than comments on graffitied highway signs and overpasses, until we reach our destination. Mount Olympus Games sits behind a narrow storefront in a suburban strip mall with a sea of parking lots in front. Beneath the fifty-foot-tall architectural sign welcoming travelers to Phoenix Point, sit six charging stalls and four gas pumps. Most drivers wait in their vehicles, one scrolls through his phone as he leans against his car. A concrete masonry wall hiding the transformers separates the charging infrastructure from the gas station for safety. Few cars occupy the parking lots. I park the car and tell the voice assistant to hold our ride for us until we're finished.

Storefronts with shiny windows are set back from the false front, beyond a row of plaster columns. Various business signs decorate the shaped parapets that rise and fall like waves. A red-painted bird graces an arched space above the anchor store's sign, glistening in the sunlight. Clean stainless-steel windows rise from ground level to at least eight feet, and behind the glass rests an enormous twenty-sided gaming die with glowing numbers. Purple and yellow tie-dye marbling swirls between the numbers. The die rests on a black felt-topped table at knee height, along with several game figurines and a case-laminate hardcover book graced with the face of an elf archer with an enraged expression. A neon 'open' sign welcomes customers. We pass rows of gaming books and other paraphernalia, while Marissa glances at a deck of tarot cards on a shelf behind the glass-topped counter display next to collectible booster sets.

"Help you?" A woman with purple hair says. She wears a black T-shirt featuring a heavy metal band's logo, and a half-dozen glittering eyebrow rings.

There's a wide entrance to a back room decorated with gaming heroes and photographs.

Seeing where we're going, the cashier nods toward the entrance. "Gaming room. Tournament starting at noon if you want to join for ten bucks."

"What game?" Marissa asks, not waiting for an answer.

Only five people occupy the gaming room. When we enter, Prometheus breaks off a discussion with his brother Epimetheus and summons a flame in his palm before letting it subside. He rests in the folding metal chair as though he owns it, stretching his feet beneath a huge flat-topped table with a wooden-slat perimeter. A painted and textured green landscape, complete with artificial ruins, provides the setting for an epic battle between good and evil, just without any characters depicted.

"Welcome," he says. Prometheus wears a business-casual polo shirt with all the buttons undone, revealing a vee of ashen skin. He frowns at us and points at a pair of chairs opposite the table.

"Good place for a tactical session," I say with a frown. "Get on with it, we gotta be in New York today."

"Yes," he says, flexing his neck muscles, "we heard about your trip to Greece. But we have urgent matters to discuss today."

A short woman leans forward in her chair. She is sporting a floral-pattern skirt, a plain red T-shirt, a golden necklace, and brass hoop earrings. Her hair is tangled into a braid behind her head, and her makeup is gaudy. They've done a good job cosplaying as mortals.

"Titans," Dione says, shaking her head. "They have gone into hiding for now, but we have reports of a coming meeting, and evidence points to them organizing something big, possibly another war."

"So?" I grate. "That son-of-a-bitch Cronus is still rotting in Tartarus where he belongs, right?"

Epimetheus frowns. In his black T-shirt and leatherette pants, he looks like a bouncer at a dance club. "Sure of it. But even without him, you have to respect their powers. We're debating a preemptive strike, weighing whether it will delay their plans or result in starting a war."

I frown, and Marissa peers at her feet while resting her hand on my arm. Leaning forward, I stare at him before glancing over at Prometheus. "We just got done with a war, and they lost. Their leader must be an idiot."

"I would not call Coeus a fool," Dione says. "After all, he wrested control from Cronus's sister-wife Rhea."

"Incest," Marissa whispers. "That tracks."

"Rhea still carries a lot of power," Epimetheus warns. "And so does Themis."

"Rumors for now," Prometheus observes. "But still, we must be cautious. We think they may be assembling where Gibraltar's rock once stood."

"Why Spain?"

He shrugs and flexes his forearms. "Mouth of the Mediterranean, an important body of water separating Greece and Rome from Africa. They may wish to provoke this NATO group, which includes your United States—"

"World War Three," I splutter.

A major war hasn't occurred in over a century. The second Titan war and Philadelphia's destruction didn't even cause a massive armed conflict between nations. Either our diplomats were more diplomatic than we expected, or we're overdue. I can't decide which is worse.

"War is the last resort," Dione says, glancing at Eos, who is listening, her expression pensive.

"But intelligence suggests they're still loyal to Cronus and Erebus. And that's a big problem." Epimetheus narrows his eyes, hesitating.

The more he speaks, the darker my mood becomes. A headache is building under my skull, and I'm cracking my knuckles, glaring at the other five members of the New Titan Order.

"You don't need to be angry," Prometheus says. "But be careful on your journey to Greece—Delphi is a cursed place."

"Cursed? What are you talking about?"

"The oracle has foretold of something terrible lurking beneath the mountains, a power so great that it could cause panic across Europe."

I growl at him, "She didn't tell me anything."

"We will assess our next steps with caution," Eos says wearily. "We don't want to start a war, either. The other eleven Titans know you're still alive, Kerry. And they know about your son."

Balling my fist and grimacing, I lean forward and slam it down onto the battlefield so hard that it loosens the perimeter boards and sways as

Prometheus reaches to steady it. Rage flushes through me, and I can feel my face going red. Marissa grips my arm, pulling me away from the table, and takes me over to face the red and blue checkered pattern on the three windowless walls of the gaming room.

The right side of the room features six battle tables with different battlefield environments, while the room's other half has five sets of six-foot-long tables, each with black tablecloths and painted wooden benches.

Fire Guy hesitates and sighs, trying to conceal his worry. Whether concerned about Marissa and me, or the fragile state of the world, his anxiety might be a harbinger of a darker future. Collecting his nerve takes him a moment, but when he settles down, he leans forward and peers directly into my eyes.

"Your son is in excellent hands, Kerry. He has a great father. When you return, you must help him to control his gifts."

Rage rushes into my heart. "What do you know about it? Who gave him the gift? I'll hunt that bastard down and—"

"The Gods are patient," he warns, "but they do not share powers. You descended from the Six Titans of Crete. I believe you will figure it out soon enough. But until then, be vigilant."

"When I return," I growl, "I'll slap you all the way back to the fifth century BC."

"Anger will not serve you well, Kerry. You know that in your heart. Follow that knowledge."

"What do you know about my heart? You left me with a city in tatters, a dead mayor, and two authoritarian gangs, and I'm supposed to just follow my heart? Some friend you are."

"Kerry," Marissa whispers.

Instead of heeding her warning, I point my finger at Fire Guy's face and pour out all the poison I can. I can feel my body melting, teetering on the edge of solid and smoke, ready to unload every agony that rages through me.

Five minutes pass as Marissa continues to grip my arm, closing her eyes, and breathing deeply. My veins pulse with dark energy as I rage at Prometheus, who takes it all in without arguing back. Each beat of my heart comes with a flash of dark. *Thump*—black. *Thump-thump*—shade. And then a tiny flicker of red interrupts the pulsing, chasing the frigid darkness with a warm ether.

I will never let you down. Because you never let me down.

Warmth spreads through my body as I open my eyes, meet Marissa's gaze, and stand.

22

Strix Flight 3712

Moments after we left Phoenixville, Marissa falls asleep. Feeling weary myself, I glance at her between long stretches of staring at the road, weaving through the thickening traffic, and cursing at bad drivers under my breath, careful not to give them the finger. Becky and I used to joke that flipping off New Jersey drivers was akin to pulling a pin from a grenade and then holding onto it. The way drivers hurry to their destinations as though their lives are the only important thing in the universe reminds me of the way I view my own family. I would do anything for them, including taking the lives of the people of Philadelphia, according to Ash.

I grip the steering wheel harder when I think of her and Gus, tied up in the FB throne room, forced to endure torture on my behalf. If she survives, she might smash in my face with the butt of her handgun.

When a driver flies around me well over the speed limit, a surge of hot adrenaline flows through me, causing me to press harder on the accelerator. The car's infotainment system dings at me the moment I do. Glancing at the driver's assist screen, I see nothing, but then the annoying assistance voice chimes in, "You will only make it forty percent of the way to your destination. May I find a charging station for you?"

This prompts me to give it a nickname. Marissa shifts her legs, raises her head, and glances at the dashboard as I say, "Yes, please, Blenda."

"Good one," Marissa mumbles.

"Ok," Blenda says, "setting course for ChargeNation in Union. Stay on Interstate 78 for twenty-four miles."

Marissa doesn't move until we take the exit ramp, and Blenda continues with her annoyingly cheery directions. When we reach the charger, I glance at Marissa, plug in, and wait. According to Blenda, we will reach eighty percent battery capacity within ten minutes, an improvement on older technology.

"You should find a phone," Marissa says, rolling down the window. "Call Becky."

Public payphones were discontinued fifty years ago. The best I can do is enter a convenience store and ask to use their landline, or maybe find a prepaid disposable in a trash can.

Deciding to stretch my legs, I walk to the small convenience store a few hundred yards away, pausing when a driver in an old pickup truck tears through the parking lot, showing me his middle finger. In my experience, if I return the gesture, he's likely to stop, do a three-point turn, and try it again. The store's cashier has a bored expression, glancing between her phone screen and the cash register before greeting me with a weary smile. I peruse the aisles and grab two bags of chips for Marissa and me before approaching the counter.

"Just that?"

"Actually," I say, "I was hoping to use your phone."

A quizzical expression crosses her face. "No cellphone? Don't hear that much anymore. That will be an extra five bucks. Fifteen-minute limit."

"Fine."

She gestures for me to follow her into a tiny back room with a folding plastic table holding stacks of junk, one of those old scroll-pad desk calculators with a missing paper roll, and a simple cordless landline. When she leaves the room, I punch in Becky's number and wait, hoping she picks up, but knowing the odds are slim. If the caller or voice system masks its identity, Becky never answers. But she does this time.

"Hey," I say, rubbing my eyelids.

A pause at the other end suggests she wasn't expecting it to be me. "Ker? Jeez, where have you been? Are you all right?"

I grimace. Fifteen minutes will not be enough time for me to explain everything that has happened, and just giving her the basics will only confuse her. I've never been able to get away with lying to her either on the phone or in person, because she's better at detecting lies than any known law-enforcement agency.

"Well ... I'm alive, if that's what you're asking."

"*Really?*"

I'm rolling my eyes at myself and feel extra stupid. "I mean, the gangs found out I've been in Philly, and they know who I am. Marissa saved my life, though."

As if I can see her eyes light up, I let her answer with the brand of sarcasm only she can pull off. "Why would she do that?"

I chuckle, switch ears, glance at the junk pile on the table, and lean against the door.

"Our son called me the other day," she says. "Thanks for stopping by to reassure him. I didn't think having a baby would hit him this way."

"There's a reason for that," I say, although I don't want to explain it right now. "But listen, Beck, I only have a few minutes to tell you I love you before I fly out to Athens this evening. I'll tell you all about it when I get home."

Another pause, but this one drips with anger. "Athens? You and Marissa are going away together already?"

"Can't explain it now," I admit.

"Do it anyway, Ker."

"You were right. Philadelphia is a sewer, fully stocked with rats. We found evidence that the thugs want to set up their own empire, and we're going there to stop it. I wish I could tell you more."

"Ker," she says with another pause, this one touched with sadness, "come home. I miss you. We can rent a paddleboat, or even go up to Lake Erie—"

"I wish I could. Listen, Beck, I lost my phone somewhere, and I'm pretty sure it's dead anyway. Whatever you do, don't answer if someone calls from my number."

"I miss you, Ker," she repeats "but I can't stop you. Stay safe."

"I will," I say, not really trusting myself. Having lost count of how many times I've told her I'll be careful, caution has proven so elusive that this promise has all but become meaningless. Nothing I can say will reassure her when the only person I need to convince is myself. And because Becky is a human lie detector, at least with me, she must know I'm in greater danger than I'm telling. True to form, I can hear it in her voice.

"You know what I'm saying. No matter what, I will always love you."

I just hope she'll feel that way when she has to scrape bits of me off the mountains in Delphi and scour the Aegean for the rest. Saying that to her will bring further terror, an emotion I've spent years trying to curtail.

"Love you too," I say, swallowing my sadness.

As I hang up I'm wiping a tear away from my cheek. I collect the two bags of chips, and rejoin Marissa in the car.

I hurry across the parking lot, hand her a bag of chips, and let Blenda navigate us to JFK. We speak little during the drive, sharing only observations and a few memories. Once there, we find a place to park, hurry through the terminal, buy our tickets and a duffel bag at the gift shop, stand in line at security, and board the plane, in what feels like one movement.

Carpeted in red felt, the aisle might only be wide enough to wheel a two-foot appetizer cart without bumping into passengers' legs or running over their toes. Embarking on this journey with only a caduceus and a metal ball in the duffel makes me feel somewhat unprepared. Marissa carries nothing. We find our seats and relax as the plane taxis to the runway, makes a wide turn, and we're in the air. I gaze out the window as we climb above New York. The buildings shrink and blend into a haze of tiny gray squares before the clouds cover it all, and then there are only glimpses of the Atlantic Ocean as we cross the globe.

Marissa fumbles through the keypad to find the meal menu, asks if we can order food, and then rests her hands on her lap. I use the tap feature to pay. Now we can have a heart-to-heart. I look directly into her eyes, and let my soul do the talking.

"Theres a lot you haven't been telling me. If you don't trust me, I understand. I can make peace with that."

"Do you tell Becky everything that's on your mind? Does every question have to have a definitive answer, where everything else is just noise and you can get to the heart of everything in a few sentences? Or do you opt for the catch-all 'I don't know?'"

Appreciating her point, I nod and glance at the back of the head of the woman seated in front of me. She wears blue and purple butterfly clips in her hair to keep her plaited ponytail from moving. Her partner eyes the flight-attendant cart that's already halfway down the aisle. Becky has used that point in conversation with me a million times, and once I even tried to explain to her that sometimes, I really *don't* know. The very question "what are you thinking" tends to erase my thoughts, because it catches me off guard.

"All the time," I admit. "But I've seen you do things I never thought possible."

"Anything is possible, if you put your mind to it."

That won't work on me. I've experienced enough to know that many things are impossible no matter how much thought and faith you put into them. Hearing her offering what sounds like a quote from a motivational poster hits me the wrong way. I know that Marissa has never been one to confuse rationality with inspiration.

"Then explain how you learned do to these things. Because communicating with the dead isn't the same thing as summoning them to fight on your behalf. A year ago, you hypnotized me and confused warriors into attacking each other. And now you're summoning ash nymphs out of thin air."

"Our city was sacked, Kerry. Don't you think you'd fight as hard as you could to return it to what it should be? I understand your family's needs, but everyone has needs, and you can't satisfy everyone, no matter how hard you try."

"Doesn't that disprove the 'everything is possible' theory?"

She looks down. A few feet away, the flight attendant pours drinks into shatterproof stemware from her cart.

"It proves that every theory has an exception," Marissa corrects me, paying no mind to the attendant.

Looking out the window, I allow myself time to process what she's just said, but this just dulls its meaning, leaving a void in my mind. A man stands across the aisle, wrestles open the overhead carrying compartment, and drags out one of those magnetic travel games.

If she's going to argue about concepts of physics, I might bolt up from my seat and run for the bathroom and be sick. Secretary Harley isn't the only one capable of understanding them. "You know, I won't make you say it. You said yourself that it's better if it surprises me, but what if that surprise gets me killed? Aren't we friends?"

"Are we? You spent an entire year away from the city, never bothering to call or write. I needed your help. And that wasn't the only thing."

"Tell me."

"Miriam is dying, she's foreseen it. And dammit, I hate being alone in a city where everyone's your enemy. It does things to you."

I frown, but keep my attention focused on her eyes. Somewhere deep within, they plead with me, searching for way to empty all the toxic thoughts and come clean. The tattoo on the back of her hand catches the light peculiarly, spreading a warm look through her arm. My whole life I'd believed the pentagram was a symbol of evil, but Marissa uses it to keep her safe.

"She's—can't she heal herself?"

Marissa rests her head against the backrest and sighs. "Doesn't work that way. This kind of magic can only go outward. Sort of the opposite of how yours works."

"Magic?"

"She's been teaching me. You know she's related to a Greek sorceress? All those secrets. I thought she was born with certain gifts. Circe could transform people into animals, but Miriam has foresight, too."

"I know that."

"But you've never seen her put it to use. I can't believe I'm telling you this."

"You can tell me anything."

Her eye sparkle with tears as she explains, "That's just the thing. I can't say some things because I'm unsure how it all works. She's good at teaching me control, but not the mechanics behind it. And she warned me not to explain it to anyone because it could stop the magic."

"I mean—"

"It's real," she says, closing her eyes. "You don't know what it takes out of me. She's passing the torch. Life and death define us as humans; there are limits everywhere. But certain people can rise above them."

The flight attendant wheels her cart from row to row, offering drinks, while another cart starts behind us, serving meals. Hunger pings at my stomach as I wait for our food to arrive. Dividing my attention between her and the need for sustenance makes me lose the momentum of our conversation. Marissa clasps her hands together, interlocking her fingers and cracking her thumbs.

Twenty seconds later, the meaning of what she said hits me. "You mean ... Sarah?"

"The Phoenix. Lots of stories and symbolism circulate about her. She doesn't need to obey the limits of life and death, because she's part of it. Connected with immortality. Transcended. That's why you can still feel her energy and hear her voice."

"I thought it was entanglement."

"The quantum aspects of that still obey the laws of physics. That was what connected you when she was alive, but now she's something more."

I gaze into her eyes for a long time, squeezing out the emotion that drives into her with every breath she takes.

"The ash nymphs are more of a spiritual personification of a Greek legend you and I first heard about a year ago—they're called the Meliae. I can commune with them. And you remember what they're famous for, don't you?"

"Oh God," I say, understanding it all. Cronus castrated his father Uranus, spreading his blood over the land, giving rise to men. "That's insane."

"The Meliae are the ones who nursed Zeus in the mountains of Crete." She shares a different thought. "I just never understood the way you and I are connected."

I frown as I try to understand everything she's just said. It circles around my brain, snagging in dark recesses where my most rigid thoughts and beliefs are harbored. "Marissa?"

She stares at me as a shadow moves in my peripheral vision. "Please promise me you won't let me misuse the caduceus."

When the shadow darkens, I glance through the window at the darkness encroaching in all directions, spreading like an oil stain through the skies. The shadow sprouts wings as it swoops over the ocean, matching the plane's pace, and seeding panic in my mind. Chaos is about to unfold. Omens always mean something; the Oracle of Delphi was right.

23

Secrets of Clytemnestra

Flying is a convenience many take for granted, both the safest and most worrisome means of travel. As a child, I never enjoyed the speed and reliability because of financial burdens, and I can count on one hand the number of times I'd been on a plane since. Just before I moved to Philadelphia, I boarded a small jet bound for a smaller Midwest airport, disembarked an hour later, and forgot about the experience.

An hour after my conversation with Marissa fizzled out, I fall asleep. Dreams plow through my subconscious like wildfire, interrupted by mid-flight bumps.

My eyes still feel droopy when I awake. I glance up at Marissa, who has taken an interest in the Athenian weather on her device screen and is using both fingers to enlarge the radar. She sighs and leans her head back as the plane bounces like an old pop-up tent trailer.

"We are experiencing a bit of turbulence," the pilot announces over the PA system. "Please stay in your seats until it passes. We will arrive in Athens by four-fifteen a.m. Eastern Time. Thank you."

"Good morning," Marissa whispers "Looks like rain."

Various passengers stir as the turbulence bounces us around. How they sleep through it, I may never know. A man four rows in front of us scrolls through the seat-back tablet computer, playing a repetitive game before becoming frustrated and folding it up. He rests his head on his partner's shoulder.

Years ago, I'd marveled at how weather forecasts could aim at being precise, when they sometimes couldn't even get the current conditions right. I'd noted an overcast sky and a pesky breeze, while all the weather outlets insisted it was sunny and calm. Yet, most days the forecast temperature was off by only a degree or two. Traveling in the rain does not interest me.

When the flight lands, we disembark and follow the signs for the baggage claim. The carousel, an ovular ribbed-steel conveyor encased in polished chrome walls, surrounds the double-sided return hatch, draped with rubber strips. I watch for my bag with the caduceus in it while Marissa watches a tall guy chasing three kids through the terminal.

"American Airlines Flight 3712 from New York, please continue to the baggage claim area," a pleasant, artificial female voice says, then repeats the message in Greek.

I step forward and watch bags pop out of the hatch while the AI voice continues.

"Jeran Dobson, your bag is now ready. Jasmine or George Delano, your bag is now ready."

She rattles off ten other names before I see my duffel emerge from the hatch. Marissa doesn't notice, as she continues to watch the man chasing the children before looking at a sign twenty feet overhead.

"Kerry Gearhardt," the voice says, "your bag is now ready."

A slender woman standing behind Marissa gasps as I step forward to claim my bag, and as I reach down, she speaks loud enough for everyone around the carousel to hear, "*The* Kerry Gearhardt?"

Strangers knowing my name doesn't surprise me, but here in the Athens airport so far away from home, it's jarring. Marissa pretends not to notice, but her shoulders twitch and I know she's heard the woman repeating my name. I ignore the woman and Marissa and head to the rental car stations.

Dozens of agitated tourists grumble over the length of the line, and that only a single cashier is managing the chaos in the rental car section. One of the larger firms has a half-dozen self-service terminals where drivers can specify features and schedule the ride for pickup a half mile away in the rental lot. Without asking, Marissa takes over and settles on a compact, affordable electric with four hundred miles of range. After I pay, Marissa taps the screen and shrugs. "Wants an email address or phone number to send the confirmation," she whispers.

"Do they have Batterycars?"

She shakes her head. "User-appointed luxuries cut into their profits. No phone, no confirmation."

I find an airport employee who can speak decent English, explaining to her we wish to rent a car but that we're electronics deprived. When she agrees to help, she sets us up with a printed receipt we can hand over to the lot attendant when we check out. This experience takes so long that it makes me never want to fly again, but we'll have to do it again when we return home—if we return.

Marissa and I make small-talk as we use the vehicle's navigation system to guide us toward Delphi. It warns us of excessive traffic on our route but assures us we're on the fastest route.

The rainfall intensifies the farther we travel from Athens. Crossing a picturesque countryside featuring rocky hills, sparse forest, and grassland, we get stuck behind a heavy truck that sprays our windshield with bits of mud and pebbles. The damage will cost us, so I cringe every time a stone bounces off the window. Twenty or thirty miles later, we enter a long valley with scattered villages and farmhouses interspersed with big, leafy poplar trees. The landscape changes as the road bends into the rocky hills. Now it's sparse trees and pockets of green-flecked shrubs we see through the deluge. I think the area is asking for erosion damage. At one-mile intervals, corrugated metal culverts parallel one side of the road, where deep canyons carry mud into larger streams. Where the rainfall becomes heavier, asphalt curls over abrupt overhangs, cracking with the weight of passing traffic.

The Greek highways show signs of inadequate maintenance, but I don't let it bother me. I switch the wipers on high, swishing away sheets of rain and still struggling with visibility behind the truck. Slowing down, I slacken my foot on the accelerator and use gravity to my advantage. Traffic slows to a crawl ahead of us before coming to a halt. A half mile ahead, I glance at the aftermath of the rain, where a jack-knifed truck blocks the lanes. It seems to have rammed a wooden-post railing, snapping the timbers under its weight, and the truck lost its load into the drainage ditch.

As I stop the car, before I can mutter an expletive under my breath, I see movement from the corner of my eye on the mountaintop. Hundreds of cars have stopped, and a small town lies below us, nestled in the folding fan of a steeper slope. The movement intensifies as I gaze at it.

Multiple tons of rock and mud pour down the hillside, smashing and burying everything in their path. Enormous boulders bounce down, crushing homes and cars. The sounds of rock battering against metal and shattering windows fill my eardrums. Terror congeals in my veins as I put the car in reverse, but it's no use; we're pinned. The truck driver behind us abandons his vehicle and runs.

"Get down!" I warn Marissa, but she's seen it coming and is already burying her head under her hands and curling over.

Rocks and mud smash into the railing, shoving it right into the halted traffic, while the mass's weight shoves us to the other shoulder, shattering the side windows as it advances. Two cars in front of us flip, tumble over the embankment and crash to a halt at the bottom of a vee-shaped ravine that's gathering boulders and mud. The landslide will bury drivers alive if the deluge doesn't stop. I curse while I shield my face from the mud and rainfall in the typhoon.

I can't stop this from happening, no matter how deeply I reach into the darkness of my soul. I hear Marissa whimpering even as a cascade of mud buries me waist deep. A two-ton hunk of granite rolls to rest against our demolished car with an ear-crushing roar. It presses us against the railing, which luckily holds until the landslide subsides.

Voices shout and moan as desperate survivors are already sloshing through the mud to get to people buried under the debris. An uprooted poplar tree lies on top of a sedan four cars away. Marissa struggles to free herself from the seatbelt, climbs out the broken window, and anchors her feet against the muddy railing, reaching for me. I can't crawl out of the ooze on my own, but when I touch Marissa's fingers, a foreign power builds within me.

The impact has popped the trunk, and gravel and mud cover my bag, but I can grip it by the shoulder strap. I rush through the mud and ruins to check the sedan for survivors. A truck driver is wedging a crowbar into the crack between the doors, struggling for traction as he pries it open. I tackle the rocks before pushing the tree away, so that I can reach through the shattered windows.

Behind the driver's seat, a child struggles to breathe as the mud is already solidifying around him neck deep. He looks at me with desperation, trying to move his head around, even as I tell him to calm down. Digging in the mud through the open window is doing me no good, so I sink my arms in to grab for his hands. When I'm pulling at him, I notice a gaping wound atop his head, where a ripped-out patch of hair dangles from his bloody scalp. He might require a miracle, but I avoid thinking about that.

When a woman from a few cars behind us sees me struggling to free the boy, she climbs over the debris to help. Together, we pull the boy from the window while Marissa helps the truck driver to rescue the other passenger. The woman in the front seat sits motionless, covered in mud, with a hundred-pound boulder resting against her head. Her eyes flit open as if pleading with the sky for relief. As the rain slows, the woman and I work to free her but we know she's already dead. Her son is lucky to have survived.

I pick up the duffel from the mud where I'd dropped it, unzip it, and pull out the caduceus. If Marissa was correct about the lore associated with it, I may be able to revive this woman. I swallow nervously as I turn the staff in my hand, watching the serpents coil around in their embrace.

The woman helping me stands back wide-eyed when she sees what I'm holding.

As I turn the staff, the snakes' eyes begin to glow while the wings rise and fall, as if to take flight. The force tugs at my arms as I stand there, as if pulling toward the child's mother. Horror pulses through my veins when the woman's head tilts sideways to rest on her shoulder.

Although I understand she can't die again, I feel a surge of guilt flash through me until I see her shoulder move. She opens her eyes and squirms in the chest-deep mud. The boulder has trapped her, but when the stranger scurries to my aid again, we work to wedge her free through the shattered window. It doesn't work. Trying the passenger side, we help the truck driver and Marissa pull the man out before dragging the driver through the mud with her good arm. As her torso emerges from the muck, I can see that her arm is broken above the elbow. We might be hurting her more by moving her, but if we leave her in the car, the first responders might not get to her until it's too late.

I put the caduceus back in the duffel while Marissa and the truck driver move on to the next car in line, working to rescue stranded motorists buried in the mountainside. Ahead of us, the jack-knifed truck lies on its side, teetering over a steep drop-off on the left side of the road. Unable to help with rescuing those we can see, some people are sifting through the debris for any who might be buried.

Rescue crews arrive to help clear the highway, and I introduce myself to the woman. She has a strong Greek accent but speaks English. After telling her my name, I debate about adding the "Conveyor of Light and Shade," opting for my last name instead.

"Nice to meet you, Kerry," she says, mopping mud from her face and hair. "You're American?"

"From Philadelphia," I mutter, almost biting my tongue in shame.

She shakes her head as she props herself against a boulder where the railing used to be. "Sad what has happened to your city. We watch with great empathy here, even as your government ignores you."

I want to empty my heart of every angry swear word I can utter to tell her how the criminal gangs have taken over, killing anyone who gets in their way, while Washington and Harrisburg collectively decide our once-great city deserved its fate and is better off alone. But she doesn't need to hear it.

"Uh ... yeah," I say, "it's a big problem. What's your name?"

She closes her eyes for a moment, as if thinking about it. Mud drips into her face as she speaks, slurring her words. "You can call me Helen."

I grimace as I bury a sense of irony and try help her get over her shock by keeping the conversation going.

The truck driver works with emergency personnel up and down the washed-out road, helping survivors to safety. Marissa limps to my side, wrings out her hair with her free hands, and looks at Helen.

"The caduceus is real," Helen muses, holding back a gasp. "How did you get it?"

Ignoring her question, I introduce Marissa to her, and an idea pops into my mind. "You speak Greek? Like the ancient kind?"

"Few can these days," she laments after a quick half-nod, then speaks a line of ancient Greek without translating it.

"Great," I say.

"It's a learned skill, but you could say I was born with it, my sister and brother being who they are. I sometimes wonder about my lineage. There are many stories, from Zeus and Hera, to my mother. My brother's name is Paul, but he calls himself Pollux. But he says I'm only his half-sister. I don't know what that means."

I frown when I hear Zeus's name. Although he helped bring Ian back, it isn't enough to forgive his duplicity and arrogance. I was aware at the time that if I took my anger out on him, he could have zapped me with his lightning bolt and erased me entirely. "Hell of a guy, Zeus," I growl.

Helen looks confused as she addresses Marissa. "Are you from Philadelphia, too? You know, your city was named after a Greek ruler of Egypt."

"Ptolemy Philadelphus the Second," I finish, grimacing. "City of brotherly love. There isn't much love there now, brotherly or any other."

"We were on our way to Delphi," Marissa says, peering at the demolished mountaintop and the swathes of mud and boulders burying the valley, "to learn about something that might be hidden in a temple there."

"I have been many times," Helen says, "studying the writings, reading about the oracle and everything. There is so much to see and learn. As it happens, I was going there myself. If you're still hoping to learn about it, I can guide you."

"Really, I don't think we can accept," Marissa says dismissively.

But I interrupt her, "Yes, we can. We're looking for Atlantis, and something called an Antikythera mechanism."

"The Antikythera," Helen repeats, raising her eyebrows. "Lots of supposition about what it does. Some say Archimedes invented it to predict the movements of the stars and gauge the passage of time, but the ancient Greeks shouldn't have had technology advanced enough to do that."

"There's a working copy of it hidden somewhere."

"Athens Museum," Helen says. "Although they haven't said it actually works. Let me help you unlock the secrets of Delphi."

"Really," Marissa says, "it's too much to ask."

"Of course it isn't. Reaching the mountains through this disaster won't be easy for a while. But we can use another route. We can borrow a car?"

I try to picture what the ruins might look like now, millennia after I saw them last. Imaging limestone pillars and lintels, statues, and millions of rectangular bricks strewn around the hillside, I close my eyes, feeling a surprising surge of warmth in my skin. A silent, subconscious voice speaks in Sarah's soft voice.

They will be safe.

Swallowing, I stand upright, grasp Marissa's hand, and follow Helen through the destruction. Even she has anything to do with Hera and Zeus, her kindness and eagerness to help have surprised me. Entrusting her with our secrets feels natural, and I hope I won't regret it later. We follow her for over a mile until she finds an abandoned car in working order downstream of the landslide. Without entering Delphi into the navigation system, Helen turns back and hurries along the highway toward Athens. After a few minutes, she turns onto a narrow side road that twists through hairpin bends as it ascends the hillsides. Marissa and I whisper to one another during the journey.

Sorrow runs through my veins as I consider the devastation we've just witnessed. What if a Titan caused it? I try to dismiss the thought, but it has merit. I don't dare bring it up to Marissa. I can't predict how she will react, but it won't be favorable. If a Titan did it, Prometheus will have reason for concern, and the oracle will have foretold another devastating truth, the ramifications of which I'd rather not think about.

Focusing on my thoughts distracts me from the landscape and the fact that Helen is explaining something, which I only pick up halfway through.

"...so my brother says my sister and I were really swapped at birth, to different parents, and that Zeus is our real father. My brother has always disagreed with Christian beliefs. He thinks the gods are real, but I'm not so sure."

"That sounds tough," Marissa says. Her voice is flat, like she doesn't really care.

"We tolerate one another, mostly," Helen says. "Our actual mother, of course, isn't old enough, and our father disappeared when I was a toddler after our country's financial collapse. They say he got involved in a violent altercation with a pro-austerity activist and died in a hospital a week later. But even I don't know the whole truth. It's just the way Paul likes to accuse me of being someone I'm not. He says I'm 'Tainted with Clytemnestra's blood' whatever that means. But I have ways of getting back at him."

"Zeus is a bastard!" I blurt out, earning a surprised expression from both women.

Although we've driven away from the landslide, it's still raining as we drive deeper into the foothills toward the ancient city of Delphi, where every secret concerning Philadelphia's future hides within the ruins. I don't know whether it will lead us to Atlantis, but the mixture of hope and dread that I'm feeling mix into an agonizing potion that poisons my mood.

They will be safe.

24

The Omphalos Curse

The road to the historic ruins of Delphi winds through limestone boulder-strewn mountains, with sparse vegetation where some topsoil persists. Between the rocks, groves of poplars shade low shrubs and thick tufts of grass that look like verdant islands in a sea of tan. Helen frowns as she keeps pace with a minivan with Italian license plates that is driving slower than necessary, negotiating the tight curves. She enters an oblong parking lot filled with cars, a few tour vans, and a long bus. Avoiding the bus, Helen parks the car near a long bicycle rack harboring at least twenty mountain bikes. A male rider in black spandex wraps a chain lock around his bike's frame before jogging up a rocky trail toward the monument.

Storm clouds hang low over the hillside, their dark gray bulging underbellies threatening rain. Unperturbed, men, women and children hike up and down the wide trail. Marissa lags behind as I follow Helen up the trail. My legs ache, and my breath shortens halfway up the trail, allowing Marissa to catch up, slap me on the back, and urge me onward.

An American boy crouches to pick up a round stone and shoves it into his shorts pocket. A man hurries past him steps at the edge of the trail, scraping his skin on a shrub branch before springing toward a set of wooden stairs zigzagging up the slope.

"It's a big site," Helen explains as I stop to catch my breath. "Ancient Delphi was a large city with thousands of residents. And the temple of Apollo—I think we should investigate there first."

Marissa agrees with a cool nod, glancing at me. I bend over with my hands on my knees and pant. The top of the rocky trail gives way to more wooden stairs. Stumbling over a protruding hunk of rock, I stop myself from tumbling face first into the brush by stepping in a hole in the dirt. When my foot twists, I regain my balance but Marissa grasps my right hand to stabilize me. She's proving more agile than I would have expected; maybe scrambling through the Philadelphia rubble to escape the gangs has made her fit.

A drop on my forehead signals rain. I use the rough plank railing to help myself up the stairs, hoping the Temple of Apollo still has a roof. Five minutes later, the rain puddles on the plank steps. Their roughness gives good traction despite the wet. On the last switchback, a woman in stretch pants and a bright green fanny pack hurries past us, punching her phone in search of a signal. Although when we reach the top, I spy what can only be a cellular service tower disguised as a poplar tree high up a rocky slope.

The Acropolis complex sprawls over about eighty acres. On the outskirts, demolished walls form rigid squares in the hillside. The collapsed blocks create a dubious exploration experience for the five or six kids who mill about the ancient homes in search of relics. From this vantage point, the Temple of Apollo is hard to miss. Most of its roof has collapsed, leaving cracked, fluted pillars with curved capstones supporting hefty lintels and a refurbished pediment depicting the gods battling giants. The central figure wields a long bow with feathered arrows stuffed in a sleeve on his back. In the background, snakes slither.

Ignoring much of the ruins, we meander through the complex to the limestone steps. The columns stretch upward at least forty feet, capped with pairs of snakes similar to the caduceus. The weapon is still stowed in the duffel I carry. I turn around to gaze at the city nestled in the Greek hills.

None of us have phones or cameras, so we won't be able to capture it. As we walk, people do double-takes as they note our mud-covered clothes and faces. Marissa stands next to me, draws in a deep breath, and says, "Never thought I'd stand here. Apollo is one of my favorite gods. Because you know, I love music, and..."

She'd never told me that. But then again, I might have assumed it, with her trendy black clothes, tattoos, and piercings.

"Not much music in Philly anymore," I muse. "Street performers used to enchant tourists on Market Street every day."

She nods. "And Beau used to strum bass along with a guitarist with wicked chops and the coolest goatee. I remember his take on Stairway to Heaven. Contrary to urban legend the record never had a Satanic message on the back. I listened to it forward and backward a hundred times."

"Temple of Apollo," Helen announces, reading a glossy sheet of paper she took from a pine box on the fencepost surrounding the site. "Home of the oracular cult, the Pythian Apollo."

"Pythian?"

She nods, reading the Greek writing on the sheet then stowing it in her back pocket for later. "It's called the oracular cult because an oracle used to live here. One of the most celebrated seers in history."

"I met her," I mumble, unzipping the bag and showing her the caduceus.

Helen stares. "Uh-huh. And she gave it to you?"

"Care to explain it to her?" I ask, nudging Marissa.

"I wasn't there, remember? I was out fighting the UPP, giving you cover. You only told me part of the story."

"The oracle was there," I say, glancing into the shade of a corner column. "In Philly. She introduced herself and said another war is brewing, after I won this from her. And she gave me a warning. 'Success cannot undo gravity.' I'm still trying to figure out what that means."

"Let us see if we can give you some clues," Helen says. She leads us between the central pillars at the top of the steps. Their ornate flutes shimmer in the gray atmosphere, blurring into thin fog at the capstones.

The remaining walls carry Greek pictograms featuring snakes and dancing satyrs. I scrutinize them while Helen studies an etching along the base of the crumbling wall. The foundation stone stretches in eight-foot-long rectangular limestone bricks, where carved Greek characters encircle the sanctuary.

"Priests gather at the ancient spring to see the pneuma, the breath of the spirits here at Delphi, home to the Pythian Apollo..."

I watch her as she stumbles over a few words and crouches to make out the next line. "Uh...you can read it?"

"Didn't I tell you?"

"Go on."

Marissa wanders between the pillars while Helen continues to translate.

"The oracle is wise and sees all. She foretells a war of the Titans and the destruction of the evil winged serpent Typhon at Olympus. Sister Claria—" Helen pauses to translate the next word. "—or it could be Priestess, given the context.... She fell before Typhon to shield her daughter Io from the wreckage. She broke her knee on the stones and sacrificed her life so that the girl could enjoy great fortune in the court of Hera.

"But a sorceress transformed her into a heifer before she arrived. To protect Io from the wrath of Zeus, Hera dispatched a hero who died to save her. When Hera heard the news of her servant's death, she placed his eyes in a peacock's tail feathers."

I say, "Argus. That means they were here. They know. Marissa, the tail feather...It *looked* at me."

"Right," Marissa says, tossing her hair behind her shoulder. "Just before I saved your life *again,* which you still haven't thanked me for."

Biting my lip, I focus on the writing as Helen glances back and forth between us, unsure whom to believe. "It's connected. That's why the mayor wants to see Hera. He believes Hera to be just, and that she'll help him achieve his goals."

"Okay, I guess I'm convinced," Marissa says, glancing at the etching on the foundation stone, "but you must have imagined the feather looking at you. I mean, it makes no sense, because evidence points to him being mortal."

"But the magic..."

"I'm sorry," Helen interrupts, straightening her back as she kneels on the dusty floor. She inches forward to read the smaller writing. "Should I continue?"

We nod.

"After the war, Typhon was slain and cast into Hades to guard the entrance of Tartarus forever. And Io communed with Julian from Rome, an apostate Christian who tried to save the Delphic Oracle but failed before he became emperor of Constantinople."

"Keep reading," I tell her as Marissa and I scan the temple for more carvings.

Helen's words fade into silence as we make our laps, looking at the central dais, a platform of rock for worship. The floors around the dais crack in a radial pattern as though construction workers had dropped a monolith and forgotten to patch the damage. Tiny weeds sprout from the cracks, making rivers of green amongst the rocks.

Helen continues, "The map shows the way … according to the oracle, a final clue lies in the catacombs beneath the temple of Poseidon. The map—"

"Kerry," Marissa whispers, "something feels wrong here. The spirits are stirring. We need to leave this place."

"The MAP!" Helen calls out, regaining our attention. "Come see."

As we hurry to her side, the stones beneath us vibrate. Something evil lurks under this temple. But the map will guide us—if it's complete.

"Look here," Helen says, "this circle. That's Crete. And you'll recognize this one." She points at an egg-shaped irregular island. "It's Sicily. This line traces across the Mediterranean to the Iberian Peninsula."

"The Rock of Gibraltar?" I gasp.

Prometheus had noted the remaining Titans were assembling at the Rock of Gibraltar to plan for another war. And the oracle of Delphi foresaw it.

"Pro—" Marissa starts.

"I'll crush his skull!" I snarl, my fingers shaking in rhythm with the trembling floor. Prometheus will deserve his fate, as will the other four members of the New Titan Order. I resolve to punish him after we defeat the Titans, although another war is the last thing this world needs.

"Kerry!" Marissa shouts. "Run!"

I snap Helen out of her daze. "Come with us if you want to live."

The overhead lintels emit ribbons of falling dust, which whip in the humid breeze to create tiny sand dunes within the temple. Marissa, Helen, and I sprint toward the limestone steps, descend them two at a time, and dart toward the site exit.

Confused tourists scurry in every direction, while a family gathered around a gigantic egg-shaped stone gathers their belongings, tripping on shifting bricks as they hurry away. Rain pelts my forehead as I shout at

Helen to hurry. She trips on a broken stone, smashing her knee against the foundation bricks. She moans in agony as she cups her hands around her knee. Marissa backtracks to help her, wedging her hands under Helen's armpits to hoist her to her feet. Her resultant limp slows us down, but we see the family escape as the rocks around the stone tumble and collapse into a fiery pit.

I grasp Helen's hand. Fifty yards away from the top of the plank steps, the ground crumbles and shifts, blocking our escape. Struggling to chart an alternative course, I see a stone lip along the perimeter fence. Getting to it will require leaping a narrow canyon with collapsing walls. I steel my nerves and sprint in that direction as the pit expands. A river of molten lava bubbles twelve feet below us, eroding the channel until it's too wide to leap.

A loud rumble interspersed with cracking rain-soaked rocks echoes across the hillside behind us. Doubling back to find a safer route, we look up at the shifting monolith as the pillars lean one by one. The temple collapses into a gigantic dust cloud billowing a quarter mile into the hazy sky, where it blends with the falling rain.

The lava river boils, encircling the ovular stone in the center. We're trapped, but the Omphalos stone remains undamaged, even as the paving stones surrounding it have crumbled into rubble. A hissing sound like jets of water flashing into steam rips across the site, while the surrounding ruins crumble and tourists flee. A tour guide escorts terrified people down the steps, glancing backward as canyons open across the stone surface. Scaly green and black skin slithers through the canyon, growing spiny appendages along the ridge of a long, snaky body. The beast bubbles in the lava, spitting steam as it climbs out of the canyons and twists around the Omphalos stone.

Baring bloody fangs, it dances around us, eyeing us evilly as it locks onto us as prey. The body grows four bulky feet, each tipped with razor-sharp claws. The talons scrape across the stone as it towers over us. Standing twenty feet high and as long as a football field, the monster licks its scaly lips with a long, forked tongue, hissing.

Then it lunges, sinking its foot-long fangs into the limestone inches from Helen's feet. Trying to drag her away is no use. The assaulting monster wants a fight. Lifting its hind leg, it swipes its spiny tail at us. To avoid it throwing us down the slope, I tackle Marissa and Helen. The tail flies over our heads as fast as a whip.

The creature sinks its talons into the earth as I unzip the duffel, pulling out the caduceus with my bloody hand. Marissa shrieks when she sees me holding it aloft. "Kerry, NO!"

Her warning hits me in the chest. The monster hisses, eyeing the caduceus with envy. Its splinter eyes blink as its pink tongue slips out of its mouth between the fangs. Another lunge carries five claws toward my face. Dodging them, I curl my fingers around the snakes and threaten the monster with it. But instead of lashing out at the beast, the snakes go limp in my hands.

The lizard demon strikes again with its tail, tripping me and sending Marissa hurtling toward the canyon from whence it emerged. Bouncing back to my feet, I sprint towards it as it swipes at my leg. Fresh blood oozes out of four new gashes beneath my shredded jeans. I spew curse words at it, beckoning it to strike again.

Reaching out with the limp caduceus, I try to pulverize its face with the magic, but the staff will not respond. The weapon is useless, as though drained of life. I cling to it anyway to defend myself, but it can't stop the monster from sinking its fangs into my left hand.

Screaming, I twist myself out of its grasp while Marissa runs up behind me with both arms raised like she's shoving an invisible stone towards the demon. It hisses at her and strikes with its claws, missing her midsection by less than an inch.

"COME ON," I howl, brandishing the caduceus. "Is that all you got?"

"KERRY!"

From the corner of my eye, I see a spot of blood on her brow trickling down her nose. The monster slashes at her with its claws, hesitates, and locks its focus on the caduceus again. With its forked tongue lashing at the air like a whip, the monster dances around us, knocking us off our feet with its hulking body before raising its snake-like neck fifty feet above us. Ready to pounce, it follows the caduceus with its eyes as I wave it under its snout.

I see its reaction before it happens; it coils its tail around us to squeeze us closer, and its four clawed feet dangle above our heads. Bits of molten rock spatter onto the ground at my feet, almost igniting my jeans. I have the monster right where I want it.

The dark energy pulses in my veins as I allow the memories of harrowing tears to shred my emotions. In the back of my mind, I can hear Ash taunting me, intermittent with Sarah's terrified scream as she slides off the muddy cliff into the ocean.

Sarah's image erupts into flames as she crashes down, and when I wedge my eyes open, something insane happens. The beast cowers above us, its eyes on a red bird circling overhead. My body keeps its form, failing to become a black dust cloud this time. Attempting to unleash lighting does me no good. I struggle in its tail's grasp as Marissa whimpers at me.

"The spirits are on her side!"

I swear as the tail wriggles around me. When the bird swoops from the heavens, the monster relinquishes its grip to defend itself from the Phoenix. On the first pass, the avian misses, dragging her flaming tail feathers across the demon's head.

Rearing back for the attack, the monster unhinges its jaws, revealing rows of serrated teeth and the slender, forked tongue. The tail smashes into the ground nearby, lifts us off our feet, and throws us backward fifteen feet as the bird once again zeroes in on the monster.

The lizard licks its chops as the attacker aims at its open maw and then flashes into a flaming missile, streaking from the heavens so fast I cannot see her wings. When her beak contacts the creature's skull, her whole body explodes into a fireball that knocks the monster off its feet and sends it careening to the ground. Scooping up Marissa to flee, I watch as the beast's flaming head flails against the rocks, bouncing like a boulder in the rubble around the Omphalos.

The canyons emit smoke as Marissa and I steer clear of its thrashing tail. The monster hisses and growls as its claws and limbs fall to rest. Hurrying to Helen's aid, we find a path through the canyon, scale the craggy walls, and reach the top steps of the wooden stairs. The creature lunges again as its eyes catch fire. Next to its head, a pile of black ashes settles and shifts before sprouting red and orange flames reminiscent of Sarah's golden locks.

As we descend the stairs, the monster's lifeless body disappears beyond the hillside. Helen and Marissa whimper and moan as we make our way toward the car. A throng of tourists with cameras and phones chatter in the parking lot as we limp to our vehicle.

Once we're inside, I start the motor and dab at the blood on my hand. It stings as though acid is leeching into my flesh. I grit my teeth and drive away before asking Helen the question that has been needling at my brain for the last hour.

"What did your brother mean when he said you were tainted with Clytemnestra's blood?

Helen shrinks in her seat and gazes out the window as we drive leave the way we came, refusing to answer. My heart feels like it's beating a million miles an hour. The Phoenix might have saved us this time, but can I count on her again? If we can make it back to the Athens airport in one piece, I'll rejoice, even though I plan to pummel Fire Guy afterward.

25

Orestes and the Circle

Nursing wounds from the serpent's attack, I drive through the mountains without pressing Helen for any further information. The stinging in my hand grows into a persistent ache as we wind through the curves to modern Delphi, in order to charge the car battery before we return to Athens. I can see the antipathy on Helen's face, but I must know the truth. If she never tells me, our journey may not go as planned. It could just become another distraction in a quest that's full of them. Still, the longer she stews in silence, the longer I can unwind the lore in my head.

I shouldn't be surprised that a serpent demon had guarded Delphi, home of the oracle and the cult of Apollo, but what caused it to attack us instead of the millions of tourists who flock to the ruins every year? Perverse ancient magic might explain it, but even after the Titans, I refuse to believe in mysticism.

By the time the car nears the fifty percent battery mark, Helen is frowning as she gazes at the hillsides around the city, pondering a way to explain something.

"You ... I think I heard you ... mention the Antikythera mechanism? If there's a working copy, it must be in the Athens Museum, which of course centers on the legendary goddess Athena and the Pantheon."

"If it actually works," I mumble, "and if it really exists, we need it to help chart a course for Atlantis. If *that* even exists."

"You never told me why you're looking for it," Helen says, still focusing her gaze outside the car.

I glance at the GPS screen on the dashboard. I'm not sure if I should trust her. Her body language suggests more than meets the eye, but I don't get a sense she's being deceitful. "The corrupt gang controlling our city—they ironically call themselves the Freedom Brothers—wants something from Hera, along with the Ouroboros ring a friend of mine wears. All the symbolism is there. The snakes in the caduceus, everything involving Delphi, the serpent eating its own tail. It's all there. And we found an underground chamber with a replica of the Omphalos stone, symbolizing Rhea's trick to deceive the Titan Cronus, a *real* swell guy. We believe they seek the treasure in Atlantis to establish a new empire, isolated from the rest of the United States and the Western world. That's why we're trying to save our city."

"Good a reason as any," Helen says, raising her eyebrows. I can see her face reflected in the passenger window, and despite her inner despair, I see her eyes flicker with interest in the story.

"What about the feather?" Marissa leans forward in the backseat. She glances back and forth between us and then focuses on my forehead. "And that stone with the etchings?"

I'd almost forgotten. Gulping, I realize I no longer have it. Had I lost it before we boarded the plane, or did I lose it in the mudslide? "Not that it matters now. It only had two characters on it—*theta* and *upsilon*. And the eye ... it belonged to Argus, the guardian of Io, whose eyes Hera placed in a peacock's tail."

"Both letters of the Greek alphabet, but served different archaic uses, deriving from Phoenician characters—"

"Phoenician, as in the Phoenix?"

Helen tilts her head and twists her body so that she can glance at me from the corner of her eyes. "Yes, and no. Since I'm guessing you're interested in the symbolism behind them, I can share some details there. Scholars assume *theta* to be the symbol of death, since its original form contained a cross. And *upsilon* is even more complicated. Known as Pythagoras's letter because he used it as an emblem of virtue and vice, which Christians later interpreted as the course of human life."

"Life and death," Marissa says, holding her breath.

"Reincarnation," I add.

"The Phoenician civilization produced purple dyes from murex shells, according to historians," Helen says, frowning. "Thus, only tangentially related to the mythical bird."

"The Phoenix is real," I say, trying to hide the sadness in my expression. Referring to Sarah as a myth derails the thoughts in my head, making her guidance seem trivial, even when my heart knows otherwise.

"They had trade routes all across the Mediterranean," she explains, accentuating the name of the sea. "From the Strait of Gibraltar to present-day Lebanon."

Marissa clasps her hands on her knees. Dried mud from the landslide still cakes her jeans, and now that the skies are clearing, I see our filthy clothes in a different light. "Didn't Fire Guy say something about Gibraltar?" she says.

I can only manage a nod, and Helen stares at me, hoping for an explanation. Despite the reverence in his demeanor, the casual way he carried Sarah's body to the pyre he built still stains my mind with anger.

The estimated mileage range on the dashboard increases faster the closer we get to a full state of charge. Deciding to stop at eighty percent, I unbuckle my seat belt, get out of the car, and unplug.

When I turn the power on again, the GPS updates its route, showing public charging destinations and restaurants along the way. Deciding to use the two-plus hours thinking about Ian and his family, I pull out of the charging stall and follow the directions to Athens and the museum.

As I drive, the silence seems to change course, veering us away from the focus on Greek lore and into more emotive territory. Once or twice, I catch reflections of Helen's turned away face in the car window, and I glance in the mirror at Marissa. I refocus on the curving highway as it rises into the mountains past the ancient temple of Apollo, and into a narrow gorge before opening into the mud-swallowed valley, where stranded motorists sift through the wreckage and dig for survivors.

"Of course, I researched Clytemnestra," Helen says suddenly, "Eventually. She was a murderer—killed her husband, the king of Mycenae, or Argos, depending on the region. She started an affair and plotted to kill her husband, and ruled over Mycenae until her son killed them both for revenge. Before she did, Agamemnon sacrificed his daughter, and after Helen was kidnapped from King Menelaus of Sparta, the war started."

I peel my eyes away from the road and slow down as instinct grinds my gears to powder. "And your namesake. That's why your name sounded familiar."

She nods and frowns. "If I'm really Helen, then Clytemnestra is my half-sister. But Paul likes to call himself Pollux—Clytemnestra's brother."

"You don't say."

"You think the Phoenicians had contact with the Greeks at sea?" Marissa says, leaning back in the seat and crossing her arms. "I mean, same general region, same general era."

"They traded throughout the Mediterranean," says Helen. "Of course they had contact with the Greeks, because many characters from the Greek alphabet derive directly from the Phoenician language."

Finally, it hits me. If *theta* and *upsilon* symbolize life and death, the stone suggests they might be intertwined. And the phoenix rises above it all in its rebirth, completing the cycle and starting anew, just like the Ouroboros. I process through this information until we reach the Greek capital. Our conversation centers on the sprawling modern city and the confusing network of streets as the nav system guides us to the Hellenic Archaeological Museum.

When we arrive, finding a parking space is difficult despite the ease of sighting the building. Its fluted pillars frame a veranda in front of thick wooden doors. The columns' curled capstones resemble those the Freedom Brothers had reused from the Second Bank of the United States. They support a flat roof adorned with bronze-colored statues of Greek gods and goddesses. Tiered stair sections rise ten feet to the elevated entryway and the grand second-floor lobby. Inside, intricate stone carvings line a wall. Helen guides us through dozens of displays depicting heroes and legends, until we reach a modern room lit by elegant track lights pivoted to illuminate glass display cases.

Ancient relics are labelled with translucent plastic. In the center of the case, a broken green dial with double spokes accompanies a dozen smaller pinions, shattered gears, and the wooden remnants of a box. Next to the display, a hand-crank lever lies on its side. Directing our attention to the central dial, the plaque explains the meanings behind the symbols etched in the metal. The Antikythera mechanism, it says, was discovered on a dive near the rocky coast of the Greek island of Antikythera over sixty years ago, and archeologists have determined it to be a sophisticated time-keeping device that can predict the positions of the planets and constellations during any season.

"Beautiful, isn't it?" A white-haired man says, approaching from the other side of the display case. "The real thing. Modern historians say the Greeks shouldn't have had technology this advanced. The divers determined the mechanism had been recovered from a Roman raid and was being transported back to Rome. Astronomers marvel at its accuracy to this day, even suggesting that seafarers could use it to keep track of their position in the sea."

"You're an archaeologist?" I ask. "I heard there was a working replica here."

"The rumors are true," the white-haired man says, stroking his gray stubble. "Would you like to see it?"

"Of course," I say, following him into an eight-foot-square office. His desk is covered with a plastic laminate cover littered with overstuffed folders. Behind his desk, a wooden display cabinet features cloth-bound books, various knickknacks, and even a bust of Apollo. Next to the bust stands an oblong box. Steel gear wheels interlock, punching through holes in the plywood surface. A metal crank on the side wall controls the gears, looking like the wind-up handle on a jack-in-the-box.

"I helped build it myself, following the specifications and everything the archeologists discovered. Sometimes understanding how something works depends on building a copy."

I look up. "And it works?"

His eyes light up at the suggestion. "It took a few years of tweaking to get it to register astronomically correct outputs consistently, but once we worked it out, it became clearer. Only the most intelligent of the ancient Greeks could have designed it."

"Archimedes?"

He smiles. "In fact, evidence suggests it's older than that. We know of an advanced civilization that predates Athens itself, known for the brightest, if not the most immoral, society in ancient lore."

His insinuation makes my spine tingle. "Atlantis?"

"The only evidence Atlantis even existed was from literature written hundreds of years later. But if even a fraction is true, and Atlantis does exist, can you imagine the knowledge it must contain?"

"Unfortunately, I do," I say. "We're taking it."

Marissa gasps, "Kerry!"

"I'm afraid you're mistaken," he says, scowling at me as though I've just told the crassest joke he'd ever heard. "Now if you would please move along..."

Gritting my teeth, I consider that getting him to part with his life's work may be a masterclass in foolishness, but I've had enough of negotiating and waiting for things to materialize. I exit the building with Marissa and Helen in tow, hurry down the steps, and rummage through the duffel. Curling my fingers around the cool steel staff, an idea explodes in my mind. I grip the rod until my knuckles are white, glowering until my lips tremble with rage, and dart back to the stone steps to give the white-haired archeologist a piece of my mind.

Marissa barks at me as I stagger away from them, leaving Helen dumbfounded. "Kerry Gearhardt, STOP!"

"I'll give him a reason to part with it," I snarl, breaking into a run.

"Kerry!"

Her warning stops me in my tracks when I reach the bottom of the steps. Turning, I watch Marissa reaching out to me through the dead.

Success cannot undo gravity.

The words of the Delphic Oracle press into my head, eliminating the urge to lash out in anger.

Still, the resident scientist might want to see the masterpiece I've stolen. And now, a different plan enters my mind. If Marissa and I show it to him and demonstrate how it works, we can convince him to go with us across the Mediterranean in search of the famous lost city of Atlantis.

The clouds hang low over Athens like residual banks of fog clinging to the mountains after a winter snowstorm. Breaks in the clouds let occasional golden rays from the sun illuminate the city, and one such patch warms the area around the museum as we climb the steps. To avoid security throwing us out, I try to keep the caduceus hidden behind my back, which makes me feel more awkward.

"Kerry," Marissa complains when we reach the top of the steps. "You must understand, I stopped you the best way I know how—because you were about to disobey the oracle's warning. I could see it in your eyes."

I scowl at her. She has often used her powers to get us out of sticky predicaments, but never against me. That is a fact I cannot ignore, and it doesn't make me feel much better.

"I'm sorry," Helen says, "but did I miss something?"

"Long story," Marissa says.

"But it might be beneficial."

Before we break our conversation to enter, a group of younger women push open the heavy doors from the inside, chattering and laughing as they bounce down the stairs. The museum's top step offers a panoramic city view, where thousands of flat roofs cover the hillsides, the landscape growing steeper approaching the Acropolis. At this distance, only the most famous features stand out. Dozens of fluted columns with curved capstones beneath a pair of pediments hide the smaller structures flanking them.

"Do you think the Titans know we're searching for Atlantis?" Marissa asks.

I narrow my eyes. "I'd put money on it. I don't know how the Rock of Gibraltar plays into it, but something tells me we'll find out. And if the Titans are aware, you better believe the gods are. Not a good combination."

Helen swallows. "The Titans? I thought they were imprisoned."

"For trying to prevent the Olympians from taking over. They went to war with the Titans and blamed them for it. The height of arrogance, only the Titans are worse."

"You *met* them?"

Another long story. If I told her everything, she'd have the Athens police arrest me for being a menace to society. Then again, I don't need her to stay. She's following us around because she wants to, and the longer she does, the more she puts herself in danger.

"They'll try making a play for it," I say. "I don't know how to stop them, or even if I can. We're no match for them."

"We have one advantage," Marissa says. "They're missing their best leaders."

Glancing at her, I feel the blood pressure surge in my veins. "Coeus may not harness the raw power Cronus did, but he's smarter. And it's not like the other ten are total slouches."

"You know Coeus is in charge?"

"Based on what we saw of him during the last war, I'd say that's a fair assumption."

Marissa sneers. "You know what they say about assumption."

Helen leads the way through the twenty-foot-tall doors, past the statues, and into a corridor approaching the archaeologist's office. When we round the corner, three security officers in white uniforms confront us.

"I'm afraid I'll have to escort you outside," says one man in a thick accent. The other two nod silently.

"I need to speak with the archaeologist," I say, turning the caduceus in my palm.

"That supposed to intimidate me? Dr. Katsakis is not available."

Knowing he'd counter that way, I sneer and tighten my grip on the metal staff between the coiling snakes, whose eyes begin to glow. "I'd prefer not to use it on you."

The security guard inches backward when he sees the eyes, but is not relenting.

Marissa closes her eyes. A moment later, the officers slink back toward the wall, as if remembering they need to guard another wing of the museum. The moment allows us to walk past them and find Dr. Katsakis's door. It's locked. Seeing through the opaque glass is difficult. A hazy blob of gray and brown shifts when I tap the door. Caution and patience rarely get me where I want with most people. Then again, being assertive never works on Becky. I don't know how to approach this man, but it works this time.

As though he's expecting his security detail or graduate students to interrupt him, he rises from the chair, swings the door open, and glares at the caduceus. A split second before he slams the door, I wedge the staff into the frame to stop him. The door bounces off the snakes' heads and swings back toward Dr. Katsakis.

He doesn't bother letting us in before he speaks. "Where did you get that?"

"Unimportant," I say. "But I can assure you, it's the real thing."

The scientist frowns defiantly before letting us in. He rests back in his leather chair and laces his fingers together over the transparent plastic desk topper before uttering another word.

"I can show you what it does if you doubt me. I'm only asking you to let us borrow the mechanism. We'll bring it back as good as new."

Assuming the Titans don't destroy it while battling us for Atlantis, or the Olympians don't take it.

"And what do you propose I do with it?"

"Nothing," I say. "When we return with the device, we'll let you photograph it, weigh it, determine its composition, whatever you want. But we need it for now."

"You have no leverage," he scoffs. "I do not take kindly to being treated like ... how do you say? A chump?"

"Then, by all means, come with us."

As he strokes his stubble, I can see the wheels churning in his brain. Furrowing his eyebrows, he mumbles something I don't understand, shifts in his seat, and straightens his back.

"I'm too old for that sort of thing, and I get seasick. But I know a crew of divers who owe me a favor. They're planning an expedition searching for a shipwreck off Sicily, and I believe they leave tonight. If I make some calls, I want your word, you will keep me informed and let me keep the caduceus after you return. Those are my terms."

Anger flashes through me, but instead of showing it I sigh and glance at the snakes' eyes, which have stopped glowing. As if she knows I'm about to relent, Marissa grips me by the crook of my arm and whispers in my ear. "It's a ruse. Let's get out of here."

"A promise is a promise," the doctor pleads.

Hesitating, I examine his offer in my head before nodding and shrugging. "Make the call right now, and we'll consider it a deal."

"Kerry?"

Ignoring her only makes her grip my arm tighter. "The Olympians will want to claim the caduceus, too. And probably your Neato friends. You can't be so brazen."

I've made a living on snap judgements. Being timid on a construction site only causes delays, angry subcontractors, and even angrier owners. So far, I've done everything Marissa's way. But not this time.

Dr. Katsakis fumbles through his contacts, scanning the list until he finds the relevant one. Using the computer to dial the number, he waits and lets it ring aloud before an older-sounding woman answers, "Good evening, doctor. To what do I owe the pleasure?"

Her accent sounds like a mashup of fast-talking New York and the soft dignity of Oxford English.

"I wonder if you have space on your vessel for three students."

The woman hesitates. "I don't know about that. Safety concerns ..."

"They will comply with every order," the doctor says. "Let them aboard and consider us even."

A longer silence resumes while the line crackles with static. Her tone confirms my suspicion. "Very well. Send them to Pier 74 by nine this evening. We must leave by 10 so that we can get everything set up for our dive by early morning."

I breathe a sigh of relief as Dr. Katsakis clears his throat. "Hem. Thank you, Ms. Paris. Expect them on time. Oh, and I should tell you—they're searching for Atlantis."

26

Flotsam and Nereids

Floodlights illuminate the harbor and the anchored ships; everything from tugs, motorized sloops, fishing vessels, and an Aegean cruise-liner. Marissa and I lead the way through a maze of brown, red, and yellow cargo containers triple stacked beneath two-legged loading cranes standing a hundred feet high. The floodlights cast oblique shadows over the piers and the boardwalk, a haven for souvenir shops and late-night bars. Across the calm water, the light of an incoming ship cuts through the mist, reflecting off the tiny waves lapping at the pilings.

Finding Pier 74 isn't easy; half the piers don't have any visible numbers. The first numbered anchor bay bears a six-foot-high 26. Beyond that, there is a wooden archway with a printed 29 in the red-stained wood with faded blue paint. The next three bays give us no number, but as we pass a canvas-sailed yacht, I spy an enormous, backlit 74 in the distance. Even late at night, the boardwalk carries many lurking visitors. Behind Pier 34, a line of women clad in sundresses chatters with a man in a pilot's cap and a maroon vest. Men in smart casual clothing join them, waiting to board the ocean-liner for the night.

Between bouts of staring at the waters and frowning, Helen glances at me as though she wants to say something. I realize what she's thinking, but I'm not in the mood to fill her in with the information she wants, and I saunter along as though I'm deep in thought.

"There's so much you haven't told me," Helen drones.

A helicopter's silently turning blades distract me. Parked a quarter mile away from Pier 74, the aircraft waits for its passengers and crewmembers to return.

"*The* Kerry Gearhardt," Marissa explains, "is pretty famous these days, especially on the Eastern Seaboard. For what, I'll never understand." She grins and then continues. "Something to do with time travel. Portals and such. And Titans. Epic story if you have five to seven hours."

I've never talked for over ten or fifteen minutes at a time, at least not in front of a human being. Not even Becky has heard me do it, and she once talked me into speaking at church. Marissa has her own brand of sarcasm, just as sharp as Becky's.

"Titans?"

"Where do I start?" I say.

Marissa shakes her head. "Maybe from the beginning."

"Huh. Good one." I don't even know where the beginning is, because time travel has so distorted my reality that my timeline includes loops and gaps.

Pier 74 looms ahead. The research vessel sways beneath an overhang that shelters the decks from wind and rain. Recessed lights high overhead mark the deck with hazy yellow circles. Men carrying crates and tools aboard scurry through the lights, casting shadows.

"They call him the Conveyor of Light and Shade," Marissa says. "Or Titan, depending on the day. Because he's a descendant of the Titans of Crete, and a princess gave him his gifts."

"Ariadne?" Helen speaks in a monotone of disbelief. I can't convince her without showing off, and I never do that.

"But Marissa has powers too," I say. "Spiritualist. Occult dealer. And one of the smartest women I've ever met."

Marissa replies with her trademark snark. "Gee, thanks. I'm number two."

"You ... you know what I mean."

"He's chained to a religious woman ... what did you say she does for a living?"

"Becky's an interesting case," I explain. "Believes in Jesus and God, but also in the ancient Greek gods, because she has no choice."

As we draw nearer to the research vessel, I hear the shouts of crew members as they load pallets onto a forklift, maneuver it onto a narrow diamond-plate ramp, and organize supplies for the expedition. A woman in a yellow hardhat carries a clipboard, tapping her pen and counting entries on the manifest. She looks up from her work as we approach, waiting for us to introduce ourselves.

Marissa speaks first. "Do you know a Dr. Katsakis?"

The woman slips the clipboard under her arm and glances at our filthy clothes and greasy hair. "You must be the three treasure hunters. My name's Emma, but you can call me Dr. Weingart. We're loading the last supplies. In the meantime, you may board, take the yellow stairs below deck. Relax, take a shower. We've got a long night ahead."

"Thank you, doctor," I say, looking away.

The three of us ascend the ramp, holding onto the bent-pipe railings as we board the vessel. The ship's hulking bridge tower has captain's quarters with wide windows beneath mounted megaphones and searchlights. A central mast with a limp Greek flag stands atop the tower. Below deck, a series of unlabeled doors jut from a narrow corridor with plain white walls. Further on, unmarked rooms encircle a void with a single, round-windowed door. A faded chrome plate labels it as the lab. The ship's single bathroom is at the end of the hallway. Set in the low ceilings, a row of bright recess lights runs along the left side of the hall.

"I think I will hit the shower," Marissa says, swiping a hand through her tangled hair.

"Me too," I say, feeling my eyelids droop.

She raises her eyebrows. "Gee, I don't know what to say."

Awkward.

"I mean, after you."

The quarters are tiny, though there are enough rooms to house a dozen crew members and scientists working in shifts. Helen disappears into one near the bathroom without another word, while I pick one three doors away, lock the door, and collapse into the low twin bed. A single mirror is fixed to the wall. A wire-meshed wastebasket in the corner carries only a few scraps of paper. Rolling over and waiting for Marissa to finish her shower, I let my head rest on the flat pillow, close my eyes, and drift off to sleep.

"Coffee!" someone in the halls says hours later.

I throw the blankets off, feel the boat sway, and get to my feet. As I do every morning, I stumble to the mirror, rub my eyes, and look at my crumpled expression. A scientist and a crew member amble through the hallway when I emerge from my room, tiptoe past Helen's quarters, and lock myself in the bathroom. A change of clothes awaits me, labelled with a tiny, wrinkled, sticky note.

After the shower, I dry myself, slip into the clothes, and sigh happily. The warm, clean fabric against my skin sends a pleasant feeling through me.

I meet Marissa as I open the door, and together we enter a small break room with a silver-banded round table and four folding chairs. A single cabinet crowded with an oven, a microwave, an ice machine, and a coffeemaker inhabits the left side of the room. A single-drain sink abuts a 1970s refrigerator.

Marissa pours me a small cup of coffee, sips hers, and waits for me to speak. I allow myself a moment to feel the craft swaying on the sea.

"Have you seen Helen?"

"Oh," Marissa says. "I think she's still asleep. Should I wake her?"

The door bursts open a half second later, and Emma stands in the hallway, to pull us away. She allows us to wander the corridors and orders her crew to prepare for a dive. Swallowing a mouthful of coffee, I stand up and raise my palm to stop her from walking away.

"I brought a couple of things aboard," I say, "and I want to use one to chart our course tonight. After you've completed your daily assignment."

Dr. Weingart tightens her ponytail. She wears a neon-blue windbreaker with white reflective strips down both arms. "We can't deviate much. How far do you think it is?"

"Uh—"

"That's what I thought."

To study the Antikythera mechanism, I'll need darkness, but then again, determining the positions of the sun and moon may help me more.

I return to my room to fetch the device, carry it up to the bridge, and join Marissa at a long conference room table. She folds her hand across the fluted wood bandings and scowls.

The chair I choose offers an impressive view through the windows, which wrap around the front of the tower, allowing panoramic views of the vast Mediterranean. Noting the position of the sun and moon, I roll the crank until I have the correct date, mark my spot, and push it aside. Resting the caduceus on the table, I attempt to make sense of it.

"We're in the middle of nowhere," she says. "Looking at it on the map, you don't realize how big it is. Maybe an inherent flaw of the Mercator projection, but still ... how can it pinpoint the location?"

"I don't think it can," I say. "We'll have to look for other signs."

"Or we can just ask Poseidon." Marissa lowers her voice as Helen enters the room, pulls out a chair, and sits.

"Poseidon doesn't even know," Helen says. "It says so in his temple."

Marissa scoffs. "Great."

We fiddle with the device at various times throughout the day. The divers take turns jumping into the sea, equipped with underwater cameras, cables, and breathing tanks. As the hours pass, I grow more and more frustrated with the device, but keep it near us. Until dusk.

The flat sea affords a perfect view of the sunset as the vessel continues westward. Marissa comes back from the breakroom carrying a single box of crackers. She dumps them out on the table, divvying them up, and shoves two into her mouth.

As the fading orange and yellow light in the wispy clouds fades to blue and then to black, Helen clicks the crank into another groove and wheels it around.

With the naked eye, high clouds obscure many stars. Asking the captain to lower the lights may improve visibility. He agrees to power them down for a few minutes at a time as we work the gears on the device, pushing Mars and Jupiter into place, and continuing with the North Star and Sirius. When the map of the sky takes shape, I double check the date and point out an anomaly to Marissa.

"See that? The Big Dipper?"

She nods.

"It's pointing downward in a straight line between here and Gibraltar."

"Great observation, but I don't see how it helps."

I gulp as the revelation hits me. "Of course it helps. Because ... the Big Dipper. The Great Bear. Ursula Major. Callisto."

Vanessa.

I remember hearing her crying out as my fist-sized rock pierces Typhon's skull. Her eyes flutter as she gasps my name. I plead with her to stay with me, but she falls, the light leaving her eyes as she hits the turf outside the cabin.

"I don't know how that—"

Helen doesn't have a chance to finish—we see movement across the ship's bow. The captain flashes the leading lights to warn off the intruders, but they've already caught up with us. It is a wooden, motorized craft speeding toward us, bouncing over the choppy waters.

"Unidentified vessel," the captain warns over the loudspeaker in English, "please stay back or we will sink you."

My heart sinks and my veins turn to ice when a series of flashes and sounds of gunfire burst over the water. When the captain spins the wheel hard to port, the Antikythera replica slides to the end of the table. Marissa dives to catch it just before it crashes to the floor, struggling to regain her balance. Crew members scurry across the deck, one of them uttering a piercing scream amidst the blasts. He limps toward the tower door, turns to face the intruders, and shouts.

The shots peel paint and pierce metal as the pirates attack, pulverizing the craft with high-caliber bullets.

"Get out!" The captain screeches. "We have no money! Call off your—"

CRASH!!

The window shatters, scattering shards of glass across the control console and the narrow walkway. Marissa and I dive below the console as the captain ducks behind the wheel, spinning it to correct our route.

The pirates expect this move, toss ropes over the rails, and climb up our ship's hull with their guns clenched in their teeth. I hear another shriek, and more gunfire erupts. The vessel lists to our starboard side, sending everything on the tabletop skidding to the floor. Still cradling the device, Marissa rolls in the glass to shield Helen from falling debris. Blood stains her new clothes, expanding into red spots near her knees. The gunfire stops when a dozen pirates advance on the barricaded tower, pulling knives from their pockets. Emma and her colleagues are the last to enter the bridge. They shout to each other as stomping feet clang against the metal stairs. They're coming for us, and we're defenseless.

Marissa and Helen hide behind the table as three scientists barricade the door. They'll kill us all, and for what? I gather the caduceus in my hands, spin the handle in my fist, and jump to my feet when the criminals pound at the door.

Outside in the water, the lights from the boat illuminate a splash from a surfacing whale, only it's not a whale.

It has tentacles and spiny fins. Five of them emerge from the water, raising their hulking bodies to attack. The enormous hydra smashes the pirates' boat into splinters as the finned creatures encircle the research vessel. As it lists, the scientist stumbles. But the monsters have drawn the pirates' attention.

Another volley of gunfire erupts, but it does nothing to deter the creatures. More of them emerge from the deep, pressing for the attack.

"We're going DOWN!" the captain shouts before screaming a series of Greek curses.

The pirates chatter in their own language as they hurry toward the port side to look at the monsters. They're slinking under the surface one at a time, and a few seconds later, they all arise at once, spraying the deck with saltwater as they attack. Razor-sharp spines rip through the hull as the serpentine creatures crowd the boat from all sides.

The hydra waits to finish us off, wielding a hundred black tentacles as it rises twenty feet above the surface. It spits out seawater, baring innumerable serrated teeth. Understanding that we're out-manned, a few pirates dive over the aft rails, disappearing into the deep where hungry jaws close around them, swallowing them whole.

Even lowering the lifeboat will not save us. Darkness invades me. I stagger side to side as I push open the bridge tower door, bouncing off the walls as I descend to face our threats. The monsters break the surface as the hydra slaps the water with its gigantic tentacles. Swallowing a gasp of humid air, I see a tiny red flash tear across the sky like a meteor before disappearing beneath the horizon.

The hydra curls one of its tentacles around the mast and entangles another with the port-side framing tugging the ship back to a level position as it pulls us closer. Energy floods my soul in an instant, and when I open my eyes, lighting is forking in all directions, piercing the waves, and setting the monsters alight.

Seeing this, the hydra dives below the water, swoops below us, and lifts us out of the water. Its hundreds of suckers slide across the deck, making loud slurping noises as the creature angles the bow toward its maw.

Behind me, Marissa and Helen scream as they tumble down the angled deck. Holding on tight, I raise the caduceus high overhead, watching the snakes curl around the staff as their red eyes blaze with newfound power.

The magic blasts one monster with an enormous splash, pushing it under, before another wave severs a tentacle swirling above us. Scowling, I aim at the serpent's eyes, in every direction, blowing up sea monsters with every pulse.

"KERRY!"

I can hear Becky's voice echo in my ears as Marissa clings to the rail with both hands. Helen has her arms wrapped around Marissa's waist, dangling over the violent waters. The ship lurches again when another blast hits the hydra between the eyes.

It retaliates by dropping us. A split second of weightlessness precedes a violent crash as the hull splits in two. Seawater pours in through the open gash, swallowing the crew. When the front end hits the water, the change of momentum sends Marissa and Helen overboard. As her fingers slip from the railing, I remember Sarah sliding into the abyss after Cronus attacked the seashore.

"MARISSA!"

Pirates dive overboard to take their chances with the sea as the water swallows the hull inch by inch. Still, the hydra twists its tentacles in front of the stars. I realize the Antikythera mechanism is gone, lost to the churning Mediterranean.

Serpentine sea monsters coil in the ocean, eating pirates and crew whole. When Marissa pops her head out of the water, Helen gasps as the nearest monster swoops in for the kill. I have little time to react. My first shot with the caduceus misses, causing a ten-foot-plume of water to shoot above the surface. The ship lurches deeper into the waves, as I give in to the warm water.

I spit out saltwater as I swim to save Marissa and Helen from the creatures, but something has distracted them. I blink in horror when I see it.

A thousand women swim nude through the deep, carrying spears to take out the sea monsters. The hydra flips at least eight women out of the water, sending them flying toward the African coast as hundreds more replace them.

The women swarm like locusts, chasing away the serpents with spiny fins and burying their spears in the hydra's tentacles. They slide up around us, lifting us out of the water as they form a churning sea of bubbles. My eyes sting as the saltwater floods my throat. The water mutes the residual ringing of the gunshots as the thousand women rescue nine of us, including Marissa, Helen, and myself.

I try to gargle a "thank you" but one woman places a spindly long-nailed finger against her chapped lips to hush me. Three metal prongs jut from the waves three hundred feet away, gathering the women into a conference. When a man emerges carrying the trident, he commands the women to take the survivors to safety. I breathe a premature sigh of relief as they take us away from the wreckage.

They make it only ten feet when the surface erupts with a geyser of warm water shooting a hundred feet into the air. The surface bulges, and a thousand bodies flee. My eyes widen and terror grips me as I watch the biggest monster I've ever seen create towering waves as it surfaces.

Marissa and Helen scream in unison as they float, abandoned with only me to save them. The sea god disappears behind the waves as the towering beast lunges toward us.

27

Leviathan Armageddon

The bulging surface breaks into a towering tsunami, sending hundred-foot waves toward the coastlines. In the blink of an eye, the clouds grow into a spiraling gale, whipping the waves into a saline spray. A field-length ridge on the monster's back carries hundreds of enormous plated spikes, each twenty feet tall. The waves thrash as the creature's back emerges, one dripping spine at a time. Attached to a neck longer than three city blocks, the massive head twists as it shoots out of the water, reaching dizzying heights as it roars.

Forked lightning zaps its body from the spinning typhoon, further charging the beast. Transforming lightning into heat, the demon blinks its fireball eyes as it searches for the people responsible for waking it. From a mouth large enough to swallow a cruise liner, a fifty-foot-long tongue licks its scaled lips, slithering past hundreds of five-foot hooked teeth. Its tail whips above the thrashing sea foam faster than I can blink.

You might think a creature this large would move slowly enough to allow us time to escape, but you'd be wrong. Before I can scream, the tail coils around us. Twenty feet in diameter, its hulking scales reek of death and seawater, flashing with the reflections of lightning. Three separate blasts of electricity pulse into the craggy spines atop its head, sending spasms of energy from the neck to the tail. Hooked barbs along the tail's midsection interlock around us, preventing our escape.

Spewing seawater, Marissa grabs Helen and tries to move, but the monster has other plans. It lurches high above, focusing its fiery eyes on the surface as though to shoot meteors at us. Another surge of electricity from the sky amplifies its first strike. Moving at sonic speeds, it zeroes in on us, raining down from the sky like a twenty-ton boulder. It doesn't need to be perfect; its hulking maw could swallow us whole with a million gallons of water even if it misses the mark by ten feet. Marissa can't hope to move fast enough while trying to rescue a stunned Helen.

I have no choice. I must engage the beast before it can devour them, but my powers cannot stack up to its electricity-resistant outer shell. Raising the caduceus above my head, I distract it when a bolt of lightning plunges into the towering waves, but the wave of energy can't do enough damage to cause the creature more than a brief annoyance. A single wave tosses me fifty feet high, separating the three of us by orders of magnitude. The serpent's eyes glow when it prepares to attack.

I swear as I keep my weapon above the waves, shooting concussive blasts as fast as it will charge. Each time, another jagged bolt of lightning further energizes the monster. My wave crests and falls, dragging me under before I can manage another shot. Stinging with saline water, my eyes burn under the surface as the waves' power drags me deeper. Flashing lightning illuminates enough of the scene to see the creature's true breadth. This thing might be big enough to swallow the Empire State Building. Five hundred feet away, the darkness conceals its head and tail.

Whipping the caduceus toward it, I unleash another attack, but the water's density slows and mutes it. The weapon is useless.

The sounds of weeping fills my ears as the demon plunges its head below the waves, slithering like a mile-long serpent. My bones ache from the pressure and electricity. The source of the crying becomes clear. Above me, I can see Becky's lifeless body rising and falling in the titanic waves. A man swims through the water, trying to save her, but a millisecond later, Becky disappears, transforming into scales and sadness. From somewhere overhead, her teeth gnash. Desperate to intervene, I clutch the caduceus harder and swim toward the surface. With each stroke, another monster wave crashes over me, pushing me further into the depths. I'll never save her.

Her sobs transform the foamy sea into an acid that corrodes my flesh. Marissa and Helen must try to swim away if the sea serpent hasn't already swallowed them. A rasping moan gurgles from my stomach up through my throat as the creature pushes me downward. In a matter of seconds, I will drown.

Nothing can stop me from gathering every bit of darkness I've ever felt, but will it be enough? My eyes gloss over when I attempt to surface again. A break in the current shoots me to the tip of a frothy wave, allowing only seconds to catch my breath before the ebb drags me under once again.

I see no sign of Becky or anyone else. A solitary flash of lightning dips into the violent waters a mile away, distracting the beast. As though it has seen other intruders, it whips its head around, sawing its spiny tail through the brackish water. It slams into me so fast I can't even see it moving. Just one hit is enough to push me lower, and one of its tail spikes rips through my abdomen as the monster jolts away to new prey. The last thing I can hear is a ship's foghorn before I'm too deep to hear anything.

As the darkness envelopes me, undulating with a circular current, I feel the pressure increase. My heart rate slows as I go down, and before the world turns black, I make out streaks of velvety red floating through the water—my own blood. I'm about to become shark food.

The calls of a whale pass me by as saltwater enters my lungs. Before I can adjust, something huge collides with my body, carrying me upwards. The beast's slippery body lifts me above the surface where it emits a towering plume of water before vanishing.

I'm flailing my limbs, I'm trying to see Marissa and Helen, but it seems the waves have dragged them under.

Moaning with fury, I clench my fists as my body melts into an ash cloud floating on the foamy waves. Somehow, I can now see clearly.

The sawtooth tail of the sea demon whips and thrashes above the water as it defeats its nemesis. Faster than I can perceive, the monster flips into a hair-pin U-turn, its head snaking through the water as fast as a bullet train. It catches up to me as I drift away. Confused that its prey has dissipated into thin air, it raises its head above the waves, growling and spraying me with silty water.

Another shot of lightning feeds it more energy, and before I can understand what's happening, the coal dust comprising my body clings to the beast's scales. As I inch higher and higher along its body, I fear it might see me creeping up its backside like an oil slick. Its head thrashes as it bares a hundred razor-sharp teeth, each long enough to turn me into a shish kebab. It eyes me as it zeroes in for the attack. The monster sinks its fangs into its own hide, drawing soupy globs of cold blood. The blood thins as it fuses with my remains, going black as it melts away.

When it realizes what it has done, the creature draws its head back, sticks out its forked tongue and twists into an underwater spiral. Still, I cling to its scaly body as it barrel-rolls through the turbid waves. Another blast of pressure sends me seeping through pores in its body. I begin to erode the demon atom by atom, which, given its size, might take me a hundred years.

A fresh batch of agony makes it coil in the water, emitting ear-piercing screeches. Digging into its soul, I feel a massive pressure wave building within what's left of me. Lurching away, the creature speeds toward the French coast, but I'm still attached to it.

After a mile or two, I explode into light—or at least, what I perceive as light. Another bolt of lightning boils me as I climb through its spikes, pool on top of its head, and drill into its skull.

Screaming echoes from far below—Marissa and Helen are still alive. The monster sees them before I zone out. It jabs at the surface with its fangs, missing them before rearing back for another strike. My body has become coal dust, and I'm tearing the beast apart as fast as I can.

The journey to the center of the monster's brain might take me a week at this rate, but it feels me leeching through its enormous head. With every pulse of lightning further building within me, everything goes dark.

Sinking. Faster than a bullet-shaped boulder, I plummet into eternal darkness. My body tumbles and rolls, gathering seaweed and salt, slowing me down. When the nightmares flash around me, my blood turns to ice. Waves of unrelenting torture claw at my midsection, sending barbs of pain through every inch of my body.

Without light, my mind invents imagery violent enough to crush my soul. I see Sarah sliding into the abyss, before a solemn Prometheus carries her to the pyre. In an instant, the scene transforms into a thousand bodies melting into blood and oil, falling as darkness destroys an entire army. Arrows arc through the sky, needling my flesh with rivers of acid. I see Marissa tied to a wooden monolith, unconscious, and moments away from catching fire. And then Philadelphia collapses, a thousand skyscrapers succumbing to the wrath of the Titans. A crater spreads through the streets, resulting from the explosion of light and shade in my soul.

Becky sobs and heaves on the arm of a couch, over Ian's body. He curls his arms around a lifeless infant, a victim of his own power. The acid creeps deeper into my skin. White-hot tears flood my eyes when I attempt to console her, but I cannot reach; an invisible barrier separates us.

"No, Ian...Don't—"

"Becky."

Another figure emerges from a thick gray fog. Carrying an aura of light, the intruder's soul emits warmth and illuminates a gray abyss roiled with sorrow. The image eats away at me. I know the intruder; I've seen her at our wedding, in the hospital when Ian was born, at a dozen Christmases, and a handful of vacations. Her cheery demeanor clashes with the dreadful atmosphere in this room. Cobwebs cling in every corner, shrouded in dust as a million spiders skitter across the decaying floorboards.

Before I can react, I collapse to the floor, a crater in Downtown Philadelphia. Curling asphalt and shifting rubble tumble into the pit as it fills with water.

And before my body materializes, I can hear Sarah's crystal voice clinging to the insides of my skull.

They are within you now. Part of everything you are, and everything you will be. Do not abandon them, Kerry. They need you more than you know.

My eyes flit open as the undertow takes me deeper into the vast darkness. I cannot be alone; muffled voices ride the current to the bottom of the sea, as gigantic bubbles encircle their heads. Marissa swipes her hands and feet through the water, trying to surface, but we're too deep. The growing pressure might pop our bubbles at any moment, drowning us all at once.

Marissa and Helen sink faster than I do, as though buoyancy works in reverse. The air pockets surrounding them tug them deeper. When I realize that I'm breathing in my own bubble, I try to think fast. Pain jabs at my midsection as my blood trail dilutes in the water above me.

Light emanates from below, and when I see it, relief courses through me. My pupils dilate before reacting to the sudden burst of radiance. The lower we descend, the faster we sink, and the surrounding bubbles enlarge with every meter.

Below us, a transparent diaphragm of surface tension refracts the light's rays, exaggerating the bubbles and turning our bodies into bent and bloated abstract art.

Our bubbles break on contact with the surface tension. The environment draws us in; our popping bubbles are absorbed. When we emerge into a cool air mass, the sea drops away, and we tumble onto tufts of grass in a sea of limestone bricks. The ruins have kept the city intact for millennia. Damaged structures tower around us, poking up at the bubble canopy surrounding the mountain.

The island looks like a volcano that has collapsed. In every direction, beyond the stone buildings, a gray earthen wall ripples as the bubble distorts.

When my knees slam into the grass, I crawl over to Marissa and Helen. They are staring at an open pit under a tall brick bell tower. The darkness seems to reach out to us, pulling us closer. We struggle to our feet and hurry toward it. As we walk, I notice empty eye sockets watching us from the shadows, and a feeling of decay fills the air. The closer we get to the pit, the more bodies we see piled up. The darkness beckons us, and we can't help but move forward, even as pain shoots through our bodies. As we enter the cave, my eyes widen, and a heavy sadness wraps around us.

It is perfect blackness. My foot collides with something oblong, sending it rolling across the gravel floor. Bending to pick it up with my free hand, I kneel on the floor while feeling for the object I've kicked. Jagged bone slides under my fingertips, then a smooth river rock, then I clutch something wooden, curling my fingers around the handle.

Marissa kicks a pile of bones that scatter across the floor. In that moment, I realize what I'm holding—a torch like the ones shown in the adventure movies. If we can ignite it, we can see where we're going. But there's nothing. When I rise to my feet, I grip the caduceus staff in my left hand, hoping to use the glowing eyes to navigate. Instead, they seem to gather darkness.

Ten feet away, I can hear Marissa and Helen breathing as they wander deeper into the cave. A flash of orange light precedes a burst of flame at the end of my torch, and as my eyes adjust to the firelight, terror sinks into my bones.

Thousands of skeletons call this cavern a tomb. The darkness of their souls leeches into the air like humidity from a dense forest, spreading sadness and despair. Beneath shattered ribcages and a thousand skulls, a faint glimmer of yellow collects the firelight. And a man stalks next to me.

Or at least, he was once a man. His skin and clothes have eroded and frayed over centuries. Decaying muscle rots on his filthy bones. He looks at me through gemstone eyes. Above the jagged cracks crisscrossing his skull, he wears a golden crown encrusted with diamonds. He grins at me through dingy teeth as a vat of green venom vapor pours from his mouth. The fire at the end of his bony arm extinguishes itself as I see that Marissa and Helen have waded through the bones into a sea of shimmering gold.

Golden coins scatter yellow light through the cavern, and as I watch, the man beside me morphs into a living human. Growing new skin and fresh clothing to cover his bones and muscles, he watches me through the emeralds glittering in his eye sockets.

"He who enters this lair must be pure of heart," he says, his voice clacking in his throat as though a wooden togue beats jaw bone. "I have ruled this ancient domain for over four thousand years, before the Olympians knew of us. Welcome, Kerry, Conveyor of Light and Shade. You shall have all you ever wish in our glorious city, but you can never leave."

"Thanks, but no thanks," I rasp. "I gotta get home. The wife is getting worried."

"Your companions," he rattles, "shall accompany you for a time, until they die, but you will find ten thousand friendly souls here to share our spoils forever."

I grit my teeth, glowering at him. "I'm not immortal. I belong on dry land."

"You cannot leave," the king reiterates. "You are my subjects forever."

I grip the caduceus in my right hand and scowl at him, inching closer to his face as the firelight at the end of my stick curls the thin batch of hairs on his scalp. Enraged, I press the caduceus into his face as the eyes begin to glow. One shot will end him. But then again, can the weapon kill someone who's already dead?

"KERRY!" Marissa turns around in shock when she sees what I'm doing.

I'm going to kill him if I can. A flood of hot rage courses through my veins as my heart blackens.

"NO! DON'T!!!" Marissa can't scream loud enough, because I have broken the Delphic Oracle's warning. It's too late. And the consequences materialize immediately.

28
The Bony King of Atlantis

The skeleton wearing the crown closes his gemstone eyes, relaxes, and inhales. His ribcage expands as though invisible lungs exert air pressure from inside his chest. When he straightens his spine, the eyes morph into green human eyes, attached to the skinless eye sockets via a red, stringy membrane. Baring his teeth, he glares at me as Marissa speaks. "Kerry, what have you done?"

Glowering at her, I lower my eyebrows. "Me? I didn't do—wasn't it supposed to kill him?"

The king cracks his knuckles and utters a dusty laugh. "The caduceus cannot kill the dead. Not even the ancient Titans can do that."

"It seems to have had the opposite effect," Marissa snaps, earning shocked expressions from myself and Helen. "You remember what the oracle told you?"

Bony uses the momentary confusion to give me a cockeyed sneer before breaking into a mirthless laugh. "Fools."

"You know what?" I say, narrowing my eyes. "We're gonna take off. Nice to meet you, Skeletor."

His laugh sputters and his pupils dilate. "Who are you to show such disrespect? You will never leave. From this moment, you shall refer to me as Your Majesty, King Hynas the Great."

My feet crunch on bones as I inch backward, golden coins clinking together as they roll away. Helen can't stop staring at the king. Marissa surveys the legions of skeleton parts guarding an enormous fortune scattered throughout the catacomb. As she glances around, I can sense more movement to my right. Body parts materialize out of the scattered bones, functioning feet, legs, and pelvises. The nearest skeleton pauses its own assembly, teetering on its wobbly legs, which contain several missing bones.

"Great, Sire," I say. "Tell your royal subjects I said goodbye."

"You SHALL NOT LEAVE!"

I tilt my head sideways and watch a pair of arms coalesce amidst the treasure. Their attached carpals and finger bones clench to pull them across the floor in search of a newly assembled body. They're up for a fight, but can they die?

"I just—maybe you'll reconsider." For me, stuttering only comes naturally when I have nothing of value to say and I'm letting in a bit of timidity. "See, my—I'm from Philadelphia, a mostly deserted place thanks to the Titans. But the man who calls himself mayor seeks your treasure to enrich himself and build a new empire in the United States of America. And the federal government, as inept as they are, will let it happen. They'll find your sanctuary, plunder it, and use it for evil."

"My boy," the king snarls, "the mortals know not where we rest. Our domain remains hidden from even the Olympians. Pride makes them think they can lay claim to this fallen city, but they shall never see its spoils. We're safe here, despite what your 'mayor' believes."

Helen stammers, attempting to gather her senses.

"And you blame the Titans for the demise of your city? Believe what you wish about my ancestors, Kerry, but the Titans are builders. Some of the finest architects ever known. Our city's graceful columns are reminiscent of their talents."

"I met them," I say, watching a pair of hands grab a skull by the mandible, lift it to the top of a skeleton body, and attach it to the neck. "Their grandmaster is in Tartarus, while the rest of them flee in defeat. Their new leader Coeus thinks he's got superior intellect, but they're nothing without Cronus."

The bony king adjusts his crown by pushing it down to his ear holes to cover a zigzagging crack that expands from the cheek to the eye socket, and over his cranium. "And who let them out of their prison?"

I swallow. "I did."

The mirthless laugh returns as the king tilts his head back and squares his elbows like a boxer preparing a nasty jab. "You, a mortal, in Tartarus?"

Frowning, I decide to challenge him. "What, haven't you heard of me? *The* Kerry Gearhardt, Conveyor of Light and Shade?"

If he had eyebrows, he'd angle them downward like one of those caricatures from a street artist. Instead, he bares his teeth, advancing toward me while his army constructs itself out of loose bones.

My heart sinks through my chest, but when I see a blur of red beyond the watery horizon line, energy pulses through my veins, causing my fingers to glow. I glance at Marissa and Helen.

"Run."

"Haven't you listened to me, Conveyor? None can betray me. The blood of Atlas and Pleione runs through my veins."

I wedge my eyes closed while the tempest of energy sparks in my heart. "You haven't *got* veins, *Your Majesty.*"

The skeletons throw themselves at me one by one as Marissa and Helen sprint towards the cave's mouth, where they meet a hundred sword-wielding skeleton soldiers intent on tearing them apart.

"Tiberius," King Hynas says without turning his head and flexing his bony fingers. "Kill them."

Tiberius launches himself at me, spearing me in the gut with his skeleton fist while summoning a golden blade from the loot beneath our feet. Bracing for impact, I feel my body turn to ash. Before I know what's happened, lightning fills the entire cavern. The moment Tiberius strikes me, his bones explode into splinters as blasts of lightning crush the advancing waves of skeletons.

A man wearing a sagging burlap loincloth concealing rotten flesh throws himself at me as the energy rebounds from the cave's ceiling. His assembled bones sparkle and glow when the lightning fuses his arms to his side and blows his skull off his spine. Still, he lowers his stature to impale me with his spine, which crumbles when it clashes with my body.

Confusion runs through the bony cohort and they back off. Behind me, guards hold Helen and Marissa captive. I spin on the balls of my feet, draw in a sharp breath, and lunge at them. Taking me as a more impactful threat, they release their captives and prepare for battle. I knock two of them off their feet, hearing their bones clatter against the floor, while spinning at the hip and grasping one sentry by the arm bones. When I yank at them, I expect them to come loose, but an unseen energy force binds them to the shoulders. Instead of breaking away, the arm spins with enough force to send the soldier back flipping toward the ceiling. I let go halfway through the motion, sending a blinding shot of energy through its bones. It glows as it blasts its two closest companions, who shatter on impact. The rest of them race toward me, as more and more skeletons assemble themselves from the cavern's floor to engage me.

Wrestling themselves free from the chaos, Marissa and Helen bolt to the catacomb's entrance, screaming as they fend off a horde of skeleton foes. When the king sees that I have defeated his chief warrior, he seizes a golden staff near his feet, aims it at my midsection, and shoots a slimy green liquid toward me.

I throw myself on the ground, causing the ooze to stream over my head straight toward Marissa's back. To warn her, I screech through a raspy voice, but before the glob of acid tears through her clothes, another skeleton builds itself out of the bones to intervene. The soupy attack crashes through its ribcage, sending splattering orbs of green throughout his bones, which steam like hydrochloric acid.

The distraction allows Marissa and Helen to escape, but something grabs onto my feet to prevent me from scuttling out with them. A dozen hands, detached from bodies, pin my legs to the cave floor. I claw at them to escape, but I cannot move. King Hynas marches toward me with two brand new guards wielding long shields and spears. He snarls and chatters through his teeth as his eyeballs roll around in their sockets.

"Die—honorably or dishonorably," the king warns.

"Not today," I growl, grabbing a fistful of coins in my right hand before the skeleton hands pin my arms to the floor.

Gathering the energy from deep within, I hurl the gold at him, watching it sparkle as it accelerates past the speed of sound. To accompany the flash of acceleration, an ear-crushing wave of thunder vibrates the ceiling and the floor. As though the gold coins can sense movement, they form waves that flood through the caverns, carrying a thousand bones deeper into the darkness. The treasure carries the king into the depths while I fight off the bony hands that pin me down.

"The Titans shall destroy you!" The king roars as I stagger to my feet, sprint toward the exit, and join Marissa and Helen on a grassy terrace where a spring water fountain flows from pristine white marble. I recognize the winged creature as a harpy before we reach it. As though it senses us, the statue flaps its wings and bends its knees to take off.

Before it launches itself into the air, the flowing water stops, and I point the caduceus' snake heads toward it. The eyes glow as the statue bolts off the ground, beating its stone wings in the air.

The magic stuns it for a moment as the life force inside it flickers. Grabbing its outstretched talons with one hand and gathering Marissa and Helen into an embrace, I steel my nerves.

In an instant, the fountain harpy bolts above the city's ruins, carrying us toward the surface tension bubble high overhead.

Grappling with us, the beast lunges its wings and exhales a powerful gust of wind just as our bodies crash into the water. The sound dulls my senses when the wind blows a bubble around us. Seeing that it has allowed us to escape, the harpy statue claws at the water, sending splatters of rain onto the stone street.

The three of us rise as the bubble carries us up through the dark water, past rotting vats of seaweed, floating sea life, and bits of plankton. Our bubble shatters as we surface. We gasp in the chilly water as the violent waves toss us up and down amongst the research vessel's wooden remains. The monster has not finished searching for its prey. When it senses us, it sizes us up, coils its enormous tail and arches its back skyward. Lightning flashes behind the serpent demon's unhinged jaw, highlighting a forked togue twenty feet long. It licks its chops when it sees us and charges.

Moving faster than the waves itself, it catches up to us before we can try to swim to safety. It zeroes in on us, and a goopy trail of drool coalesces on its ten-foot-long fang before dropping into the frothy water.

It lunges at us and misses, sending a plume of water up from the surface. Beneath us, the beast coils its tail into a spiral, straightens itself, and launches up out of the water. But the moment it splashes out of the depths, a pressure wave of light slams into it, disorienting it. To assess its new enemy, the monster recoils and saws its plated armor spines across the surface to attack. The pressure wave returns, gathering into a violent tsunami with enough force to confuse the demon. The monster teeters high above us before the wave sends it hurtling toward the distant coastline.

Marissa, Helen, and I thrash in the towering waves as they launch us towards Ibiza. Only one thing could have caused this kind of disturbance; my blood freezes when I hear the distant voice of a Titan beckoning me to surrender.

Marissa screams when she sees something dragging Helen under. She dives into the sloshing sea to save her, but I know it's too late. Gloom builds over the Mediterranean as a different kind of darkness spreads throughout the region. The Titans have grown powerful enough to destroy entire countries. If they set their sights on humanity, they will wipe us out for good. The only point of light I can see is their wish for ultimate power. And I'll use that against them one last time.

The Delphic oracle warned me not to use the power of the caduceus for ill purposes. Coeus laughs in the distance as eleven streaking balls of light circle over the rough seas, lifting the surf into a vortex. The whirlpool sucks Marissa and me downward, pulling us closer to a point of low pressure in the eye of a hurricane. Lightning forks across the sky, and before long, a robed figure with muscular legs and bare feet drifts out of the storm to settle above the water vortex Oceanus has summoned. His voice is cold and methodical, carrying across the waters.

"Kerry Gearhardt, Conveyor of Light and Shade. We know you have found the lost city of Atlantis. To make sure it stays lost, we shall destroy you bit by bit so that your mourners cannot identify a single piece. The Olympians will never know you existed. We will free the world of the Olympians' reign, ensuring peace while The One rises again."

I gasp, coughing up a stream of saltwater as I scream. The blackness invades my soul as Marissa swirls into the darkness, just out of reach. I can use the caduceus to fight back, letting Marissa drown, or I can save her, allowing the remaining eleven Titans to reestablish their despotic rule over humankind. Terror sears through my heart, crushing me with misery. Understanding at last what I've unleashed, I wallow in self-pity.

King Hynas, the son of Atlas and Pleione, and brother of the Seven Sisters, had descended from the Titan Iapetus. He alerted them that we'd found Atlantis. And now, I can do nothing to undo the worldwide damage I have caused. I let the Shade within me swirl into a cloud of coal dust to dissolve in the sea as I dive to rescue Marissa from evil.

29

Delphinus Circle

Saltwater begins dissolving the soot that my body has become. Without limbs, I cannot swim into the abyss to retrieve Marissa, making what's left of my heart wretched. Remembering that I'm mortal doesn't help. The moment Ian and Becky enter my mind, I concede to the gut-wrenching truth that I'm alone and outnumbered. While my abilities have gotten me out of many sticky circumstances, they cannot go toe-to-toe with eleven Titans whose powers have been magnified.

And since I don't have a voice, I can't call out to her. Somewhere beneath me, her spirit tries to wrestle free from the prison of her body, floating like an aimless speck of dust in the vast ocean.

Marissa, I try to say, *Listen to me. You're strong. Fight it.*

The Phoenix swoops overhead, her majestic amber wings ascending like the sun over the violent sea. Her song penetrates the chaos as though to drive it away, but when our enemies see her, they redirect their attacks. She dodges the first volley by diving, and the second by flipping upside down in midair, pulling her wings tight against her body and tucking her talons into her feathers. She makes herself into a torpedo, rocketing toward the whirlpool that sucks me down.

The moment her feathers touch the water, warmth spreads through me. Clarity beats its way through the darkness within, and when my dissolving ash pulls itself into a human form, my eyesight shifts.

For a split second, I can see for miles. Ian rows a canoe away from the shore, siphoning the circling winds the Titans have created. My heart leaps in my chest when I see the dark clouds towering over him like a sudden thunderstorm. Hoping that he has come to save my life, I dig deep for energy. Instead, something odd transpires; my extremities won't glow, because the seawater is absorbing the energy necessary to launch a counterattack against the Titans.

Even reaching for my happiest memories with Becky gives me nothing. The Phoenix has given me the power to fight on—to survive—even with the deck stacked against me. My heart murmurs in my chest and the world goes black.

When I open my eyes, I can see Marissa's hair floating like detached bits of stringy kelp. The hurricane overhead may carry enough power to dilute gravity's effects. The winds carry spray into the storm. Within the circling clouds, I see Oceanus spitting a deluge back into the sea. A flash of light tells me the other Titans are preparing to attack.

The first wave corkscrews into the vortex. The energy feeds into bioluminescent creatures, swimming away from the terrible storm. Aglae species burst with life as the towering waves glow green. Another flash of light blends into the water, and when I look toward Marissa again, I can't believe my eyes.

Faint blue creatures dance around her, blowing a million tiny bubbles to lift her to the surface. Dolphins. A dozen pairs of fins slap at the whirlpool as she surfaces. Floating face-down with her limbs splayed out, she's unconscious.

Hoping to thank the dolphins, I wave at them with my free hand as I swim to Marissa's aid. She is alive but has swallowed seawater. I try to compress her chest and blow into her mouth, but I can only make her fingers twitch.

A serene song echoes through the wind above me. The Phoenix will help rescue us somehow. But when a fiery body hovers beneath the clouds, anger flushes through my veins.

Fire Guy hasn't come alone. He's brought the NTO, his four Titan companions. When they arrive, the storm churns gray while a distant yellow and orange orb blasts it with solar energy. Heat makes the evaporation increase, causing the storm to grow.

Eos brings another kind of dawn. A calming presence permeates the seas, but the Titans have noted their arrival. To blast Eos out of the sky, Iapetus sends a shockwave toward her, but Prometheus blocks it with a fireball before it hits her. The pressure rebounds towards Iapetus, and Epimetheus launches a counterstrike. A shifting black mass of birds swarms in the storm, millions of wings casting pale shadows on the frothy waves. When Oceanus tries to send an attack his way, he misses the mark, loosening his grip on the whirlpool. The slowing water velocity should help me awaken Marissa, but the lack of centripetal force makes the task more difficult. I try to gauge what the NTO will try next.

Glowing sea foam floats around us, sticking to our skin and hair. Behind closed lids, Marissa's eyes roll as spiritual energy zaps her awake. The dead have helped revive her. I peer upward at the aerial battle while I wrap Marissa's arms around my back, swimming in the crashing waves away from the chaos. The sea foam pulses in rhythm with my heart, bubbling like a cauldron of soap. As if the whirlpool is reforming, the foam spins around us, glowing as it assumes the form of a woman. Her foamy hair tosses in the wind. She blinks in the seawater when she sees me. I remember.

She's an oceanid and a valuable part of the New Titan Order. Dione wipes the foam away from Marissa's mouth while spinning above the waves. A long shawl tatters from her neck and shoulders, highlighting her pale skin from head to toe. Trying not to stare at her, I swim up a monster wave to help her, but she carries Marissa too high for me to reach.

BOOM!

A black mushroom cloud expands through the storm when an errant fireball from Prometheus meets something concrete high above. One of the

Titans splashes into the sea as Dione floats away from the battle, cradling Marissa in her arms.

Trying to flee the chaos does me little good. The rolling waves make it difficult to discern direction. I can only rely on Eos and the sun to give me clues. No matter what position she takes in the melee, she always faces away from the rising sun. She launches fusillades of energy at the eleven Titan attackers, but they parry every blow.

Prometheus ramps up the speed with a pair of fireballs. He locks his eyes on the Titans' leader. Coeus sneers at him. He vibrates the waves and water vapor to mimic a human voice, groaning like an earthquake in the sea.

You are a traitor. Your service to Zeus is beneath you. Join us or die.

"He's immortal," I gasp, batting my arms against the crest of a fifty-foot wave.

SILENCE, you fool!

Never one to let wisdom intimidate him, Prometheus launches a flame-thrower wave of napalm toward the Titan leader, which evaporates into gray and black smoke when Coeus spins around it. He curls his lip at Prometheus, gathers a ball of blue liquid like a water balloon in his hands, and studies its weight.

The immortal may die in battle. A smooth feminine voice splits the swirling hurricane. A sudden memory leaps into my mind at the familiar voice. Theia, the progenitor of religion and justice. Her words are like poison. She is spinning circles around Ophion; even the Titan god of wisdom is no match for her. A string of white light wraps him tighter and tighter, cocooning him in the stuff of his own powers.

He's not strong enough to fight back. My heart lurches when I see him fall into the foamy seas. Eos, still with her back to the morning sun, reaches out to slow his descent, but too late to stop the turbid waters from devouring him. With his forces down to three, Prometheus sends another fireball at Coeus when Crius appears at his side, but the Titan defuses it by transforming his head into bighorn's rack. When he charges Fire Guy, he moves at the speed of sound, faster than flames can travel.

Crius rams Prometheus in the stomach, but Fire Guy is prepared for the assault. The Titan's horns burst into flames and evaporate on contact. Unharmed, he circles around Prometheus like a boxer studying his opponent's weaknesses. A white flash of light illuminates the battle in an explosion of blinding light. Bright enough to beat out the sun, it pulses as Themis exerts her powers. The light disorients everyone. I sink my head into the waves, searching for Dione, but she's disappeared in order to carry Marissa to safety, leaving only Prometheus, Epimetheus, and Eos to battle on my behalf. The seawater eats away the energy I need to fight back. I've used up my energy to fight the serpent demon. The longer I spend in the water, the weaker I'll become.

A sudden idea springs into my mind. When Epimetheus swoops closer to avoid a pressure wave from Iapetus, he emits a trail of smoke. I scream at him over the sound of the lashing waves. "Get me out of the water!"

He streaks away without helping me, but within moments, an enormous bird coalesces out of nothing, streaking toward me. To stop its momentum, the avian beats its wings, flipping sparkling droplets of water out of its feathers. The creature tilts its head sideways to peer at me as it plunges its talons into my shoulders. The saltwater magnifies the pain as the bird flaps its ten-foot wings, taking me skyward. Themis tries to blast it with light, but misses.

When she teams up with Hyperion, the Titan storm explodes. I can see nothing as the creature carries me away from the battle. Trying to dry off while in flight, I draw energy from the bird. It feels its life force pulsing into my veins, makes a beeline for the battle, releases me, and crashes into the sea when a pressure wave smashes into it.

Oceanus cackles with laughter as Coeus duels Fire Guy in the sky before making another wave leap out of the sea. Catching me by surprise, the descent makes a surge of energy shoot through my fingers. Lighting forks across the sky, blazing with heat and radiance, while Hyperion seeks to absorb it. My outburst hits Coeus square in the chest, along with at least three other Titans.

I cannot sustain the attack. I sink into the violent waters as the energy runs out of me. Eos sees me and sends out a bit of energy to keep me from drowning, but she's engaged with the enemy, the titan Mnemosyne, who pulls her hair into a bun behind her, and mouths my name as she erases every trace of evidence that Atlantis ever existed.

Mnemosyne pulses as the wind whips strands of her hair behind her and the front of her dress presses to her abdomen and thighs. She turns to aim an attack at me, but an undertow grabs me and pulls me under, making Mnemosyne's memory attack glance off the waves.

When Hyperion and Themis combine for another flash of light, Prometheus launches a flaming meteor at them. It burns into smoke when Iapetus tries to diffuse it with a pressure wave. The projectile slows down and splashes into the sea a hundred yards from me. Crius rams Prometheus in the chest again as he recoils.

Fire Guy collapses into the sea. A geyser of steam erupts from the surface as Coeus and the other Titans whoop in victory. Epimetheus dives into the sea to save his brother while Eos darts toward me, scoops me out of the water, and flees in defeat.

The Titans roar with laughter as we streak across the sky, their cheering voices joining the chorus of the whipping waves. Even without Cronus, the Titans may enjoy enough power to rule the world. My heart sinks when I remember Ian canoeing away from the Italian coast to save me. I can no longer decide if that was a dream or a result of the Phoenix's powers, but I know I can't take it for granted.

For some reason, Sarah wants me to comfort him, to train him to use his powers. I still haven't told Becky. Will she ever forgive me for keeping it a secret if he accidentally floods the lake house?

The truth stings deeper than any hurt I could have imagined, lingering with me as Eos streaks toward Libya. The Titans remain loyal to The One True God of Darkness, Erebus. And if they get their way, evil will thrive, and humanity will face its last war. Nothing can stop that from happening now. All because of me. The Delphic Oracle never fails to predict the future. Her master Apollo must now join another war after enduring tragedy and the fall of his temple at Delphi.

I'm not powerful enough to join an epic fight. I must rely on Ian and the twelve Olympians. My next move will be to warn Zeus about what's coming, and tell him where I'd found Atlantis, but coping with the loss of so many friends burdens me.

I never had a strong relationship with Ophion or Prometheus, my allies, but Marissa has always stood with me, ever since I met her. Sarah has guided me through it all, a loyal speck of firelight traversing the skies to watch over me. But the loss that hurts the worst is Helen. Whether descended from Helen of Troy or Clytemnestra, her life was in my hands. Her death will weigh on me forever.

30

The Tutelary Goddess

I pass out during the flight, having lost consciousness as we approached what must be Africa. The shipwreck, the darkness, and the battles had destroyed my sense of direction, and only Eos' arrival helped right my bearings.

I cough as she stands over me, gazing down at me in pity. She wears a single-shoulder white dress with a brass ring clasp at her right shoulder, and she carries a slender staff with a carved knob. As though checking for the time, she glances skyward once or twice as the end of the hurricane blows out beyond the rocky shore. Sand surrounds us. I cannot guess how far from civilization we must be, or whether I'll ever make it back to Athens.

My throat aches from coughing up saltwater. Eos lowers her eyes to scan the vast Mediterranean. Thirty feet below us, the water crashes into the jumbled rocks, and towering waves smash the shore, sending plumes of spray high into the air. I can feel the spume landing on my face as I struggle to my knees in the sand.

"I do not understand," she says, as though contemplating something bigger than herself. "Why did you not fight?"

"Couldn't," I cough. "I think the saltwater sapped my ... it doesn't matter. I need to speak with Hera and Zeus, tell them where I found Atlantis."

She glances at me and draws in a breath. "You found it? It's real?"

Nothing feels like an acceptable answer, so I bow my head forward and lay my forehead on the sand, closing my eyes.

"All this time ... and you remember it, so Mnemosyne didn't hit you."

"That's what I figured," I say. "Where's Marissa?"

Eos frowns, relaxes her shoulders, and lets the hem of her dress rest on the sand next to me. Her buckled sandals are caked with wet and dry sand. Beneath her soles, irregular gravel clicks when she moves her feet. "I was not aware you had a companion."

"My friend," I correct her. "The same one I was with during our emergency meeting in the suburbs ... Phoenixville. Which I'm sure they chose for a reason. She was alive. Dione saved her."

"We must regroup," she says, lowering her voice and touching it with a glimmer of sadness. "Though only four of us remain."

My voice cracks when I ask, "Are Ophion and Prometheus really—"

"Their fate will be revealed soon," she says, "but we must go on as though we've lost them. Though we are immortal, we are not immune to battle."

"Get me to Olympus, or wherever they hang out. But not without Marissa."

"You realize another war has begun. Flawed as their means are, the Olympians will wish to seize the lost city, while the Titans aim to preserve its secrets. For what ends, I know not. But we shall soon find out."

I'm not interested in another war. Her tone of voice suggests empathy, or at least an incentive to state the facts so they don't hurt. Even if this war is my fault—again—I must not fight. My family needs me, and so does Philadelphia.

"I'm going home after I talk to Hera. I'll stop by Reading before making my way upstate, where Becky is pacing in the living room, chewing her split ends."

"Your motives are pure," Eos says, "but one thing I wish to know ... assuming the inhabitants of Atlantis are dead, how did the Titans know where to find you?"

I haven't had time to form a solid explanation, but I tell her everything I know about the king, his relationship to the Titans, and his wish to keep us forever. Leaving out the part about using the caduceus on him makes me feel dishonest, but she sees through it straight away.

She watches a flock of seagulls circling overhead, she lets her shoulders slump and breathes in the moist air. "You made a mistake. And the caduceus ... will the gods find it in Atlantis?"

I cough as I realize I've lost it. Dr. Katsakis in Athens might write Marissa, Helen, and me off as shipwreck victims. But with his prize possessions gone, will he forgive us if he learns we've survived? My heart pangs in my chest when I remember Helen. She didn't deserve her fate. If I get back to Philadelphia to rescue her and Gus, Ash might beat in my face with the butt end of her handgun, but I'll have earned worse.

"So ... Marissa? Dione?"

"Your friend will be safe. Dione is a sea nymph. We shall wait here for her and Epimetheus. We agreed to come here if the battle turned ill."

"The Titans are stronger than ever," I say. "We—the Olympians—had their hands full last time they faced off. I hate the thought they can reunite with Cronus and Erebus, but it might be possible."

"We will strategize around that possibility. The Titans will strike again soon, and when they do, we will respond. With only three of us left, battle will be more difficult, but we have won under worse circumstances."

Another enormous wave rolls ashore. I see it building from a mile away. It crashes into a tubular half pipe more than a half mile from the rocks. As I watch it, an uneasy feeling grows over me. The wave collapses into foam, and after ten minutes, Dione emerges from it, still carrying Marissa.

I gasp when I see them. Eos takes off and flies to their aid, leaving me behind. Moments later, a dung beetle rolls across the sand to flee a scorpion while the seagulls squawk overhead. Epimetheus lands in a puff of sand, shakes it off, and wrings it out of his hair before he speaks. I can see the sadness in his face, as if he knows his brother won't return. This information should be devastating, but my emotions cannot cope with losses this steep and frequent. Helen, Ophion, and Prometheus are gone before I can internalize any of it, because I still haven't gotten over the loss of Sarah.

"What shall we do now?" he asks, as though I'm the leader.

"Olympus," I say. Sometimes a single word is enough to release the trauma in my heart. I curl my knees up and interlock my fingers around them. Tears roll down my cheeks. He sits next to me and rests his hand on my shoulder to comfort me.

"We will go. I must report to Zeus."

I have no interest in speaking to the father of the gods. He may have earned my loyalty by stepping in to help save Ian and Sarah, but his arrogance annoys me more than any job foreman I've ever met, and some have had the ego to run for office.

"What is the next step in your quest?"

Shuddering, I try to form a complete sentence, but the only word that doesn't come out garbled is "Hera."

Rising out of the waves, Dione and Eos float above the frothy surface, draped in their white gowns. From where I sit, I think they resemble a religious image two gentlemen once shared with Becky and me. Something about a father and a son.

They float down and Dione lays Marissa next to me. As though she's dying, her eyes bore into my soul without moving as she wheezes.

"God, you look,"—*cough*—"terrible." Her voice is raspy and distorted, but her sense of humor is intact.

"You're one to talk."

"Ready to fly when you are," Eos announces.

They scoop us up off the sand. As we soar over the Mediterranean towards the dying cyclone, I can hear Marissa's voice echoing through my mind.

We've emerged on the other side. Marissa rasps, clears her throat, and continues. *Do I need to explain what this means? Miriam was right all along. Sarah has outlasted it all. The war, the strife, even mortality. The Phoenix represents a progression of time but is immune to its effects.*

I let my heart speak to her. *You mean Miriam has been teaching you—how to defeat time?*

It's more complicated than that. She knows how the Phoenix works. Her tears can heal wounds, her appearance can guide us to the best choices and offer protection from harm. And every time she's reborn, her ashes bring life. And energy. A gift.

Rushing through the air at hundreds of miles per hour makes hearing speech impossible, but I can read the emotion on her face. Her words hit me right where it hurts the most, but where I most need to feel them.

Are you saying she *gave Ian his ability?*

Her eyes are haunting. They sparkle with the energy in her spirt, dancing to the understated melodies between the movements of a symphony. *In a way. But you were the one who gave him the ability to harness it. If your powers work on emotional energy, you can assume his do, too.*

Because he's a Titan.

A Titan of Storm and Sun.

When traveling near the speed of sound, time feels like it's standing still. Eos, Dione, and Epimetheus land on their feet on an expansive marble floor that stretches between ornate limestone pillars. Archways supporting molded lintel beams cut through the breezeway like a grand corridor. The New Titan Order members ascend the granite steps. The journey has allowed Marissa and me to recover enough to walk. I run my hands along the smooth, white stone railings as we ascend to a twenty-foot-wide walkway. At the top of the curving steps, the staircase flares to make a curved T-shape opposite the carved double doors that lead into the throne room where I first met Zeus.

Marissa remembers it, too. She grips my hand, helping me into the hall while the three surviving members of the NTO cross, nodding at a man carrying a chrome serving tray at the other end of the corridor. He gives them a smile and disappears into a hallway as we enter the throne room.

I expect to see Zeus sitting in the claw-footed chair at the end of a long row of marble columns, but a woman sits there instead. Her robes glimmer with flecks of gold, and her brown hair glows in the distorted rays of sun pouring through the glass panes. The gilded curtains are open, fluttering near the floor. She watches us approach and Eos, Epimetheus, and Dione all bow humbly before her.

The goddess wears a silver diadem in her hair, with a matching set of right-angle spiral earrings dangling from her ears. Her expression changes from dismay to sadness.

"My lady Hera," Eos, greets her, "we come before you in desperation. The remaining Titans have evaded capture for a year, growing more and more powerful. We defended our newest member from their attack."

Hera's voice is firm, her face expressionless as she looks at me. To avoid eye contact, I glance at the swirling marble floor and the golden gleam of reflected sunlight. "Kerry, Conveyor of Light and Shade. You should have stayed home with your family."

I don't dare speak to her. "I'm afraid you can blame me for that, M'Lady," Marissa says. "He came to help me investigate the death of a beloved mayor, and our quest led us here."

"We seek an audience with Zeus," Dione says. "We must make plans."

"And you wish me to go with them?" Hera says, staring at me.

I step forward a few paces and allow myself to glance at her face. Her skin is pale and warm, as though the sunrise has magnified her matronly powers. I look down at the white-strapped sandals beneath the hem of her robe, which gathers flecks of dust from the marble.

"I must speak to you alone," I say, trying to smooth my voice.

Marissa stands next to me and nods. I don't have the heart to tell the goddess everything, but Marissa speaks for me. She lays the groundwork by revealing how the Freedom Brothers and United Philadelphians for Progress have tightened their rule over the afflicted city. When she finishes filling in the background, I feel my emotion increase the tension.

I explain the FB's penchant for murder, their captives, and what they plan to do with the riches in Atlantis. Telling her everything sounds like a bullet-point list of events leading up to this moment, but I know Hera is following me.

"It is a curious position to take," Hera concedes. "I would say that he mistakes me for another, but Carlos indeed knows who I am—my virtues and my vengeance. I protect women in childbirth, celebrate marriage and unity, and help heal those afflicted by battle. Building empires is not in my repertoire."

"But his reasons for wanting your help are obvious," I remind her, hoping to make her think about the Omphalos stone, the Ouroboros ring, and the oracle at Delphi.

"The cow and the peacock are sacred to me," Hera admits, "for my husband had an affair with Io, my priestess in Argos. In my vengeance, I turned her into a heifer, but she was my servant. Zeus gifted the heifer at the behest of Mother Gaia and created the violet. I contracted the giant Argus Panoptes to watch over Io and prevent Zeus from visiting her. But Hermes slew him. To thank Argus for his service, I decorated my peacock with his many eyes."

I knew part of the story, but then I ask her about the Omphalos stone, the temple at Delphi, and her demeanor changes from regret to hope. She arches her eyebrows and continues, "My mother Rhea wrapped the stone in swaddling clothes to deceive Cronus into thinking it was Zeus, to prevent him from being eaten. The Omphalos is the navel stone placed at Delphi, the center of the earth. Apollo defeated the earth spirit Python and buried it beneath the stone when he built his temple."

I frown when the images of serpents pass through my mind. "But why the snakes? They're everywhere. The Ouroboros, Python, the caduceus."

"Snakes represent eternity. They symbolize wisdom, healing and prophecy. The Delphic cult of Apollo idolized them. The caduceus and Ouroboros for rebirth, and the cyclical nature of life and death. Serpents guard Athena's palace to keep her safe and grant her wisdom."

"Mayor Carlos wants the Ouroboros ring," I blurt out. "He knows who wears it—a friend of mine who ... who shouldn't have even lived this long. He wants you to help embolden his reign because of your connection to life and childbirth."

"But without the alleged treasure in Atlantis, you believe he won't succeed?"

"I believe there's something bigger at play. Because we found another Omphalos sealed in an underground chamber in our city. He knows your parents were Titans, and he knows the Titans were the ones responsible for creating the power vacuum that he used to gain control. Allied with the Titans, he can reign with terrible might."

"My father is no ordinary Titan," Hera warns.

"He's evil," I say, hurrying through my sentence to focus on what matters the most, "but he's in Tartarus, where he belongs, with his master. Get Hades to increase the guard, because the Titans aim to release them for world domination."

Hera furrows her brows as I finish my warning.

"The oracle foresaw this war. She warned you not to use the caduceus for ill, and you did so anyway."

I stammer, "I was angry because the king wanted to keep us locked in Atlantis forever. I was defending my friends."

"But the caduceus cannot kill the dead," Hera argues. "Thus, it reanimated him so that he could send the message to Atlas that a Titan of Light and Shade had discovered Atlantis and the treasure within. You are reckless, Kerry."

"My wife agrees with that," I say. "But don't you see? You have no choice but to help, because not just Philadelphia is at stake. The entire world is ... again."

She winces in the sun driving through the high, arched windows. "Because of you, *again*. If I could strip you of your powers, Kerry, I would—because you do not use them for good. You have allowed yourself to become an agent of the same evil you seek to defeat."

She sighs a final, exasperated breath, adjusts her diadem, and combs her ringed fingers through her silky, curled hair. "But alas, you are right, I now have no choice. I will go with you to Philadelphia and help you restore order to your city. After this war abates, you shall never again interfere with the world. Zeus will not stand for it, and he will kill you."

31

Serpent's Tail

The Parthenon floats in the clouds, letting bright sunlight shine through its tall arched windows. The light makes pie-shaped patterns on the floor. Marissa looks out at the thick fog below the palace. The mist makes the ancient city feel like a heaven, filled with powerful gods and goddesses who can be both angry and proud. If Becky could see this place, she'd notice the irony at first glance, whereas it had taken me two visits to understand the nuance. I don't mention it to Marissa. She's silent, maybe contemplating humanity's future. If Hera is right, we may last less than a decade. This is true regardless of the Titans' wrathful plans. Blaming everything on the Titans is like saying the destruction itself has an evil plot.

Of course, Hera was right to blame me. Over the years, I have honed my talent for screwing up, and that's one ability I may never learn to control, even with Becky's help.

Ten minutes ago, Hera stepped away to consult with her husband, whom I imagine is arguing with Epimetheus, Eos, and Dione about what the coming war entails. I want to avoid getting involved, and not just because I despise Zeus.

Marissa taps her toes near the dental-patterned baseboard along the wall. The arched windows illuminate stone statues of the goddess Athena and her exploits. One carving depicts her with wings and a crown of vines, but upon closer inspection, the real subject must be Nike, the goddess of victory. Shown without Ares, it could symbolize many things.

"How do you expect we'll get to Philly?" I say in a monotone so low Marissa might not hear me. "I mean, I guess the rental car company might have to cut their losses if we don't go through the airport."

"Hopefully we'll fly," Marissa jokes. "But the Neato are no better at flight than Transnational Air."

"Faster, though," I say.

"No in-flight meals, or infotainment screens, or flight attendants serving alcoholic beverages."

"Uh…"

"Which I could really use right now. You?"

"I don't suppose the gods will offer us wine."

Tilting her head as though tipsy from too much alcohol, she slurs her speech. "Might have to sacrifice a firstborn if you think Dionysus isn't generous. But I hear he was a party animal."

"Maybe we live it up with him on our next trip."

She chuckles. "*Your* next trip might well end with your head on a silver platter."

Shrugging, I hit back. "Better than Cronus eating me alive."

Fifteen minutes later, Hera pushes open a set of double doors on the opposite side of the great hall. If Zeus takes the Titan threat as seriously as he should, he will assemble the major gods to plot a course of action.

Hera waits for a muscular guard to enter from the corridor. He wears a pair of suspenders attached to dingy corduroys with brass carabiners, over a tight white T-shirt.

He matches our pace through the hallway, down the curving steps, and onto the veranda. A line of high pillars marks the back border of the plaza, behind which grow vines and rosebushes along the rocky edge. The cliffs drop into white fog and we cannot see far, but overhead the deepest azure stretches to the horizon.

"What shall be our destination in Philadelphia?" Hera asks.

I waste no time thinking. "Independence Hall. The historic district."

"Brash move," Marissa sneers "Maybe they won't kill us."

"It will be late at night," Hera says. "I do not come to fight for you. Only to negotiate with your leader."

"Mayor Carlos is not *my* leader," I retort, scowling.

The well-built stranger flexes his pectorals, making his T-shirt ripple. He towers over us, at least seven feet tall. "Ajax, you will bring Kerry. I will fly with Marissa."

I exhale to prepare for Ajax's iron grip, and close my eyes. Liftoff is more gradual than I expect, although we're leaving the fog-shrouded palace behind as fast as a rocket. Ajax takes me higher and higher, and I wheeze in the thin air.

My escort laughs above the howling winds, and barks my name, telling me to blink. I do as he says.

When I open my eyes, we're floating westward in darkness above a row of thunderstorms that march off the East Coast. Unimpeded by high pressure air, cloud cover, and light pollution, the stars decorate the earthly dome with a million points of light. Marissa and Hera drift next to us, and I take a moment to gaze at the Big Dipper, trying to remember its significance. For some reason, the name Vanessa lurks in the back of my mind.

We dart through the clouds, slowing as we barrel down from the heavens into a sea of light surrounding a gaping black hole—Philadelphia's halo—and we descend into the heart of our city. The moment we touch down on Market Street, the city erupts into chaos. Armed agents flow from the shadows all around us, pointing automatic weapons at our heads. The Freedom Brothers have been expecting us. A shroud of dark spirituality lingers in the streets, emanating from the Second Bank building.

I feel my throat tighten as a procession of men and women wearing camouflage march along the center of the street, carrying a cherry wood coffin. I know what it means before anyone speaks. Misery crushes me. It's like a boulder in a mudslide. I can't breathe.

I surrender. The men bind our hands and we are marched into the refurbished building. Our heels squeak on the polished granite floor. Renaissance art adorns the chartreuse walls interspersed with white-painted half pillars spaced fifteen feet apart. Clicking heels and firearms haunt the Freedom Brothers headquarters.

The men escort us into a narrow pass-through, an unmarked inlet with a pewter knob door and a peephole. I don't remember Carlos's throne room allowing passage from the main halls, but then again, I had just crawled out of the sewer and hadn't adjusted to the dim lighting.

A man with broad shoulders and a chiseled jaw kicks the door open and pushes Ajax inside. He's so tall his head hits the top frame. Marissa steps in right after him, accompanied by a tattooed man with a flattop haircut who's leading her. Hera slips through the opening on her own, while a stocky woman shoves me from behind.

Mayor Carlos watches me from his upholstered throne, crossing his legs and sharpening his menacing stare. Misti stands beside him, wearing her black leather pants and a band T-shirt. Her dirty blonde mohawk lies limp over her tattooed scalp, and a studded choker is clasped around her neck. She snarls furiously at me as Carlos begins to speak to his new captives.

My eyes flit to where Ash, Gus, and Liana had been tied. The walls still bear the shackles that tied them, but the FB thugs have moved the prisoners—I can't tell if they're still alive.

"Fine day for a funeral," Carlos says, speaking with a false air of patience. "Would be a shame if we had to soil the occasion with more senseless deaths."

"What do you want?" I croak.

"Do you not understand whose life of service we are commemorating here today? Military fanfare, with our permission of course, never looked so good in this city. You might remember him as that flea-ridden hobo you once communed with right out there on Market Street. Secretary Harley K. Whitworth, Jr. A man of honor. And the former owner of this."

He reaches into a pocket in his dark purple robe, withdraws the iron ring, and turns it in his fingers before slipping it on.

"The Ouroboros grants eternal life. And now, with you all here, I'm going to persuade the mother goddess Hera to endorse our grand government. Such a monumental day, wouldn't you agree?"

My heart ignites with fury the longer I look at him. Without the woman restraining me, I might just leap across the room and strangle him. Energy crackles in my veins as a profound blackness envelops my spirit. I never got the chance to introduce Becky and Ian to the wisest man I ever knew. Feelings of regret swirl through me like a raging storm of agony over a scarred, barren landscape. I can feel my bones vibrate as the dark energy overtakes me.

A moment later, I'm lying flat on the floor, and a hundred enraged voices scream through the halls and the throne room. Encircled in darkness, I read cursive words scrawled on yellowed paper, laying out the will to the secretary's estate. It names me as the sole heir to Calvert Manor, and Mayor Carlos is wearing my ring.

32

The Coup

Darkness defines me. It leeches into every thought, devours every emotion, and claws at the inside of my skull like someone trapped in a casket. I cannot speak or comprehend words. Searching in the black, desperate to escape, I picture the Phoenix. As time swirls into an endless hurricane, I might succumb, but then I hear Becky's voice, a distinct murmur instilling a ray of hope. A crack appears in the dark, allowing a flash of white light to zigzag through me. When the storm expands, I can see Ian clinging to life as he begs me to make it stop. The daemons are shredding him, yet his emotions only enrage the storm.

Another flash, this one red and orange, makes me crackle with energy. A foreign power builds within me even while Ian's voice cries out in the dark. A torrent of rain unleashes a flood that will punish the grieving city. Ian is mouthing my name.

Before the flood sweeps me away, a flame circles in the dark. I watch the bird as it soars overhead, gliding in the chaos and swooping lower.

Grab ahold.

My blood turns to ice, but her voice still reaches me. Denying her might be a death sentence, but I'm all out of tricks.

Trust me.

Trust is the ultimate double-edged sword. It can soothe a wounded ego and bring possibility to the dire, or it can poison the last vestiges of hope. I have no choice but to trust the Phoenix.

I reach both hands over my head and she does the rest. As she wraps her feet around my fingers, I can feel her hot feathers. She lifts me from the abyss and in a brilliant flash of red, returns me to the FB headquarters.

Marissa kneels over me as my eyes adjust to the brightness in the room. She places her hands on my chest as though she's about to administer CPR. This moment tells me more about myself than I could ever learn about her.

She doesn't need to speak his name. I can feel him in her heart, see him through her eyes. The former watcher of Market Street and Secretary of Defense resides in her soul, transcribing a new identity in my heart.

Harley K. Whitworth, Jr. is a demigod, a descendant of Zeus himself. But his passing still floods me with misery.

Hera refuses to look at me. She stands before the mayor like a prisoner awaiting her sentence, her arms slack at her sides, and loose strands of her hair swaying in the draft. I hear a metallic screech behind me and contort my body on the floor as the service hole cover scrapes across the floor. The body of the dead woman who resembled Miriam is gone, yet the stench of her corpse remains.

"Don't tell me," the mayor says to Hera, "that your powers of retribution are now impotent."

"I do not follow your wishes," she mutters, causing Carlos to sneer. "Violence never made a society great."

"We will bring an *end* to violence!" the mayor says. "And make our city as peaceful as ever, truly earning its nickname."

Marissa whispers in my ear as the first armed thug climbs out of the sewer, wielding a sawed-off shotgun, which he points at Ajax. Right behind him, another soldier climbs through the hole. I can hear raspy breathing as the black tentacles of an arm tattoo reach out of the dark.

"They've been discussing a treaty for at least ten minutes," Marissa says. "I think she's stalling."

"Your misdirection," Hera says, squaring her shoulders, "will not work on me. Release the prisoners and abdicate your throne."

"This *throne* is a culmination of responsibility, Your Highness. An assertion of control in a city devoid of order. If we allow lawlessness to continue unabated, it will threaten the world at large. Everything will crumble. And your self-righteousness will have achieved nothing."

Mayor Carlos deals in English like a renaissance painter deals in light. His words are those of a seasoned, well-educated politician. When rhetoric became the guiding principle of the American experiment, order began circling the drain. Yet no matter how bleak things got, there was always a battle to fight. Left against right, light against darkness, and morality against corruption. I've been following the public disappointment for over a year now, and have grown weary. If the mayor is seen to be offering a vision of light, he will attract more followers.More FB thugs climb from the hole and from a secret entrance to the right of the throne. With no visible door, the wall section cuts away from the surface, folding on itself, wainscoting and all. A sconce light hinges outward with the wall, and another band of henchmen bound through the gap.

"But then again," Hera is saying, "people want to believe in good, no matter the evil that surrounds them. You, of all people, should know that. Building a fragile façade of strength cannot crush hope. Darkness begets only darkness."Carlos glances at Ajax, then refocuses on Hera. "And that's where you come in. The matronly goddess will absolve the sins of a once great city. The people will bow to you, and together we will restore greatness from the ashes."

"Can you believe this garbage?" I croak at Marissa.

The mayor breaks eye contact from Hera, frowns, and addresses me. Even before he speaks, his contempt is obvious. "The Titan returns much too late to make any impact. How does it feel to watch everything you love die?"

Energy crackles in my heart. My fingers twitch as I stare at the Ouroboros ring on his finger.

"Careful, *The* Kerry Gearhardt. You wouldn't want to electrocute your friends."

I gasp. Behind me, a hazy white light shoots through the dusty air, projecting a bleak image on the black wall behind the mayor's head. He stares without raising his eyes, because he knows the exact picture that will saw a hole in my emotions. I blink as it comes into focus.

Ash, Gus, Liana, and Sparta gaze over the darkened, destroyed city with expressions of shock covering their faces. They struggle with the ropes binding them to a single power pole. Their hands yank at cords tying them to the wooden cross-members while power lines coil around their wrists. Through the image, I can hear Ash commanding Gus to kill Marissa and me. The venom in her voice is intense.

Before I can think about what I'm doing, I gaze into the upper corners where the walls meet the ceiling. Wires fixed to the wall with electrical tape run from the light sconces to the cornice, the bronze fixtures acting as grounding rods. If I lash out with lightning, the system will send a current through the closed circuit that will instantly execute the four freedom fighters.

"This is hardly the behavior one looks for in a leader," Hera admonishes, frowning and looking away from the flickering projector image. "If you want me to help restore love and glory to your city, you must release them, and every other prisoner you hold captive."

Is she proposing a compromise? I curse under my breath. What was that word I once accused Zeus and the Olympians of harboring? Hubris? She's just like her worthless husband.

"All is not lost," Marissa whispers to me.

Three dozen armed henchmen surround us, training a variety of guns on our faces. Ajax flinches as the gunman presses the barrel of a shotgun into his back.

"Very well," Mayor Carlos agrees. "Misti, send a cherry picker to get them down. Allow them to come and witness the show."

Trust me.

The Phoenix is speaking in Marissa's voice, planting the words directly into my brain.

Marissa closes her eyes, and when she opens them, an army of souls fills the room; they peer out through floating, glowing eyeballs. With a flinch of her eyebrows, she summons more spirits, terrifying the guards.

Hera snaps her attention from the mayor to Marissa as she blinks again. When she opens her eyes, six ash nymphs advance on the soldiers.

The gunmen open fire to destroy the new enemies, but their bullets only fly through them, to punch holes in the wall. As the violence blooms, the ghostly eyeballs flit back and forth angrily. To shield myself, I can feel that dark energy coiling within me. But Harley's power makes my fingers glow, preventing me from succumbing to the dark.

"Shall I have them kill your son in Reading?" Carlos sneers.

I'm going to kill him and take the ring for myself; the glow in my fingers sparkles and energy pulses through my body. Self-contained lightning bolts fry my hair and make my clothing smoke. Blue energy cycles through me as the true power of the Phoenix's trust blazes through me.

"Kill them!" The mayor snarls.

Gunfire blasts holes in the walls, punching through floorboards and ceilings. Marissa pushes herself against the floor as I writhe amidst the chaos. The gunmen aim at me but the bullets catch the lightning and send jolts of energy through the room. Three gangsters collapse as blinding currents hit them.

Ajax twists a thug's arm and sends him toppling into the man holding the gun to his back, seconds before the gun goes off. The bullet splinters the granite floor, and Ajax bludgeons three FB fighters on his way to the exit before he disappears.

The ash nymphs swallow eight more, pulling them into the underworld as the hovering eyeballs watch it all unfold.

From beside the mayor, Misti rushes toward me. I don't know how she's doing it, but she's attracting the lighting. It zaps out of me and into her, sending a million volts right into her flesh—but it doesn't stop her.

Misti grunts as she wraps her clawed fingernails around my wrists. The lighting flashing from my fingers plunges directly into her chest. I recoil when I see reflected blue light glinting off metal under her shirt. I can see links of metallic armor resting against her flesh, poking out from her T-shirt.

Chainmail. She's turned herself into a Faraday cage. My enemy knows me well. Guns continue to fire as another band of gangsters burst into the room to replace those lost to the ash nymphs.

I hold my breath as I hear hooves clicking in the hallway, just before Chiron comes into view. The Freedom Brothers open fire on the invading forces, cutting them down one by one even as Chiron tramples a gunman. A second later, a bullet rips into his abdomen, and he falls. His dying gaze rests on my eyes, a flicker of compassion in a blackened heart.

Misti flexes her fingers and digs her nails into my wrists as the lighting in me subsides. The eyeballs chant a chilling melody carried on a haunted wind, trying to distract as many as they can. As I watch it unfold, the mayor grips a television remote, ready to press a button.

Pretending to attack me, Hera blinks twice. The diadem on her head tilts slightly, revealing strands of gray in her hair. She extends one hand towards me, as though to stop the lightning. When she sees Hera helping to subdue us, Misti laughs, a hollow cackle that taunts the eyeballs.

With a flick of her wrist, Hera absorbs all the energy pulsing through me. Just before I collapse, I gasp when I see her other hand is outstretched behind her like a relay sprinter accepting a baton. In a flash, she transfers every bit of energy that she's absorbed from me and redirects it into the mayor's chest.

He doesn't have time to scream. His clothes burst into flames as the electricity plasters him to his chair. Dozens of armed soldiers point their guns at me, ready to shoot.

In that moment, all hell breaks loose. The ceiling collapses, raining crumbling tiles onto the granite floor. I roll away a millisecond before it crushes me. Marissa shields herself with her hands over her head, but seven more FB mercenaries collapse. The mayor's screams flood the air as Hera releases the energy stream.

Misti brushes off ceiling debris to confront the goddess, releasing my arm. Nothing I can do will stop the carnage. But when the overhead ducts rattle, I realize what's happening. Ten armed soldiers descend into the room, opening fire on the Freedom Brothers as they come down.

I recognize Baldy when he lands, pulls a hood off his scalp and stares at his enemies. An all-out battle is raging through the room. The United Philadelphians for Progress kill six more FB thugs with ease, and then the walls catch fire. The wires from the sconces into the corners burn, spreading flames through the walls. In a matter of moments, everything is filled with smoke as the fire spreads. Coughing while I attempt to shield myself from the burning debris, I feel Marissa gripping me under my armpits. Misti engages a younger man with a Glock pointed at her scalp, but he never opens fire. She squeezes his neck with her fingernails, causing him to unleash several wild shots. My ears are ringing. Another UPP fighter accosts her, but Misti slugs him in the forehead before he can shoot. Five, six, eight more bodies collapse into bloody heaps on the floor as the fighters volley gunfire between them.

When Hera closes her eyes, I can feel something pulsing through the room. The floating eyeballs blink out of existence and the walls fall into flaming ruins. Fire spreads into the corridors to devour the FB headquarters and the last remnants of the Second Bank of the United States. Spinning her hands, Hera harnesses the spirits' combined power and pulverizes everyone. Ten more bodies fall to the floor as Misti duels the last UPP fighter to the death.

She punches him in the face, but he parries and pummels her midsection. Her chainmail armor protects her from body blows and draws blood from her attacker's fingers. Realizing he's up against someone he can't beat, he backs away and sprints through the flames into the corridor, his clothes igniting.

In a flash of light, Hera disappears, leaving me, Misti and Marissa as the only survivors.

Misti dances around me, grunting with glee. With Hera having fled the melee, I cannot trust anyone else to get me out of this. I swallow my rage as the last of the wall collapses over the mayor's smoking body.

Misti cackles and Marissa scoots me backwards.

"You can't win, Kerry Gearhardt," Misti scoffs. "The city is hell because of you. They will hate you and kill you. The anarchy and street brawls will lead to mortal combat. The last one standing will rule this empire. And that will be me."

Marissa closes her eyes. "Maybe another day," she says.

And before my eyes, the Phoenix materializes, gathering the flames toward her. Misti has no time to react. She trips over my extended knees and flails over bleeding bodies, causing spent bullet casings to roll through the mangled T-bar grid and the broken ceiling tiles. She drapes herself over me, trying to choke me.

I can feel the life force exit my lungs as she squeezes. Powerless to intervene, Marissa pleads with her to spare me. Misti will become emperor of Philadelphia—but the Phoenix has other ideas.

The firebird lands on her shoulders. Bits of ash fall to the floor as its tail feathers ignite. The flames explode into a dissipating fireball, setting Misti's mohawk on fire.

Misti screams as she bats at her head, trying to pat down the flames, but the Phoenix is no more. She kicks at the bird's ashes as the fire devours her hair. Darting over to the mayor's body, I exchange punches with her, kicking in her face with a violent thrust of my leg. As I pull the Ouroboros ring from Carlos's blackened fingers, newfound energy pulses through me. Misti claws at my legs; blood pours from a cut above her brow onto the Phoenix's ashes.

The cycle of life and death sends a surge of energy through my veins, just enough for one last punch at Misti's chest.

She sees it coming before my fist can land. Instead, I transfer the full power of my energy into her neck. The power from my assault crushes her trachea. She keels over, gasping for air as her eyes glaze over.

Our only escape from the flames is into the sewers. Marissa drags me toward the service hole entrance, pulls me into the black, and we tumble into the turgid, sloshing water below us.

I gasp as smoky tears sting my eyes. If the mayor sent goons after Becky and Ian, will they survive? Somewhere overhead, as the former FB headquarters burns, the infant Phoenix shifts in the ashes. A sudden revelation hits me.

Breathless, I fight away the tears and the stench to say, "That was the UPP leader fleeing down the hallway. Let's find him and end the reign of terror once and for all."

"I can only hope Hera's on that one," Marissa says.

I shake my head, shivering in the water. "No. She's going back to Olympus to plan for war."

"We'll find him," she promises. "And if Ash and the gang are alive, they'll hunt him down and make him beg for his life."

By now, I know Ash. If she finds him, she'll kill him. No matter her motives, passion drives Ash's actions, and that will be her last visit to this city.

"That will create a power vacuum," I say as we crawl through the sewer. A soggy newspaper presses itself against me, and when I push it away, I swear I can see my own face gazing back at me through the black ink. The paper floats away, leaving bits of gunk on my arms as we slither through the sewers toward freedom.

"Our next step," Marissa says, "although it pains me to say it, will be to take control. We'll establish a new democracy and invite citizens to rebuild."

We crawl in silence as I consider the revelation the only way it makes sense. Sarah has become bigger than herself—bigger than life—and more important than even the Phoenix. She has transcended everything. And Marissa and Miriam understand how it works. Before morning, they will explain it to me.

I take big breaths as we climb to the street. The Ouroboros coils around my finger, wriggling as it sends life-giving energy into my bones. The Phoenix's abilities and the seal of the Ouroboros intertwine, binding Sarah and me forever.

33

Ion Lost

As night transitions into the early hours before dawn, Marissa and I wander the streets. An alley cat darts into a shadowy gap between two hulking beams bearing the weight of a crumbling slab under several stories' worth of rubble. From the street, I can see several smashed cars buried ten feet above me. My heart races when I hear a screeching meow, as if two cats are dueling over a dead rat.

"What now?" Marissa asks through clenched teeth. She looks a few blocks ahead, squinting at a row of leaning power poles that fade into darkness as they extend away from the downtown area. That type of question has never been unclear. I've always anticipated the next steps, even when it felt like conflict was impossible to resolve. Now there's a ruined city with no leadership structure, and everything feels uncertain. I can't give Marissa any answers, she must figure it out on her own.

"I mean with the Neato and everything," she says, not quite achieving solemnity. "With Fire Guy and Whatshisname down, there are only four left. Are you recruiting?"

I squint into the darkness. Along the river, the horizon is lit with a pale blue glow, reminding me that the sun always rises. "Looking for a job?"

"I know about a guy," she whispers, "that I think you should train."

"Ian?"

She shrugs.

"I won't let him fight our war. His family needs him." If I had nothing more to add, I'd just shrug it off and move on, but my feelings keep me connected to the idea. Everything that has happened so far can be traced back to my decisions, and regardless of whether he wants to be involved in the war or deserves to be, he can't escape the conflict. Just as Becky has always believed that everything happens for a reason, I understand that every action leads to consequences.

"But say you try to ignore his abilities. Bury them deep so no one ever knows. What happens when he causes another Hurricane Sandy?"

"They'll blame it on global warming," I quip.

"I'm serious. And don't you see? The Phoenix gifted him with powers for a reason. Because she believes in you. Are you going to deny her now, after everything? That isn't *The* Kerry Gearhardt I know."

A headache swells in my forehead as I gaze over the New Jersey horizon in search of yellow and orange hues. The longer the blue glow lingers, the more my nerves vibrate.

"Our first mission should be to save what's left of this hellhole of a city."

She raises her eyebrows and glances at my face. "You're the de facto mayor. What's your first official act?"

The only next step I can think of is to find Ash, Gus, Liana, and Sparta. I'm hoping my electrical outburst didn't fry them. If Ash is alive, she'll still try to kill me, though. For at least five minutes, the silence amplifies in my heart. It feels as though speaking will disrupt the rhythm of life itself. Marissa already knows we need to find the four, and she also knows Philadelphia needs urgent solutions. Even if she wants to impart the mayoral powers on me, I cannot accept. Because *my* next step is to find my way home.

A fallen skyscraper a few blocks ahead once glowed yellow as the rising sun glinted off its glass face. Now a cage of twisted steel and crushed concrete, it cowers in the shadows, entombing mangled cars and dead bodies. Once home to over a million and a half residents, Philadelphia probably has thousands of dead bodies. The next mayor will need to do more than rebuild supply lines, or nothing will change.

"There," she says, nodding at a distant power pole standing fifty feet high, beyond the financial district. While that single lodgepole column looks intact, it has no companions between which to suspend wires.

I can't remember whether the image Carlos showed me had other power poles in the shot, but I remember wires.

"Got a bad feeling about that one," Marissa says. "Let's go check it out."

After trekking several blocks nearer, we can see it from another angle. No other pole stands in the line, suggesting the Freedom Brothers had recently constructed it. As we continue plodding toward it, I make out a black form near the cross-member. Looking for the connecting wire, I trace a frayed black line from the pole until it disappears behind the skeletal remains of an eight-story building. Scanning the opposite side of the edifice to find the line again, I guess the wire terminates within the structure, and therefore connects to a transformer.

The circuit must be open, because Carlos and Misti had understood and planned for my powers. If they'd completed the project, they could have zapped the four suburban freedom fighters instead of using them to threaten me. In that scenario, I would be the energy source and represent the closure of the loop. They'd rigged the trap well, but left a minor problem. Without people guarding the pole, anyone could have climbed up to save them. The Freedom Brothers may be without a leader, but they have enough followers to pose a threat to any new mayoral candidate. They will regroup by morning, and Marissa and I cannot hope to prevent it without help.

"I see them," Marissa says. "In the mood for climbing?"

I shake my head. We could use the help of someone who can fly.

The last six blocks take longer than they should. Trying to avoid a source of commotion takes us several blocks out of line. A crowd is cheering on a duel between two evenly matched competitors. The whoops and jeers drown out the sounds of punches landing or weapons clinking, yet the violence leaves a mark on my heart.

When we're almost there, I sense motion in a black alley. Before I can react, the shadow sees me, and growls.

"Run," I breathe. But Marissa is closing her eyes. The wind shifts, and when the stranger sees a chilly reflection stirring in the air, he panics and backs away—right into the hands of a gunman. The assailant presses a handgun against the man's temple and dares me to approach.

"I'll blow his head off," he barks, "and then I'll hunt you down."

My hand flinches when I try to adjust my eyes to the light. During the journey, the horizon has lightened, allowing the warm yellow hues to shine through. The light adds detail to the victim's face. My heart races when I realize who it is.

"Quin," I mutter. Raising my voice, I shout at the gunman. "Let him go!"

"Yeah, what are you and your girlfriend gonna do about it?"

"You don't want to know."

Joaquin wrestles in the warrior's grip, kicking at his shins but failing to escape.

"That's what I thought. Run away like you always do. You're still powerless, Gearhardt."

The shimmering spirit Marissa summoned still hovers overhead. She tilts her head, preparing to summon another, but I already know she can't stop a bullet. I'll have to use intelligence to save Quin's life.

The FB remnant is identifiable by his clothing. His cut-off shorts are mostly clean, although dirt collects around his ankles and there are spots of blood at his elbows. He wears a black T-shirt, crisp enough to suggest it's new from the UPP storehouse.

"I won't take no for an answer," I snarl. "Let him go."

"You and what army?"

In an instant, the sun flashes, as though a giant bird's shadow crosses in front of it.

"Unhand him," a female voice says from behind me. Marissa opens her eyes to gape at the woman who has appeared behind me. I recognize her voice, yet the urban decay lends it a more earthen, less ethereal appeal.

The gunman releases Quin and tears through the dark alley, disappearing into the destruction.

Eos, the embodiment of dawn, stands behind me. Her three companions materialize out of the sun and land around us for a spontaneous forum.

"You are brave, Kerry," Eos says. "We are here to discuss the results of the Olympian meeting."

"I'm not ready for another war," I say, shuddering. "I'm going home. Try and stop me."

Epimetheus folds his arms across his chest. I can tell by his expression that Prometheus didn't survive falling into the sea. "We're going to give it to you straight this time. The Olympians have asked us to patrol the African coastline. Should any of the Titans turn up, we're to apprehend them. Zeus has decided to mount a European defense, dispatching heroes and goddesses to the Swiss countryside, and sending spies into Paris and Berlin. We don't know the Titans' plans, but this should get us some information."

My voice darkens as I speak to Epimetheus and Dione. "They remain faithful to Erebus. I think they intend to break him out of Tartarus."

"The Titans will fail," Dione says. "Hades has ensured that no one—mortal or immortal—can access the pit."

"Hades is a liar!" I snarl. "He's weak."

"And yet he captured Erebus using the Keres. I think it's a mistake to not show a little trust. Hades knows you destroyed his tower. He knows why you did it, and why it had to happen. It turns out that may have been Erebus's biggest miscalculation. We shall explain it to you in due time."

I glance up at the four motionless figures tethered near the power pole's cross-member. The wires still coil around their wrists. "I must go home. Becky needs me. And so do my son and my grandchild. I'm retiring forever, and nothing you can say will stop me."

Epimetheus struggles with what he wants to say. "I wanted to tell you something my brother told me." His voice trembles as though he's about to shed tears, yet his eyes stay dry.

I wait for him to explain.

"He saw something in you the day you broke him out of Tartarus."

"I *what*?"

"That's right," he says, "you can't remember it. Prometheus saw a man who values what's most precious to him. The bonds of love were pure, and it reminded him he once had a family—one to which he later pledged loyalty because of you. Your light turned him away from the shade. He promised to serve Zeus in life and death."

"We know how you feel about Zeus and the other Olympians, Kerry," Eos says, "and we realize you may never agree with him. But here and now, we must trust him, because the world's fate hangs in the balance."

"Easy for you to say," I rasp.

"Kerry," Marissa whispers, nudging me in the side and gazing at the sky.

Destruction has erased the light pollution Philadelphia once created, granting a broader view of the heavens. With much of the sky still dark, finding the Big Dipper in the Ursa Major constellation is easy. I stare at it while Marissa summons the courage to tell me what she's thinking.

"You owe a lot of people a lot of things; the former mayor, your friend Harley, the Phoenix, Becky, and probably even me. You'll never give everyone what they need, but you can find peace within yourself. I will start a new government and drive out the FB and UPP remnants. I know just the woman who can help. You may remember her as a descendant of a sorceress called Circe."

"Miriam's alive?"

She curls the corners of her mouth. "For now. She may have a year left, or maybe six months. We've spent the last year learning together. You were right; that's the secret I've been keeping from you. Miriam thinks she may have unlocked one secret not even the gods believe. And the Phoenix proves it."

"I respect your decision," Eos says, squaring her shoulders. "If we should meet again, please consider what we've told you."

The three remaining members of the New Titan Order prepare to take off. Before he lifts off the ground, Epimetheus grabs me by the hand and smiles down at the ring on my finger. "You hold the secret. Prometheus will rise again."

Before he can explain, he shifts his balance and flies away like a rocket. The moment we're alone, Marissa shrugs and breaks eye contact.

Quin struggles to his feet with a look of shock on his face. Marissa and I must now determine how to rescue Ash and her friends.

Climbing invigorates me. After deciding the dangers of retrieving the freedom fighters aren't worth the delay, I climb while Marissa and Quin guide me from the ground.

The pole narrows as it rises. At its base, reflective white stripes identify a hazard to prospective motorists, showing that the FB had repurposed it. Gripping the rusted, railroad-spike handles, I ascend while glancing down at Marissa every other step.

Reaching them takes a few minutes, and when I get within a few feet of them, I can sense Liana's feet twitching. She rolls her head around on her shoulders and opens her eyes a crack. She says nothing as I untangle the wires from her hands, disturbing Gus. He jolts his eyes open and glances at Ash.

Purple-black lacerations encircle Ash's wrists, throbbing beneath the wires as if her body has absorbed the latent electricity in the system. Still motionless, her eyes stay closed as her chin rests on her chest. After I untie Liana, I'm startled to hear Quin ascending the pole behind me. He climbs faster than I can, despite being older in real years.

Quin wraps Liana's arm around his shoulder and climbs back down. Marissa tends to her as Quin climbs up again behind me.

Understanding that Ash would want to be the last one we rescue, I loosen the wires around Sparta's hands. She flinches when I tug at the ropes around her waist but can grunt half-consciously as I hoist her over my shoulder. When Quin reaches me, I hand her to him, taking care not to let her slip. then I begin untying Gus.

Gus stirs as I unravel the ropes around his waist and feet. "I can do it," he rasps. "I'll get her down."

Quin leaps to the ground with Sparta's arms wrapped around his shoulders. Glancing up to make sure I don't need help, he leans as if to kiss her. She protests the moment his mouth touches hers, rolls him off, and coughs.

"Really?" Marissa jokes. "Mouth-to-mouth?"

"I'm CPR certified," Joaquin says.

Liana rolls to face Sparta as I help Gus to free Ash from the wires and ropes. She offers no resistance as Gus hoists her onto his shoulder and climbs down the ladder after me. If he falls, he could knock me off the spike on the way down, injuring or killing all three of us. His grip stays strong until we reach the ground.

He lays Ash face-up on the dirty sidewalk and purses his lips. Just before I look away, I see him leaning to resuscitate her. Keeping her eyes on Liana, Marissa shifts on her knees and hunches her shoulders.

We have a long night ahead, making plans to set up a new government, meeting Miriam, and escorting Ash and her gang to safety, but I'm ready for it. The Ouroboros ring pulses on my finger, and an idea comes to me.

Gus whispers to Ash to awaken, but she's not responsive. Tears run down his cheeks as he recognizes her fate. "No, please don't go like this. I never told you I love you."

Touching, Marissa mouths, glancing at Quin and Sparta.

Sparta coughs again, clutches her hand on her ribs, and tries to roll away from Joaquin as if trying to help Gus save his true love.

Nothing they can do will bring her back, but my heart flushes when I feel the ring pulse on my finger. Its energy transfers into my hand, carrying it toward Ash's lifeless body. Knowing I can do nothing to stop myself, I crawl to a stop even as Gus bats my hand away. He cradles her head against his chest and sobs as the tears pour down his cheeks.

The Ouroboros guides me. Slipping the ring off my finger, I feel the energy stagnate in my veins. The snake chases its own tail as it wraps itself around Ash's finger. In a rhythmic dance, the serpent fills her with its energy.

Gus shelters her head against his chest, tangling loose strands of her hair in his fingers. The energy from the ring brings color to Ash's cheeks, she opens her eyes, and now the ring rests on her finger as it completes its job. When she struggles against Gus's grasp, he utters a great sob of relief.

The emotion of strangers never hit me like this before. Sparta turns to face her leader while Liana watches. There is pain in her expression. Gus holds Ash until she wrestles free from his grip.

She elbows his face and scowls at me with all the hate I deserve. If she had the strength, she'd pummel me right now, but for a long time she doesn't move.

Her expression tells me everything I need to know. In my heart, I can hear her caustic words shouting at me: *You burn in hell, you bastard! I'll hunt you down and kill you for this.*

With my heart aching and tears welling in my eyes, I let my shoulders slouch. If Becky were here, she'd know what to do and might even try to console Ash. But Ash wouldn't have it. By now, I know enough about her. With her energy back to full strength, she sees the Ouroboros ring around her finger, slips it onto her palm, and gapes at it. Her lip quivers as her eyes burn with fury.

She balls her fist around the ring, bends back her arm and hurls it at me as though hoping it might explode as it contacts my head. I try to catch it, but it hits me in the forehead with a *pop* before clinking onto the sidewalk and rolling under a thin, splintered slat of wood. I retrieve it and immediately push it back onto my finger.

But rather than punching me in the gut, Ash lets her fury wane. Her lip quivers, and she closes her eyes, rolling into a fetal position on the ground. She fights Gus away when he rests his hand on her shoulder. Covering her face with her scarred hands, she screams, pouring out all the rage she can muster. The vibrations in the air hit my spine and scrape through my eardrums, provoking dread.

I can't endure how much pain she feels. She screams again, letting tears seep through her fingers while her uneven fingernails dig into her forehead with enough pressure to draw blood. Again Gus tries to console her, but she bucks him off and kicks him in the groin.

Over the course of my life, I have encountered few circumstances where I can say nothing to defuse the tension. Yet this tops every experience. When Becky first told me she was pregnant, I gaped at her and swallowed and my mouth went dry. And when she had to relate the news that her mother had passed away, the tears made her eyes so swollen she couldn't see straight. She didn't need my words; she only needed my presence. I held her until she fell asleep, never uttering a single word.

No matter what I say, I can never make Ash forgive me. Perhaps understanding that the Ouroboros had saved her life because of me, she refrains from attacking me. But I can never soothe a rage that deep.

Marissa places her hand on my shoulder to tell me we need to move on. Gus is rolling over, clutching his groin with both hands while Liana and Sparta give me silent thanks for saving their leader's life.

Liana coughs as Marissa helps her to her feet, and Quin gives Sparta his hand to help her. I dare not touch Ash. She rolls over, growls into her palms, and gets to her knees as I help Gus to his feet.

Together, the six of us limp among the ruins to the suburbs without speaking as the sun rises high over the eastern horizon. War is returning, but Marissa will generate Philadelphia's revival.

34

The Order of Cleisthenes

The former historical district is abuzz with rumors of a new order. A man with a white beard and a bell proclaims truths. Every few seconds, he hits the bronze bell with a stick, drawing a crowd to his sermon. Within half an hour, Market Street fills with weary humanity. They scowl and mutter as he speaks, but as he nears the end of his address, the energy starts to shift from frustration to hope.

I rest on a splintered wooden lintel that once invited customers into Miriam's shop. Although the building is reduced to rubble, something in the ambiance permeates my soul, finding a place it can blossom. For over an hour, I sit and watch the streets the way Harley once had. A couple limps along the sidewalk without speaking, and when they approach the man giving the sermon, they share a brief kiss and the first two steps of a slow dance.

"The United States of America was founded right here, only a few blocks away," the preacher reminds the growing crowd, "when we as a nation forged peace and a lasting vision of freedom. Somewhere, we diverged from that, and what remained devolved into tyranny after our great city fell."

The crowd groans.

"Now we stand on the doorstep of a new era, one promising those same inspiring principles our founding fathers sought in the beginning. Freedom! Justice!" He strikes the bell harder after each sentence.

"Philadelphia! The gangs must not rebuild. Fight for truth and be ever vigilant. Together, we can rebuild a democratic city. I want to introduce the man who will shape our destiny for a new age. He's a scholar, a gentleman, and one of the finest tacticians our city has ever known."

I know what he's about to say, but I can't let excitement reach a point where everything hurts less, because I have too much work to do before heading home. Marissa and Miriam are arranging one last meeting before the sun goes down. But for now, I sip from a flask of purified water and wait for the speaker to introduce the new mayor.

The crowd jeers, as though this puts them under the thumb of only a slightly better dictator. To encourage calm, he strikes the bell once more.

"My fellow citizens, meet Joaquin D. Robinson!"

Quin pushes open a ceremonial door they'd fished from the rubble hours earlier and built a frame around. He waves at the throng of hundreds and they become quiet.

"We must move quickly to establish a police force," Quin says. "If you are interested in keeping the peace, please approach me afterwards. I assure you we will rise together. This fall, we will resume elections for police chief, city council, and mayor. I have already assembled a small team of ambassadors to speak for us in Harrisburg and Washington. They will have their feet on the ground here, and you can speak to them in person any time you wish. Please be respectful. In this transition period, we cannot tolerate violence. Our police force will remove any instigators while we open our borders for supplies and aid so that we can rebuild."

I wince in the sunlight, take a swig of water, and close my eyes.

"Thank you for your sympathy, my fellow citizens."

As if they don't believe him, the crowd murmurs. I expect the man with the bell to start a chant of freedom, but as the crowd disperses, I detect an air of indifference. A woman with a cane hobbles past me, mumbling to no one. "More despotic rule," I hear her say. Her words seem like a harsh reality. A people trampled under the heels of ruthlessness can't immediately trust words of hope and reform, because the history of reform presents a timeline of decay, where society devolves year after year, bringing more and more chaos. To convince the citizens to change their minds, Quin will need to seek the people's approval for everything, down to the construction of a new fence. Only by leading by example and involving the citizens can he break the cycle of misery and distrust the FB and UPP wrought.

Quin shakes hands with a young woman, and when I see who she is, my heart stops. Ash has cleaned herself up, wears her hair in a braided bun, and has changed her clothes. Unsmiling, she accepts Quin's pat on her shoulder, turns her back without looking at me, and disappears into the crowd.

After deciding that no one else wishes to speak, he approaches me.

"Good afternoon, Mayor," I say.

He forces a smile. "Still feels dirty being appointed. The next six months will be busy. We're going big, building a new library, a new City Hall, police, fire, and emergency services. A hospital. I only hope Marissa can talk Harrisburg into opening their wallets."

"You'll make a fine leader," I say, "What did Ash tell you?"

"Just a quick thank you," he says, tilting his head sideways. Now in the daylight, I can see the gray in his hair. Age has hardened his face, putting wrinkles and lines into his cheeks and around his eyes. He looks wiser, but I still recognize him as a friend. Many years ago, we used to design characters, play video games, drink beer, and watch football. "She asked me to not be a stranger and to reach out if we need help."

"There won't be a *we,*" I say, frowning. "You and Marissa can always call, InstaText, whatever. But I'm going home."

"Family first," he says, shaking my hand and resting a hand on my shoulder.

"How will you do all that while running for re-election?"

He chuckles. "I've already decided I won't run again. I wasn't installed democratically. We must let the people decide."

I smirk. "You realize what that makes you?"

"A bleeding heart, hipster, communist traitor who can't be trusted, I'm sure," he says, grinning and then letting his expression droop. "Nothing we haven't heard for forty years. It takes a thin skin to do this job."

I don't have the heart to laugh at his play on words. "Don't let it become *too thin.* The people won't trust you."

"You've seen their faces," he says. "They already don't, and who can blame them? I wouldn't trust me, either, after what this city has been through."

I'm still surprised he survived the Titan attack. For a year, I didn't think he had. When we used to hang out, chat about strange women disappearing and even stranger "street watchers," he was always the brains of the pair of us. His gaming strategies always worked, a skill he'd learned in high school when he was in a role-playing-game club with our friend Kel.

"I have one more stop before I leave," I grumble. "You'll need to set up a communication and electric network I'm sure. I'll try to gather volunteers to engineer for you."

"If we get Harrisburg and Washington involved, we'll have all the engineers we need. But that will take time. And money, which we don't have."

"If I know Becky, she's already setting up a national donation drive so people across the country can help."

"You're a lucky man," he says, frowning. "Still miss Jamira. Never found her body, but it's been a long time."

I pat him on the shoulder, then wrap an arm around him before gazing to the sky and exhaling. "You know what happens when something ends? It opens the door for something else to begin."

Miriam has done some housekeeping. The swept entry way between crumpled building skin, steel, and concrete now lacks dirt, gravel, and clever booby traps. She leads me through the triangular doorway, pulls aside a makeshift curtain that hadn't been there last time, and pushes open the door to her lair next to the elevator shaft. A trio of candles flickers on the door table, and the polished knob reflects a golden halo that radiates through the room, bringing warmth. Marissa sits on a stool made of broken concrete and splintered wood. Carpet underlay is draped across its smooth surface, covered by a sheet.

Marissa motions me to sit next to her, while Miriam takes a plush red velvet pillow from beneath the tabletop, fluffs it, and sits on the ground. She wears the signs of accelerated aging from a year of chaos. I can't comprehend how she can sit on the floor and get up again. I'm far younger and I have trouble doing that.

"How's the new Mayor?" Marissa asks.

"I'd assumed you'd start hiring mercenaries," I reply.

"Considered it," she says, "but we need leadership first. If he's half as competent as you claim, he'll set that up in no time. And I'm sure Ash, Gus, and her crew will help keep the FB remnants out. What did she tell you when we left them at the city limits?"

I shake my head. "Some variation of 'I never want to see you again' interspersed with a few well-deserved F-words."

"She'll forgive you."

I shrug. How can I expect her to do that when I can't forgive myself? My meddling with time and space has caused everything. The war wouldn't have happened, and Philadelphia would be less of a sinkhole had I not released the Titans, even if I did do it for what I considered to be a noble purpose.

"How's Ambassador Marissa?" I ask, changing the subject.

"I made a few calls this morning, first to Governor Black, asking him to send in the National Guard. Can you believe he complained about how bad that would look politically? Like helping the citizens of your own state is a bad thing."

"Most people would just as soon remove Philly and most of its suburbs from the state entirely."

"And then getting on the horn with Senator Sherman isn't easy. Most of the time, no one even bothers answering, so you gotta call ten times, assuring the switchboard lady that you're someone important, and possibly lie about your wealth."

"God," I say.

Miriam sets a thick book on the table and thumbs through pages as though she's looking for a particular spell. Her white eyebrows are drawn together as she listens to Marissa and me discuss our city's political future, which I still don't have the heart for.

At least Marissa agrees with me.

"He said he'd talk to the president and try to build a multi-partisan coalition to assess our city's needs. Didn't promise anything, but maybe that's a good thing."

I nod. "And how much did you say said you'd donate to his reelection campaign?"

"Hey, if he's not making any promises, neither am I."

"How far out is the National Guard?"

She stretches her back. "A few hours, give or take. Sounds like Governor Black values people who are down-to-earth. I'm surprised he's lasted two terms."

"Ah!" Miriam croons. "The elixir of enchantment. Should work even better with that ring on your finger."

"Uhh..." I gape at Marissa. "What's she doing?"

"You may address me directly, Kerry," Miriam snaps. "The elixir of enchantment does three things: First, it evens out your energy needs. It makes your powers more predictable. And third, it fills you with the spiritual blood of the Phoenix."

"Right," I say, looking for a secret stash of potion. "You're talking about efficiency. Like how a water heater works."

"No, silly!"

She doesn't care how modern water heaters work, and who can blame her?

"Then where is this elixir?"

"It's metaphysical," Miriam says.

Marissa rolls her eyes at me.

"Of course it is."

"It requires the power of three," Miriam says. "We must join hands and invoke the Phoenix in our hearts. Emotions of darkness and despair will weaken it. And when we finish, we must speak the name of the Phoenix."

I grasp Marissa's hand while Miriam leans over the door and touches my right hand. The Ouroboros ring wriggles when it feels the heat of Marissa's grasp, and when Miriam holds Marissa's left hand, the lair spins, sending us into a dark ether lit by a single brazier.

The Phoenix swoops overhead, propelling thoughts through my brain. Becky's smile and her penchant for lighthearted jabs at my expense join with images of Ian running in the sand, while a blue disc hurtles toward him. As he leaps to catch it, I glimpse Sarah's auburn hair and the freckles on her face. She smiles while I stammer out words that can never make sense. Her spirit vanishes, evaporating into a sparkling red cloud that our bodies absorb. We close our eyes and spin through the night, and when I wake up, I'm lying next to Becky, resting my head on her shoulder and weeping into her pajama top while she holds me.

"Sarah," the three of us say in unison when the spinning brings us back to Miriam's lair. For a moment, nothing happens, but then I feel the Ouroboros ring transferring energy from me to Marissa. My heart melts when I sense her gathering energy from me. Her spiritual abilities will strengthen with the power in the ring. I hope Miriam can experience it too.

"Everything shall be different from this time forward," Miriam says. "We cannot stop the coming war. But we can pull through it stronger than ever, for we have transcended the mortal with the immortal."

I never wanted immortality. Lowering my eyebrows, I sense Miriam studying my expression for several seconds. "The living can never become immortal, of course."

That's a relief.

"The power of the Phoenix is in both of you now. You cannot be reborn from ashes, but through spiritual reawakening. Each time you do it, you will experience renewal. Do not let it go to waste."

"What about you?" I raise my eyebrows upward as though I'm about to sneeze and run my fingers along the beaded rim of the brass doorknob between my knees.

"I am an old crone," she says dryly, "I shall not last the year. Sadly, I'm the last of my line."

I close my eyes and let my heart sink. Age is driving all my allies to death, because time travel distorted my perception, and made me younger than I should be.

"Marissa," Miriam continues, "your spiritual sensitivity is already far greater than mine. Great things are in your future. You shall excel in your role as ambassador to Philadelphia and assume the mantle of Mother Circe as her new heir. Do you accept?"

Marissa turns her head to stare into my eyes. The Ouroboros wriggles on my finger, and energy spreads through my body.

"I do," she says. "I will use it for good. You have my word."

The session winds down faster than I expect. With every passing word, warmth spreads through my heart. I don't want to leave, but I must. I have a long drive ahead of me.

Ian doesn't come when I knock on his door. The dog barks and hurries through the room, beating its enormous tail on the door as it goes past. A few minutes later, Brianne opens the door. She's showing no visible signs of pregnancy. She greets me with a smile and tells me that Ian isn't home.

"We just had a terrible storm. Rain, lightning, wind. I hear a tree fell on an old woman's house here in Reading. Ian said he had to leave to protect me. I still don't know what he meant, but he might have gone to the lake house."

I gaze at Brianne and wrap my right arm around her. "You're going to be a fantastic mother."

"So he told you?"

"Of course he did," I say, trying to show her a false sense of comfort while the dog gallops through the living room, rattling shelves and tracking dog food across the carpet. Its tail knocks over an empty glass, which bounces off the table and rolls to a stop on the floor. "Listen, I know he's scared. For more than one reason. I'll talk to him, send him back home, and have him explain everything. Don't let it shock you."

"Why would it?"

"That's between him and you," I say. "He'll tell you everything you want to know, because he loves you."

Before I leave, I give her a hug, return to my car, and speed across the countryside to reach home.

The house is silent and dark. A pair of sailboats skulks between the island and the beach, gathering moonlight in the blue and white sails that send rippling shadows over the shimmering surface of the lake. Passing the bay window, I pause in the hallway, turn into the bedroom, and draw a silent breath before I change into my pajamas and slip between the sheets, careful not to wake Becky.

The floor creaks when I lift my right foot from the carpet and pull it beneath the bedspread. I let the darkness fill my heart with sweet shade as I close my eyes and feel Becky's hand on my chest.

A moment later, she kisses me and snuggles closer. I can't stop the tears from running off my face into her hair, wetting the sheets and the pillows. Everything hurts, and dread fills every corner of my heart. Yet the Ouroboros and the Phoenix give me strength, while the elixir of enchantment regulates my energy.

Just as it was with Ash, I can say nothing, because words will only hurt. Becky's presence is all I need. Her chest rises and falls next to me as she drifts back to sleep. I plant a gentle kiss on her forehead and wrap my arm around her. Moments before I fall asleep, I can hear the Phoenix calling me through time and space.

Becky rolls over, kisses my cheek, and mumbles a simple sentence that spreads fire through my soul, filling me with power. "Welcome home."

Glossary

Algea—The daemon spirits of pain, grief, and suffering.

Aphaia—A goddess worshipped exclusively on the island of Aegina. She is associated with fertility and agriculture.

Achaean—One of the names in Homer's works used to refer to the Greeks collectively.

Argus—A giant protector of the princess Io, he had a hundred eyes. In mythology, he served at the behest of Hera, after Zeus killed him to cover up his affair with Io, Hera put his eyes in the tail feathers of a peacock to memorialize his service.

Astraeus—The son of the Titan Crius and the god of the stars and astrology.

Atlantis—An island nation first mentioned in Plato's works as an allegory on the hubris of nations, theorized to have inhabited either the Mediterranean Sea or Atlantic Ocean.

Batterycar—A app-based ride sharing company that allows drivers to rent electric vehicles for short term use, similar to present-day bicycle and scooter rental firms.

Caduceus—A wand topped with wings and wrapped in two intertwined snakes, it was a symbol of the god Hermes. It is associated with various stories and lore describing where it came from and its magical properties.

Cleisthenes—Often referred to as the father of Athenian democracy, he played a pivotal role in developing a system where the people ruled, instead of the elite classes of society.

Clytemnestra—A central figure in Greek legend, known for her role in the events leading to the Trojan War. She was the half-sister of Helen of Sparta.

Colossus—One of the seven wonders of the world, it was a giant statue of the sun god Helios in the ancient city of Rhodes.

Delphinus—A dolphin-shaped sea daemon that served the god Poseidon.

Hynas—The son of Atlas and Pleione, and brother of the Seven Sisters, descended from the Titan Iapetus.

Icarus—The son of inventor Daedalus, who attempted to leave Crete using a set of wings made of wax that his father invented. He was warned not to fly too close to the sun or the wax would melt, leading to his death.

InstaText—An advanced text message system that sends encrypted text through local radio airspace instantly as the sender speaks or types.

Ion—The illegitimate child of Creusa and Apollo. Creusa abandoned him in his cradle and Apollo asked Hermes to take him to the Delphic Oracle, where he was raised by a priestess.

Leviathan—Sea-serpent demon.

Nemesis—The goddess of retribution, justice, and wrath, punishing hubris before the gods.

Nereids—The sea nymphs, known for their kindness and benevolence to sailors.

Omphalos—The stone Zeus placed at a location deemed to be the center of the earth, in Delphi. When the Titan Cronus ate his children, his sister-wife Rhea wrapped a stone in a blanket and disguised it as Zeus so that Cronus could not devour him.

Oracle of Delphi—An ancient Greek fortune teller and messenger of Apollo who served at his temple in Delphi.

Orestes—The son of Agamemnon and Clytemnestra, he is known for avenging his father's murder by killing his mother after the Trojan War.

Owl—Associated with the goddess Athena, it symbolizes wisdom, knowledge, and insight. It is often depicted protecting Athena.

Meliae—The ash tree nymphs, born from the blood of Uranus after Cronus castrated him. They are associated with the natural world and symbolize the cycle of life and death.

Mercury—The Roman equivalent to Hermes. He is associated with the element Mercury in alchemy, which symbolizes the transformative nature of knowledge and communication.

Pheme—The personification of fame and renown, her wrath was associated with scandalous rumors. She is often depicted playing a trumpet.

Phonoi—The personifications of murder and killing originating from Eris, the goddess off strife.

Plato's Forms—A type of philosophical realism claiming that certain ideas are literally real. Such forms are described as perfect, eternal entities that transcend the physical world.

Ptolemaic—A Macedonian Greek dynasty that ruled Egypt between 323 and 30 B.C.E, with the last ruler being Cleopatra VII.

Pyrophoric—Materials that combust in air at certain temperatures. Notable pyrophoric materials include alkali metals such as potassium. The term derives from the Greek word *pyro*.

Second Bank of the United States—A historic structure in Philadelphia, inspired by classical Greek architecture.

Strix—A bird of ill-omen. A chapter in this book uses the numbers 3712. The numbers 3, 7, and 12 are significant in many religions including Greek mythology.

Ten Labors—A series of tasks carried out by the greatest Greek hero Heracles in service of the King Eurystheus.

Theseus—Hero of Greek mythology and son of Aegeus, the King of Athens, and known for his many heroic deeds, including defeating the Minotaur in the labyrinth.

WalleTap—A company that uses a digital scanner, allowing users to wirelessly send payment without contact by swiping a physical or digital wallet without interacting with a human being.

Acknowledgements

I don't release two books in a year often and may not do so again. This year has been a whirlwind—one of the best years of my career.

Since avid readers have long asked about my writing process, let me lay it out here. As always, the journey starts with a concept. At the end of book three, I left one or two questions unanswered, not intending on a fourth book, trusting fans to use their own judgment about what happens next. Instead, the original concept was a stand-alone spinoff story about Philadelphia reinventing itself after the events of *Reincarnation*.

With that in mind, I tinker with ideas regarding where the story might go and rely on instinct to guide me there. As I often tell those curious enough to ask, I don't bother creating an outline, opting instead to let the plot build itself, and the characters to shape their own destinies. This leads to wonderful surprises, which I can't wait to share with you.

Near what I determine to be the halfway mark in the plot, I hammer out a basic outline of what might happen in the latter chapters. Because things don't always go according to plan, the process requires fact checking against itself to ensure consistency. Unexpected twists tend to cast previous chapters in a new light, forcing me to revise them to fit the overall plot.

I call it an imperfect strategy for crafting a story as perfect as possible.

At various stages, I rely on beta readers and send review copies for those interested in posting a review on Amazon or Goodreads. This serves two purposes: to gauge reader interest in the characters, and to identify possible weak points in the plot. I would like to thank author Bernard K.

Finnigan as well as Siren, Fire, and the rest of the ARC group. You're all amazing!

My journey as an author has grown as time has advanced. I've met dozens of local and national authors during events and made some incredible friends, who have helped refine my marketing strategies by giving me new ideas. My fellow Treasure Valley Authors, April, Merri, Jeanette, and Chris have proved to be invaluable resources.

As always, Jeanine Henning created the unbelievable artwork for all formats, keeping to the theme she established with *Revelation* while adding new elements as the story dictates. She turns a brief description of my words into stunning art and nails it every single time.

For editing assistance, I once again turned to Tarryn Thomas. Along with her associate Angela Tuson, they helped strengthen prose and tighten the narrative pacing, as well as catch the numerous typographical errors that somehow survive two previous passes. They do amazing work, and I'm thankful for their help.

Again, I want to offer my sincerest thanks for the tremendous support from book dragons across Idaho and Utah. I have a blast talking to everyone and meeting new people. Next year, I hope to expand my reach into other states, although I have yet to finalize anything. Nevada, Washington, Oregon, and Maryland are on the radar, and I'm hoping for the best!

I would also like to express thanks to the organizers and promoters of Gem State Comic Con, Border Town Comic Con, DarknessCon, FanX, Goddess Fest, and the City of Nampa for building great events. Also, thank you to the managers of the various bookstores at which I have appeared, for organizing exciting signing events.

The final chapter of this series is well underway. While I can't pin down a release date, schedule constraints may push Book 5 into 2027 if I sign with a new publisher. I have gone to great lengths to get *Transcendence* released on an expedited schedule, and I'm psyched to share it with all you loyal fans.

For more updates, check my social media page, and if you have signed up for my mailing list, be sure to check your spam filter to make sure they're getting through. My website, which is undergoing maintenance issues, will be up again soon with any luck. See you soon!

-bm

About the Author

Brad Mathews bends genre rules by creating dynamic, unorthodox characters thrust into criminal investigations.

He is known to use abstract imagery to construct striking realities that build into suspenseful mystery tales.

Mathews is Certified in Plumbing design, and his extensive Building Information Modeling experience gives him a unique ability to detail mechanical and industrial settings in his novels.

Mathews resides in Boise, Idaho with his family.